Nov 2008
EWD

DIRTY WHITE

Further Titles by Brian Freemantle from Severn House

BETRAYALS
DIRTY WHITE
O'FARRELL'S LAW

DIRTY WHITE

Brian Freemantle

This title first published in Great Britain 1996 by
SEVERN HOUSE PUBLISHERS LTD of
9–15 High Street, Sutton, Surrey SM1 1DF.
Previously published in 1985 under the title
The Laundryman and pseudonym *Jonathan Evans*.

British Library Cataloguing in Publication Data

Freemantle, Brian, 1936–
  Dirty white
  1. English fiction – 20th century
  I. Title
  823.9'14 [F]

ISBN 0-7278-4938-7

Typeset by Palimpsest Book Production Limited,
Polmont, Stirlingshire, Scotland.
Printed and bound in Great Britain by
Hartnolls Ltd, Bodmin, Cornwall.

*F*or Gordon and Joyce, with love

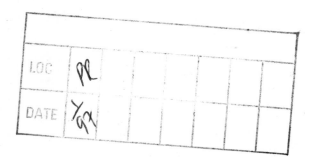

Poetic Justice, with her lifted scale:
Where, in nice balance, truth with gold she weighs.
                    ALEXANDER POPE, *The Dunciad*

1

Becage made a performance ordering the wine and spent a lot of time with the menu as well, while Walter Farr sat relaxed in the paneled room, enjoying the Texan's flamboyance.

Becage was one of the earliest clients, going back a lot of years: there wasn't actually friendship between them but the relationship was more than one of investor and broker.

Becage swirled and then tasted the wine, nodding approval. He kept the glass in his hand while more was added and then raised it toward Farr and said, "To the best investment man in Manhattan."

Farr smiled, appreciating the gratitude. "That's my job," he said.

Becage shook his head. "Cut out the modesty, Walter. Who else in this town has got your track record?"

"Quite a few," said Farr.

Becage pulled back for the food to be served and said, "Not in my book. So how about it?"

"I don't think so," said Farr. "I've thought about it, of course. Actually went out to the West Coast a couple of years back, to see what it was like. Even thought of Dallas. But I'm not interested in getting any bigger. I've got all I'll ever want, and by staying concentrated here in New York and limiting the clients I can go on providing what I always have: personalized, individual service."

9

"You could make a lot more money," said Becage.

"I don't need a lot more money."

"The complete and satisfied man!" said Becage. The mockery was friendly.

"I suppose so," said Farr. But not complacent, he thought. He maintained the same care with and attention to Becage's portfolios now as he had when they'd first met. Just as he did with every other client.

"I wish you'd think some more about it," persisted the Texan. "I'd back you all the way and I could guarantee as many clients as you could handle."

"I appreciate what you're saying, really I do," said Farr. "But I've already told you, I've got all the clients I can handle. And I like my independence."

"Take Rawlings on, at least," said the other man. "As a personal favor to me. Poor bastard has got badly burned with two brokers and has started to lose faith."

They stopped talking while the plates were cleared. Farr shook his head to anything more than coffee, considering the request. He really could do without more clients but he liked Becage and didn't want completely to reject everything the man suggested. "Tell him to get in touch, so I can find out what he wants. I'll work out a prospectus or two and maybe we can talk about it."

Becage smiled across the table at him. "Thanks, Walt. I knew you'd do it."

"Only as a personal favor," insisted Farr. "And only this time. The list is closed."

"Just this time," agreed the Texan.

Becage took brandy with his coffee but Farr refused. Becage said he had some risk capital available and fancied some commodity futures, maybe grain or pork belly through the Chicago market. But Farr said he thought metals, particularly gold and silver, were going to recover because of people's traditional confidence in gold and silver when the Latin American countries, Brazil and certainly Argentina, had difficulty in meeting their IMF loan requirements, which he guessed would happen in about three months' time. Becage immediately deferred to the broker, pledging 200,000 dollars. The Texan made one last effort to get Farr to consider expanding into Houston and, as firmly as he had before, Farr refused. Becage embarked upon another eulogy of gratitude and Farr sat through it as he had on the first occasion, vaguely embarrassed and glad there was no one else listening. Becage walked with him to the foyer of the Union Club, offering the use of his own limousine, but Farr declined, deciding on impulse to walk a little before picking up a cab to take him back to Wall Street.

He paused at the corner of Park Avenue, staring in both directions along the broad highway, breathing deeply as if he were physically savoring the city. It was one of the early days of spring. The pale yellow wash of sun was not warm enough to make a topcoat unnecessary, but there was no smear of smog, and on Park at least there wasn't the dirt and collapsing decay of the other parts of New York. In fact it looked new and fresh, and Farr breathed in deeply again, finding easy the stir of excitement that the place always gave him. He set out toward the straddle of the Pan Am building, thinking of the lunchtime conversation with Harry Becage and knowing that it would be impossible for him to consider operating out of anywhere other than New York. The Texan's argument that he wouldn't necessarily have to live in Houston or anywhere else where he established branch divisions was valid, of course, but Farr had never liked situations that he couldn't personally control—and from New York he could not have been able personally to control something a thousand or two thousand miles away. Far better to stay as he was. And he was complete and satisfied, he thought, remembering Becage's jibe. Business, at least. Privately it wasn't so, but he thought he'd adjusted pretty well to that. How much different—not just in his private life but maybe in business as well—would things have been if Ann had lived? It was a familiar—practically daily—reflection, the prod of grief as sharp now as it had been in the shaded ward eight years before when he'd sat holding her listless hand and suddenly realized that there wasn't any longer any breathing and that she'd died without opening her eyes for that last time, for him to say goodbye. Maybe he would have expanded, if Ann were still alive. It had always been important, to prove himself to her: for her to be aware of how successful he was. Among all the regrets, he was sorry she hadn't lived to see come true all the dreams and fantasies they'd had, in the cold-water apartment on 34th, where the pipes knocked and the roaches were fearless and Howard slept in the perambulator beside the pull-down couch-bed because they hadn't been able to afford a cot.

Farr paused, waiting for the lights to change so that he could go on toward the Waldorf-Astoria on the cross street. Things would certainly be different with Howard if Ann hadn't died. Farr knew he hadn't failed with Howard— such a fear was clichéd anyway—but he didn't think he'd succeeded either. He'd made a home and done the things fathers were supposed to do with their sons, like camping and sailing and baseball, and there had never been anything the boy wanted that he hadn't got; Farr loved Howard and knew that Howard loved him in return. But Farr had always been conscious of a distance between them, an embarrassment or difficulty that neither could identify or surmount. Farr could not think of anything more that he could have done; surely, to have considered remarrying, to have provided a surrogate mother, wouldn't have helped? Not that Farr had ever seriously thought of it. He had adored Ann with a consuming, all-enveloping love and when she died there had been no love left for anyone else. Maybe that was the problem with Howard. Maybe, despite Farr's thinking otherwise, Howard did not believe himself sufficiently loved. How long had it been? The last letter had been about two weeks ago, although Farr thought it might have been a little longer, and he was unsure if the last telephone call had been just before or just after the letter. Whatever, it wasn't enough. He should make more effort, instead of expecting it always to come from the boy. Boston was only an hour away on the shuttle, for God's sake! This weekend, Farr determined. He'd call, to make sure Howard didn't have anything on, and suggest this weekend. Go up on Friday and make a couple of days out of it—and try to spend more time with the boy, in the future.

Feeling he had walked enough, Farr turned in the shadow of the huge building topping Grand Central Station, seeking a taxi, happy at the decision he'd made about his son. When he got over or around whatever barrier there was between himself and Howard, he would be complete and satisfied. Farr missed the first cab but got the second, settling back for the ride downtown. There was no reason, he thought, why he shouldn't make the call as soon as he got back to the office.

Farr's organization occupied a complete floor on the ninth story of a building with a view of Battery Park and the World Trade Center; it was a rigidly controlled setup consisting of eight other investment brokers apart from himself, each with their own support staffs but ultimately answerable to him. The one directly answerable was a tightly corseted, tightly coiffeured woman named Angela Nolan who had entered the firm of the newly bereaved Farr hoping for more than a career in investment, sadly accepted his lack of interest and long ago reconciled herself to finance in the daytime and a regular Tuesday and Friday night affair with a married stockbroker in Scarsdale.

"Anything?" he said, entering her office, which was linked to his.

"I'm not sure," replied the woman.

Farr stopped, frowning at the oddness of her reply. "What do you mean?

"There are two men waiting for you in your office," she said. "From the FBI. They showed me their shields, for identification."

"The FBI!"

"Yes."

"What the hell do they want?"

"They wouldn't say."

Farr thrust into his room. It was a corner suite, with a better view of the twin towers than of the park. One man was quite relaxed in a visitor's chair to the side of Farr's desk and the other was at the window, gazing out. They both turned, at his entry, and the man who had been sitting rose.

"Mr. Farr?" he said.

"Yes."

"My name is Brennan, Peter Brennan . . ." He nodded to the man at the window. "My partner is Jim Seymour."

"What's this about?" demanded Farr.

Brennan offered his shield, which Farr didn't bother examining. "FBI," said the man, with strict formality. "You have a son named Howard Farr, a senior at St. Marks in Boston? Hoping to go to Harvard?"

"What's happened to him?" said Farr.

"He's been arrested," said the FBI man at the window. "For conspiracy to import and distribute cocaine."

2

Farr had to concentrate in order to comprehend every word and every implication, but initially he found it difficult. Brennan, the elder of the two FBI men, his already sparse hair carefully arranged over a balding pate, his suit matchingly careful in muted checks, hopefully moved a narrow pencil between his fingers as he talked—as if expecting some revelation from the uncertain broker that would shed light on a difficult point. Brennan was the person who talked, his delivery as precise as everything else about him, while Farr fought against a feeling of unreality, positively holding onto his chair beneath the concealment of the desk edge, as he listened to an account of observation of his son after the seizure of a cocaine delivery and the setting-up of an arrest involving an FBI undercover agent. Farr couldn't believe what he was hearing. Brennan used expressions such as mother ship and snow and cutting and of things going down and paymasters and couriers, and Farr decided that there had been some terrible mistake because what was supposed to have happened to his son only happened to other people's kids. But then he recognized another barrier he was trying to erect—erect for his benefit, not Howard's—and realized that there hadn't been any mistake. Not on the part of the police and interception authorities, at least.

"Surely it was just kid's stuff—experimenting?" he

15

intruded, hopefully, when Brennan paused. "Howard wasn't actually trafficking!"

"It was kilos," came in Seymour, who had moved to a chair adjoining that of his partner. "The full analysis isn't complete yet, but it's coming out at something like seventy percent pure. He was putting $100,000 up front. Cut to street level, he was looking at a million. Maybe more."

"That's ridiculous!" protested Farr at once, imagining an opening. "He hasn't got $100,000; wouldn't know how to get it!"

"He had it," came back Seymour with quiet insistence. "It's obvious to me where he got it, but we can't prove it."

"You mean this wasn't the first time!"

"You got any other idea where he could have got his hands on $100,000? Cash?" demanded the FBI man. Seymour was taller than Brennan and seemed uneasy with his size, frequently shifting in his chair. The heavy spectacles did not appear to help his myopia and he blinked and squinted frequently.

"I've told you there was a previous surveillance, before this arrest," said Brennan, supporting his partner. "It's a pretty thick dossier and your son figures in an awful lot of it."

"Jesus!" said Farr. It hadn't been a cliché to think of failing the boy: he had failed him. And not just Howard; Ann too. The promise had always been, before she got too bad, that he would care absolutely for their son. He swallowed against growing despair. He said, "You certain there can't have been a mistake?"

Brennan sighed at the broker's attitude. "Mr. Farr," he said, with forced patience. "We've had a tap on your son's telephone for the past two and a half months. We've transcripts of conversation between him and a known and convicted drug trafficker in Orlando, Florida. Those conversations openly refer to a ship called the *Della Maria*. We've got AWAC surveillance data on the *Della Maria* coming through the Caribbean. Our coastguard service tracked it, too. Right up the East Coast, avoiding the normal offloading places in Florida or the Carolinas. It put in five days ago at Newburyport, just north of Boston. We've surveillance photographs—still, as well as movie—of the entire operation. We followed the car down into Boston and we photographed the handover to an intermediary, a man named Chavez. It was Chavez with whom Howard was arrested two nights ago, in a car parked on Tremont Street, on the edge of the Common. Chavez had a sample from the *Della Maria* and your son had a hot box . . . do you know what a hot box is, Mr. Farr?''

"No," said Farr dully.

"It's a made-for-the-job testing kit," explained Seymour, coming back into the conversation. "The impurities and cutting agents used in coke manufacture burn off at certain temperatures. So you just put your sample into the box, create the temperatures, and it's simple chemistry to work out how pure your purchase is."

"Howard was doing that!"

"Your son's a dealer, Mr. Farr," said Brennan. "He's got all the connections, all the works. And a hell of a marketplace. There's hundreds of kids on the campus of Boston University and Harvard just across the river."

"He was trading in the universities!"

"Where else do you think he was selling!" said Brennan. "An important dealer is called 'The Man' and in Boston your son was The Man!"

"But not a very clever one," said Seymour.

"What's that mean?" asked Farr.

"There are rules, to being a good dealer," said the taller FBI man. "The most important is that you don't start using your own shit!"

"You saying he's addicted?"

"You know what freebasing is?" asked Seymour.

"No."

"Speedballing?"

"No!"

"You snort coke, Mr. Farr," said Brennan. "But you can get a bigger rush by burning off the impurities with ether or with alcohol and inhaling the pure cocaine alkaloid. It's usually done with a water pipe. For speedballing, you need heroin as well. Heroin is a soporific: you go on the nod. Cocaine is the opposite, a stimulant. Speedballing is mixing the two, to get a rollercoaster . . ."

"You telling me Howard was doing that? Freebasing and speedballing?"

"Yes," said Seymour.

"When did you see your son last, Mr. Farr?" asked Brennan.

The broker hesitated, making the calculation. "Two months, I suppose. Maybe a little longer."

"He seem OK to you then?"

Again Farr did not respond at once. Then he said, "Yes. Fine. Maybe a little disheveled, untidy. But he's a student. I didn't think anything of it."

"How long were you with him?"

"Quite a long time, over a Sunday. Flew up from here in the morning. We had lunch at the Locke-Ober, drove around awhile and I came back on the afternoon plane."

"He excuse himself from you much? Need to go to the washroom?" asked Brennan.

"I don't know," said Farr, almost irritably. Then the recollection came and he admitted, "Yes. Said he thought he might have some kind of bug. Didn't eat a lot, either."

"Drugs suppress the appetite—heroin certainly," said Seymour. "Sometimes there's a craving for junk food."

"You mean he was . . . he was injecting himself? Taking drugs while we were together?"

"He sure as hell couldn't have got through without taking some sort of fix," said Brennan.

Farr felt physically sick and was angry at the feeling because it somehow seemed theatrical. "Where is he?"

"In custody."

"Does the school know?"

"Not yet," said Seymour.

"What's going to happen to him?"

The two men exchanged looks before replying. Then

Brennan, who appeared to be the spokesman, said, "That's why we've come to see you, Mr. Farr. What happens to your son really depends upon you."

"I don't understand."

"We're offering you a deal," said Seymour.

"A deal!"

"There's two ways this can go down," said Brennan. "One way, we charge your son, produce everything we've got and go for the maximum sentence, plus the seizure of all his assets, which the law allows us to do. Which would mean the end of any career or future, of course . . ." The agent paused. "The other way is for you to do what we ask. Which means no charges, no exposure. Howard will need a lot of treatment and a lot of help but you could afford it. And he might just be able to get to Harvard."

Farr looked between the two men, confused. Surely a bribe wasn't demanded as blatantly as this! But what else could the bastards want? He needed time to think, someone with whom he could talk it through. He didn't think they'd give him time and there was no one with whom he could discuss it. Cautiously he asked, "How does the second way work?"

"Howard was into a million-buck deal but the fact is that that was popcorn stuff," said Brennan. "We want to set up an operation to go after the traffickers who really matter. The guys operating out of Colombia and the truly organized-crime people working with them here!"

Farr's relief that he wasn't being asked for a bribe was immediately overwhelmed by a fresh feeling of confusion. "What do you want me to do?"

"We want you to set it all up. And make it work for us," said Seymour simply. Farr didn't feel complete or satisfied any longer. He felt very frightened.

3

The need to concentrate was even more important than before. He'd had to understand before—which he did, fully.

Now he had to grasp what these two inconspicuous, almost clerklike men were proposing. To save Howard, whom he'd neglected. And what about himself? The question intruded irritatingly—deflecting him—but Farr forced himself to confront it, to begin purging himself of the guilt. Himself, too, he conceded. If he had to look deeply into the hidden rooms behind the always locked doors, Farr recognized that, although he disdained professional expansion and responded modestly to the sort of praise that had been piled on him only hours before by the Texan millionaire, he enjoyed—in the way that a favorite court confidant or even courtesan enjoyed—his esoteric fame. The loss of such a reputation as his would hurt as much as it would hurt the court confidant or courtesan to be discarded.

So, yes, if there were a way to avoid Howard being hauled before a court and exposed as a drug trafficker, there was as great a reason for him to do it for himself as do it for the boy. Farr felt a burn of embarrassment at his thoughts and was glad there would never be a circumstance in which they would have to be revealed to any living person. He took off his jacket—feeling encumbered, despite the meticulous temperature control—and told An-

21

gela through the intercom that all his calls had either to be held or transferred. As an afterthought, he offered the two FBI men a drink. Dutifully, they took coffee, and Farr joined them, wondering if his control might have been better if he'd accepted the brandy Becage had offered at lunch; he certainly needed something stronger than coffee. The woman was as efficient as always, so the coffee came quickly and they didn't attempt to speak until after it was served. Brennan, in his role as spokesman, set out the proposal and Farr sat tensed forward over a desk that held separate framed photographs of Ann and Howard.

"Entrapment?" said the broker, when the balding man stopped talking.

"No!" said Seymour at once, coming in before his partner. "Entrapment—or causing it to occur—has become the best established defense on any drug charge. We've lost more cases than we've made because some smart-assed lawyer has been able to convince a judge that their client was drawn by enticement into committing an offense he might otherwise have never considered or even dreamed of considering."

"Then what you want me to do doesn't make sense," said Farr.

Brennan smiled, his patience this time not as forced as before. "This makes so much sense it's practically a treatise for a Ph.D. in logic," he said. "You're not American: you live and work here as is your right, having married an American woman, now deceased?"

Farr frowned at the description, which sounded as if it had come verbatim from some official dossier—which, he supposed, it probably had. "Yes," he said, in tight agreement: Ann wasn't—had never been—"an American woman."

"You have no connection whatsoever with any enforcement agency—particularly a drug enforcement agency—of the United States of America?" persisted Brennan.

"Of course not!" said Farr, allowing the irritability.

"You are an investment broker practically unique in Wall Street; anywhere else, for that matter. Someone who has become a millionaire not by shotgun expansion but by concentration on a selected and favored group of clients for few of whom—if any—you've ever created a losing portfolio?''

Farr remembered that ''not by shotgun expansion but by concentration on a selected and favored group of clients'' had been an expression he particularly admired in a profile written about him in *Barron's* about six months earlier; they'd done a great deal of research. He said, predictably modest, ''That's the way I've always preferred to work. *It* works.''

''Sure we've done these sort of things before,'' said Seymour. ''There was Operation Greenback which became Operation Eldorado—which is still running—and Operation Bancoshares; but in all of them there's been a failing. It looks good in print and on television, because Joe Six-Pack, Mr. Average America, reading the newspaper in Des Moines or watching *60 Minutes,* has got to believe it's good. And to be able to say we've seized six million or sixty million bucks' worth of drugs and property *does* look good, until you know that's a piss—and a very small piss—into the bucket for what's being made every day of every week of every year by guys to whom losing sixty million is a budgeted-for expense, like IBM or ITT allow a few bucks for stolen paperclips and pencils. It's made to look good and important because we need *our* budgets maintained by Congress, and the Drug Enforcement Administration needs their budgets maintained by Congress, like the Customs does and the coastguard does and the Internal Revenue Service does.''

Farr's hands were beneath the table again, out of sight, grasping his chair, as he tried to hold onto what the two men were saying. ''You telling me it isn't working?''

Seymour snorted a laugh. ''I said a piss in the bucket, Mr. Farr: if you blink, you miss it.''

''Why is my cooperation important?'' asked Farr, who thought he understood but was determined to get everything spelled out.

"I said Howard was The Man in Boston," reminded Brennan. "In a very small part of Boston. A million bucks might sound a lot—although, I suppose, to you it doesn't, not necessarily—but in the sort of figures and the sort of trafficking that we're thinking about, and more importantly trying to stop, it's another hardly heard piss into the bucket. Which is why all the sting operations are insignificant. We seize a few million bucks' worth of shit and we arraign a few people and talk about a million-buck buy and—shall I tell you what that is! It's important, certainly. It lets Joe Six-Pack know we're out there in the dark streets and the dark alleys, pitching. Makes him feel safe. But twenty-four hours after we roll up punks like Howard . . ." The FBI agent hesitated, the irritation at the lapse obvious. Farr waited for the apology and respected the man for not attempting one. Instead, Brennan said, "That's what he is, Mr. Farr. A drug-taking punk who thought he could make the big time. I'm not going to lie to you about anything; certainly not that. Like I was saying, twenty-four hours after we roll up people like Howard, he's replaced by someone else. We've seized maybe two kilos, probably more, in arresting Howard. Logic decrees that there should be a shortage on the streets; panic buying and panic price hikes. It hasn't happened. *Won't* happen. Because whatever's been lost can be replaced. At once."

"You want the people who matter?" anticipated Farr.

Brennan smiled, coming forward in his chair to match in intensity Farr's head-bent attention. "*Exactly* that!" he said. "We want the guys in Colombia and Bolivia and Peru. And the organized-crime people here. The *names*. Like Escabar and Lehder and O'Campo and Moreno and Suarez in Latin America. And the Gambinos and the Genoveses and the Bonnanos and the Trafficantes and the Brunos here, at home . . ." The man had to pause, breathless in his urgency. ". . . We don't want to sting; we want to *burn* the bastards. Get the biggest names possible and make sure they're arraigned and that we can get not just a criminal conviction to put them in jail but get also the sort

of seizure decision we could go for against Howard. This
time I'm not talking about millions, Mr. Farr. I'm talking
about *billions*. We want to create an operation to take the
big guys, the really big guys, by the neck and frighten the
living shit out of them. Make them realize that they're not
as invulnerable as they've been for far too long.''

"Which is why you're important, Mr. Farr," interrupted Seymour, constantly hurrying the discussion. "The
Escabars and the Lehders have stayed rich and free because they're careful. Clever and cunning. All the other
operations like this have been set up entirely in-house; it's
been our accountants and our agents spending a few months
setting up a front and coming on strong. The Colombian
and the Bolivian and the Mafia barons have *knowingly*
used us—aware that we needed time to establish ourselves
and operate as we are supposed to—but they're never
within a thousand miles of the front operation when the
trap's sprung. They can afford to employ the best lawyers
available, to make sure everything is kosher.''

"And I'm kosher?" said Farr, who was a gentile.

"Kosher and established, to anyone who makes any sort
of inquiry. We'll put behind you an operation that will
make the invasion of Europe look like a Boy Scout practice, but you'll be the bona fide, one hundred percent
financial investor they can trust to wash their drugs money
and make them richer still.''

"If it works," said Farr. "If I agree to set up the sort of
scheme you want and there are arrests, there will be a
trial?''

"A sensational one," agreed Brennan.

Farr gestured around the luxurious office. "To the detriment of this business.''

Seymour shook his head. "One of the undertakings
we're prepared to give you right here, today, is that without any reference to Howard or his arrest you agreed
willingly to act for us. Any reflection upon you or your
business will be one of admiration, not condemnation
. . .'' The FBI man's pause was exactly the right length.

"The detriment to yourself and possibly to this business will be if the case goes ahead against Howard and he faces a court on the charges that could be made against him—and you're called into that court. I told you earlier that I couldn't account for where he got the buy money. I think it's from an earlier drugs deal, but I couldn't say that as evidence in court because I couldn't prove it. The court—and the public—would be left to conjecture where the money came from."

"Bastard!" erupted Farr, seeing the blackmail.

"I'm trying to catch the bastards, Mr. Farr," said Seymour, unperturbed at the outburst. "If I've got to cut some corners to achieve that, pull a few shitty tricks, then I'm prepared to do that. All I've just said is that I won't perjure or conjecture in a court of American law."

"I know what you've just said," insisted Farr. "You're prepared for it to be inferred that I was financier of the deal."

"We've no control whatsoever over what people infer from any court hearing," said Brennan. "I said earlier that I wouldn't lie to you. I'm not lying to you now . . ." He gestured sideways to his partner. ". . . Neither's Jim. He's setting it out, clear and simple."

Farr knew well enough that he didn't have a choice but he determined against giving them the satisfaction of an immediate capitulation. "I want to see Howard," he said. "I won't make any decision until I see my son."

"We didn't expect you to," said Brennan, denying him even that small satisfaction.

4

Walter Farr was a meticulous man and he acted in a meticulous way, despite having to face the biggest crisis in his life since Ann's death. He told Angela Nolan that he would be away for a few days and asked her to advise the other brokers of his absence—remembering even to warn her of an approach from someone named Donald Rawlings, who would be coming to them with Becage's recommendation. While the FBI men waited patiently in an outer office, he called the Dean of Admissions at Harvard, arranged a meeting, considered calling his lawyer, and then abandoned the idea. Farr had already decided what to do so there was no need for any criminal attorney. The preparations made, he became impatient to reach Boston.

At his suggestion, the three men helicoptered to La Guardia, enabling a shuttle connection far earlier than they could have managed if they had traveled out to the airport by road. No one bothered with conversation on the crowded commuter flight. As they touched down at Logan, Farr decided he should have rented a car, but an FBI vehicle was already waiting.

"You know I'm going to do it, of course," said Farr, as the car moved out of the airport complex.

"Thank you," said Brennan politely, as if the broker had been allowed an independent decision.

"Could Howard be released into my custody today?"

27

"I could try to fix it," said Brennan.

"I'd like to get him into care as soon as possible."

"Sure," said the FBI man.

"He'll have been seen by the court's medical people," offered Seymour. "Maybe they could recommend a place. I guess you'd want him treated somewhere close to school."

Farr's half-considered intention was to take the boy back to New York, so that he could personally keep an eye on him, but then he realized that, if he went along with the deal, it was likely he would be away from the city for long periods at a time. "I guess so," he said. "I haven't really thought it through."

Boston began to take shape ahead, and Farr looked out at the initial straggle of clapboard and shingle houses, as if he were seeing them for the first time—which he probably was, he thought: he certainly hadn't been aware of them during the last visit. Forcing honesty, Farr admitted to himself that the last time had been a duty visit: the to-and-from flights planned and the car planned and the restaurant planned, and the conversation between himself and his son stilted and difficult, with gaps while each sought for something to say, as if they were courteous strangers encountering each other on a train or a plane, just passing the time.

"We're here," announced Seymour, breaking into the reverie.

Farr followed the two men past the bustle of the other desk and rooms, down a corridor off which ran a honey-comb of boxlike squared offices which Farr thought fitting for the beehive atmosphere.

Toward the end of the corridor the construction became more solid and he realized they were approaching the detention section. Howard's room was numbered 6; there were no obvious bars but, even so, Farr decided it was a cell. Brennan nodded to a uniformed man sitting at a control desk and the man unlocked the door, standing back for them to enter.

At the door Farr said, "Can I see him alone?" and Seymour said, "Sure."

The room was fetid with Howard's smell, sweat and urine and, unaccountably, cabbage. Farr was a fastidious man who sometimes showered twice a day and who had always believed that he had inculcated at least the habit of cleanliness into his son. He swallowed against the distaste and realized that that was something else about which he had been wrong. Howard sat balled up on the top of a disheveled bunk, hands clasped around his legs, which were pulled up tight against his chest, knees hard against his chin: a childlike position of comfort. Scuffed, dirty track shoes were haphazardly discarded by the side of the bunk and Farr saw that there was a hole in the boy's left sock. He wore jeans and a thick woolen shirt. Farr remembered Howard wearing the same shirt when they last met and was surprised at the unimportant recollection. From the smell in the room he wondered if the boy had bothered to change it, since that time.

"Hello," said Farr, not knowing what else to say at the moment of confrontation.

"Wondered if you'd come," said the boy. His skin was greased waxlike with perspiration; the dampness had spread up to his hair, which hung lankily because of it. He was rocking back and forth very gently in his hunched-up position, as if he couldn't bear to be still.

"Was it likely that I wouldn't!" Farr tried to keep the annoyance from his voice; he'd decided on the flight that fighting wouldn't achieve anything.

"Don't know," said Howard. While he talked, he stared down at his holed sock, refusing to meet his father's gaze.

"How long?" said Farr.

"How long what?"

"Have you been taking drugs?"

The boy shrugged as if it were unimportant. "Year, I guess, maybe longer . . ." He looked at his father at last.

"I feel like hell . . . like I'm coming apart. I burn, deep in my stomach. The bastards won't give me anything."

Farr bit against the instinctive angry response. "They said you were freebasing. Speedballing, too. So you're addicted."

"Kick it if I want to," said Howard, with little-boy bravado.

There was a hardbacked, upright chair against the wall opposite the bed. Farr looked intently at it, to see that it was clean, and sat down uncertainly. "You're a mess," he said. "You *look* like hell."

Howard tightened his lock around his legs, physically holding on. "Need something," he said, denying his boast of seconds before.

"You were dealing," accused Farr. "Setting up a buy with $100,000. Where the hell did you get $100,000?"

"Friend," said the boy.

"Liar!" said Farr, despite the earlier determination. "You're a trafficker, infecting other kids like you're infected."

"No!" said Howard, defiantly. "Didn't sell to anyone who didn't know what they were doing."

"Is that your defense, your justification!" demanded Farr, disgusted.

"If I hadn't done it, someone else would have."

"Jesus!" said Farr. How much, he wondered, was he responsible?

Howard released his legs, carefully, as if he feared any different position might cause him pain. He turned to look more directly at his father, and he did it leaning forward, urgently. "Help me!" came the sudden plea. "Tell them I hurt . . . that I need something. Just to get me over today. Just for today."

Farr wanted physically to hit him. He'd rarely struck him, not even when as a tiny kid, he'd done stupid, irritating things. Maybe he should have. He said, "I'm going to help you. But not by trying to get you any drugs. I'm going to get you better."

"I *can* get better, if you get me something. Fix me up, just for today." He smiled, conspiratorially. "I'll tell you where to go. Say you've got an appointment but that you want to come back to see me later. Didn't search you when you came in, did they . . . ?"

"Stop it!" said Farr. "For Christ's sake, stop it! Don't you realize what's happened! Where you are? What could happen to you? You've destroyed everything. Your schooling. Your future. Everything. You could go to jail, for years. And all you can think about is a fix!"

"Need help," insisted the boy, looking away, his mind blocked by a single thought.

Farr had not expected this. He had not necessarily disbelieved the FBI men, but he'd thought that when he got to the boy there would be some reasonable explanation, an excuse or mitigation. But not this—not this shaking, smelly whining thing who was supposed to be his son, who wasn't sorry or contrite about what he'd done, but interested only in sticking something in his arm or up his nose. Farr's revulsion was physical, an acid sourness at the back of his throat, and he knew he easily could have been sick and added to the stink in the room. "You thought about what's going to happen?"

There was another uninterested shrug. "Busted," said the boy, in apathetic acceptance. "Court, I guess. Jail, like you said."

"Doesn't that mean anything?" demanded Farr, incredulously.

"Haven't thought about it."

It was pointless, decided Farr. Howard was beyond reason; beyond reach. He needed treatment—long, professional treatment—and then maybe they'd be able to reestablish something between them, although at the moment Farr didn't know what that something was.

But he'd do anything—everything—to get Howard better and to keep him better. He stared across the room at the boy, who had returned to his fetal position and was rocking back and forth once more. What, Farr wondered, would be involved in that commitment? He stood abruptly, and said, "I meant what I said, about helping you."

For the first time, there was something like an animated reaction from his son. Howard unfolded himself and came up from the bed in a single movement, reaching out for his father's arm. "Knew you'd do it!" he said excitedly. "There is a bar, on Hanover, near the Paul Revere statue . . . red awning . . . Guy's always in the third booth . . . Knows me. Just say you're from me . . . it's called . . ."

"Shut up!" shouted Farr, jerking himself uncomfortably from his son's grip. "That's not what I meant. I meant proper help."

"Bastard!" Howard shouted back. "Fucking bastard!"

Farr tensed, the fist already made, positively straining against hitting out. The commitment was going to take a lot; he hoped he would be able to sustain it. He knocked against the door, not feeling any personal embarrassment at his anxiety to get away. Brennan must have been waiting directly outside because it opened at once. Farr walked out without saying anything to his son, hurrying some way along the corridor before coming abruptly to a stop. He inhaled deeply, taking the first full breath for a long time.

"Difficult, isn't it?"

Farr was aware of Seymour beside him. "Yes," he said shortly.

"We arranged a meeting while you were in there," said the FBI man. "District attorney in charge of the case. And the doctor I told you about earlier."

"Thanks," said the broker sincerely.

When Brennan came up from the detention area, Farr walked between the two men to an elevator which took them up three floors. Here the offices were less boxlike and didn't conform to the beehive pattern. Brennan led the way into a spacious suite where two men were already waiting, making the introductions as Farr entered. The district attorney was a balding, rotund man named Alvin Schuster. The doctor, who wore a sagged tweed sports jacket and shapeless trousers, was introduced as William Silver.

"The Bureau is proposing an unusual course of action," said Schuster at once.

"Yes," said Farr.

"And one in which I understand you're prepared to cooperate?"

"Yes," said the broker again.

"This comes down to plea bargaining, I suppose," said the lawyer. "I don't like plea bargaining. Never have. I think criminals should be prosecuted for the crimes they've committed and properly punished. From the evidence I've considered, your son is a criminal, Mr. Farr. I could make a case against him and I'm quite sure I could get a conviction, a jail sentence for a number of years. What I'm being asked to agree to means your son is going to get off—go free, instead of being properly punished for a crime of which I believe he's as guilty as hell . . ."

"I understand all this," said Farr, unhappy with the lecture.

"Understand something else," said Schuster. "I've been told, assured, that letting him go will be worthwhile because, as a result, an operation will be mounted that's going to hurt and punish criminals far bigger than him. If that happens, maybe I can see the justification for what I'm being asked to allow. But I want to hear it from you: I want you to tell me that you can set up and front this operation, and that at the end of it I'm going to see the sort of convictions I want."

Frowning, Farr looked away from the district attorney, toward Brennan. Then he turned back to the lawyer and said, "I can't give you that undertaking! How can you expect me to? I can set up an investment company and run it to make people a lot of money, but there's no way I can guarantee that those people will be drug dealers whom at some stage you'll be able to arrest and charge."

"We've got some people," came in Brennan, hurriedly. "People in Colombia and here in America that these organized-crime guys trust. Once things are properly set up, we can guide them to Farr."

"You sure of that?" asked Schuster, still doubtful.

"Absolutely," replied the FBI man. "How else could we make it work?"

Schuster gazed down at a dossier lying before him on his desk. Farr supposed it was the file on Howard. After several moments, the attorney raised his eyes again and said, "There's a lot of uncertainty; too much uncertainty."

Farr was confused by the encounter. From the New York approach, he'd imagined everything arranged. Now it didn't look that way at all—which meant that, if Schuster did not agree, there would be the prosecution and the public humiliation and Howard really would be destroyed, further destroyed than he was at present. As quickly as Brennan before him, Farr said, "If the Bureau can guide them to me, I can do the rest. I *can* guarantee that."

Schuster remained doubtful. "If I proceed now, I get a conviction. Your way, I'm gambling."

"For a hell of a prize," said Seymour, entering the debate. "Prosecutions of people like Howard Farr are so commonplace they rate a paragraph in the newspapers. And they've been replaced on the streets before the first arraignment: they don't matter a damn. We're going for the important people."

Maybe the argument to him in New York had been a rehearsal for this meeting, thought Farr.

Schuster said dogmatically, "The law's the law."

"To be used to the best effect to protect the public," pounced Brennan. "If we get this operation right, we'll be safeguarding hundreds more than we would be by taking Howard Farr off the streets."

The man nodded sideways, indicating Farr. "And he's off the streets anyway. His father knows the score now and can get him into care. There's no risk of his setting up again if you agree not to prosecute."

"Want me to tell you something?" said the district attorney rhetorically. "There were two 'ifs' in what you just said, and the first was the more important: *if* you get the operation right."

"We won't be able to try unless you let us," said Seymour.

Schuster looked directly at Farr. "He addicted?"

"Badly so, from what little I've seen downstairs in the detention rooms," agreed Farr.

"You want to put him through some form of detoxification?"

"Yes."

Schuster went back to the unopened dossier. "I just talked about gambling," he said. "I'm not a gambler. I like black and white, with a clear, definable line drawn down the middle. I'm not going to gamble. I'll hedge my bet. I'll agree not to proceed at the moment, to enable the kid to undergo some treatment course. That'll give you time to set up the sort of operation you've been talking about—and time, too, for me to be convinced you're getting the bigtime clients into the net. But I'm going to sit as tight as hell upon everything, and if I'm not satisfied after a reasonable period that it's working, I'll press charges against him . . ." Confirming Farr's earlier impression, Schuster tapped the document folder in front of him. "I'm leaving this file open. I'm marking it pending, for possible prosecution, and I'll make that prosecution the moment I decide you've fouled up . . ." The lawyer paused again, looking toward the physician, who had so far remained silent. "How long, for a detoxification?"

"There's no established period," said Silver. "I've seen him and I've made a preliminary examination. The urine samples show a high level of toxicity. With any cure—and cure isn't a word I like using because I don't think an addictively inclined person is ever cured of his habit, any more than an alcoholic ever ceases to be an alcoholic—it comes down to the motivation of the person concerned. If he wants to be taken off, then it's possible. If he doesn't, then forget it.''

''I'll not let it run forever,'' insisted Schuster. ''I'm prepared to give it six months, which I think is damned generous. If you haven't anything positive to show me in six months, then Howard Farr gets taken to court . . .'' He looked carefully from Brennan to Seymour and then to Farr. ''Understand?''

''Perfectly,'' accepted Brennan.

Farr had lost immediate interest in the dispute, concentrating instead on the doctor. ''You saying that Howard might never be cured?''

''Yes,'' said Silver. ''You get the impression down there this afternoon that he wanted to be?''

''No,'' answered Farr honestly. ''All he wanted was for me to arrange some sort of fix for him.''

''Then he's got a long way to go,'' said the doctor. He allowed the pause. ''You both have, if you're going to stand by him.''

''Of course I'm going to stand by him!'' said Farr, experiencing the same indignation he'd felt at the attitude from his son immediately after he entered the detention room.

''Let me tell you something,'' said Silver. ''Drug addiction isn't like any other illness—not something for which you can feel the sort of sympathy you might for any other sickness. Drug addicts will cheat and lie and deceive and steal and promise not to do it again when they get caught— and the moment you blink they'll do it all over again.''

An idea occurred to Farr. ''Do you know of any residential facility here, in Massachusetts . . .'' He hesitated. ''*Secure* residential facility?''

''There's a place in Eastham,'' said Silver, at once.

''I want him committed there, by force or by law if necessary,'' said Farr, talking more to the district attorney than to Silver. ''You've got an open file on him, so use it. I don't care what the binding order is, so long as it *is*

binding. And he knows it. If I'm going to meet your
six-month deadline, I won't have time personally to care
for him, and I don't know how to, anyway. If he hasn't
got the will to detoxify himself, then I want the will
enforced upon him.''

"You want a legal commitment?" asked Schuster.

"Yes," said Farr. "I want him better."

To the doctor, Schuster said, "Could you get him into
Eastham?"

"I think so."

"I'll make all the legal arrangements," promised Schuster,
coming back to the investment broker. "But I meant what
I said. Six months."

As they walked back toward the elevator, to leave the
building, Farr said to Brennan, "There's a bar on Hanover
Street, near the Paul Revere statue. I don't know its name
but it's got a red awning. There's a trafficker who always
sits in the third booth . . .''

Brennan consulted his watch. "We should have hit it
about two hours ago," he said.

Farr turned, to face the man. "You were listening!"

"The room's wired, Mr. Farr," said Brennan. He nodded sideways, to his partner. "Like Jim told you in New
York, we'll cut corners and pull shitty tricks if it means we
can win.''

They reached the ground floor and started walking out
toward the now darkened streets. "You set this up, didn't
you?" said Farr, remembering something else about the
New York meeting and the extent of the detail they appeared to know about him. "You said there'd been previous surveillance. You knew where he got the $100,000
from because you'd seen him pull previous deals. You just
let him run while you worked out a scheme where I'd be
useful to you, and when you were ready, you pulled him
in. That's it, isn't it?"

At the exit Brennan stopped, to meet the accusation.
"Yes," he said. "That's exactly it. Like I said. Any shitty
trick that's necessary.''

*　　*　　*

There had not been many meetings between Farr and the Dean of Admissions, just information occasions, for the future, so Farr hardly knew Wilbur Jennings. The academic was a dried-out, aloof man with thinning white hair who'd developed the mannerism of repeatedly lowering his head in apparent reproof to stare out over his half-moon spectacles at whomever he was addressing. Farr thought that the funereal black of his suit was the only color in which he could imagine the man.

Farr rehearsed the story, wanting to minimize as much as possible any action the school might consider taking against his son. Sure—for six months at least—of there being no publicly announced charges, he omitted completely any mention of Howard's trafficking and dealing, limiting himself to the disclosure of the boy's addiction and the need for treatment.

Showing neither surprise nor shock, Jennings did not speak for several minutes after Farr had finished.

"You've my sympathy," he said at last.

Farr wondered what the man's reaction would be to discovering his sin of omission. "Thank you."

"Drugs seem to be the scourge of modern society." Jennings delivered the platitude in a sonorous, unmodulated voice.

"It's always easy to imagine it happening to someone else's child, never one's own," said Farr, in matching platitude.

"You said you sought my help and understanding?"

"I want to reduce as much as possible the harm that might be done to Howard's schooling."

"This is the final term at St. Marks," reminded Jennings. "He has to graduate to be able to enter here."

"He's in treatment," said Farr. "The final examinations will be impossible this semester."

"Then it's impossible," insisted the dean.

"The doctors say he could be cured in six months," exaggerated Farr.

Jennings pursed his lips. "If he could cram a remedial course, obtain a General Education Certificate, he could possibly enter for the semester after the one that we anticipated."

Farr felt a surge of relief. "Thank you," he said.

"I've set out the possibilities," qualified Jennings. "Howard has to be able to do it."

That, thought Farr, was the problem.

5

Howard Farr was formally charged with conspiracy to import cocaine into the United States. After consultation with Alvin Schuster, his father signed the undertaking that he had no objection to a preliminary in-camera hearing and waived the right for legal representation.

This meant that a closed hearing was possible in judge's chambers, with only the district attorney, the arresting FBI agents, Farr and Howard present.

Schuster gave the briefest outline of the alleged charge against the boy and said he was making a commitment request, with which Farr agreed, to a rehabilitation sanatorium to enable treatment and that he wanted a *sine die* adjournment of the case, which he nevertheless intended to pursue.

There had been an earlier consultation between Schuster and the judge, a surprisingly motherly woman named Telford. At the hearing she made Howard stand before her and asked him if he understood what was being said; Farr sat hot with embarrassment at the stumbling, practically incoherent responses from a boy who had once been so intelligent. The judge then called Farr to ask if he was in agreement with the course being requested by the prosecution, and Farr said that he was. She returned to Howard, formally ordering the committal, and then, for a full five minutes—the time seemed much longer in the confined

41

space of her chambers—she lectured Howard upon the penalties and of her reaction if he attempted to abscond. She stopped frequently, demanding confirmation that he understood. Each time, there was a mumble of words inaudible except to the woman.

After the hearing the impression of enforceable legality was maintained, Howard being taken to Eastham by Brennan and Seymour with Farr to follow separately. This gave Farr the opportunity to thank the district attorney.

"It was as much for my benefit as yours," said Schuster. "There was a lot of theatricality, but there was a formal charge, and my ability to bring him before a court at any time I see fit is established."

"I still appreciate it," said Farr.

Schuster smiled—the first time the man had relaxed since they'd met. He said, "I've got a son just two years younger than Howard. It frightens the hell out of me that the same thing could happen to him. I wish you luck, with what you're doing."

"I'm not sure where I'll need it most: with Howard's cure or with the investment operation they want me to set up."

"I think you're going to need a lot of luck. Period," said Schuster. "I meant what I said."

"I know," said Farr.

An hour after the departure of the FBI men with his son, Farr set out but he did not hurry, wanting Howard to be formally admitted and settled in before he arrived. Outside Boston he recognized signs for such places as Martha's Vineyard and Nantucket—to both of which he'd ferried with Howard when he first came up to St. Marks—and Hyannis and Chatham. They'd particularly enjoyed Chatham, he remembered, liking the way it had been maintained by the zoning restrictions and not spoiled by hamburger parlors and shopping malls. He wondered if they'd ever do things like that again. He drove for almost an hour along Route 6 until he saw the first turnoff to Eastham and realized he hadn't bothered to get directions to the sanatorium. He chanced exiting and was relieved when he stopped at the nearest gas station to learn he'd made the right choice. Following the guidance of the attendant, he found the correct side-road and then an even smaller lane without difficulty.

Brennan's car was parked on the graveled area that ballooned out at the top of the drive, but Farr was more intent upon the drive itself and the entrance through which he'd had to pass to reach it. The gates were controlled from a small guardhouse and had to be opened and closed after each arrival or departure, but they were only about twelve feet high and the guard who admitted him was a white-haired, frail old man who was obviously eking out some retirement benefit. The wall which stretched away on either side of the gate and presumably encircled the premises was even lower—not more than ten feet, Farr guessed. The grounds were heavily wooded, restful, he thought, for people recuperating, but it seemed to him that the foliage and undergrowth provided excellent cover for anyone who decided to escape.

Farr went past Brennan's vehicle and found the FBI man waiting for him in the entrance hall. Beside Brennan there was a tall, bald, dome-headed man who had adopted an apologetic stoop in an attempt to minimize his height. He wore a striped blue suit that had clearly been ready made: the sleeves were far too short, so that his arms projected bonily beyond them.

"Dr. Morton Halpern, the director," identified Brennan. As Farr shook hands with the head of the sanatorium, Brennan added, "I've explained to Dr. Halpern about this morning's hearing . . ." Seeing Farr's frown, he went on, "About the commitment being binding."

"Why don't we talk about it in my office?" invited Halpern.

"Jim and I will wait outside," said Brennan.

Farr followed the stooped figure into an office directly adjacent to the hallway with a view from the front of the house down the driveway, practically as far as the gate.

"Can I get you anything?"

"No, thank you," said Farr. "Have you heard from Dr. Silver?"

Halpern nodded. "He telephoned and sent the case notes up with Brennan."

"I don't think it's going to be easy."

"It rarely is," said Halpern.

"Dr. Silver said you had to want to give it up. From what I've seen of Howard, I don't think he does."

"I don't think any of us can guess at this early stage what he does or doesn't want to do," said the doctor, with professional caution.

"He seems to be in a great deal of pain. Discomfort, certainly."

Halpern shook his head. "It's one of the greatest problems, at the beginning of a detoxification. Heroin is the only physically addictive drug and that fact is vastly magnified in the mind of every addict. Actually, it's more difficult to give up cigarettes than it is to kick heroin. The discomfort is no worse—and often far less—than with bad flu. I sometimes prescribe a tranquilizer, and from what I've been told it might be necessary in this case, but more often than not the supposed pain that these people suffer is self-induced. They *make* themselves hurt, believing that they're going to anyway. That's the real problem, not just with heroin but with cocaine abuse, as well. Psychological dependence is always greater than the physical. It's no problem getting them off. All you need for that is a locked room. The problem arises when they finally accept that their upset is self-induced and we have to convince them not to *want* to use anything again. That they don't need it . . ." Halpern gave another of his habitual headshakes. "Which really compounds the difficulty, sometimes, particularly with an intelligent addict—and all the indication from the reports is that Howard is intelligent. You can get that sort of person off and you can counsel and talk, and nine times out of ten their reaction is 'Hey, this is easy. If

I can get off as easy at this, then why shouldn't I do it again because now I know how easy it is to stop?' ''

"That isn't very encouraging," said Farr.

"I'm not trying to be encouraging. I'm trying to be totally honest and totally objective, so that you understand from the outset how it's going to be."

"Dr. Silver said it was difficult to estimate how long it might take."

"It's impossible," confirmed Halpern.

"You said you wanted to be totally honest?"

"Yes."

"So what's the relapse rate? What could I expect from Howard if you straighten him out and he's cured?"

Halpern looked down at his desk before replying, head shaking again. "About ten percent," he said. "Some of my people say fifteen."

"Relapse?" pressed Farr.

"No," said the director. "Having gone through detoxification, only about ten percent stay clean afterward."

"Dear God!"

"Howard might be one of the ten percent," said Halpern.

Farr couldn't imagine so, from what he'd already seen.

"I'm frightened he'll try to run," he said. "Everything was set out for him by the judge, but he seemed stupid, mumbling like some fool. I'm not sure he understood."

"It's not uncommon for them to try to run, certainly in the early days," admitted Halpern.

Farr gazed beyond the director through the window and into the grounds. "It doesn't look particularly secure."

Halpern smiled, unoffended. "It's not a prison, Mr. Farr. It doesn't set out to be and neither should it appear to be. When it comes to the bottom line, these people have got to help themselves, and they couldn't be convinced to do that in a completely prisonlike atmosphere. Because of Howard's particlar circumstances, for the initial period— two or three weeks, maybe—he'll sleep in a locked and constantly monitored dormitory ward. My staff is extremely efficient. It won't be obvious to him, as it isn't obvious to

anyone else, but during the day he'll be under pretty
constant surveillance. I told you that it isn't uncommon for
people to try to run. The last one really to succeed was
nine months ago—a girl, and we recovered her with the
help of the local police in five hours.''

"I'm not sure Howard will make it." Farr needed the
confessional. "In fact, I doubt it very much. And I'm
extremely worried.''

"That's pretty common, too, among parents," assured
Halpern. "You shouldn't feel embarrassed or ashamed.
Stop asking yourself where you failed: what's happened to
Howard doesn't mean that you have, not particularly.''

"I could have given him more time.''

"We could all give our kids more time," said Halpern.
"Maybe it would help. Maybe it wouldn't. I've treated
kids who've been cosseted and pampered and rarely out of
their parents' sight and who've started to score *because*
their family was too attentive.''

"What *should* I do?''

"Come to visit, although not too often, which would
overpower him. Don't sit in judgment and have 'how
could you?' conversations, which I know is difficult but is
important. Start trying to think about it as an illness, which
it often—although not always—is.''

"I'd like to see him, before I go?''

"Of course," said Halpern at once.

Howard's room was at the back of the building and, as
Farr proceeded along the corridor behind the director, the
gradual transition from ordinary hospital to the tighter-
security unit was as obvious as it had been in the Boston
detention cells. In Howard's ward area there was even a
man at a control desk with a closed-circuit television monitor suspended in front of him. It was the man at the control
desk who unlocked the door to let Farr in to see the boy.

Howard was in his familiar hunched pose, the filthy
training shoes kicked off and lying in the center of the
room. There was a wide-apart mesh over the windows

and, beyond, the window was open, so the smell had not yet had the opportunity to permeate the room.

"They going to look after me here? Give me something?" demanded the boy, without any greeting. "Christ, I hurt." He whimpered, as if some audible proof were necessary.

"It's a hospital," said Farr. "They'll look after you."

"I *want* something," whined Howard. "Tell them to give me something." .

"You understood what was said in court?" demanded Farr, wanting to get out of the cul-de-sac.

"That wasn't a court."

"It was an official hearing, before a judge. You were ordered here and I've agreed to it."

"Do a deal? Spread a little money around maybe?" smirked Howard.

"No," said Farr, remembering Halpern's injunction and refusing to be annoyed. "I did not do a deal. All I tried to do was to get you sorted out."

"Told you how to do that in the other cell," said the boy.

"I want you to do something," said Farr. "I want you to promise me that you'll cooperate. That you'll do everything they ask of you here and not try to fight them or anything stupid like that. If you don't—if you're stupid— you'll end up back in court. You understand that?" As he spoke, Farr remembered the warning from Silver: *Drug addicts will cheat and lie and deceive and steal and promise not to do it again when they get caught—and the moment you blink they'll do it all over again.*

"Sure," said Howard, glib despite his discomfort.

"I've seen the Dean at Harvard. There's still a chance of a place," said Farr.

"For an ex-con!"

Shit, thought Farr; it had been a mistake to tell him. He said, "I thought if you showed an effort here . . . if the court could be told you were genuinely cured and properly contrite . . . that some sort of probation might be possible."

"You've got to be joking!" sneered the boy.

It was better to appear naive, decided Farr. He said, "That's what I thought. We'll have to see."

Howard's look of curiosity heightened Farr's unease. "You tell Jennings everything?" he demanded. "About the buy?"

"No," said Farr, continuing the part of the fool. "I just said I hoped to get you treatment."

"You sure you haven't set up some deal!"

"No deal," insisted Farr. "Don't think you're getting any special breaks."

"How long do I stay in this dump?"

"The doctors decide that."

"Great!" said Howard. "I go through a detox to get me fit to appear before a court that's going to throw me into the slammer and lose the key. What a choice!"

"It's a choice you made," said Farr. Halpern had advised against criticism: damn! He said, "I'll come up to see you as often as I can."

"Don't go to any trouble."

"If I considered it any trouble, I wouldn't," said Farr. "Stop trying to be hip and smart. You're neither." Careful, he thought.

"Were those the words in your day? Hip and smart?"

"They still translate."

"We going to do the generation-gap bit?"

"Not unless you want to."

"You know what I want."

"Why!" He was going against all the advice and they were the experts and he wasn't, so perhaps it was wrong, but surely he was allowed the one question?

Howard smirked again, unfolding his body, delaying the reply. "Because it feels good," he said.

"No. It can't be that. That's too trite. You can't have done what you've done—*everything* you done—just because it *feels* good! Children suck sweets and eat ice cream because it feels good."

"And they masturbate and try to touch girls' tits and do dope because it feels good, too."

Farr stood staring down at his son, helpless to reply. He'd behaved exactly as Dr. Halpern had told him not to, which meant he was a fool. But the conversation had convinced him that Howard was more likely to be among the ninety percent failures rather than among the ten percent successes. He said, "I'm going to leave you now."

"The man with the key to freedom!"

"I'll come—" Farr stopped short of saying "often," remembering Halpern's warning. "Like I said I would," he finished awkwardly.

"Like the song says, I'll tie a yellow ribbon around the old oak tree!"

Farr recognized that Howard was openly goading him now, prodding for some outburst. "It's a song about a hero," he allowed himself; then he strode from the room and stood directly outside, watching the attendant resecure the door.

The walk back to the front of the sanatorium allowed Farr sufficient time to recover, so that he was completely in control of himself by the time he reached Halpern's office and thanked the man.

Only Brennan remained, patient as always, in the front hall. "Jim's gone on ahead, to get things organized."

"Organized?"

"I told you that you were going to get backing," reminded Brennan. "Thought you might like to meet the team."

"Fine," said Farr, his mind still occupied by the latest encounter and not really interested in what the FBI man was suggesting.

With Brennan in the passenger seat, he regained Route 6; they drove for some way back toward Boston before there was any conversation. It was Brennan who initiated it.

"So Howard's in care."

"I'm sorry," said Farr. "I've already thanked Schuster,

this morning. I guess I owe you some thanks, too. So thank you.''

"We've kept our side of the bargain," said Brennan.

"Yes."

"Now we expect you to keep yours."

Farr looked quickly sideways and then back toward the road. "Just wait to see how well I do it!" he said, with a determination hardened by the recent confrontation with his son.

Brennan gave the directions when they regained Boston, guiding him not to the FBI offices as Farr had expected but to a small feeder road off Bedford Street. It was dark by now, so Farr wasn't properly able to study the outside, but from the surroundings he guessed it was one of the old Boston houses, with a history attached to it. Brennan opened the door with his own key, shouted "Hi!" and, without waiting for an answer, carried on across the hallway and thrust open double doors leading into a large central living room. Farr saw Seymour first, already approaching to greet them. Behind the lofty man were four other people. One was a woman, and disoriented as he was, Farr still thought at once how attractive she was. Beautiful in fact.

6

He seemed to be going through a period of constant introductions, thought Farr. This time it was Seymour, already
established in the room, who made them, politely bringing
the woman forward first. Her name was Harriet Becker
and she had an easy smile, a firm handshake and dark hair
which fell fully to her shoulders. Farr wondered what part
she was to play, but it was a fleeting reflection, because
Seymour hurried him on. Harvey Mann, the next in line,
was a thickset, bespectacled man who didn't smile and
whose handshake was cursory. William Batty, by comparison, grinned eagerly out of a young, anxious face and
said, "Hi, good to meet you." The last of the party was
Harry Jones, older than Batty, with a distracted demeanor
and spectacles secured at one arm by a twisted paperclip.
Farr wasn't sure he'd got all the names right, apart from
the woman's, but decided they would emerge during whatever conversation they had, so he didn't seek any repetition. He stood slightly back from the group after the initial
greetings, aware for the first time of a well-stocked drinks
tray to the left, near heavily draped windows. With its
fully stuffed furniture and flocked velvet wallpaper, the
room resembled, Farr thought, some dated film set; he
supposed that this was what he'd read about in books and
newspapers as being a "safe house." Such an idea seemed
theatrical, like the setting itself. Brennan offered drinks

51

and Farr accepted gratefully, needing one after the latest
encounter with Howard. Jones and Mann took drinks too,
but Batty and the woman declined. An embarrassed atmosphere developed, of which Brennan appeared to become
aware.

"OK," he said, enthusiastically. "Now that we've met,
let's set out the positions. For this to work—as it must
work—everyone up front has to be squeaky clean as far as
the bad guys are concerned. Not the slightest risk of
identification . . ." He nodded sideways, to Seymour.
"Which is why Jim and I have got to stay buried deep in
the woodwork. We've made narcotics cases not just here
but out on the West Coast as well. For us to be visible
would be far too risky." Brennan paused once more,
indicating Batty and Jones in the one gesture. "Bill and
Harry are the technical side of the operation. When we
finally make a case—or cases—we want as much video-
film and tape-recorded supportive evidence as we can
get." Brennan moved on to Mann. "I guess Harvey is
technical, too, but in a different way. Harvey's the accountant, who's going to keep the books and chart the
money and bring the house tumbling down, when the right
moment comes." Farr was already looking forward to
hearing about the woman before Brennan spoke. "Harriet's the decorative part," grinned the FBI supervisor.
"There'll need to be some sort of office setup, and an
office without a woman is suspicious. She can be de-
scribed as a secretary or personal assistant or whatever
and, apart from allaying any suspicion, she'll have the far
more important function of maintaining the liaison with me
and with Jim—" The man raised his hand, attempting
reassurance. "We'll never be far away, don't worry," he
said. "There just might be a time when you'd like us a
little closer. And quickly."

"When they start shooting, you mean?" Batty tried to
make the question sound like a joke, but Farr detected the
concern in the technical man's voice.

"It's been known," came in Seymour. "The Colombians—and it's the Colombians we're particularly targeting—are vicious bastards. And since it's come up, let's talk it through. This isn't an operation that anyone can lay back on. Not for a moment. Make one mistake—just let a suspicion arise—and they could come in shooting." He paused, to let the warning settle. "Don't think I'm being dramatic," he insisted. "They'll kill, just like that." He snapped his fingers.

Farr hoped his concern was not showing, particularly to the woman. Until this moment the possibility of physical harm hadn't occurred to him; in fact, he hadn't even considered the technicalities of what he was being asked to do. Farr had never knowingly had to face the prospect of physical pain or injury: to enter or put himself into a situation where it was a likelihood. He didn't know if he was brave—if, indeed, physical danger was a test of bravery. Would they let him be armed? Whether he was or not didn't depend entirely upon them, he realized; as a private citizen he could apply for and most probably obtain a weapon. But what would he do with it, if he got it? He didn't know how to shoot a gun, had never wanted to and didn't want to now. Seymour *was* being overly dramatic, despite the denial. Farr glanced around the room, at the serious faces of the people with whom he would be working.

"What sort of protective backup will there be, besides you two?" Mann asked Seymour.

It was a question he himself wanted answered, but Farr was glad it came from the accountant.

"That'll be an on-ground decision," said Brennan. "We start amassing armies and we're going to become too visible." He nodded at the woman. "We'll make the decisions on a day-to-day basis, depending upon what Harriet tells us. Don't worry. If things start getting heavy, then we'll get heavy, too."

"Don't forget," said Harriet.

Her accent was difficult to place, but Farr guessed she was from somewhere in the South. She'd smiled when she spoke and Farr thought that, of the assembled FBI personnel, she seemed the least worried; he decided again how glad he was that the nervous question had come from Mann.

"We won't," said Seymour. "Believe us, we won't."

"How long's all this likely to take?" demanded Jones. "I'd like to tell my wife how long I'll be away from home."

"To get it right, I don't care how long it takes," said Brennan. "Elsewhere there's been talk about six months, but that period was really to judge progress or otherwise. We've not overlooked the personal difficulties . . ." He stopped again, turning to Batty. "You're married, too, aren't you, Bill?"

The technician nodded and Farr, interested, waited for a similar confirmation from the woman. She said nothing and Brennan didn't question.

"I'd quite like to know, for the same reason," said Mann.

"We'll try to get you home as often as possible," promised Seymour. "That's a commitment."

"I appreciate it," said Jones.

"Me, too," said Batty.

"Would there be a chance of bringing my wife down to Florida, maybe?" asked Mann.

"I think that's got to be another on-ground decision, to be made as we go along."

"What's Florida got to do with it?" interjected Farr.

"That's where we're going to set up the front," said the accountant.

"Who decided that?" persisted Farr.

"I thought . . . well, it's obvious," said Mann.

"Yes," said Farr. "That's exactly what it is. Obvious." He turned to Brennan. "What's my part in this?" he demanded.

"We've already talked that through. You're setting up the investment company."

"*I'm* setting it up?" Looking at Mann, he said, "So I'm running it?"

Brennan became aware of the atmosphere between the two financial experts. "Yes," he said. "You're running it. That's the deal."

"So Florida's out," decided Farr, with intentional forcefulness. "From what we've discussed so far, we're not going for the penny-ante street vendors, with a few million dollars. We're going for the big guys. There have been too many false-front financial operations already in Florida ever to hope to get the sort of people you want involved. If you want big, you're going to have to think big."

Mann colored and Farr wondered if it was the remark he resented or the confirmation from the FBI supervisor that he was going to be subservient to someone outside the Bureau.

"OK," said the accountant, belligerently. "What's your idea?"

Farr didn't respond at once, belatedly regretting any bad feeling arising between himself and a man with whom he was going to have to work closely in the coming weeks and months—regretting, too, that he was obviously showing off in front of a woman he didn't know. Impressing a woman wasn't what mattered. What mattered was creating a smooth-running operation with a smooth-running team to achieve what the FBI wanted and what Alvin Schuster wanted and pulling Howard back from disaster.

"It depends on the need," he said at last, as if Mann were going to be the person who decided. "Purpose of the exercise is to attract big-time—really big-time—traffickers. To do that we've got to set up an investment corporation able to wash not millions—I've already been told millions are easy in drug trafficking—but *billions*, billions we can trace and track and seize, when the time comes. We can't do that from the American mainland. Maybe once, when the banks were sloppy about their requirements under the Currency and Foreign Transactions Act. But they're not sloppy anymore. OK, so we both know there are ways around the requirements. But they're small-time ways—

compared with what we're going for—for small-time operators."

"You mean offshore?" said Mann, anxious to prove to those in the room his understanding.

"Exactly!" said Farr. "I'm not going to bother with the marginals, like Vanuatua or Naura. For practical purposes, we've got a lot of choices . . ." He held up his hands, collapsing his fingers as he recited. "The Bahamas, Bermuda, the Caymans, Turks and Caicos, the Netherland Antilles, Monserrat, the British Virgin Islands, the Channel Islands, Panama, Liechtenstein, Monaco, Bahrein or Hong Kong."

There was a shift from the people in front of him and Batty gave one of his hope-to-please smiles which Farr decided was an expression of admiration.

"What about Switzerland?" demanded Mann, in immediate challenge.

"Good," said Farr, trying to build bridges. "The problem is the Mutual Assistance Treaty on Criminal Matters. If Washington can prove that money held in a Swiss bank comes from crime, Bern will provide all the bank and transaction details. And if the accusation is proven, the money is forfeited. So Switzerland is an important part of the chain—because we might need the provisions of that treaty—but not the beginning of it." Farr chanced a direct look at the woman. Harriet Becker was regarding him expressionlessly.

"So what are you suggesting?" asked Brennan.

"When we're operating, I shall probably channel through them all," said Farr. "It's the proper way for an investment analyst to work—the way they'd expect me to work . . ." He hesitated, talking directly to Mann. "I think the practical place to establish our corporation is in the Caymans." Mann was about to speak but Farr hurried over him. "The British and American governments have concluded an exchange-of-information agreement in the Caymans, similar to that of Switzerland. We'll use it, when the time comes. Like we'll probably use the Swiss agreement."

"I don't like it," said Brennan. "We don't have jurisdiction in the Caymans."

Farr frowned at the FBI man and felt uncomfortable
when he realized he was exaggerating his response for
Harriet's benefit. He said, "That's its *advantage*, for God's
sake! It'll make the people we're trying to catch more
relaxed. But you're not even surrendering jurisdiction, if it
works as I understand it will. Where will the money
predominantly be coming from that they'll want us to
launder?"

Brennan and Seymour exchanged awkward glances.
"America, I guess," said Seymour.

"So there's your jurisdiction!" said Farr, triumphantly.
"If it works as I plan it to work, the Caymans will be the
pivot. From America will come verifiable narcotics cash,
from verifiable emissaries. And the proof of their being
emissaries will come from the second leg of the operation,
when that cash goes into Colombia or Bolivia or to some
Mafia enterprise. The perfect pivot."

"It'll mean becoming established there, then?" queried
Mann, still seeking flaws. "Apartments, houses, stuff like
that?"

"Which will erode the budget," said Seymour, speaking more to Brennan than to the investment broker.

"What the hell are you quibbling about?" demanded
Farr, too forcefully he thought, immediately regretting it.
"You come to me and say you're planning something big;
something *really* big. We're going to get the billionaires.
And now we're talking about budgets and accommodation.
We're not going to get within miles of people used to
dealing in hundreds and thousands of millions if your
concern is rental costs and budgetary allowances. If it
comes down to that, then, personally involved though I am
in another respect, we'd better call the whole thing off,
here and now." What would happen to Howard if they
called his bluff and *did* abort? If he wasn't careful, this
inexplicable—even juvenile—wish to play the macho part
in front of a woman who was probably happily married, or

happily involved at least, could end up destroying whatever limited, uncertain future that Howard might have.

"We have to work within a budget," cautioned Seymour.

"Everybody does," said Farr. He nodded to Mann. "He's the accountant, the man who's going to keep the books. There'll be a proper accounting, at the end of every week or every month, or whatever period Washington decides they want." Farr realized that, although offered as a reassurance to the two FBI field agents, the statement reduced Mann into a clerklike role.

"It wasn't quite what we had in mind," admitted Seymour.

"Then we'd better talk it through, so there isn't any misunderstanding," insisted Farr. "And the first clear understanding must be that the Caymans are expensive: as expensive as hell. You, with a budget, may think that's a disadvantage. I see it as a positive bonus. If we're trying to impress multimillionaires that we're a company that knows exactly what it's doing and how to do it, then an address in Crewe Road, Grand Cayman, is a dozen times more impressive than Collins Avenue, Miami Beach. Just by *being* there, we prove it. So, OK, we're going to need accommodation, because it's logical to have something, but there's no domiciliary requirement for setting up on the islands—we could economize there, if economies have to be made."

"You sure it's necessary?" queried Brennan.

"Positive."

"I'm not," said Mann. "I still think we could get away with something on the mainland. In Florida."

"Get away!" sneered Farr. "Is that the principle of this! Getting away and making stupid reductions. I've already had a lecture about this operation not being to catch small-time dealers. I thought we were going beyond that . . ." Farr remembered the argument with the district attorney and linked it with this discussion. He said to Brennan, "This hasn't been thought out, has it? None of it? You came to me and made it sound as if everything had been planned and considered and formalized. But it hasn't been planned at all . . .'' He stopped again. ''Have you actually *got* a budget?''

''A provisional allocation,'' conceded Brennan.

''So let's talk about a positive allowance,'' said the increasingly disillusioned Farr. ''Most important is working capital. No one is going to come near us with a long pole unless we can satisfy their professional advisors that we're legitimate and solvent.''

''How much?'' asked Harriet, in an unexpected intrusion.

''I would consider two million the absolute minimum,'' said Farr. ''I'd prefer four million. We'll need spacious offices—which aren't easy in the Caymans—not a hole in the wall. We'll need accommodation for ourselves. It's a small, self-contained island, so we needn't invest in any large, impressive car pool. One vehicle will probably do, not necessarily anything big. Fees and setting-up costs will be in the region of a hundred to a hundred and fifty thousand.''

''We've been able to borrow from banks large sums of money—millions sometimes—when we've been feigning a buy and needed to look convincing, but I don't recall any occasions when we've wanted to take it out of the country,'' said Seymour, still cautious.

''Something else that hasn't been thought through!''

''How sure are you that—even if you go to all this trouble and expense—you can create what's necessary?'' asked the usually aloof Jones.

''Not at all,'' admitted Farr. He gestured to Brennan. ''I've already said that all I can guarantee is an investment company that I know will withstand any sort of scrutiny or examination. You're supposed to have the contacts who will lead the people you're after directly into the trap.'' Farr gazed pointedly into his empty whisky glass. Continuing his newfound role as the unchallenged expert, he got up uninvited and refilled it. Remaining by the drinks table, he said, ''If it's going to have any chance to work, then it's got to be done properly. No economies. Nothing cheap.''

"Convincing," admitted Seymour.

"I think we need further discussions with Washington," said Brennan.

"If it gets modified, then it isn't the proposal you put to me," said Farr. "Certainly it won't stand any chance of the success you've demanded."

"Florida is still possible," offered the insistent Harvey Mann.

"The sort of thing that could be set up in Florida was never part of any discussions between us," reminded Farr.

"What do you want us to do?" asked Batty.

Farr was uneasy at the degree of uncertainty that existed in the room. And not just the room, he remembered: there had been the conference with the district attorney, a warning of what was to follow. He had imagined slick, coordinated planning and knew now there wasn't any. They were stumbling forward, step by step.

"Give me twenty-four hours," said Brennan, generally. Directly to Farr he said, "Sure it's necessary—the money, particularly?"

"If you want it to work," insisted Farr. "I'm not suggesting that the three or four million will vanish, for Christ's sake! We need to be able to show we have capital. And not just—although that's essential—for any trafficker's lawyer to discover, during a credit search. This is going to be an official company and there's official liquidity requirements to satisfy in the Caymans. Eventually, it'll be returnable: there's no risk."

"Can you guarantee that?" asked the pen-twirling FBI supervisor.

"Of course I can't guarantee it." Farr was irritated by the naiveté of the question. "But I can't see what danger there would be to it. It's not for investment; I don't intend gambling with it."

"Who'd control it; be responsible for it?" said Seymour.

"I would."

"What sort of receipt would we have?"

"I thought you already had it, at Eastham."

The tall FBI man colored and said, "Sorry."

"I don't need to steal your money," said Farr, refusing him the escape. "If you don't trust me that much, then there's another reason for not bothering to go ahead."

"Just give me another twenty-four hours," repeated Brennan. "We'll all meet here again on Wednesday."

Farr moved close to the senior FBI man, not wanting his question to carry to the others. "How does this leave Howard, if everything is called off?"

"I don't know," admitted Brennan.

The two FBI men overflew New York, going direct to Washington for a meeting they arranged before they left Boston, so Farr returned to Manhattan alone. He lay back on the cramped shuttle with his eyes closed, trying to review events. The positive thing was that Howard was in care and being treated. The confusion about what he imagined to be a well-organized scheme was unsettling, but it would be wrong at this stage to consider it a failure before it even began; or try to hypothesize what might happen to Howard if it were canceled. All he could do was what Brennan had asked. Wait. Which left one unanswered question. Why had it been so important to behave as he had and attempt to impress Harriet Becker? Since Ann's death, women had occupied an unimportant role in Farr's life. There were women friends who were just that, friends: people with whom he could go out to dinner and to the theater or to the opera without the beneath-the-surface awkwardness of the relationship progressing further. And there had been the occasional—very occasional—sexual involvement. But rarely had there been such an immediate reaction as there had been to Harriet Becker. Another uncertainty, to go with all the rest. Farr disliked uncertainty.

7

Jorge Gomez decided that things were going his way. At last. Today would be the decider and it could still go wrong—which would mean the waste of almost ten months' work and manipulation, and worse, the loss of face to some very important American connections. But there was nothing more he could do: no insurance he hadn't invoked, no possible difficulty he hadn't anticipated and prepared for. So now—from today, this moment, now—everything had to take its course. If it went wrong—if Julio Navarra failed to show and Gomez still hadn't heard from his widespread contacts within the immigration and airport service of the man's arrival—then he would be made to look stupid. Antonio Scarletti would go back to the Bruno family in Philadelphia and tell everyone that he, Jorge Herrera Gomez, the prince regent of the cocaine traffickers, couldn't deliver. If it went right, then he'd look the opposite. He wouldn't be prince regent anymore; he'd be king. He'd be the sensible, thinking Colombian who'd used his intermediary expertise to corner the coca production of Bolivia's biggest and most influential grower and channel it exclusively to one of America's most important and influential Mafia families. U.S. task forces and European enforcement agencies would be fucked because what Gomez was putting together was intended to be the world's first multinational drug-dealing enterprise, the profits from which would make the rest of the minuscule multinationals look like paupers glad to collect money in cloth caps and tin cans by begging at theater queues.

It hadn't been easy—but then, he hadn't expected it to be. For him to be the *número uno*—in Latin South America as well as Latin North America—it had been important that they came to him. At first, the machismo of Julio Navarra forbade that; and the pride of the Bruno family in general, and of Antonio Scarletti in particular, made the idea preposterous. But, without conceit, Gomez knew he had done it right, after the initial, thoughtless approach.

It was more than nine months ago now—when he'd flown to La Paz and waited cap-in-hand at the Cochabamba suite, with the drinks and the canapés ready, for an entire frustrating, humiliating week, before being summoned, cap-in-hand still, to Santa Ana de Yacuma and granted as if by royal decree a meeting with Julio Cesar Navarra. And the bastard had laughed at him! *Openly* laughed, for the encouragement of the acolytes: a king disdaining the bumptious courtier who argued that the world wasn't flat and that what any of them had done so far hadn't begun to tap the revenues of the new, eagerly sniffing world over the curve of the horizon. Navarra wasn't laughing anymore. He hadn't been for months, and today was the final, unspoken—although Gomez thought something vocal might be possible later—apology for that charade at Santa Ana de Yacuma. Today Julio Cesar Navarra was coming to him, here in Medellin. Just as Antonio Scarletti—already a don in the Mafia, but aspiring to be *capo di tutti capi* of every family throughout America—was coming to him in Medellin. It had been inspired, after the Bolivian embarrassment, to ignore Navarra and concentrate instead upon America. Gomez liked Scarletti. The Italian-American wasn't interested in scoring points for the benefit of the hangers-on. Scarletti was interested in the most important thing: making money. It was when the approach came from Philadelphia that the ridiculous Navarra had changed his mind and begun to take the proposition seriously. Gomez knew he would kill the Bolivian; *wanted* to kill him. But only when the time was right—only after they'd forged the three-way link that was his concept and Gomez had learned enough about Navarra's complete operation. Gomez determined to find someone within Navarra's organization who was ambitious—although not foolishly ambitious, like so many were—and he'd nurture and encourage him, and when Gomez staged the overthrow he'd have what he'd always intended to have: the exclusive conduit from the most productive coca-growing provinces of Bolivia through his distribution chain to the equally efficient organization of a leading American Mafia family. Going my way, he thought again.

Gomez was unusual among the trafficking operators of Colombia. He complied, of course—by, for example, putting the required number of his own men into the *Muerte a Sequestradores* army that offered protection against guerrilla kidnappers who thought that the relatives of recognized traffickers were legitimate kidnap victims. He supported Pablo Escabar financially during the government elections, and attended the gatherings of Garces and Ramos and Lehder and Alverez-Moreno and Zuleta and Quintero and Davilla and Nasser and the von Griekens and the La Fauries and the Londonos—not from any hold-together commitment, but because he knew that, if he didn't, they'd consider him a breakaway opponent and, until he became established and replaced Escabar and Lehder, he ran the risk of becoming one of the daily stripped, dead and mutilated victims of the city and country's drug trade. In reality, Gomez despised the muscle-rippling machismo and the rancho motor rangers with belching flames painted along their bodywork and the need to impress with yet another delivery helicopter or yet another delivery aircraft. He thought the others were insular and self-obsessed and foolish. Jorge Herrera Gomez wasn't insular or self-obsessed, and certainly not foolish. He was a man with an ambition— an ambition he intended to achieve. He wanted to become the richest, most influential, most powerful drug trafficker, not just in Latin or North America, but throughout the world. If Julio Navarra kept today's appointment, he would become just that.

Reminded, Gomez called for the third time the immigration inspector at Medellin, and for the third time was told that there had been no arrival of anyone called Julio Navarra nor anyone answering the physical description or resembling the photograph Gomez had thoughtfully provided. Two hours remained before they were all scheduled to meet, so there was time enough—because, of course, Navarra would be using his own aircraft and not be dependent upon any civil service, but Gomez still wasn't happy about the uncertainty.

The Intercontinental is the only prestigious hotel in Medellin—the place where the traffickers stage their parties and their gatherings, each to impress the other—and it was here that Gomez had booked in the already-arrived Scarletti and the still-to-arrive Navarra. He summoned the hotel manager and repeated an earlier tour of the Bolivian's suite, ensuring that the bar was stocked and the flowers fresh from a valley that boasted the best orchids in the world. He made the manager reiterate that, if Señor Navarra sought anything the hotel felt unable to provide, they would nevertheless promise to provide it and call at once one of the four numbers he had specified, so his own people could complete the order. Gomez didn't know if Navarra used his own product—if he did, he was stupid, but then Navarra *was* stupid—but he had instantly available a supply of the purest refined cocaine. If he fucked, there were girls available. Boys, too, if that was the way he did it. The same facilities were available to Scarletti, and Gomez was impressed that neither the American nor any of the five men who accompanied him had drawn upon them. It proved he had been right in going to Scarletti and the Bruno family: they were proper businessmen, impatient with distractions—and, like proper businessmen, they were interested only in profit. Fleetingly, Gomez considered calling their suite, to inquire if everything was satisfactory, but it was *only* a fleeting reflection because he realized it would make him appear anxious.

Gomez twitched at the intrusive shrill of the telephone. Then, at once, he smiled his thanks and said of course the informant in the airport control tower should be promised a reward for the information that Navarra's private aircraft had filed an onward-flight plan from Bogotá and was already on its way. As fleetingly as he had considered approaching Scarletti's suite, Gomez mentally debated the idea of going out to the airport to meet the Bolivian producer. Instead, he stayed in his own suite, savoring what the confirmation of Navarra's arrival meant. The Bolivian *had* come. Scarletti had come. They were the supplicants: the ones who wanted, who ached, for the deal. Gomez felt warm against the cold. Anyone less controlled, less determined, might have considered something as theatrical as a meaningless, solitary drink, or— considering where they were and the subject of discussion—a celebratory snort of the product. Gomez had started using coke—although privately, so that none of his people would know—but was completely aware how wrong it would be at this moment. Maybe later. Like his other, still favorite, indulgence, which was fucking, which he did every day and rarely with the same girl, preferring it to be a financial, transitory episode. Although he felt like fucking now, Gomez decided there wasn't time. But that there would be a celebration later—and with more than one woman, as a celebration ought to be.

He stood at the window, able from the high elevation of the hotel actually to stare out over the Medellin airport, which occupied the middle of the valley, picking out his own planes among those of the other traffickers clustered at the private section of the field. He could see the dwarf-like figures of the service personnel as they readied two that were, later that day, to fly up to Barranquilla to make the marijuana collection. Although cocaine was Gomez's principal activity—and increasing personal interest—there was still sufficient profit in marijuana to make its cultivation, and its trade, very much worthwhile. Once again, ahead of everyone, Gomez had imported from California—a reverse smuggling route—*sinsemilla*, and already had two extensive plantations of the superior marijuana, in which the tetrahydrocannabinol was particularly high. Beyond the parking area, Gomez could see private as well as commercial aircraft arriving and departing. He wished it were possible to isolate it, the Bolivian's plane; he would have enjoyed seeing the moment of Navarra's arrival, the very moment of the man coming to *him*.

A thin, tightly coiled man, Gomez turned away from the window. He prepared himself for the encounter with the care with which he'd devoted to everything else. The subdued gray shirt toned in with the subdued gray trousers, and the sports jacket was a muted gray check. Just as Gomez disdained the flamboyant dress of the other traffickers, so he despised the almost universal predilection for gold jewelry and decoration. Gomez wore only a slim gold wristwatch, a discreet Piaget.

He had installed further along the corridor his immediate coterie of protectors—headed, sensibly, by his cousin; family were always safe. It would have been madness, after all, to consider moving around a city which averaged six drugs-related murders a day without protectors. But intentionally and cleverly he had dispensed with them for the meeting, wanting Navarra and Scarletti visibly to be aware that he wasn't frightened nor needed bodyguards. So, when the attentive undermanager came to check that nothing had been forgotten or overlooked, Gomez answered the door himself. He knew nothing had been forgotten, but he still enjoyed letting the man fuss about the rooms and check the bar and the refreshments and pointlessly rearrange already perfectly arranged flowers. Gomez thanked the man and tipped him in American money—a twenty-dollar bill—and then sat back, waiting. He told himself that he wasn't suffering from nerves: it was excitement at the moment of everything coming to fruition. Excitement, too, at winning. He always intended to win.

Gomez went to the door again at the knock, smiling to see Scarletti. The American had come alone. Scarletti was a small man, little over five foot tall, but he didn't have a small man's need to impress. He had an open, unworried face and was dressed as conservatively as Gomez, in unobtrusive blue.

"Navarra isn't here yet," said the Colombian. "I know he's coming; it shouldn't be long."

Scarletti nodded, showing no curiosity at Gomez's knowledge. "Don't you have a place here, in Medellin?"

Gomez gestured toward the invisible Andean range, against which the hotel was built. "Two *fincas*," he said. "I've a house on the coast, too. At Riohacha."

"I thought we might have met at your house," said the American.

Gomez had considered it but decided that it would have been too much to expect Navarra to come to his home. "The hotel was more convenient," he said. He didn't add "neutral."

"Sure it's OK?" asked Scarletti, looking around the spacious apartment. "I get uneasy in hotels."

Gomez smiled at the concern, careful against appearing patronizing. "The whole floor is ours," he said. "And the authorities aren't a problem for me, here in Medellin; in Colombia even."

"Good place to operate," said Scarletti.

There was a sound at the door. Gomez didn't hurry to respond. Four men accompanied Navarra, grouped tightly and directly behind the man, in a protective half-circle. Gomez looked briefly at the Bolivian, then beyond to the guards and said, "We're by ourselves."

He stood back, allowing Navarra to enter. The Bolivian did so with head-bent curiosity. He almost at once became uncomfortable at the realization that he had put himself at a disadvantage by bringing escorts to the room.

"Better we speak just among ourselves, don't you think?" said Gomez, wanting to heighten the Bolivian's unease.

"Sure," said Navarra, in quick, irritated agreement.

He jerked his head impatiently, dismissing his people into the corridor.

"Antonio Scarletti, Julio Navarra," said the Colombian, entering his role as host.

Scarletti nodded at the introduction and Navarra nodded back. Neither man smiled nor made any gesture, such as offering to shake hands.

"Can I get anyone a drink?" offered Gomez. Now that they were here, he could afford to appear subservient in small things.

"Scotch," said Navarra. He was indulgently fat, stomach bulging under a bright red shirt. He wore two medallioned gold necklaces and a gold wristlet band on each arm.

"Just a soda," said Scarletti. "Seven-Up will be fine."

Gomez made the drinks but didn't take one himself. "Thank you for coming," he said, as he handed them the glasses. "It's going to be worthwhile—for all of us."

"I hope so," said Scarletti.

"How worthwhile?" demanded Navarra.

"We're going to become the biggest," promised Gomez, simply. "The biggest operation there is."

"How?" said Scarletti.

"By organizing ourselves properly." Gomez nodded toward Navarra. "By guaranteeing supplies from the biggest coca manufacturer in Bolivia and channeling it through me, in established regular shipments, up to you in Philadelphia for distribution throughout America and Europe. At the moment there isn't any proper setup. Not like there should be." He indicated Navarra again. "You sell to whom you can, seeking buyers." He turned to Scarletti. "And you buy from whom you can, seeking sellers. My way will concentrate all that. Guaranteed purchaser, guaranteed supplier. No other middle men, no other involvement. We can double our income. Triple it maybe."

"How?" demanded Navarra, allowing the hostility to show.

"The most important part. I used the word 'guarantee.' I guarantee to buy all the coca you can produce, and I guarantee that I will get every shipment through to Philadelphia or wherever else you stipulate for delivery."

"There are task forces everywhere in the States now," said Scarletti. "How can you guarantee there won't be any interception?"

"I intend retaining a stockpile, here in Colombia, after refining. Any shipment intercepted will be replaced, in full, within a week. If I can't replace the order in cocaine, I'll guarantee it to you in cash. You'll have already been paid, of course," he said to Navarra.

"That's a big undertaking," said Scarletti, allowing his admiration to show.

"Which I wouldn't have given if I hadn't thought I'd be able to keep it," said Gomez. "That's the deal." He looked carefully between the two other men. "What do you think?"

"I like it," said Scarletti, at once. "How much stuff are we talking about?"

"As much as you can handle and shift. Tons. Sufficient not just for all your outlets in America but in Europe, as well. Like I said, we'll be the *biggest*."

"I get paid whatever happens to the shipment?" asked Navarra.

"On the day of delivery, here in Colombia," promised Gomez. "And I'll guarantee collection from you as well. All you have to do is cultivate the coca."

"You get the best part of the deal," Scarletti said to the Bolivian. Gomez prevented any expression of satisfaction at Navarra's role being diminished.

"And you get your supplies," he repeated to Scarletti. "The risk is in the middle and I'm the one who's taking it, with a money-back guarantee."

"You're right," said the American reflectively. "This could make us the biggest."

"*Will* make us the biggest," insisted Gomez. "All I want today is the decision."

"Yes," said Scarletti. "I'm definitely in."

"Will you be our supplier?" Gomez asked the Bolivian, phrasing the question so the man would realize that, if he didn't agree, they would go to someone else.

Navarra frowned and Gomez wondered if the man understood how he'd been trapped. "Yes," he said after a pause. "I agree."

Gomez allowed himself the theatricality of shaking hands, with Scarletti first. Navarra hesitated and then responded. Enjoying the unusual exuberance, Gomez offered more drinks and Scarletti joined in, accepting Scotch now that the business had been settled.

"To a successful and fruitful partnership," toasted Gomez.

"A successful and fruitful partnership," echoed Scarletti.

"I hope it proves to be so," said the still-doubtful Navarra.

"What are we going to do, with all the money!" enthused Scarletti.

"Make more money," said Gomez.

The director of the Eastham clinic waited patiently for the case doctor, whose name was Belson, to finish his report and then said, "As bad as that?"

"That's my opinion," said Belson.

"Tranquilizers won't be enough?" queried Halpern.

"Not for a long time," insisted the doctor into whose care Howard Farr had been entrusted. "I've prescribed clonidine and naltexone to block the narcotic craving."

"What's his general attitude?"

"Hostile," said Belson.

"Think he'll run?"

"I haven't got any doubt about it," said Belson. "He looks at the keys and the locks like he'd look at a hypodermic."

"What sort of therapy do you recommend?" asked the director.

"Nothing group, not at this stage," replied Belson. "He'd wreck any session. It'll have to be one-to-one."

Halpern sat back in his chair, sighing. "So young Howard is going to be a problem for us?"

"Unless he's stronger than we both think he is."

"I pity the father," said Halpern. "He's worried to hell. I think he still can't believe it's happened."

At that moment the telephone sounded in Farr's Manhattan townhouse. The investment broker recognized Peter Brennan's voice at once: "It's agreed. Everything your way."

Gomez did the coke by himself—because he didn't want anyone to observe his enjoyment of it—but summoned Orlando Ramos to join him with the women. Gomez decided he was lucky, having Ramos as his chief protector. They were cousins and had grown up with each other, in Medellin. Ramos was family; someone he could trust—not bright enough to be ambitious for the top job but happy always to be the loyal lieutenant.

8

The need for Brennan and Seymour to return to Washington for further consultation had caused a hiatus and Farr was glad of it. Everything had happened too quickly from the moment of his first encounter with the FBI agents, not permitting him sufficient time to think. Farr realized that, whatever happened in the coming weeks and months—and, despite his apparent confidence at the Boston planning meeting, he hadn't the remotest idea what might happen—he still had business and clients to consider, and brokers who relied upon him. What was occurring was an aberration, a nightmare intrusion into his orderly, settled, complete and satisfied life. For an indefinite period—he wished to God he knew how long—he was going to be forced into an absurd situation more fitting to a five-dollar novel or a cheap movie than to Walter James Farr, revered investment broker, pillar of Wall Street respectability. But aberrations were like hiatus; only temporary. When it was over, he would return to the life he knew and in which he felt safe—which meant taking as many precautions as possible to protect the business while he was away.

Farr had structured his business as a pyramid, so it wasn't necessary to summon everyone in the firm. Angela Nolan had to be briefed, of course—while he was away, the burden of his part of the corporation would fall predominantly upon her—and the other immediate division managers, Paul Brent, Richard Bell and Hector Faltham. Particularly Faltham.

Faltham had joined him within a year of his setting up business and Farr didn't regard him as an employee. Faltham and his wife, Nancy, still invited Farr for weekends and at Thanksgiving, although the two men's social involvement wasn't as frequent as it had been when Ann was alive and they made foursomes for dinner and for the theater.

Angela entered the conference suite first, habitually eager, obviously wanting to ask in advance of the others' arrival the reason for the summons. Brent and Faltham arrived together, shirt-sleeved and relaxed, and Bell was late, apologizing as he came into the room and explaining that he'd been held on a telephone conversation to Hong Kong. They grouped themselves familiarly around the table and Angela said, "It isn't time for the monthly conference. What's all the mystery?"

"No mystery," said Farr, hoping he'd rehearsed everything sufficiently. "I've decided upon a little expansion."

"Expansion?" queried Faltham, the man who knew him best and was therefore most familiar with his method.

Farr supposed that the reaction was predictable. And not just from Faltham. It was practically a joke among them that although they had all the business they could handle and were turning clients away every day, they were determined against becoming an uncontrollable conglomerate. Farr acknowledged his earlier reluctance to expand and said that he still regarded the Caymans as only an experiment that might not work. He'd apologize when it was all over, Farr thought; explain the reason why he'd had to lie and ask for their understanding. He was sure they'd forgive him. If they had kids in similar situations and had been asked to do what he'd been asked to do, they'd do it—and he would have understood later, when the explanations came.

"The Caymans!" said Brent, voicing everyone's surprise. "Offshore. Funny money. That's not our style."

"I'm not saying that it is," repeated Farr. It was right that he should talk to them—even as incompletely and as possibly dishonestly as this—but he reflected as he did so how fortunate it was that he'd always retained sole control of the business. Partners or directors could, and probably would, have insisted upon a fuller explanation. These people, his most intimate working companions, might question, but when it came to the bottom line they, even Faltham, were still employees—and he was the employer. They couldn't seriously challenge or stop him.

"Surely the Caymans is pretty well established now?" said Faltham, a pipe-smoking, deliberate man who was older than any of the other senior brokers—older, in fact, than Farr. "Would there be sufficient volume of business to make it worthwhile?"

"I won't know until I've explored it thoroughly," said Farr. He looked from one to the other, particularly at Angela. "It'll put an extra burden on all of you, for a time."

"You won't be working from here?" said Brent.

"Not a lot," said Farr. "If it's not feasible, then I don't want to waste my time—our time. I'm going to go down and give it my undivided attention, check it out thoroughly. If it works, then fine. If not, then I can wrap it up with the minimum amount of fuss and bother." He sat hot and uncomfortable under their obviously skeptical looks.

"How long?" demanded Angela.

"I'm not sure," said Farr, anxious to avoid positive commitment. "Maybe six months."

"Six months!" exclaimed Faltham.

"I'll be back and forth during that time. There could be daily telephone or telex liaison, if we thought it necessary."

"You'll want us to get involved?" anticipated Angela hopefully.

"No!" said Farr, regretting at once the quickness of the refusal. Trying to recover, he said, "I'm keeping everything to the minimum. Time, money, and certainly staff. I want you all here looking after the shop. This will always be the mainstay of the business. This *is* the business.'' Would he be able to keep the undertaking to commute back and forth? The FBI would have to allow him that, surely? He would create just the sort of curiosity and uncertainty they were trying to avoid if he simply vanished from a city in which, within a selected environment, he was so well known.

''Never expected this,'' said Faltham. ''Against all our previous policy.''

''So maybe I've changed my mind.'' It was too dismissive and Farr felt further regret: none of them had ever abused the employer/employee relationship and he didn't like having to remind them of it.

''It's your right; your company,'' acknowledged Faltham.

Shit, thought Farr, I'm handling it very badly. ''Like I said, I'll be in constant touch, but you guys will be running things here. I'm going to need your support. I know I'll get it.''

''Of course,'' said the loyal Angela.

''What if the Caymans works? Where after that?'' asked Brent, probably the most ambitious of the senior men.

''Let's see if the Caymans works first.'' Farr was anxious to finish the meeting and stop deceiving them.

''Sure we can make it work,'' said Bell. It was an admiring remark: the man had said ''we,'' but he'd meant ''you.''

In his growing embarrassment, Farr decided that it was inadequate to hope that they would understand and forgive him at some future, indeterminate date. ''We'll see.''

Bell asked when he would be leaving. When Farr said, ''at once,'' the persistent Faltham commented that things were happening not only unexpectedly but also very quickly. Farr lied that he'd been thinking about the project for some time, managing to remind them more subtly this time that he didn't need to discuss anything with them if he didn't choose to do so. Angela asked directly about his personal clients and Farr said they would become her responsibility.

"I'm sending out letters to the most important ones, explaining that I might not be as available as I have been in the past but that it's only temporary—" He looked beyond the woman, to the three men. "If Angela's work-load gets too heavy, I'd appreciate you pitching in."

There were nods of agreement from them all and Faltham said heavily, "Best of luck."

Farr decided that the man expected a fuller explanation. "Maybe I'll need it," he said sincerely.

They'd been very good, the Negress particularly. Professional and athletic and inventive and very good. Gomez was glad he had given them a hundred dollars more than they'd asked for: they deserved it and he was celebrating after all. He decided to have the black girl again. But on her own. Two was a fun fuck but it was distracting. Definitely on her own, next time.

"Good?" he asked, as Ramos emerged from the other bedroom.

"Great," said Ramos, knowing that the man expected gratitude for including him in the orgy.

"I want the black girl again," said Gomez.

"Any time," said Ramos, who always acted as procurer.

"They've agreed," disclosed Gomez. "Navarro and Scarletti."

"Congratulations," said Ramos. The left side of the man's face was creased by the scar of a long-ago knife fight. In a familiar gesture, he ran his finger the length of the scar.

"Scarletti I'm confident of," said Gomez. "Because he's the biggest producer, I've got to deal with Navarra."

"There are others."

"It would mean involving more than one—three, maybe four. The beauty of the whole concept is its simplicity: one supplier, one buyer, with us in the middle."

"We could always switch, if Navarra doesn't work out."

"Watch it, closely," ordered Gomez. "Navarra will try to buy someone, an informant from among our people."

"I'll be careful."

Gomez believed everyone had a price—everyone except Ramos. He thought again how lucky he was to have his cousin so close.

9

Farr's shuttle arrived in time for him to book into the Copley Plaza. Afterward, outside in the square, he considered walking to the safe house off Bedford Street but decided against it, not wanting to be late. As it was, everyone was already assembled by the time he got there.

As he entered the same large room as before, Farr thought in passing that, although he had gone to New York and Brennan and Seymour to Washington, the others in the group must have stayed on in Boston, assembled for the job and with nothing else to do. Farr made a general greeting, smiling toward Harriet, who smiled briefly back. She had very even white teeth.

Farr sat back easily as Brennan recounted the Washington meeting. Farr was conscious of the immediate tightening of Mann's face at the announcement that the operation was going to be conducted out of the Caymans rather than Florida. The man's resentment couldn't stem entirely from their one short meeting. Farr speculated that Mann had felt he could financially organize the entrapment, that there was no need for the involvement of any additional expertise, certainly not expertise from outside the Bureau. Farr conceded that this was an understandable attitude but he hoped it wouldn't become a problem between them.

"How much liquidity?" he asked Brennan.

81

"Better than I expected. Three million," said the FBI man.

"Washington must attach a great deal of importance to this," said Harriet, and Farr wondered once more about the source of her accent.

"They do," said Seymour. "They see it as one of the big ones."

"So now we're set," said Brennan, looking expectantly at Farr.

"When's the money available?" asked the investment broker.

"Whenever you want it."

"Working finance, too? There'll be expenditure on office accommodation, incorporation fees, legal expenses, stuff like that."

"All available," assured Seymour. "You said a hundred and fifty thousand at the last meeting. That's what has been allocated."

His terms appeared to have been met easily, given the vagueness and uncertainty of the last encounter, thought Farr. He said, "Looks as if we can start a business then."

"When?" said Brennan.

"Right away, I suppose. I've told my people in New York I'm going to be absent. . . . Everyone here has been gathered for the specific purpose . . ." Farr hesitated. "There'll be no need for everyone to come down, not at once. It would look unusual, in fact. I'll go down and secure some premises, go through the legal necessities." He turned to the two technical men. "You'd better make a visit before I sign any binding leases, to make sure the premises will be all right for you to work in." To Mann he said, "There's really no point in your thinking of coming down until we're all set up." He didn't intend it to sound as dismissive as it did. The accountant's face stiffened again.

"What about me?" asked Harriet.

"I think it might be an idea for us to travel together," said Farr. "Your supposed role is to be up front, after all. It would look better—more natural—for you to accompany me.'' Was that the sole reason? he asked himself. He pushed the intrusion aside, adding, ''And it's probably a good idea to have someone official with me.'' He smiled at her again. ''You're liaison, after all.''

She didn't smile back. ''All right.''

Brennan took over the conversation, talking through with Jones and Batty the possible difficulty of taking undiscovered into the island the sort of monitoring equipment that would be necessary, appearing relieved when both technicians assured him that what they needed could be stripped down to appear no more unusual than rather complicated photographic equipment with sound attachments. Such equipment wouldn't seem particularly unusual on islands with some of the best scuba water in the world and fish that were frequently photographed. Anything additional could easily be purchased locally.

''We're set then?'' asked Seymour.

''One thing won't be possible,'' disputed Mann.

''What?'' asked Brennan.

''The sort of protection you promised,'' said the accountant.

''We'll be there for a lot of the time,'' said Brennan. ''Certainly at the first indication that there might be difficulties.''

''Just you two,'' persisted Mann. ''You won't be able to have the sort of task force backup that would be possible on the mainland.''

Brennan and Seymour looked at each other. It was Seymour who spoke. ''It was discussed in Washington. You're all volunteers. If any of you feel like withdrawing, now's the time to do it. We can't afford any internal problems once the thing gets underway.''

Do I qualify as a volunteer? thought Farr, as he watched the two FBI organizers invite any of the other assembled people to speak. Farr supposed he was. Just. A reluctant volunteer. No one responded to the invitation and Mann looked away from Brennan's direct gaze.

''Everyone's fully committed then?'' insisted Seymour.

There were mumbles and nods from the men and Harriet said, "Fully committed."

Mann's embarrassment this time was entirely of his own making, thought Farr: it was understandable that the man should be properly apprehensive but if he was that nervous why had he volunteered in the first place?

The conversation continued for some time, but there was really nothing left to say, so Brennan called the meeting to a close. Farr told Harriet that he was staying at the Copley Plaza and invited her to eat with him there that night—extending the invitation to Brennan and Seymour as well, to avoid the appearance of anything more than a business meeting—but Harriet declined, saying that she had last-minute things to do. At the hotel Farr called the Eastham clinic, wanting to visit before he flew south, but the director said he didn't think that seeing Howard so soon was a good idea.

"What's wrong?" asked Farr, immediately alarmed.

"It's not my policy to lie to patients. Or to their relations," said Halpern. "At the moment everything's wrong with Howard. He's needing a lot of help with the detoxification—we're having to use blockade medication, which I didn't want to do—and he's resisting everything we try and do or say to help."

"I should come up."

"No," said Halpern. "Howard's important at the moment—not what you feel you should do. Whatever slight settling in we've managed to achieve—and it's very slight, believe me—would be destroyed by your coming. When would there be another opportunity?"

"I'm not sure." He could make time. The formation procedures—office leasing and legal necessities—would take a while, and there would be days when there was nothing to do. He said, "I'll keep in touch; as soon as you tell me it's OK, I'll come."

"Thank you for your understanding."

"The only thing that matters is helping Howard," said Farr.

Farr supposed he shouldn't have been surprised by the report from Eastham—he had predicted himself what Howard's behavior would be—but he had hoped for something better. He noticed the stationery and envelopes in the suite bureau and wondered if he should write the boy a letter. About what? There was only one subject between them at the moment and he didn't imagine that a letter about it would help Halpern and the other doctors—and he could hardly write a gossipy, newsy letter about what he was about to do.

Farr forced himself on, calling Logan to work out the flight schedules and fixing a connection for himself and Harriet for the following day which involved their transferring for the Cayman plane at Miami. Harriet had given him the number of the Ramada Inn at which she was staying and he called her there, to tell her of the timing. She said thank you and he repeated the dinner invitation; again, she declined.

Despite the circumstances, he was looking forward to it, Farr realized, surprised, as he replaced the telephone. It was a professional anticipation, he decided. Excitement didn't seem the appropriate word, but it was the only one he could think of, so he accepted that he was excited at the prospect of moving out of the financial village of Wall Street and Manhattan to test his ability to set a trap and bait a trap and bring tumbling into it men wealthier than he had ever encountered. Farr remembered Mann's nervousness at today's meeting and the previous one and honestly examined his own feelings. He decided that he *wasn't* scared—in that, at least, he wasn't disappointed.

Farr was in the bar, waiting, when Brennan and Seymour arrived, gazing around the baroque opulence in obvious admiration and attempting jokes about what was possible and not possible on an FBI salary. Brennan inquired about Howard, which Farr appreciated, and Seymour said he was sorry the initial reaction to treatment hadn't been better. In the dining room they ate fish, because they were in Boston. Brennan repeated the importance that Washington attached to what they were doing and said that headquarters was sure they had selected a good team, of which Farr was part. The broker waited for there to be some comment about Mann's uneasiness or even hostility, but it wasn't raised so he didn't mention it.

"Harry and Bill are terrific technicians," praised Seymour. "Nothing they can't do with a camera and a piece of sound equipment."

"Let's hope they'll get the opportunity to prove it," said Farr.

"Harriet's a good operator," said Brennan.

Farr had thought that the conversation would get around to the woman. He said, "Mann's an accountant; Jones and Batty are technicians. What's her specialization?"

"She's not a specialist," said Seymour. "She's a field agent, like us."

"Unusual job for a woman."

"Unusual women do it," said Brennan. "There are a lot of them: most a damned sight better than the men."

"Making sure I don't stray?" asked Farr, in sudden challenge.

"Sir?" said Brennan curiously.

"You said that Harriet was the decorative part, liaison too. And she's a field operative, used to case work. Mann's the accountant—keeping the books, you said. So I've got a case officer and an accountant maintaining a constant monitor to make sure I don't slip."

Seymour smiled in unembarrassed admission. "You're an outsider, Mr. Farr. None of our people—not even accountants like Mann—could come near to you as far as your job is concerned. But this is spreading way beyond what you're accustomed to."

Farr recognized that this didn't refer to any possible violence. "Think I might be tempted?"

"You know the checks we made," said Brennan, extending the admission. "We know the sort of money you usually handle. If this goes half right, you'll be handling more than you ever have before, even at your level. And it'll all be in untraceable cash.''

Farr supposed he should feel offended but he didn't. He *was* an outsider, so there was an argument for putting other professionals alongside him. And it was understandable they would want to maintain as close a check as possible upon the money. ''I promise I won't put my hand in the till.''

''Just doing our job,'' said Brennan.

''That's been the justification for a lot of mistakes, in the past.''

''That's what we're trying to anticipate and avoid,'' said Seymour. ''Mistakes.''

''Let's hope we're both lucky,'' said Farr.

''What about our coming down with you tomorrow?'' asked Seymour.

''I suppose that's a matter for you to decide, but there doesn't seem a lot of purpose. This is nuts and bolts; framework time. We're not going to start operating for weeks; can't operate for weeks . . .'' He permitted himself the indulgence. ''I won't even risk your three million, so you won't have to worry about temptation. I would have thought it better to limit your time there until it is absolutely necessary—when, hopefully, there will be people to see and check out.''

''I think you're right,'' said Brennan.

''Suddenly things seem to have reached an anticlimax,'' complained Seymour. ''Having lived with this idea for so long and managed to set it all up as we originally intended, this part seems to sag.''

''Why not take a vacation?'' suggested Farr. ''Like Mann and Jones and Batty should take a vacation: they made points about their families, so they should enjoy them while the opportunity exists.''

''Maybe you're right,'' said Seymour.

''Isn't that what I've got to be?'' demanded Farr. ''Right?''

*   *   *

Harriet Becker wore jeans and loafers and a wool traveling shirt and Walter Farr felt conspicuously overdressed in
a suit and tie, wishing that he found it easier to relax and
be casual. She was polite and considerate, making incon-
sequential small talk as well as responding to it, but when
the talk flagged there was a book readily available from a
bulging travel bag. It was by someone called Paul Scott
whom Farr didn't know; he wished he'd occupied the
empty hours—he considered he'd had more empty hours
than most people in the immediately preceding years—by
forcing himself to concentrate in the hollow, echoing townhouse on the novels and books he'd begun but was never
able to finish. Harriet refused any drinks on the flight to
Miami. There was a three-hour layover before the Cayman
connection. They studied the menus of the airport restaurants and decided against eating. At the bar she took only a
soda. His martini was weak.

"Do you resent my involvement too?" he said.

"I don't understand the question."

"I get the impression you're holding back a lot."

"I don't understand that, either," she said. "I thought
we were on a job."

"We are," agreed Farr. "Chances are that it'll be a job
that lasts a long time."

"Then over the course of a long time I guess we'll get
to know each other better," she said. She didn't speak for
several moments, then she said, "There's a kind of unwritten rule, in the Bureau. Don't develop friendships that
are too close in case something happens to the person
you're friendly with."

"I'm sorry," said Farr. "Have I strayed onto forbidden
ground?"

"Still-painful ground."

"I'm sorry," he repeated.

"It didn't properly qualify, not according to the rules."

"If it hurts, I don't expect you to tell me."

"It was messy," she said. "Messy in every way. His
name was Jack, Jack Bossy. He had dark hair and nearly

always a five o'clock shadow and he was the supervisor in the San Diego bureau where I was first posted. He was married to a lovely girl called Julie and they had a little boy called John, who had a brace which made him lisp. I used to go to parties—even at their own house—and try to make John like me because I wanted to be his stepmother, and try to hate her, which I couldn't, and try not to let what was happening show.''

She was talking in monotone, staring into a glass in which the ice had long ago melted. "It was a stakeout," she started again. "Drugs, like everything seems to be drugs. We had a tip about a drop and we set it all up but nothing happened. He was control that night so he called it off about one o'clock and I expected us to go back to my place, because the stakeout meant he wasn't due home at any time and it was the sort of thing we'd done before. But he said no. He said he loved me and that he loved Julie and that he loved John and he realized he had to make a decision—and the decision was that he was going to stay with her." She looked directly at him but her eyes were still distant. "You know San Diego?"

"No."

"We were in a late bar, near Balboa Park. I was pleading and he was saying no and we kept drinking. It got so that there wasn't anything for us to say to each other anymore; what we were saying wasn't making any sense. We started to argue, of course, saying silly things, things I can't even remember, not properly, although I've tried to, a lot of times since . . . Wish so much that I could. In the books and the movies it's always supposed to be the girl who runs out first, but it was Jack who left. He said it had to end and that he was sorry and that we'd have to decide something about the office: about his getting transferred or me getting transferred. There's a street that runs through Balboa called Pepper Grove Drive. The clock on the car jammed, so they know he was doing 70 mph when he hit the truck. He shot an intersection and went right into the side of it. It was an early-morning garbage truck . . .''

Harriet looked at him again, shaking her head. "It had a
new driver and he'd started ahead of time and shouldn't
have been there at all. If he'd been driving on schedule, he
wouldn't have been crossing the intersection and Jack
would still have been alive now. Isn't that the funniest
thing?"

Farr could only nod, not knowing what else to say.

"I went with Julie and little John to the funeral. As her
friend. Let her cry on my shoulder and hugged him and
cried with them and they didn't know. Do you think that
was hypocritical of me?"

"I don't know," said Farr, hot with embarrassment.
"Maybe not."

"Thanks for trying to be kind," said the woman. "I felt
like a hypocrite."

"Why?" said Farr.

"Why what?"

"Until half an hour ago I've rarely known anyone so
distant. Now this. It doesn't make sense."

"Didn't you have dinner last night with Peter and Jim?"

"Yes."

"Didn't they tell you?"

"They said you were a hell of an operator."

"That's all?"

"That's all."

She gave an empty laugh, shaking her head. "I thought
they would have told you . . . wanted you to hear it my
way."

"It wasn't necessary."

"Anyway," she said, with forced lightness. "Now you
know."

"I won't say I'm sorry. That's never enough, is it?
Worst cliché in the world, in fact."

"No," she agreed. "Never enough."

"How long?" he asked.

"Nine months."

"Still hurts?"

"Like hell."

"So now it's work, work, work?"

"It helps, I suppose. I think I'll have that drink now. Proper drink, I mean."

"Why not before?"

She shrugged. "I don't know. No reason."

"The martinis aren't good."

"With tonic then."

Farr changed his drink as well, and this time the gin was slightly stronger, but only slightly.

"Know the irony?" she said bitterly.

"What?"

"The bust we were supposed to be making? The drop was made half an hour after we called everything off. They'd made us and were just waiting for us to pull out . . . Informant told us, weeks later." She snorted a laugh. "Can you believe that!"

They remained silent, neither looking at the other, for several moments, and then Farr said, "Aren't you surprised at my being involved? An outsider."

"I know how it happened," she said. "I won't say I'm sorry, either. About the boy, I mean. Like you said, not enough . . ." She drank deeply. "If you want me to say so, I think forcing you along is a bit shitty."

"I don't want you to say so unless you feel that way yourself."

"It's a bit shitty," she insisted. She took another drink. "But if I were trying to pull up trees and ring bells, like Brennan and Seymour are trying, I guess I'd do the same thing. It's a good opportunity." She finished the drink and Farr gestured for more, for both of them. As they were being served, she said, "I'm embarrassed now about telling you. I wish I hadn't."

"We're going to have to work together for maybe a long time," he said. "Guess we'll all discover a lot about each other."

"Is that going to be a problem?"

Farr frowned, not immediately understanding the question. He said, "The court's given me six months. Howard doesn't seem to be responding well to treatment, so I guess it's going to take a long time. The terms are residential."

"I didn't mean that," she said.

Farr finally comprehended. He said, "Her name was Ann. I loved her more than I'll ever be able to make anyone understand. It was cancer of the liver, so at least there wasn't any pain. She just kind of wasted away. She went into a coma, the last week. The doctors said that it was the actual termination but I expected her to come around, just briefly. I wanted to tell her how I felt. But she didn't. She just died—died without my being able to tell her that I loved her."

"Don't you think she knew?"

"I wanted to tell her at the end. She shouldn't have died without my being able to tell her. That wasn't fair."

"Things aren't. Ever."

"No," he said. "Never."

"When?"

"Eight years ago."

"No one since?"

"Not really."

"If this were a movie, there'd be a lot of violin music and one of us would reach for the other's hand and say something like how much alike it all was."

Farr looked at her, frowning at the bitter cynicism. "It must still hurt a lot."

"I said it did."

"You can't stop hurting," said Farr. "I haven't been able to. But don't shrivel up inside."

"Thanks," she said.

"I'm not patronizing you."

"I didn't think you were."

Their flight was called. Farr paid for the drinks and together they walked toward the embarkation gate. He gestured her ahead of him to put her cabin baggage on the televised carousel and then through the electronic security monitor.

She waited for him on the other side of the checks and,

as they began walking toward the designated pier, she said, "You won't, will you?"

"Won't what?"

"Reach out for my hand. I don't want this to become difficult."

"No," said Farr. "I won't make it difficult."

As they belted themselves in for takeoff, she said, "Do you always wear a suit?"

"Why?" asked Farr.

"Jack did."

10

Gomez's remark to the American Mafia chief about using the money they would make to earn more money had not been a casual aside. Gomez regarded the creation of the network as only part of the achievement; properly using the money—putting it to work—was the completion, and he went about doing that with the care he devoted to everything else. In the capital, Bogotá, there was the lawyer José Rivera whom Gomez had used, but Gomez decided that he'd bring very little, if any, money into Colombia. The already earned narcotic dollars and José Rivera had created the shopping plaza on the north side of town, with the supermarkets and the imported European and American fashion shops and the car salesrooms— imported vehicles which gave him cash tills and more than sufficient liquidity for anything he wanted in Medellin. The money from the new venture would stay outside and be handled by experts. He would get a higher return outside the country and it made financial sense to diversify as widely as possible. Nothing was going to go wrong, having got so far.

It meant using Scarletti. At first Gomez was reluctant, seeking every alternative to making himself beholden to the American. But finally practical necessity outweighed his hesitation. Scarletti had the contacts and the liaison network nationwide through the other families. He would be able to recommend the understanding lawyers and financiers who knew what to ask and what not to ask about the sums of money he wanted moved without awkwardness or interference from the authorities.

Gomez was fully aware that people from the cocaine-producing countries of Peru and Bolivia and Colombia were targeted by United States immigration and checked out on the computer links at customs headquarters. Although he was not personally transporting cocaine—nor had any outstanding indictments against him in America, which would have shown up on the checks—Gomez still entered the country by a circuitous route, to create as little interest as possible. He flew from the Colombian capital to Caracas and then to Brazil. From Brazil he crossed the Atlantic to Switzerland and, after a week in Bern, added another leg to his journey, flying to Stockholm. He spent a further week there, time-wasting to support his cover story, before flying finally to New York. By the time he got to America, Gomez had valid order books that customs and immigration could see if they wanted to—which they didn't—of European cars and clothes for his Medellin shopping complex. Passed through perfunctorily and told to have a nice day, Gomez was as sure as he could be that his name and visit hadn't been entered on any computer bank. Despite which he remained careful, knowing that if the FBI or any of the task forces were suspicious, they wouldn't have intercepted him at Kennedy airport anyway but let him run—to guide them to his people in America. Alert for any surveillance, he toured the New York supply houses, placing more orders for the clothes shops, making only business calls from his suite at the Plaza.

He made contact with Scarletti from a pay phone after four days, confident by then that he was clean and unobserved. The meeting was arranged for the following day. Gomez went by Amtrak; still concerned about being followed, he had decided that he had a better chance of isolating observers on a railway train than in an airport. He detected none. At Scarletti's suggestion, he booked into the Latham and they ate at Bogart's, the hotel's excellent restaurant. Scarletti insisted upon a table in the center of the room, because he felt it was easier for listening wires and microphones to be trailed around wall areas. Two groups of his people sat at the immediately adjoining tables. Gomez approved of the caution—admired it as professionalism—and told the American of his convoluted journey to Philadelphia.

"*That's* careful," said Scarletti, in reciprocal admiration.

Gomez was pleased at the praise. "I told you at the beginning how it was going to be."

"Can we rely upon Navarra to do the same?"

"Perhaps we won't have to reply upon Navarra forever," said Gomez.

Scarletti looked directly across the table at the other man, waiting for Gomez to continue. The Colombian didn't and Scarletti refrained from asking the direct question. Instead he said, "When are you planning the first shipment?"

"Navarra says he'll have about five hundred kilos ready in a fortnight. I can refine that down and have it ready to move here about a week after that."

"The whole half-ton?" asked Scarletti.

Gomez shook his head, guessing that the American was testing him. "That wouldn't make good sense," he said. "I plan to do it in fours, 125 kilos at a time. That way we're insured for replacement, if there's any interception: and it'll be easier, moving that amount at any one time." Wanting to balance the demands, he continued, "I plan to get the whole lot here in under a month. Sure you can move half a ton?"

Scarletti smiled, unoffended. "You ship it, I'll move it," he said. He smiled again. "On the streets that's going to come out at something like forty-three million."

"I've told Navarra that five hundred kilos at a time isn't enough; that if we're going to corner the market it's got to be much more."

"Can he supply?"

"He says so."

"It would make sense to split from source from you," said Scarletti. "Could you transport directly to Italy?"

"Of course."

"What's the optimum?"

"No one knows the full figure, but the estimates at the moment are that about fifty-five to sixty tons move through Colombia a year: that's about forty-five for here and the rest for Europe. I'd like to see us with two thirds—say, thirty tons."

"On the streets, that's two thousand, four hundred and fifty million," said Scarletti.

Now it was Gomez who smiled, briefly, at another challenge. "I think, at the current prices, the truer figure would be two thousand, five hundred and fifty?"

"You've really worked everything out, haven't you?"

"Carefully," reminded Gomez. "And I'm pitching it at slightly less than two thirds on the minimum figure on fifty tons. We would go higher."

"A lot of money," said Scarletti.

"Which is one of the reasons I'm here," said the Colombian. It would have been wrong to let Scarletti think it was the principal reason.

"What?" said the American. And then sat nodding, his face serious because he always considered money to be serious. When Gomez had finished, he said, "No problem."

"I want the best."

"I only ever use the best," said Scarletti, with a hint of rebuke. "There's a man here, in Philadelphia. Probart, Harry Probart. And one I use in New York. Norman Lang."

"Difficult to get to?"

"Not with the right introduction," said Scarletti, demanding the recognition.

"I'd appreciate it," said Gomez, providing it.

"Here or New York?"

Gomez didn't foresee frequent visits but there would obviously have to be some. And the garment industry, which was his cover, was based in Manhattan. "New York," he said.

"I'll make a call," promised Scarletti. "When you going back up?"

"Tomorrow," said Gomez.

"It'll be fixed, by the time you get there," assured the American, enjoying his supremacy.

"I appreciate it," repeated Gomez.

"All part of the partnership," said Scarletti.

Norman Lang's office suite was on Pearl Street on the top floor of an old building. There was a lot of mahogany and a smell of polish. It was a discreet place of thick carpets and subdued voices and conservative dress and quiet typewriters. Having been granted access at the receptionist's desk, the visitor was automatically assumed to belong; the smiles and the acceptance were as discreet as everything else. The ambiance was of old, established money and Gomez was glad he'd chosen New York. A challenge to a place like this from the FBI or an enforcement agency would have been an act of insolence.

Norman Lang fitted the surroundings, of course—as if he'd styled himself to form part of the decor or the decor had been styled to conform to him. He was white-haired and pink-faced. The suit was black and superb and the tie had the motif of some club that Gomez didn't recognize. Mingled with the polish was the aroma of expensive cologne and probably even more expensive cigars. The handshake was soft, almost feminine.

"I understand you're interested in investment?" said the lawyer.

Gomez noted that the formal question omitted any mention of Scarletti. "Yes, that's right."

"What sort of sums are we considering?"

"Progressive amounts," said the Colombian. "In excess of five hundred million in the first year." He paused, waiting for some expression of surprise. There was no facial reaction at all from the other man. Gomez went on. "I would expect the investment to reach a thousand in the first eighteen months."

Still there was no expression from Lang. "These investment sums will be created by activities here, in America?"

Gomez hesitated, then remembered the circumstances of his reaching this inner sanctum in the first pláce. "Yes, generated by activities entirely within the United States."

"But not sums you intend to make any return upon to the Internal Revenue Service?"

"I am a Colombian, domiciled outside the United States of America."

"There are still statutory requirements, particularly involving sums of this magnitude," insisted Lang.

"No," said Gomez. "Certainly I do not wish to make any sort of declaration to the IRS."

"I understand," said the lawyer blandly.

"This will be difficult?"

"No," said the American quickly, a hint of surprise in his voice. "Not difficult at all. There is something, however . . ."

"What?"

"There are to be no audited accounts . . . no books?"

"No."

"Then you must understand that the expenses will be high. The commission, too."

New money maintaining the privileged atmosphere of the past, thought Gomez. He said, "I understand that. How much?"

"Ten percent," replied the lawyer, quickly again.

Which meant that Lang's cut would be fifty million. Gomez said, "That's very high."

"So are the expenses," insisted Lang.

Would Probart, in Philadelphia, be cheaper? Possibly, Gomez supposed: things would be cheaper in a regional city. But the lawyer in Philadelphia would know his strength and his bargaining power just as much as this man sitting across the desk. And would a regional city be as impressive as this? He'd told Scarletti he wanted the best and this was unquestionably the best. "All right," conceded Gomez.

"How will this money originate?" asked the lawyer. "Check or cash?"

"Cash," said Gomez. "All cash."

"High-denomination bills?"

"Not particularly," said the experienced Gomez. "Twenty-dollar bills would be the average."

Lang made a slightly disparaging sound, drawing air through tight-together teeth. He said, "That creates difficulties through simple practicalities. Have you any idea how much bulk—and weight—is occupied by several million dollars? The sheer *weight* of paper?"

"I think so," said Gomez.

"I'd guess brokerage houses would be best," said Lang.

"You could find one?"

"I could try."

"I don't want any mistakes."

"I'm sure neither of us wants any mistakes," said the lawyer smoothly. "What sort of investments are you considering?"

It was a question Gomez had already prepared for. "As high yield as possible. But this isn't risk money. None of it. Nothing bizarre, just because it's got a high return."

"I'm not in the business of the bizarre," said Lang. "For your needs—and because of the circumstances of the money's availability—I consider it will have to be something offshore."

"Like what?"

"I'll have to study the market closer," said the lawyer. "When could we expect the first deposit?"

"A month," estimated Gomez. "After that, perhaps more frequently."

"It may take me a little longer than that. There'll need to be arrangements between us, giving me power of attorney."

"Now?"

"It would finalize matters. I have a notary in the office. It could be witnessed by one of my staff."

Gomez shifted uncomfortably at other people being involved. "All right," he agreed, with no alternative.

The notary was a balding man named Hatchard and the

witness, one of Lang's outer-office secretaries, was never introduced. The formalities took only minutes. When they left the room, the lawyer said, "Now everything is complete. The woman witnessed Hatchard's signature, not yours."

Complete! thought Gomez exultantly. He was going to become the biggest there was!

They considered the Holiday Inn first, on Seven Mile Beach, but Farr decided they needed more privacy, so they went back toward Georgetown and took a limited booking at the Royal Palms—not in one of the apartments but in the Coral Gables annex, in one of the three-bedroom duplexes.

Farr stood in the middle of the more-than-adequate kitchen and said, "We'll be self-contained enough here while we look around. But I suppose it would make more sense to hire a house. Houses even."

"Certainly, when the others come in," said Harriet professionally. "This is still a hotel, although it's got all these facilities. Five or six people moving in and out would attract far too much attention."

"It's off-season," said Farr. "It shouldn't be too difficult to rent."

The woman stood at the window, unable from the way the complex was built to see the beach or the sea beyond. "From what I've seen so far, it seems a pretty place."

"There'll be time to enjoy ourselves."

She turned back into the room to face him. "We're not here to enjoy ourselves," she said.

11

Farr did not need Harriet's encouragement to work. He began the day after settling into the Coral Gables. The company he intended forming was to be a legitimate subsidiary of his legitimate New York corporation, so he set about its creation in a completely legal way, engaging one of the best incorporation lawyers on the island, an easy-mannered man named Richard Belling. With Belling, Farr went carefully through the implications of the full range of applicable legislation, covering the Companies' Law, the Trusts Law, the licensing requirements for Bank and Trust Companies and the Confidential Relationships (Preservation) Law. Farr initially intended applying for a category A classification, which would have allowed him an unrestricted general license, but abandoned the idea when Belling told him that the local Cayman office would have to employ a local financial expert fully conversant with all the intricacies of the internal tax legislation. Farr knew theirs had to be a restricted office, so he settled instead for a category B unrestricted offshore license. The capital requirement was a minimum of two hundred and fifty thousand but he pledged the full FBI allocation of three million. Properly to incorporate the company required Belling to have certified evidence of the incorporation of the New York parent; this allowed Farr two twenty-four-hour returns to Manhattan, where he was able to chair brief meetings with Angela Nolan and the four other division heads, to ensure that everything was running smoothly in his absence—which it was. During the Manhattan visits—and also weekly from the Caymans—Farr maintained contact with Eastham, wanting to visit Howard. Every time, Halpern advised against his coming, insisting upon no immediate distraction in their efforts to motivate the boy into agreeing to treatment.

Farr concentrated particularly upon the Confidential Relationships Law of 1976—the legislation that attracted investors to the island and would be the lure to any trafficker. He didn't imagine that the island government would move against him—particularly in view of the access agreement between the United States and Britain—but he decided that the wording of the law allowed prosecution against him personally on the grounds that he knowingly set up the company to obtain confidential information and then communicated it to others. Compared to the other risks he was taking, Farr decided, it was not a major consideration.

The early days were crowded, but when all the legal necessities had been complied with there was a lull, during which the formal application was made to the Caymans government and examined by the Inspector of Banks and Trust Companies. This allowed Farr more time with Harriet, who had been working just as hard as he. She had narrowed down to three the possible office sites in Georgetown; two were near the fort, the third near the post office. Farr thought the post-office site best, but they deferred final decision until the arrival of Batty and Jones, in preparation for which they set about looking for houses. They made extensive tours of the island, considering going as far away as Bodden Town before settling on something more conveniently near to the capital: a sprawling bungalow and an equally large house, each in their own concealing grounds between Southwest Point and Coconut Valley Bar. The bungalow fronted on to the sea and, although the beach wasn't as good as the shoreline along Seven Mile beach, having more rocks than sand, it was still possible to swim and sunbathe there, and it had the advantage of privacy.

Farr was glad the shopping was so good in Georgetown. He worked at diminishing the suit and tie image, but did so gradually, not wanting Harriet to realize that he was making any effort. He was equally careful to avoid forcing any social involvement, although circumstances dictated that they should be frequently together. There were times when she announced—in a way that made it quite clear that she did not want company—that she was going to the cinema or to the theater along West Bay Road, and Farr never made any attempt to accompany her. Sometimes she simply said she was going out and drove off in the car; he never questioned where she went. When he suggested their going out together, however, Harriet never refused. They were disappointed with the Grand Old House, although they agreed that the plantation surroundings were attractive, and preferred the Lobster Pot for lunch rather than dinner. The Caribbean Club became a favorite. With whole days with nothing to do, while the company application was being processed and the office and houses selected, he planned outings he hoped she'd like; one day they went to the turtle farm and he laughed with her as she nervously held one of the young turtles with which visitors were allowed to be photographed. On another occasion they leisurely drove around the island as far as Rum Point, just before the road ceased, and then backtracked to an almost empty hotel where they had the beach to themselves.

They swam and sunbathed a lot from their bungalow beach as well, which Farr preferred because, although it was out of season and the public beaches were not heavily used, there *were* still people on them. On their own tiny rocky inlet, he didn't have to share her with anyone. It was a conscious thought and one Farr knew was ridiculous—they'd made the pact after their individual confessions and Harriet maintained a studied distance—but it was one that he couldn't avoid. On their own beach, and any other beach, Harriet was particular—it was always a one-piece suit, never a more revealing bikini. Nevertheless, he could see—and he tried to see as often as he could without her realizing it—that she was very firm and quite heavy-busted and flat-stomached and long-legged. He was very careful about himself, always trying to hold his own stomach tight and wishing like hell he hadn't stopped bothering about the workouts at the racquet club.

Belling said he thought that it was the reputation and the prestige of Farr's well-established New York practice that approval for the application was secured far sooner than he expected. Farr traveled into town to receive the official document and sign the remaining forms, and Belling said, "Welcome to tax-free Utopia," and that he hoped everything would work out. Farr said, sincerely, that he hoped so too.

Farr had left his car in the street, that day, rather than in a parking lot, and his return to it took him past the Passman black-coral shop. He spent a long time at the window, undecided, and then, beginning to sweat in the growing heat of the day, he went gratefully into the air conditioning, telling himself that he was only taking relief from the sun but knowing he was going to do more than that. His first thought was to buy something expensive and obviously impressive, but he discarded it very quickly, aware of how she would react. He shied away from rings, too, because in Farr's mind rings always meant engagements and marriage, and he was frightened that she might think the same. He finally chose a simple gold-linked strand of black pearls fashioned into a necklace, with matching earrings.

It had been a morning meeting, so she knew he would return for lunch, and by the time he reached the bungalow she had come in from their tiny beach, to make the meal. She was wearing a shirt-wrap over her suit but it stopped at mid-thigh; she couldn't have been inside long because, when he passed close to her, by the breakfast bar, he detected the heat still emanating from her body.

"I used the blender to make some lemonade," she said, aware of his reaction to the midday sun.

"Do you celebrate with lemonade?"

"Everything?" she said excitedly.

"Everything," he confirmed. "Properly incorporated, legally in existence . . . We're in business!"

She moved without any direction around the sectioned-off kitchen with jerky uncertainty, apparently as aware as he was that it was a time for arms-around-the-necks congratulation but keeping the barrier of the breakfast bar between them.

"Terrific!" she said. "Wonderful!"

"Belling expected it to take much longer—weeks at least," said Farr, hoping she would be impressed. "The New York reputation clinched it, he thinks."

"I think lemonade would be OK," she said.

"Lemonade's fine."

She came around from the security of the kitchen area and handed him the glass; he couldn't feel the sun's heat from her any longer.

"I'll have to call Brennan; we must get Batty and Jones down to look at the offices and make the final decision."

"Yes," he said. The thought of the others arriving—like sharing a beach—seemed intrusive. "The air conditioning is on high. Careful you don't catch cold."

"I'm OK."

"Sure?"

"Don't fuss."

She seemed to become aware that they were standing too close together and moved away.

"I'll call Eastham, too," he said, hurrying for neutral territory. "See if I can visit before it becomes busy."

"How long might that be? Before we become busy, I mean?"

"There's no knowing," said Farr. Suddenly wondering if there was a point to the question, he said, "You got somewhere you want to go, first?"

She smiled at him. "No." She wasn't wearing any makeup and her face and legs were shiny with sun oil.

"So here's to us," he said, raising the lemonade glass.

"Here's to us," she responded.

"Don't get mad."

"About what?"

"Just don't get mad."

She looked at him curiously, face serious. "I don't make any promises when I don't know what I'm promising."

"It's harmless."

"Still no."

"Honestly."

"Still no."

"We're celebrating, right?"

"Right," she agreed, still doubtful.

He took the coral jewelry box from his pocket and handed it to her. "Celebration," he said.

Harriet didn't open it at first; and glanced down only fleetingly at the box. She remained instead looking directly at him holding the container in such a way as to suggest that she hadn't actually accepted it. "Why?" she asked.

"Celebration, like I said."

"I heard what you said."

"That's what it is . . ." Anxious to ease the tightness between them Farr said, "I bought it on my American Express card; it didn't come out of operating funds. We don't stand a chance of getting caught in one of Mann's auditing inquiries."

She allowed the smile, briefly rewarding his effort. "I thought we reached an understanding?"

"We did," agreed Farr. "What's this got to do with it?"

"Nothing?" she said.

"Nothing."

She opened it at last and remained looking down at the pinned and arranged set longer than he expected she would. When she finally looked up, she said, quiet-voiced, "They're beautiful. Thank you." Abruptly, she shivered.

"I told you about getting cold. Shall I turn the air conditioning down?"

She shook her head. "It wasn't that sort of cold."

"You going to try them on?"

"Of course, I'm sorry."

Farr realized that he hadn't known whether or not she had pierced ears and was glad that she had. She had trouble with the necklace and accepted his offer of help. He carefully stood apart from her, ensuring that his hands didn't come into any contact with the back of her neck, only the clasp itself.

"Thank you." She moved away the moment it was secured to the small mirror against the far wall. "They're beautiful," she said, without turning to him. "They look very nice."

"I'm glad you like them."

She turned back into the room. "I wish you hadn't."

"Why?"

"Because," she said awkwardly.

She looked little-girl lost and Farr wanted to reach out and pull her to him—actually, for the briefest, passing moment, considering it. But he didn't. The silence between them solidified. Then he said, "I'm glad I did."

Suddenly reminded—and suddenly busy—she said, "I made salad for lunch. And chilled soup."

"Sounds good."

"Maybe I should change?" She contemplated the short top.

"It's very cool in here," he agreed, wanting to help her.

"I'll be a minute."

Farr remained where he was, watching her enter the bedroom and firmly close the door behind her. Without thought, he went to the window, gazing out at the furrowed water, silvered by the sun, popping at the shingle. Far out to sea an unknown cruise liner approached on its bus-stop tour of the Caribbean, heading toward unseen Georgetown just beyond the headland. Farr wondered how many more black-coral necklaces and matching earrings Passman's would sell before the day was out. He heard her reenter the room. By the time he turned, she had regained the redoubt of the kitchen and was smiling at him across the breakfast-bar barrier. She had cleansed her face, so that it was no longer shiny with oil and perspiration, and combed her hair, straining it back from her face into a chignon behind. The style showed off the necklaces and the earrings, which, he supposed, was deliberate.

"I guess the others will come down quite soon, now that it's all set up?" she said.

"When will you call?"

"This afternoon, I suppose."

"Won't they think this is funny?"

"What?"

"Us in the same house?"

"They'll learn soon enough that nothing *is* funny," she said. "We need cover. Occupying the same house stops any outsider trying to get involved with me. And removes the need for you to appear like any normal man and seek company elsewhere. It's practical."

"As long as they see it as just practical."

She laughed at him openly. "Worried about your reputation, Mr. Farr?"

He laughed back at her. "No, yours."

"My problem," she said. After a pause, she went on, "Although I haven't done too well with it so far, have I?"

Farr ignored the invitation to self-pity. "So you don't want any different arrangements?"

"Not unless you do," she said. "There's something else, too."

"What?"

"This way I'm protected, against the others."

"Do you think you need protection?"

"I don't know. I think Mann could become a nuisance."

"This wasn't a role I had foreseen for myself," he said.

Harriet immediately became serious. She half moved, as if to reach across the narrow divide for his hand, and then held back. "That was selfish of me and I'm sorry. If you want to move out, then of course you must. Bloody selfish."

"I don't want to move out."

"There's something I want to say before the others

come. I think you've been fabulous. Not just the way you've set things up so quickly. To me, too."

"I've enjoyed being with you," said Farr. "All the time."

"I've enjoyed being with you, too . . ." She fingered the necklace. "I appreciate it—all of it."

Farr completed the gesture she had been unable to make, feeling across the minuscule dining area for her hand. She let him take it, leaving it lifeless under his touch. Embarrassed, he withdrew. "Sorry," he said. "I forgot I said I wouldn't do that."

She smiled at him sadly. "It's still too soon," she said. "I wish it wasn't, but it's still far too soon."

He was about to reply when the telephone shrilled. It was still rare for them to get any calls and they both jumped. Farr answered it, because he was actually in the lounge. It was a short, clipped conversation, because there was not a lot to say. Farr thanked Halpern and said he'd make arrangements to come up right away; he wasn't sure of the flights, but thought he could possibly make it late that night or certainly early the following morning, depending on the connections.

"What is it?" said Harriet, coming out into the main room.

"Howard's made a run for it," said Farr. "They thought they could relax security and he's made a run for it."

It wasn't working; not as Gomez intended—the final part, that was. The shipping arrangements were perfect. Despite Gomez's distrust of the man, Navarra fully supplied the first transaction, providing a total of five hundred and eighty-five kilos, all of which reached Scarletti's distribution network without any difficulty. Scarletti paid promptly as arranged, so by the end of the first month, the agreement showed Gomez a personal profit of four million dollars. Moving it on—putting it to work, which was as important as everything else—was the problem. Advised by the urbane New York lawyer, Gomez opened safe deposit accounts in five Manhattan banks and had to rent additional boxes at three of them to accommodate the growing bulk of the money. Keeping it static annoyed him and he was worried by the need for frequent trips to New York, although he remained confident that no agency established any sort of make upon him. To minimize the risk he had Ramos, the only one he could trust, make a collection run. Gomez naturally saw Lang on every visit he made, not bothering to conceal his impatience. By the fourth meeting, that impatience had become anger.

"This isn't what I wanted; what was agreed to."

"As high yield as possible, but this isn't risk money. Nothing bizarre, just because it's got a high return," quoted the lawyer verbatim.

"Just that," said Gomez. "Which doesn't mean dead money locked up in cash boxes."

"I'm well aware of what it means and what it doesn't mean," said Lang calmly. "Do you want an investment that's solid and productive or something we've got to cut and run from?"

"You don't have to ask me a question like that."

"And you don't have to become impatient and challenge me. We'll move when it's right. When it's safe and profitable and right. Which is how we safeguard what you've got and make it grow, as you want it to."

"When?" persisted Gomez.

"Soon," promised Lang. "Very soon now."

It was too slow, thought Gomez. Maybe he'd made a mistake in not using José Rivera, like he'd always done. He'd make contact as soon as he got back to Colombia.

12

Howard sat balled up in the customary fetal position but no longer was he rocking back and forth, and there were other, more marked differences: his face and hands and arms weren't greased with sweat and his hair appeared to be freshly washed, and no smell permeated the room.

"So I fucked it," announced the boy.

"What do you think you fucked?" said Farr, refusing the invitation to outrage at the defiant obscenity.

"Getting out, what else?"

"I would have thought you would have fucked it *by* getting out," said Farr.

Howard looked at him, shaking his head in exaggerated contempt. "They wouldn't have caught me."

"They did catch you, stupid!"

"Hadn't got time to get clear."

"So they caught you!" persisted Farr. "So you didn't make it and you couldn't have made it. And what would you have done if you had?"

"Made out OK."

"How, to feed your habit? Stealing? Pimping maybe, persuading some girl as much a mess as yourself that she could earn enough for both of you on her back with her legs spread out?"

"Maybe."

"That's your ambition? To be a thief? Or a pimp?"

There was a shrug. "Maybe."

The attitude—a mix of apathy and insolence—was as calculated to upset him as the use of the word fuck, Farr decided. He said sneeringly, "And you couldn't even succeed in that, could you? They caught you, just two hours after the big breakout, doing something stupid and obvious like hanging around the Greyhound bus center waiting for the Boston departure. Thieves and pimps are smart some of the time, streetwise for a while. You don't even qualify to be a thief and a pimp, do you, Howard?"

"Fuck you!"

"Say it," demanded Farr.

Howard frowned at him. "Say what?"

"Go on," urged Farr. "Show me what a great big hard guy you are. Keep saying fuck until I become convinced."

The boy looked away, hands white as they gripped around his legs. "Son of a bitch!"

"An extensive vocabulary!" said Farr, riding his son. "Bet you know some more: words that are really going to shock me. Going to try for them!"

"Why don't you fuck off?"

"Why don't you grow up? Why don't you accept that you've fucked up—it's your word, so let's use it—and you're back among people trying to help you, and that you can't get out; you tried it and you failed, and if you try again you'll eventually be caught and the judge who didn't think much of you anyway is going to send you away for a long time."

"That supposed to frighten me?"

"It frightens me. For you," said Farr.

"I'll get by OK."

"But you can't, Howard," said Farr. "You're a failure. The original big no-no. You couldn't be a student, because it was too hard for you when you actually had to work. So you tried to become the big-time dealer and you couldn't do that either, so you got caught. You tried to break out of here and you couldn't manage that either. You can't get by. You can't do anything. You know your only ability?

The only thing you're good at? Being a failure . . ." Farr
stopped holding up his hand. "Wrong expression," he
said. "We're talking tough-guy language, aren't we? You're
only good at fucking up . . ." Farr made a circle from his
thumb and forefinger. "The original Mr. No-no," he
repeated.

"You all through?"

"No."

"You're a pain in the ass."

"You're a pain in the ass, Howard. You're the stupid
little prick who's so frightened of growing up that he's got
to block out the nasty fairies by pumping shit into his arm
or shit up his nose, who thinks the way to solve everything
is by running away."

"Is that what you think?"

"That's what I think."

"So why'd you bother?"

"Bother about what?"

"To come."

"Because it isn't a bother. Because you're my son.
Because, unlike you, I *don't* run away, just because something is unpleasant."

Howard unwrapped his legs, freeing his hands, and gave
a slow, mocking round of applause.

"That's another failure."

"What the hell are you talking about now?"

"Cynicism," said Farr. "You're lousy at it."

"You really don't like me, do you?"

"At the moment it's difficult," said the broker. "Very
difficult. And it's not liking anyway. It's love. At the
moment I despise you. I feel sick, physically sick, knowing what you've done and how pitiful you are, when you
talk. Ashamed, too. Very ashamed. Because I know I
haven't done enough and because I think that, had I tried
harder, then maybe, just maybe, you wouldn't have become the shitty mess that you are now. But none of it is
stopping me loving you. When you were a baby and
helpless, I wiped your ass and dried your nose and sat with

you until you went to sleep. *Because* you were a baby and
helpless. Which is what I think you are now. A baby, who
doesn't know any better.''

. "I'd say that was chapter three or perhaps chapter four
of the *Family Psychology Manual:* the bit under the heading 'Bringing the Recalcitrant Son to his Senses,' '' said
Howard.

"Jesus, what an asshole you are!'' said Farr. "You sit
crunched up like a scene out of about a hundred French
movies. The whole thing's a charade, an attention getter!
And your dialogue's the same! You haven't said anything
original since I came into the room.''

"Some of your lines have been pretty corny, too.''

"OK, so they're corny! At least they're sincere. Yours
are bullshit, straight from some script you thought was
good at the time.''

"At the risk of it actually sounding like a film script,
just where is this getting us?''

"Nowhere,'' said Farr. "Just like the treatment and the
help you're receiving here is getting nowhere. Because
we're still going through the film-script macho shit.''

"So if it's getting nowhere, why stay? Like I said
before, why not fuck off?''

"Because, like *I* said before, I don't run away from
something just because it looks difficult. That's your way.''

Howard unfolded himself elaborately, stretching out on
his bunk. "So! What do we talk about? How about the
future of the world?''

"What's the future of your world?''

The boy turned his head sideways quickly. "Sharp, Dad!
Very sharp!''

"Cop out, asshole! Cop out! Answer the question!''

The boy's head jerked back—so that he didn't have to
look at his father—as quickly as it had come around when
he thought he had a point to score. "You've done the
conscience number, Dad. You've interrupted a busy work
schedule and done the boring shuttle run to show me that
you care and, if it helps a little, OK, I'm grateful for your

interest. But we haven't got anything to say to each other
like we haven't had for a long time. So why don't we call
it a day?''

Farr couldn't see any purpose in remaining either but he
refused to leave on terms of dismissal: when he left, he
wanted it to be his decision. Was that right? He wished
he'd had more time with Halpern, had more guidance. But
then he hadn't been able to anticipate how bad this encounter would be. "Run! run! run!'' he taunted.

Still staring up at the ceiling, Howard said, "I can't
understand what the fuck you're trying to prove.''

"I'm not trying to prove anything,'' said Farr. "I *am*
trying to tell you something. I'm trying to tell you how
much you've hurt me and how disappointed I am, but most
of all how frightened *I* am. I am frightened, Howard.
Frightened to fuck. I guessed you were going to run; said
so. Said that I didn't think you wanted to be cured—which
is what frightens me most. Because I don't understand. I
don't understand how a kid with all the advantages you've
had does dope to the extent that you've done. I *can*
understand the curiosity and the experimentation. Like
everyone gets drunk. But they don't stay drunk, not all the
time. I can't understand why you need to speedball and
freebase, like I couldn't understand it if you became an
alcoholic. No one can enjoy being an addict, like you're
an addict. You've got a chance that a lot of kids haven't.
A chance to kick the habit and go straight. Yet you don't
want to know! That's what I can't comprehend: why, having been helped out of the hole, you're so determined to
jump back in. So tell me! I know I haven't been as close to
you as I should have been—we've been through that—but
. . .'' Farr's face tightened at the artificial way in which
Howard was keeping his eyes closed, as if he were asleep.
"So, tell me,'' he repeated. "Tell me the reasons for
doing what you're doing.''

Howard remained where he was, stretched out on his
back, eyes flickering with feigned sleep. Farr waited, refusing to be dismissed that way either. Howard lay unmov-

ing; once, his mouth actually broke into a quickly recovered smirk. It became a long silence, a stretched challenge. Farr snapped first. Moving as quietly as he could, he reached the bottom of the bed and, before Howard had any idea what was happening, heaved it upwards and sideways. The cot was tethered with a restraining cable-chain to the floor, but there was sufficient length in the chain to allow Farr to throw his son onto the floor. Howard was taken completely by surprise, actually screaming in fright as he was suddenly hurled to the ground. The boy landed badly on his side, jarring an elbow and a splayed leg that he had instinctively put out to save himself; he screamed out again, this time in pain.

"What the fu—" he managed to shout before Farr kicked him. All the broker had intended by the sudden, abrupt upheaval was to bestir the stupid bloody little fool; literally to make him sit up. But when Howard hit the floor, the frustration and impotence he felt at the kid's contemptuous insolence carried him on—so the kick was instinctive. But not completely. Instinctive would have been unthinking, but in the final seconds, when the movement had actually started, Farr knew what he was doing and he wanted to make it hurt. He caught his son directly in the stomach, just below and slightly to the right of the rib cage. The boy's breath screeched from him in winded agony, and then Farr kicked him again—not so cleanly this time because Howard was already covering himself up. The boy's arm took most of the force but there was again some contact with his stomach. Howard was sick, badly, the vomit gushing from him and covering him because of the way he was curled. He was trying to cry out but, without any breath, the only sound he could make was a lost, gasping whimper.

Farr looked down, horrified at what he'd done. He wanted to say he was sorry and that he wasn't going to abandon the boy, even though Howard seemed resigned to abandoning himself; and he wanted to kneel on the floor, among the vomit, and tell him that he knew how frightened Howard was, but that it would all work out in the end. But he did none of it. He looked down at the twitching, groveling figure and felt sick himself at the stink of the vomit which was already staining the floor. Then he turned and hammered at the door to be let out.

Outside, he fell weakly against the wall, lips tight together against collapsing into tears, eyes squeezed shut to close out the last hours and the acknowledgment of where he was and what he'd seen and heard and done: running, as he'd sneered at Howard for doing.

"You all right?"

Reluctantly, Farr opened his eyes in response to the concern of the attendant at the security desk and nodded. He said, "He needs help. We had a fight. He'd been ill. Would you help him please . . . ?" After a pause, he said, "I don't think I can."

"I'll do it," said the man.

"Thank you." Farr pushed himself away from the wall's support and walked slowly back toward Halpern's office. He hesitated before entering, trying to compose himself. It didn't work; as he opened the door, Halpern looked up and frowned. "What happened?"

"I lost my temper. Beat him up—attacked him when he wasn't expecting it . . ." Farr slumped into a chair, bent forward, and began to cry. "Christ!" he said. "Oh Christ, what have I done!"

"Done what a lot of fathers would do," said Halpern evenly. "*Have* done."

"I *kicked* him!" said Farr, confused by the other man's lack of reaction. "He's back there lying in his own puke."

"I think Howard's lain in his own puke enough times for it not to be an unusual experience," said the director.

"I just walked out after I did it," continued Farr, still disbelieving. "I wanted to apologize . . . say I was sorry. But I couldn't."

"I'm glad you didn't," said Halpern.

Farr scrubbed his hand over his face, embarrassed at his collapse. "What do you mean?"

"You let him know how you feel, physically feel. Is that such a bad thing?"

"He's hurt! I kicked and hurt him!"

"Good. Now he knows you hurt, too."

"You're not upset? Think I've done something to hinder the treatment?"

"Not particularly," said Halpern, still mildly. "We've hardly got anywhere with Howard. He feels you've neglected him; which I know you feel, too." Halpern waved his hand warningly. "I don't want to talk about it, either way. There're millions of kids treated far worse than Howard who don't go on drugs. And, like I told you before, plenty better off who do turn on. That's not the point. The point is that *he* feels it. So today you kicked hell out of him. We haven't got very far with words; maybe you achieved something by causing him pain."

"That sounds like some sort of experiment," said Farr.

"A lot of drug treatment—attempted rehabilitation—is some sort of experiment," said Halpern. "Substitution—trying to maintain a heroin addict on methadone—hasn't worked because methadone is more addictive than heroin. Psychiatry can sometimes help, but no one's yet established that drug abuse is an indication of mental illness. Sometimes it is, sometimes it isn't. It comes down very simplistically to whatever works works."

"And you don't yet know what's going to work on Howard?"

"No. We think we've got some pointers but it's still too early to say. We knew he was going to run, of course."

"So did I."

"We let it happen," said Halpern.

"*Let* it happen?"

The director nodded. "Getting away was becoming his focus: all he thought about. We had to break that focus. So we let him go. We released him from security and watched him run for it and told the police, who maintained an easy surveillance—because I didn't want him to score—so we could pick him up whenever we wanted to. We let him make the bus station and think he'd succeeded and then we picked him up. I *wanted* to tilt him off balance, but only slightly. I think one of the ways of rehabilitating Howard—or any drug abuser—is to restore, not take away, their confidence. But in this case I thought I had to take away Howard's confidence about escaping.''

"How can you guarantee that he won't try again?''

"I *want* him to try again," said the director. "If he doesn't, then he'll be apathetic, and I don't want him to lose the will to fight—because it's that will I want to channel. He'll run again and we'll pick him up again, and if he does it the third time we'll pick him up a third time. We'll go on until he gets it out of his system.''

"What happens if he beats you! Actually manages to get away?''

"The court entrusted Howard into my care because they were pretty sure that wouldn't happen, Mr. Farr. We've had a lot of people far more determined and far more able than Howard, and we've managed to stop them.''

"Experimental," said Farr.

"I already admitted it was," said Halpern.

"With me, too!" said Farr in sudden realization. "Your message said Howard had escaped, was on the run. You've just told me the whole thing was set up!''

The director nodded once more, unabashed. "Howard thinks he made a run for it and that the moment you heard—you, a father whom he thinks doesn't care—you came running. By coming here today, you proved that you cared. If I'd warned you in advance, you couldn't have carried it off properly. Annoyed?''

Farr shook his head slowly. "If I'd known, I wouldn't have lost my temper like I did. Hurt him.''

"What's wrong with losing your temper!" demanded Halpern. He paused. "When you first came into this office you started to cry and you were as embarrassed as hell, because grownup men don't cry. For a time you were more worried at crying in front of me than you were at having kicked hell out of Howard, weren't you?''

"Yes," admitted Farr.

"There's nothing wrong in crying, Mr. Farr. In fact, it's a very good release. Like losing your temper occasionally is a good release. Howard thinks his escape was genuine and he thinks your concern was genuine—which it was—and he thinks your anger and your breakdown was genuine. Which it was, also."

"You going to pull any more tricks like this?" asked Farr.

"I don't know," said Halpern. "I don't plan to, not at the moment."

"Will you tell me, if you do?"

Halpern shook his head. "Not if I think you're an integral part of it and need to behave in a logical, natural way. I'm not interested in hurting or not hurting your feelings, Mr. Farr. I'm interested in rehabilitating Howard. I'm not running some sort of experimental circus here, believe me," said Halpern earnestly. "By which I mean that I'm not using Howard as some kind of guinea pig. Or you. Whatever I do will only have one object: helping Howard. Tell me something. You ever hit Howard before? When he was a kid, I mean?"

Farr stared down at the floor for few moments. "I don't think so. I can't remembering doing so."

Halpern nodded, smiling. "Must have come as a hell of a shock," he said.

Although Brennan and Seymour were not specifically attached to a particular task force—working instead directly from headquarters—they still attended the biannual review conference of task force controllers and senior personnel, because of their current involvement. It was held in the Hoover building on Washington's Pennsylvania Avenue, in one of the fourth-floor rooms large enough to hold such a gathering. The individual task force commanders each gave an address on their activities and successes of the previous six months and then a deputy director of the headquarters intelligence unit collated the separate histories into a countrywide review of the Bureau's antinarcotic efforts. The final speaker was the director himself, a soft-spoken, hesitant man who had been given control of the FBI after a career at the bar as a trial judge and who was therefore resented by professional FBI men as a political appointee. The director's speech was little more than a repetition of the earlier presented overview, but with a lawyer's ability to isolate telling points he picked up and insisted upon one fact.

"During the last six months, cocaine seizures increased by a total of practically one and a half tons over the previous six months. That can be interpreted in two ways; either our interception—our task forces—are winning. Or the traffickers are increasing their activities. It is to answer that question that I have specifically ordered the intelligence unit to prepare a report for submission to the President."

"Why the fuck bother!" Brennan demanded in a whisper to his partner. "The answer's obvious. The bad guys are winning. Like they've always won."

"At least *we're* in business," said Seymour.

"I've sent a message through to Rivera in Bogotá," said Brennan. "Asked him to get into contact."

13

The U.S. embassy in Bogotá is a bunker of a place, a mesh-protected, sealed-off building with a zigzag approach tunnel to prevent the rush of sudden attack. Harry Green had his office in the main building, part of the CIA residency to which he was nominally attached as an FBI liaison officer, but this day he did not leave from there. Because of Brennan's instruction from Washington, he went first in the morning to the offices of the Drug Enforcement Administration, whose building was across the road from the main embassy, in a separate low-rise office block. Green was an affable, eager career officer, still adolescent-plump from college junk food and a dislike of exercise, glad of the opportunity the Colombian posting gave him and determined to succeed in it. Despite his ambition, he wasn't pushy and he got the deference just right, properly respectful without being servile. The CIA bureau liked him and the professional diplomats liked him and the Drug Enforcement officers liked him.

José Rivera was Green's case, passed on to him because the Colombian lawyer had made the original approach in Washington, just after the FBI had assumed control jurisdiction of America's antinarcotic effort. Green let the DEA men know that he had somebody he hoped might be useful and indicated that he'd cooperate as much as he felt able. In return, the Enforcement officials updated him on the material they were sending to Washington, material which was anyway disseminated through the joint task forces. Green listened with his usual polite attention, letting the briefing come naturally to his point of interest, not wanting to prompt or give them any clue to whom his source and contact might be. The identities of the major cocaine traffickers were public enough to be printed on a special fact sheet and Green was assured as they went through it that there were no names missing from those he already had. The names of members of the government and judiciary who were controlled by the traffickers were also well known, but this list had higher security classification: Green was permitted access within the restrictions of the DEA office but not allowed a copy of his own. It took him only seconds to ascertain that Rivera's name did not appear under the heading of crooked lawyers.

Green was still early for the assignation—intentionally so, for he remained conscious of the lessons of training school. He strolled past the pavement sellers, discreetly checking to see if he was being followed. He decided he wasn't, but stayed careful, joining the main thoroughfare and then crossing it so that he would be on the correct side of the road when he reached the Hilton. He turned left on entering the foyer, to the ground-floor bar with its somewhat surprising Tartan decor, managing to find a corner seat at the bar which gave him a perfect view of the door and any pursuer. He ordered a beer and sat waiting. It was several minutes before anyone else came in. A young couple, apparently engrossed in each other, went immediately to one of the tables, showing no interest in him whatsoever. Next came a man, Colombian in appearance, who also showed lack of interest. He, too, went to a table and was soon busy ordering a meal from the waiter. Green's training told him that an observer, seeing that his quarry was only drinking, would not have risked a meal which he might have hurriedly to leave, drawing attention to himself. The FBI agent took his beer slowly, allowing six more people to enter and settle in various parts of the room; only one couple actually joined him at the bar and they were as caught up in each other as the original two had been.

Reasonably satisfied that there was no tail, Green paid but didn't leave the hotel at once, going instead deeper into the foyer area and pretending to look at the shops, alert for any sudden exit. There wasn't one. Green regained the road and walked further into the city, taking a right fork near the museum, heading for the meeting place. The Torquemada had been Rivera's choice, and the FBI man hoped the lawyer had been as careful as he had been approaching it. Green circled the foyer, pausing to look at the artifact shop with its assurance of guarantees, before moving along the corridor and descending to the bar, finally sure he was alone. The lawyer was waiting in a corner seat, eyes intent upon the stairway, flickering with obvious nervousness.

"It is all right?" demanded the Colombian.

"Yes."

"Are you sure?"

"I was extremely careful: made stops and checked. I wasn't followed." Green saw that the Colombian was drinking brandy and that his goblet was almost empty. When the waiter approached, Rivera finished his drink in a single, frightened gulp and nodded his acceptance of the American's offer of another.

"It isn't easy anymore," protested Rivera. "All the big men are careful, after the various operations you've mounted. It's not like it was."

"There are lists," said Green. "Records of those whom we know to be traffickers, and names too of people in the government and the law and officials who are known to be on the payroll. I checked. You're not on them. Any of them."

"I'd hope not," said the lawyer. He reached out for the returning drink and gulped at it.

"The traffickers would have a pretty good idea who we

know about and who we don't. Lists, like we have. You're
safe.''

"Nothing's happening," reported Rivera. "Nothing that
isn't obvious, without my telling you."

"Nothing at all?" pressed Green. Another academy rule
for a meeting like this was to get everything you could
before coming to your purpose for making the meet.

"Gomez wants to see me."

Green was sure he managed to hide his reaction. "What
for?"

"I don't know," said the lawyer. "A phone call yesterday, asking me to come up to Medellin. Business, he
said."

"What sort of business?"

"He didn't say." Despite his apprehension, Rivera
laughed. "What other sort of business does Gomez have?"

"I'm interested, José."

"I'm frightened," confessed the lawyer needlessly.
"They're very careful now, like I said."

"I'm very careful, like I said," reassured Green. "I'll
make sure nothing happens."

"No one can promise that, in a country like this," said
Rivera. Embarking on a familiar theme, the lawyer added
vehemently, "That's why I went to your people in the first
place. When I realized what was happening to my country,
and how I was helping to let it happen by working with
them. Colombia used to be a good and honorable country.
Look at it now!"

Green had heard it before, several times, but he allowed
the other man to talk himself out and said, scoring, "Which
is surely why you've got to help, José?"

The lawyer made an uncertain gesture with his shoulders, looking down into the already empty glass. Green
gestured for refills, although he did not want any more.

Rivera said, "I want this to be the last time, for a while.
My nerve, it's not . . . it's not good."

Green again remained impassive, this time for different
reasons. José Rivera was not just his agent: the lawyer was

his *best* agent, a man at the center of the gossip of the judiciary and the police and the army and the traffickers. Green knew that a great deal of the success for which he had received congratulations from Washington was due to this one twitching, nail-biting man. He did not want to lose him—which meant playing the man with the expertise of a fisherman, not with rod or line but with a personal touch tickling him into a sense of security. And that meant not coming on heavy with the latest instruction from headquarters about alerting Rivera to a newly set-up investment situation and asking him to guide some of the major traffickers toward it. Spring-tight as he was at present, Rivera would run and never come back if that sort of proposition were made to him. Brennan had said he wanted things organized as quickly as possible but the man would have to wait: Brennan was in Washington, where it was easy to send cables about things happening as quickly as possible and then go out for a leisurely lunch at Mellon's or Dominique's and talk to other hot-shot supervisors about "move your ass" decisions. Harry Green was at the sharp end, where the shit stuck after it hit the fan, and he decided that the right field decision was to let Rivera run until the meeting with Gomez. In the star rating, Gomez was not in the top league, but Green was realistic: an FBI or CIA or Drug Enforcement Administration rating was arbitrary; none of them actually *knew*. Gently he said to the lawyer, "Don't worry, José. Sure you should rest. I'm not pushing you."

Rivera smiled gratefully at the younger man. "You've been very good to me," he said. "From the time this began, you've been very good to me."

Psychology was an important part of the training. Green said, "How's María?"

Rivera made a seesawing motion with his hand. "Her asthma isn't good, not here in Bogotá. Sometimes I think I should move somewhere nearer the coast."

"Manuel?"

"The teachers say he's quite exceptional," beamed Rivera, with boastful pride. "Already he's talking of what he's going to do in the university."

"What's that?"

"Something modern, he hopes. Computers maybe. Myself, I don't understand any of it."

"There are some excellent universities in America," said Green.

It was an unthinking remark, made to keep the conversation going and maintain the calming of the Colombian, but Rivera seized on it, surprising the FBI man. "The Bureau could help! Getting Manuel a place, I mean?"

The question completely confused the young American. He supposed it was possible, but he had no idea whether the Bureau would involve themselves in things like that. Hoping his embarrassed coloring was not obvious to the man in the gloom of the sunken bar, Green said, "I don't see why not." He tried to reassure himself that it was not a direct lie.

"I've never asked for any money," reminded Rivera.

"I know."

"Any sort of reward?"

"No."

"I would like that to be my reward."

Green decided that he had wrapped everything up and sealed it with tape; all he had to do was to decide on the delivery. Rivera *would* come back because he wanted something. And when he came back the FBI man knew that he could set up the investment sting with the lawyer because of the man's need for a university place for his son. Not that Green intended to cheat him. He would go through Brennan or whoever was necessary and try to get the kid a place—which shouldn't be too difficult. The CIA and the FBI regarded American colleges as their kindergartens: he himself had been recruited off campus. The Bureau had enough power and influence to place a kid, if they wanted to. Green decided he would convince Washington that a college place was an inviolable condition for Rivera's continued cooperation. He said, "I promise you that I will raise it with Washington. And I promise you that I will do everything in my power to make sure it happens."

Rivera gave another sadly frightened smile. "You've always been very good to me," he repeated.

"And I will continue to be," said Green. "You'll let me know, about Gomez in Medellin?"

Rivera bit at his lip, as if he found the verbal assurance difficult, jerking his head several times in affirmation.

"Shall I contact you?"

"No!" said the Colombian at once. "Wait for me. I'll call you when I know it's safe."

"OK," said Green. "I'll wait." He'd wait, too, until the result of the Medellin visit before raising anything with Washington. Hopefully it would give him something with which to bargain.

"It will end one day, won't it!" said the lawyer, in an unexpectedly emotional demand. "One day this country will clean itself up!"

Not while a guy can make twenty-five million from a cocaine or marijuana shipment, thought Green: the money was just too much. He said, "Sure we'll clean it up. That's what we're here for. That's why the President set up all the task forces."

"Dear Mother of God that it should happen soon!" said the lawyer, vehemently. "I hate what drugs are doing to my country."

Rivera insisted upon more brandy but Green refused, concerned at the other man's intake. "You'll be careful, won't you?" said the American.

Rivera laughed once more, bitterly. "You'd be surprised how careful."

The man drank it quickly and Green was apprehensive that he was going to drink even more but Rivera suddenly tensed himself. "I must be going."

"You'll call me?" pressed Green.

"Yes."

"We'd better leave separately."

"Me first," insisted the lawyer, anxious now to break the contact.

"Of course."

The FBI man sat back, pitying the diminutive, mustachioed lawyer as he hurried away from the table and up the stairs to the foyer level. It must, thought Green, be awful to be as frightened as that: absolutely bloody awful. He took his time finishing his drink, and did not become impatient at the slowness of the waiter to settle the check.

Jorge Gomez had survived this far—and intended to continue surviving—because he took care in everything. The man at the bar, whose presence was part of that care and who had maintained a surveillance on the lawyer from the moment of his contact with Green, quietly followed Green up the stairs. There was no risk of his being identified by the FBI agent because the others were patiently waiting in the foyer area, as they had since Rivera's arrival two hours earlier: two would have already detached themselves, to accompany the lawyer wherever he was going, and there were three more to alternate the observation of the unknown man who was about to be indicated by the barroom watcher. The one with the camera hurried outside the hotel the moment he saw Green emerge from the bar, so that he was ready with a long-focus lens to capture the American as he left. Green was excited at the outcome of the meeting, convinced that important things would come from it, and he relaxed his former caution. Rivera had got away unidentified so why worry?

It was a short walk back to the embassy compound, about half an hour, and the moment the undetected surveillance team saw Green enter, the photographer knew how to put a name to the unknown person on his film. Through the immigration inspector whom Gomez kept on the payroll—the same man deputed weeks earlier to warn of Julio Navarra's arrival from Bolivia—the photographs were checked against the filed visa application forms of American personnel. Harry Green's name came up an hour later.

"Drug Enforcement Administration?" wondered Ramos, when the information was telephoned through to Medellin.

"Maybe that. Maybe CIA. Maybe FBI. It doesn't matter," said Gomez. He was disguising it very well, but the closeness to possible disaster frightened him badly.

"We were lucky we found out," said Ramos.

"No, we weren't," corrected Gomez, at once. "We found out because we took the proper precautions, watching that bastard Rivera and seeing whom he met."

"Of course," apologized the other man. "I meant, lucky to have found out before we went through with the meeting."

"We'll still go through with the meeting," decided Gomez. "I want to know what it's about."

"Of course," said the protector again. Instinctively his hand went up to the knife scar.

"The motherfucker!" erupted Gomez, the nervousness becoming anger. There was something else too: the awareness that he had made a mistake in going to the Colombian lawyer in the first place.

"Now we know we can make an example," said Ramos.

Gomez held up a warning hand. "I want to know everything first," he said. "I want to know everything he's told the Americans about me. I mean *everything*. You understand?"

"I understand."

"Personally," decided Gomez. "I'll do it personally. . ." He paused, the anger increasing. "Motherfucker!" he said again.

"The ten o'clock flight from Bogotá," said Ramos.

"Here, at the *finca*," said Gomez. "The bullring stables."

On the flight from the capital Rivera needed brandy. There was no bar service on the shuttle but he carried a hip flask and went into the lavatory twice before the plane put down in Medellin. Ramos was waiting to meet him with two other men. The greeting was friendly but reserved. On the way out of town, toward Gomez's house in the foothills, Ramos inquired politely about the flight and Rivera said he was glad to be in Medellin—as he always was—because the weather was invariably better than in cloud-engulfed Bogotá. He wanted to take some orchids back for his wife, and Ramos said that, while the lawyer had his meeting with Señor Gomez, he would personally see to it that they were purchased and packed. Rivera thanked the man for his trouble and Ramos assured him it was no trouble but a pleasure.

It was the largest of Gomez's *fincas*, a sprawling estate despite the restriction of the mountain foothills, with an enclosing wall into which were set high and heavy gates which only opened upon identification from the gatehouse. The house itself was set far back, directly against a jut of mountain rock which provided perfect protection from the rear. To the right were the garages, servants' quarters and accommodation for the guards, ten of whom Gomez kept in permanent residence, on a rotation basis. The bullring, with its tiered seats and stabling for the horses and the bulls, was to the left, where there was more land available. Centerpiece of the huge widening drive was the permanently watered, and therefore green, garden area, with a playing fountain and a blaze of the sort of flowers which made the valley famous. The gatehouse warned the main house, before the limousine even reached it, so Gomez was already waiting on the veranda when the car circled the garden area and drew up in front of the low steps.

Gomez personally opened the door to let the lawyer out. As Rivera emerged, the trafficker said, "Welcome, my friend. Welcome."

"Good to see you again, Señor Gomez," said the lawyer. He was sure he kept the nervousness from his voice. It had been sensible to bring the brandy on the plane. "Let's hope we can make some good business."

"Business later," insisted Gomez. He took the lawyer's briefcase from him, handing it to one of the escorts from the airport, and said, "First you must see the new bulls. I'm putting on a fiesta at the weekend; all the townsfolk are coming free of charge . . ." He allowed the pause for the boast to have its full weight, because it was true and because he was outdoing the other traffickers by this coup. "And I'm flying Ortega in from Madrid, to fight in the main *corrida* . . ."

Rivera looked uncertainly after his disappearing brief-case. "Should be a wonderful event," he said, letting himself be led across the forecourt toward the ring area.

As they got nearer, the noise of the animals became more pronounced, punctuated by the occasional snorted scream of protest. The unusualness of the animals being enclosed, rather than being allowed out in the fields and paddocks at the back, did not occur to Rivera until the very entrance to the stabling. He turned at the door and began, "I don't understand . . . ?" but Ramos didn't let him finish, driving his fist into the small of the man's back so that he was hurled breathless into the covered block. The lawyer's frightened squeal was lost among the louder bellowing of the angry captive animals. The second man who had come with Rivera from the airport hauled him easily to his feet and, with Ramos on the other side, they wired his wrists together using industrial fencing pincers, and then suspended his arms above his head and pulled him up on the very tip of his toes through a high-set pulley attached to one of the main beams. It was impossible for Rivera to support himself and he stumbled desperately, trying to sustain a balance and failing, so that he swung from the taut wire like an uncontrolled marionette. The wire sliced into his wrists and blood poured down his arms. Rivera screamed long, wailing, hysterical screams, further unsettling the disturbed animals, who began snuffling and making their own noise, drowning out that of the lawyer. Gomez, apparently irritated by the man's crying, stepped forward slightly and kicked directly into his unprotected groin, finding his testicles. This time, Rivera's scream of agony rose above those of the animals. His body tried to double up, but the wire stopped the movement, cutting deeper into his wrists.

The door behind them opened, thrusting a brief wedge

of sunlight into the stable, as the man who had been given the briefcase came in. The case was still in his hand, opened now, disarrayed papers obvious from its sagging top.

"Anything?" said Gomez.

"Nothing."

"Let him down, very slightly," ordered Gomez.

Ramos released the pulley, just enough for Rivera to balance on the balls of his feet; his heels were unable to reach the ground. The kick had made him sick; stained his face and chest, and there was a lot of blood. At a nod from Gomez, one of the airport escorts picked up a bucket and threw water over the man. It cleaned him only marginally. Along one of the walls, in sectioned compartments and on specially arranged hooks, was the riding equipment for the horsemen who accompanied the *corrida*. Gomez selected a riding crop, holding it before him like a pointer and raising the lawyer's head so that the man had to look directly at him. Rivera's eyes were rolling, uncoordinated. Gomez slapped him hard across the face with the crop, once. Rivera shouted, "No, please no! No more."

"What did you tell them!" demanded Gomez.

"Who?"

The crop slashed out again, along the same line as before. "What did you tell them!"

"Nothing!"

"Liar!" The crop went along the other cheek this time.

"Nothing!"

"Liar!"

Rivera hung slumped from the wire, oblivious now to the pain, sobbing incoherently, only words such as "no" and "please" discernible.

"Look up!" shouted Gomez, nodding to Ramos.

The bloodstained, sick-stained crying man forced himself upwards, blinking at the photograph that had been taken the previous day as the American left the Torquemada.

"His name is Harry Green," said Gomez. "What's his job at the embassy?"

Rivera's lips began to form a denial and then he saw the
crop twitch again and blurted out desperately, "The FBI.
He works for the FBI."

"What did you tell him?"

"There was nothing to tell."

There was another slash of the crop, further ribboning
the lawyer's face.

"That I worked for you sometimes. Escabar, too. And
Ledher. And Alvarro-Moreno," gabbled Rivera, believing
that talk would stop the agony.

"Worked how?"

"Legitimately. Creating businesses."

"Did he want to know where the money came from?"

Rivera began to shake his head, then said, "I told him
that it was cash. That I didn't inquire. That everything was
legal."

Which it was, Gomez supposed. He said, "What about
coming here today?"

"No!"

"But you were going to tell him, weren't you!" demanded Gomez. "When you got back to Bogotá, you
were going to tell him everything."

"No!"

There was so much blood on Rivera's face that it was
impossible to see whether the riding crop made a fresh
laceration or merely opened wider one that already existed.
"Weren't you!"

"Yes, yes, yes. Oh, for God's sake, stop! Yes. I was
going to tell him everything!"

Gomez turned away from the mutilated lawyer, his mind
momentarily blocked by the narrowness of his escape. If
he'd miscalculated by a day—hours—then everything that
he'd worked so hard to achieve could have been ruined.
But he *hadn't* miscalculated. He'd got this right, just like
he'd got everything else right. It was a good omen. Gomez
began walking distractedly from the stable. Ramos caught
up with him at the door and together they made their way
back toward the main house.

"We should make it an example," said Gomez.

"Unquestionably."

"The Americans will know that the man Green has been identified. I wonder if they will withdraw him?"

"Perhaps," said Ramos. "Perhaps not. They're arrogant bastards."

"Is everything ready for Ortega's arrival? I want it all to be right."

"I'm dealing with it personally."

"I'm looking forward to it. It will be a good fiesta."

"The best," agreed Ramos, who understood the other man's need to impress the barons.

The body of José Rivera was found the following day, where the bodies of drug victims are usually found: in the hinterland behind the Intercontinental hotel. It was naked. The man's penis had been severed and stitched inside his mouth. The autopsy disclosed three bullet wounds, but the cause of death was choking, after the mutilation.

In the newspaper *El Colombiano* there is daily published a whole-page feature reporting the drug murders of the previous twenty-four hours. That day there were eight other bodies found in addition to that of José Rivera, but because he was a well-known lawyer in the capital the account of his killing dominated the murder reports.

14

Farr had gone detail by detail through it all once but Harriet recognized his need to purge himself in some way, so she said nothing while the broker went over again the encounter at the Eastham clinic. She quietly made him first one and then another drink, both of which he took without apparently noticing.

"Dr. Halpern wasn't critical," she reminded him.

"I'm not concerned about what Dr. Halpern thinks. I'm interested in what Howard thinks."

"At the moment that seems to be confined to a cellophane packet and a hypodermic."

"What sort of remark is that!" he said, irritated.

"The sort of remark that you made about thirty minutes ago: I was quoting you."

He smiled at her apologetically, but then almost immediately his mood reverted to despair. "Oh Christ, Harriet! I just don't know what I'm going to do about the silly little bugger!"

She came to him on the couch, cradled his head against her and said, "Stop it, darling. Stop trying to hurt for him. Let him hurt for himself."

Through his anguish Farr became aware of the word she had used, like a bell ringing on a still day, and at the same moment she realized what she had said. He pulled away, but not too far, so that their faces were still very close.

Farr had been near crying. He managed to stop himself but he still had to sniff, and he laughed in embarrassment. He closed the distance between them, kissing her. She did nothing at first, neither responding nor withdrawing. Then Farr risked putting his arms around her, bringing her close, and she snatched out at him with surprising passion, pulling him to her and forcing herself against him. They parted finally, both breathless. She recovered first and said, "Shit! I was trying so hard to make sure nothing happened."

"Nothing has."

"But it's going to, isn't it?"

"I hope so."

She came forward, kissing him again, but more gently this time, without her former urgency. "I hope so too, my darling," she said. "I hope so very much."

Farr was nervous, frightened of disappointing her, the nervousness making it difficult for him and failure more likely. Sex with Ann had been wonderful—joyous—but after her death apart from the few occasions when it had not mattered and had therefore worked, he had put sex aside, as he had put so much else. Now was like the first time. The first time had been with Ann: they had been worried about her becoming pregnant and he had fumbled with the contraceptive and dropped it; they'd had to put on the light to find it, and when they did find it, he'd collapsed. The memory of that night came to him and he willed himself against collapsing again.

Farr trembled at the sight of Harriet's nakedness, excitement jostling his fear. Her breasts were large but they hardly sagged at all: she was narrow-waisted and hard-stomached right down to a perfect pubic wedge, sharp-edged, like the briefest of coverings. She smiled up at his wonderment, shifting sensuously under his look. He touched her, scarcely daring to, and she smiled again and said softly, "I won't break."

"You're so beautiful."

"I want to be, for you."

"You are."

Harriet appeared to realize his difficulty, taking his delicate hand in hers and putting it where she wanted it to be, around her breasts first, where she left it for a long time, her eyes half closed and her breathing becoming heavy, and then down, parting for him. He misunderstood and moved to cover her but she said, "No. No, wait. There's no hurry," guiding her hand over his, forcing it against and into her. "Harder. Make it hurt." Farr did, though he was reluctant to hurt her, and then with both hands she felt for his head and pulled that to her, bucking and groaning under his lips.

"Please," he said, muffled. "Please soon."

"Not yet."

"I don't think I can wait."

She held him tighter against her, so he could not speak. He forgot to be nervous. He drove his head where she wanted it to be, nipping at her with his lips, holding and tugging at her, and she began to jerk rhythmically, jarring into him so that he was afraid that his teeth might really hurt, more than she needed.

"Now!" she said, bringing him up at last. "Now!"

She was wetly ready, sighing as he entered her. At the beginning they both stopped for the shortest moment, resting after the first part of the race, and then started again in perfect time, unhurried for the final lap. Harriet was still slightly ahead, moving faster, urging him on at the very last. He strained to catch her and did, so that they exploded together. She screamed out and clutched at him, burying her face into his shoulder and saying "Oh, oh" over and over again.

They took a long time to come down, literally slipping from each other because both were damply hot.

"Christ!" said Farr, able to manage only one word.

Initially, Harriet could not even do that. She reached out, smoothing his face, tracing the dips and highs like a blind person trying to create a mental image. At last she managed to speak, still short-breathed. "Wonderful."

"Thank you," said Farr. "I mean, for understanding. You did understand, didn't you?"

She nodded, head against the pillow.

"I was very frightened," he confessed. "Sounds stupid, doesn't it?"

"No," she said. "Why should it?"

Farr shrugged, enjoying their closeness, conscious of the occasional touch of their bodies. "I don't know. It just does . . ." He made another movement. "Embarrassing . . ." he said awkwardly.

Harriet moved closer, so that she didn't have to look directly at him. "Shouldn't I be embarrassed, too?"

"You!"

"I enjoy it so much. And it's been so long."

"You made it possible for me."

"You weren't—" She stopped, seeking the word. "Offended?" she finished.

Now Farr smoothed her unseen face. "No. I wasn't offended. I was grateful."

"Well, I did it!" she said. "Broke the unwritten law of involvement again."

"Sorry?"

"Not at the moment. At the moment I'm very happy."

"What about later?"

"I don't want to think about later."

They held each other, fitting together comfortably. The air conditioning was on and Harriet suddenly shivered, cooling now. Farr moved the sheet with his feet until he could reach out to drag it over them, unwilling to move further away from her than necessary. She said, "Tell me about Ann," and then hurried on at once. "But not if you don't want to. Only if you want to."

"We met at Harvard . . . that's why I wanted Howard to go there, after us," Farr began, slowly. "She was a year below me at Radcliffe. I was on an exchange from Cambridge. I got a tripos there, in economics . . ."

"What's a tripos?"

"An honors examination. Ann was studying classics—"

He hesitated again, both in reflection and at the thought that the circumstances were odd for such a confessional. "She told me afterwards that at first she thought I was odd—too serious and I didn't laugh enough. Admitted that she accepted the first date because of a bet with some other girls in her dormitory, to see who could go out first with the dull Englishman." He stopped once more, wanting Harriet properly to understand what it had been like . . . "It wasn't anything dramatic. It just seemed that we liked being with each other. Felt comfortable. But I don't think either of us thought of getting married. After I graduated, I went back to England and got a job in the City in investment brokerage. In about a year they linked up with a group in New York and I was sent there as liaison. We'd written to each other a few times and so I called her up and she seemed pleased to hear from me. Started seeing each other again, like it had been at Harvard . . ." He started again. "Realizing I loved her *was* dramatic. It happened, just like that. One day I thought of her as a friend, the next I knew I loved her . . . just like that . . ." he repeated. "No," he said, in immediate contradiction. "It wasn't quite like that. I was recalled to London—or, at least told I was going to be recalled. That's when I realized I didn't want to leave her. My father died during the war and my mother during my first year in the City. I had nothing to go back for, except a junior directorship and eventual progression to a place on the board. So I resigned. She never said so, but I think she was frightened, marrying an unemployed broker; when it came down to it, she was the more conservative of the two of us. I wanted to go to Florida for a honeymoon but she worried about how much it would cost, so instead we had a weekend in the Catskills. Turned out to be a wise economy because, although I had residential qualifications from marrying an American girl, there weren't very many firms in Wall Street interested in employing a British financier, irrespective of qualifications and diplomas. The firm I'd just left didn't provide much of a recommendation either. They'd been cheating and were had up before the Security Exchange Commission within a month of my leaving. Kind of looked as if I'd left because I was aware of what was going on and wanted to get out before the problems started . . ." He looked toward her. "I didn't know, of course," he said quickly.

There was a silence while Farr assembled his thoughts. "Tramped around with the resumés and tried to lean on all the acquaintances and people I'd thought of as friends, and practically decided that we'd done things the wrong way around: that I should have stayed with the English firm and taken Ann back to London with me. I don't remember which of us suggested I try to start by myself. I suppose it must have been me. All the money came from Ann's parents, certainly. Took a mortgage on their house—they lived upstate, at a place called Ridgewood—and made their savings over as well. Nearly seventy-five thousand dollars. First year I showed a trading loss of fifty-five thousand. Ann was pregnant and we lived in an apartment where the bugs thought they had more rights than we did. Things didn't get better, not for a long time. Couldn't even afford a cot for Howard—" Farr snorted a laugh. "Had to keep up this ridiculous pretense. Had to have an office that was far too expensive and I had to wear suits that then cost two hundred dollars, so that what clients there were wouldn't lose confidence. And at night sneak home to a dump where all the neighbors knew each other because they couldn't avoid listening through the walls . . ."

Harriet drew herself closer to him, lightly kissing his cheek.

". . . Things got better after the third year, I put together a few portfolios that came good and people spoke to people and suddenly it was difficult to understand why it had been so hard before. Two years were the good times; maybe two and a half. Then Ann started to get sick . . ." He stopped, feeling the accustomed anger. "Just when it was good! Just when I could afford the things I'd always promised her—promised myself to get for her—she had to go and get sick. Did everything, of course. Even considered a transplant, although they weren't as medically proven as they are now. There was a remission once: for six whole months. Happens, with cancer, apparently. We were nervous at first but when the X-rays and the tests confirmed the remission we actually thought we'd beaten it. That everything was going to be all right. But it wasn't." Farr swallowed against the memories. "At least there wasn't any pain. I just wish so much that she'd woken up, at the end . . ."

"It was wrong of me. I'm sorry. I shouldn't have asked you."

"I'm glad you know."

"At least you had someone, for a while at least."

"People tried to talk about it like that. I found it difficult. Still do."

"Thank you for telling me."

Harriet remained quiet for a long time and then she said, "I think there is something *you* should know."

"You don't have to . . ."

"I want to tell you. It's only fair; right that you should. There was a baby. Jack didn't know, not until the night at Balboa Park. I told him when he said he had decided to go back to Julia, and he shouted at me and said I was a bitch for trapping him—which I had, I suppose. Things were drifting and I wanted him to choose between us, and I thought he would choose me if there was a baby. That's why he stormed out of the bar like he did. Angry . . ."

Farr felt her shudder against his shoulder as she began to cry. "I killed him," she said. "I killed Jack because of what I did. If I hadn't told him I was pregnant, he wouldn't have left like he did and driven like he did, and he would be alive now."

"You don't know that," said Farr. "It's ridiculous to think like that."

"I can't help it."

"What happened?" asked Farr gently. "To the baby?"

Harriet did not respond at once. "Abortion," she said.

"I had an abortion. It seemed sensible then. I wish I hadn't now. Of all the things I wish, I wish I hadn't done that."

"You didn't have to tell me."

"I wanted you to know; I told you. I wanted you to know."

"Why?"

"I'm not sure, not really . . . Yes, I am. I didn't want there to be anything hidden between us. Not from my side anyway. It's probably difficult for you to understand after what I've told you about Jack and me, and how I went to the funeral with Julia, but I don't like deceits . . ." Harriet shook herself, an angry gesture. "It *is* difficult to understand, because it's stupid to believe. But that's the way I feel. Now, at least. I'm sorry. This isn't making sense, is it?"

"Sense enough," said Farr.

"Disgusted with me?"

"No."

"How can you not be?"

"By not sitting in judgment," he said.

"That's not possible."

"What happened before happened before," he said.

"I'd like to believe you. *Want* to believe you."

"I don't want any deceits, either," said Farr. He pushed her away from him, so that she had to look up. He kissed her, gently first, then harder, and Harriet clutched at him in her anxiety.

"I wish things were different," she said. "Us being here—the reason, I mean. Like the reason for us meeting."

"We'll have to make them so."

"Do you think we can? There's a lot of it that's— Oh, I don't know. Artificial, I suppose."

"Was what happened tonight artificial?"

"No, darling. No, that wasn't artificial."

"I love you," he said.

"I think I love you, too. I wish I didn't, because it frightens me. But I think I do."

"Don't get involved with people you're working with!"
he mocked, gently.

"It's a good rule," she said. "One that shouldn't be
broken."

"We've broken it."

"That's what frightens me most of all."

"Are they all arriving tomorrow?"

"I'm not sure. Batty and Jones, certainly. To decide
upon the office."

"I don't want this to be just an affair," said Farr.
"Something that happens while we're here, and then ends
when the reason for our being here ends."

"Neither do I, my darling," said Harriet. "Love me
again. Please."

Farr did, easily. And was pleased.

Harry Green, as diligent as always, obtained photographs
of José Rivera from the Colombian police and enclosed
them with the full account of the murder which he sent
from Bogotá in the diplomatic pouch: it was important to
supply everything because he knew there had been a foul-up
and that, if there was an inquiry, he'd get the shit. They
were at the end of the dossier; when Brennan reached
them, he swallowed and said, "Jesus Christ!" and passed
them to Seymour.

The other FBI man frowned down, shaking his head.
"What sort of people are these!"

"You tell me," said Brennan. They would be completely exposed in the Caymans, he thought: maybe they
would have a little protection, but not the sort he had
glibly assured them of at the first Boston meeting.

Professionally Seymour said, "It's a bastard. Rivera
was our best hope."

Brennan looked quizzically at his partner, who knew
everything. "Practically our *only* hope."

"You think it was Gomez?"

"He's the most obvious, from what Rivera told Green
before he went to Medellin," said Brennan. "But Rivera

acted for the others, too. Escabar, certainly. And Ledher. That's *why* Rivera was so important.''

"What are we going to do now?"

"About Colombia, I don't know. I guess the DEA must have some contacts and they might just consider letting us use them, but I'm reluctant to make the approach. I want to keep this a tight, enclosed operation,'' said Brennan.

"What about the others?"

"Others?"

"Batty and Jones and Mann? The woman, too.''

"What the hell for!" said Brennan, irritated by the question. "We already know how nervous they are. There's no point in making it any worse.''

"What about Farr?"

"Him least of all," said Brennan. "I want them all to go on thinking that things are going exactly as planned.''

15

The two technicians arrived first. They examined the three offices and chose the one near the post office, in Elgin Avenue, and Farr was glad at the choice. The selection having been made, Farr allowed the already ordered furniture to be delivered—until it had, neither Batty nor Jones could start work. The installation took only a morning, so the two Americans occupied themselves settling into the rented house near Southwest Point. Harriet acted as guide, showing them over not only their own accommodation but the bungalow as well. Neither man commented about Farr and the woman living under the same roof. They lunched well at the Lobster Pot, and Batty, the more enthusiastic of the two, said he thought he was going to like the assignment. Farr saw that Jones still had one arm of his spectacles secured by the bent paperclip.

The telephone and telex lines were the last items to be fitted. The two men dismantled the telephones, inserting listening and monitoring devices to ensure that everything would be recorded. In every receiver they put a separate activating mechanism: the recordings could be started manually but a second system was voice-activated. They then did the same with the telex machine, fitting it with an extra printout facility so that there would be duplicates of every message and an additional display screen to keep a record of all numbers dialed out or in. The cameras, both still and movie, were completely concealed in what purported to be a burglar-alarm system—a series of lens-type sensors with fish-eye coverage of every room in the office suite. Even with the film equipment, the sensors still performed their true function, reacting to the body heat of anyone who came within range.

The center of the suite was a large, open-plan office area reached directly from the road. The telex room was to the right and there were three smaller rooms at the rear. Batty and Jones wired everyone with microphones, concealed inside the beading of the desks. Each was entirely automatic, triggered again by voice. They had finished their bugging by the late evening of the first day.

Batty squatted on his heels by the desk in the main room, grinned and said, "Well, folks, we're ready for business."

"Let's hope we get some, after all this," said the more doubtful Jones.

Farr contacted his New York office by telex, advising them of his intention to fly up the following day, as a test for the installation. It worked perfectly.

They dined out, as they had lunched, at the Caribbean Club, and Batty said, "We'd better enjoy it while we can. When Harvey gets here and starts scrutinizing the expenses, he won't be happy."

Farr expected there to be some embarrassment when they got home at the end of the evening but there wasn't, the technicians going to their house and Farr and Harriet to the bungalow.

"They seem to have accepted our being together," said Farr.

"It was always planned that there should be shared accommodation," she said.

"Still thought they might have said something."

"You're embarrassed!"

"I'm not."

"You are! Worried what the neighbors might say!"

He laughed with her, enjoying her lightness. "I don't give a damn about the neighbors."

Without any discussion, she walked with him to his bedroom, and the love was as good as it had been the first time. They remained holding each other tightly afterwards, neither wanting to break away. "How long will you be away?" she asked.

"A few days," said Farr. "Now we're operational, the quickest way of spreading the word is through New York."

"I expect everyone will be here when you get back."

"Will it make it difficult for us?"

"Could be a little awkward, I guess. Until they get used to it. The house will be a bit crowded."

"Some of them would expect to come and live here?" said Farr. The prospect had not occurred to him until now.

"I would have thought so," said Harriet, curious at his obvious surprise.

"I don't want that."

"Bill was only half joking tonight, about the expenses. Harvey Mann's a tight-assed little bookkeeper. I don't think he'd go along with the rental of a third property. Everything will have to be accounted for in the end, don't forget."

"I don't give a damn what Mann will or will not go along with," said Farr. "I'm not sharing this place with anyone apart from you. I'll take over the rental here and pay for it myself. Rent something else for the others. That way the Bureau will still only be paying for two places."

She pulled away from him slightly. "That's going to cost you a lot of money."

He kissed her gently. "Can't imagine a better way of spending it."

"Thank you," she said.

"Don't fall in love or have any affairs while I'm away."

"You laying claim?"

"Absolutely one hundred percent."

She looked at him in complete seriousness in the half light of the bedside lamp. "You needn't worry. I've found someone to love."

Farr caught the earliest flight from the island and man-

aged to make a connection within two hours at Miami, so
he reached Manhattan by early afternoon. Angela Nolan
was waiting dutifully, running with her usual efficiency
through everything that had occurred since his last trip. He
congratulated her on her impressive achievements.

"Flying visit?" she asked.

"I'll be around for a few days."

"What's it look like on the island?"

"Pretty good."

"Hector wants to talk to you."

"A problem?"

The woman shook her head. "Not with his section, not
as far as I know. Just said he wanted to know as soon as
you came back, so I told him when I got the telex. He said
he'd like to see you as soon as convenient."

"Guess I'd better have him in then," said Farr.

Faltham arrived in Farr's office thirty minutes later,
shirt-sleeved as usual, pipe already going. He lowered
himself with slow deliberation into the chair Farr suggested, and remained for several moments staring across
the desk. Then he said, "When we spoke you talked about
the Caymans only being a possibility: that you weren't
sure if you'd proceed or not. From the telexes and from
what I've heard from Angela, I gather you're going ahead?"

"I think it's got potential," said Farr.

"For what?" demanded the other broker sharply.

"Profit," said Farr. "Good business."

"You've got a loyal team here," said Faltham. "Good
guys, every one of them."

Farr shifted unhappily. He supposed this confrontation
had been predictable but he had hoped to avoid it. "I
know that," he said. "I hardly need reminding."

"Why isn't anyone involved in the offshore venture
then?" asked Faltham. He held up his hand in an apologetic gesture. "OK," he said. "It's your company. You
own it; can do what you like. But I thought you owed it to
us to take us a little more into your confidence than you
have done. I gather the incorporation makes this company

the parent of the Cayman situation, yet no one from here is involved—or has the slightest idea even of what's going on. You've got a completely new team—we don't know any names, for Christ's sake!—and people here are uncertain.''

"You the spokesman?"

Faltham nodded. "Oldest guy around.''

"I've got every confidence in you—in you personally, and in everyone else in the firm. Why else would I feel able to go off to the Caymans and not worry about anything that's happening back here?" said Farr. He considered the lie and went on, "There's no purpose in anyone from here getting involved in the island expansion. I want everyone back here doing what they've always done; and always done well. The Caymans is *still* experimental. I'm going to give it a run and see how it goes. If it doesn't work, I'll close it all down. And the only person to have wasted his time will be me.''

"We go back a long time, right?"

"Right," agreed Farr.

"So I'm allowed to ask," said Faltham defensively. "You sure you're leveling about this?"

Farr determined against telling a direct lie. The alternative was practically as objectionable. "This is the way it's going to be," he said. "My way.''

Faltham's face tightened at the rejection. He took his pipe from his mouth, examining it as if seeing it for the first time. "I see.''

"Hector!" said Farr, not wanting the gap to widen between them. "Let me do it my way—indulge myself, if I want to.''

"Sure," said the other man, the hurt obvious.

"I *need* everyone back here," said Farr. "I don't want any mistakes . . . anyone imagining things when there's nothing to imagine." Farr realized that, as a result of what had happened between himself and Harriet, he'd cocooned himself, momentarily cut himself off from what needed to be done. It was not taking long to come back to reality.

"Like I said, it's your company," repeated the other man.

"Which wouldn't be the sort of company it is without you and the others," said Farr urgently. "I rely upon you. All of you. You tell them that for me? Or shall I talk to everyone myself?"

"No point in making it a bigger thing than it is," said Faltham. "I'll reassure those who need reassuring."

"Everything is going to work out OK. Just give it a little time."

Faltham looked directly at him. "There's nothing wrong with the business, is there?" he asked. "I know my own division's OK but there's nothing wrong elsewhere that makes it necessary for us to go offshore and maybe attract some high-flying business?"

"No," said Farr, urgently again, well knowing how quickly rumors could start and undermine a perfectly strong and viable financial enterprise. "The business is what it's always been. Solid as a rock."

Faltham stayed staring at him, his face showing neither belief or disbelief. "Maybe I'll tell them that, too."

"I don't want any wild stories," warned Farr.

"Neither do I," said Faltham. Critically he added, "It's a problem that arises when people don't get taken into confidence."

"There's no reason for it to arise; none whatsoever!" Farr allowed his own irritation to show. What would the professional reaction be if everything worked as the FBI intended? It would be important to remind Brennan about the promise publicly to exonerate him in court.

"So it's like you said, exploratory?"

"*Precisely* that," said Farr, glad that the assurance did not involve him in further lies.

"I'll try to make it clear."

"*Make* it clear," said Farr. "You know how dangerous these things can sometimes be, particularly if they get out of hand."

The meeting with Faltham—the abrupt, harsh return to

the forgotten reality—disturbed Farr. To spread the news
that he was operating offshore he intended to use the same
rumor mills that could be so damaging if the speculation
took a wrong course; and he would have to be very
careful—if there was the sort of feeling within the firm at
which Faltham hinted—that it didn't take the wrong course.
Walter Farr going into the Caymans had to be presented
and accepted as the action of a supremely confident and
successful investment broker widening his activities. Not
as the action of a man whose company had an unknown
problem—a liquidity difficulty, for instance—which he
was trying to solve by running after quick money. He had
Angela Nolan prepare interim figures of the year's working and profit forecast; and, despite the understanding that
Faltham would spread the message that all was well, con-
vened a meeting of the division managers—Nolan and
Faltham and Paul Brent and Richard Bell—and went through
everything with them, in a positive demonstration of their
continued and increasing profitability.

Having, he hoped, satisfied his immediate staff, Farr set
about channeling the stories exactly as he wanted them to
appear. He knew the places to go—the Union Club where
he'd eaten with Becage, the luncheon club off Fulton
Street, the floor of the exchange itself, the bars nearby—
and he used them all, seeking out the key people. First, he
planted the suggestion of the year's increased trading figures, during an apparently casual exchange with the jour-
nalist who compiled the influential Notes section of the
Wall Street Journal. After the item had duly appeared he
managed to seem surprised when *Barron's* and then the
New York Times openly approached him for confirmation.
He provided it, of course, and some more facts as well,
hinting at some expansion. This brought the *Wall Street
Journal* back and to them he finally disclosed the Caymans
operation. Farr said that he had changed his earlier and
well-known attitude toward expansion *because* of his operating success. The speed and extent of the response surprised him. There were approaches from several pension-

fund managers—the biggest in Chicago—and plenty of calls from financial lawyers in the city. Farr handled everything himself, establishing a bone-aching schedule: getting into the office by seven in the morning, making every lunch a business meeting and then continuing late into the evening.

By the end of the first fortnight, Farr had channeled business worth fifty million dollars to the Caymans corporation. It all came from reputable financiers and institutions in whose reputations Farr personally had complete faith, long before the result of any FBI probe from the islands. It was not, Farr knew, the sort of business the Bureau wanted but it was the sort of business a newly established company wanted, because it confirmed with remarkable speed their own good standing. It meant, too, that the operation was not only self-financing but actually profitable—which, he supposed, would satisfy Harvey Mann. From his several-times-a-day contact with Georgetown, Farr learned from Harriet that the accountant had arrived and taken personal control of the books. There had been approaches from and some contracts signed with lawyers and other investment outlets on the island, which she had handled and which Brennan and Seymour were processing. Farr decided, in passing, that he was definitely in breach of the 1976 law governing confidential relationships. Conscious of the eavesdropping devices, Farr found his conversations with Harriet frustratingly difficult and guessed that she did too. Working as he was consistently late, Farr took to calling her at the bungalow and they had several aimless, meandering conversations before Harriet announced that Batty had now decided to wire their houses as well as the office. She had rented a bungalow for Mann, Brennan and Seymour just beyond Southwest Point, near Jackson Point. Mann had raised the expected objection to three houses and she enjoyed cutting him off by saying that the charge for the first bungalow would not be set against the Bureau's expense. Mann had suggested she move into the bungalow she'd found for the others, but Harriet said she'd told him to go to hell.

"They realize what's happening?" asked Farr.

"Brennan asked outright," replied Harriet. "I told him my personal life was none of his business."

"What did he say?"

"That what we were doing and where we were meant we didn't have any personal life."

"How's it been left?"

"Kind of up in the air," said Harriet. "I guess it'll stay that way until you get back. When's that going to be?"

"As soon as I can make it," promised Farr. "I didn't expect to be here as long as I have."

"Nor did I," she said. "I miss you."

"I miss you too," said Farr. "I love you."

"I love you," she said. "Which'll probably be the last time I'm able to tell you because they're wiring this telephone tomorrow. So hurry back."

"I will."

Farr remained sitting in the office after replacing the receiver, gazing out over a Manhattan skyline glittering defiantly against the night. He supposed he'd achieved all he had intended: there was no need for him to remain much longer in New York. There was still Howard, of course. Farr had called several times and been stalled by Halpern, who said he thought a visit would be premature, but tonight Farr had explained that he was leaving shortly, and the director said he guessed a brief visit might be all right. It was arranged for the following day.

Farr was at the office early as usual. As soon as Angela Nolan arrived, he briefed her about continuing the island liaison he had already established. Before setting out for La Guardia—by helicopter, because he disliked the traffic-clogged Van Wyck Expressway—he saw Faltham for the last time.

"Everyone happier now?"

"I guess so," said the man.

"What about you, personally?"

"Seems OK," said Faltham, the lack of conviction obvious. "Early indications certainly make it look good."

"I appreciate what you do here, while I'm away. I really do." Maybe when it was all over he would consider involving Faltham in some sort of partnership, Farr thought.

"How long will that be—you being away, I mean?"

Farr did not respond at once. The trap was set and baited. All they had to do now was wait for the right approach. He hoped it wouldn't take long. Or did he? The sooner it came and the entrapment occurred, the quicker his idyll with Harriet would end. No it wouldn't, Farr determined. The Caymans might end, but his involvement with Harriet wouldn't. Would she marry him? He had not considered marriage until this moment, but certainly that was what he wanted. Did she? Their involvement had not come about particularly quickly, but the circumstances of it were unnatural. Would she feel the same when things were more normal? Farr had not rushed the affair and he did not intend pushing it into the sort of commitment that he wanted. Anyway, neither of them could sensibly discuss their future until there had been some resolution of the operation. Replying to Faltham, Farr said, "I'm not sure. I'll be commuting up and down from time to time. Angela will look after this end, channeling the inquiries to me."

"Just passing them on?" Faltham was alert for greater involvement.

"That's all," insisted Farr. He did not want anyone in the firm getting more involved than that.

"I think maybe I got hold of the wrong end of the stick earlier," said Faltham, in unexpected apology. "Sorry if I ran off at the mouth a little."

"You've nothing to apologize for," said Farr.

But did he need to apologize, to Howard? wondered Farr as he entered the shuttle helicopter thirty minutes later: Halpern had assured him there was no physical injury from the beating he'd inflicted upon the boy but Farr still wished that he had not lost control.

Farr spoke first to Halpern and learned that Howard was

medically detoxified. The director advised him against saying he was sorry for the beating during the last visit. Howard's clothes were clean and he looked freshly showered, and the windows beyond the restrictive bars were open. The boy was not sweating with any discomfort; in fact his face had a healthy flush to it—the result, Farr guessed, of the basketball that Halpern had earlier told him Howard was playing most evenings. Howard still maintained the hunched-up sitting position and did not stand when his father entered.

"Hello, Howard," said Farr.

"Hello."

"How do you feel?"

Howard shrugged without interest. "OK, I guess."

"Dr. Halpern tells me you're taking part in some activities."

"Trying to stop myself going mad," said the boy. "Any idea what it's like, being locked up inside four unchanging walls?"

"Like prison, I'd guess. Dr. Halpern also said your system's been cleansed."

"The all-knowing, all-wise Dr. Halpern."

Farr clenched his hands against a repeat of the outburst that had happened last time. "He doesn't think you can be allowed out of the secure section yet."

"He's the boss."

"What would you do if you could get out?" demanded Farr, abruptly curious.

"You really want to know?"

"Of course I do."

"Score—as quickly as I could."

16

The sort of approach for which they were looking came a
week after Farr's return from New York and it was Harriet
who recognized it: a seemingly vague contact from a
Georgetown-based investment service, followed within days
by a telephone call and then a personal visit from a Houston accountant, a clearly nervous man named Briars. Farr
conducted the interview, self-consciously aware of per-
forming before all the recording devices. There was a lot
of discussion about cash surpluses and available liquidity,
and Farr did not try to help the Texan, letting Briars set the
pace, wondering idly if Becage, his own Texas client,
knew of the accountant. It took an hour for Farr to discover that the accountant was acting for a construction
millionaire who appeared over a period of years to have
creamed cash payments off the top of purposely reduced
contracts, and a further thirty minutes to establish the sum
at something like five hundred thousand dollars. Farr recommended an interlinked discretionary trust, under which
the Houston developer would establish a trustee through
the Cayman islands, with instruction to create a holding
company in the nearby Netherland Antilles. Only the trustee
would be listed on documentation in the Caymans: the
directorship of the holding company could be anonymous
because the appointment would be the responsibility of the
trustee. Once established through the Antilles, the tax-

161

avoiding company could trade with the man's American corporation, enabling him to claim, through his Antilles holding, American tax relief for foreign investments. It further meant that, if he wanted to invest the five hundred thousand in some building project, then the money was "clean" and represented a disposable asset. Briars took notes and clarified some uncertainties and left promising to be in touch within days. At a later conference, after they had studied the film and the recordings, Brennan said that Farr had made the tax avoidance appear remarkably easy and the investment broker replied that in reality it was. Brennan spent a lot of time in contact with Washington, who checked out Briars through their Houston office and identified the construction millionaire in less than twenty-four hours. Briars came back, as promised, with a named lawyer who had agreed to act as nominee trustee and Farr set up a company.

"Small time," judged Brennan. "If it's an offense, then it's a matter for the Internal Revenue Service and I guess this is one they've lost."

The atmosphere between Brennan and Farr was slightly better than it had been upon his immediate return, but only slightly. With the easygoing Batty alone did he enjoy anything like the earlier relationship, because Batty remained neutral. Jones fell in naturally with the unspoken criticism of the other Bureau people; Harvey Mann was the most obviously hostile. Farr realized at once that Mann would attempt to find financial mistakes anyway and was particularly cautious in this situation—Mann's demeanor became one of almost permanent anger.

Farr did not give a damn about any of the men but he was concerned at the effect Mann's behavior might have upon Harriet. She insisted that she didn't give a damn either.

"There are times when I really think Harvey would like to punch me out," said Farr.

"I think you're right," said the woman.

"Why?"

"I told you before I thought there might have been

trouble for me, from him,'' she said. ''I think he had me marked out as his.''

Farr felt an immediate burn of jealousy. ''What right had he to imagine that?'' he demanded, regretting at once the way it sounded.

She frowned at him. ''None,'' she said. ''None whatsoever.''

''I didn't mean that,'' apologized Farr at once. It was the night they had confirmed she was right about the Texas approach, and they'd celebrated, this time at the Grand Old House. He did not want to spoil the evening with an argument.

''Don't let it get to you,'' she said.

''I thought the difficulty might be more yours than mine,'' said Farr. ''They're guys you've got to work with.''

''So I'll work with them; and what I do when I'm not working is my business.''

Was this the time to share with her his thoughts about what would happen when it was all over? Farr felt the temptation but held back. Instead he said, ''Could it have any adverse effect on the job? If someone made a report, I mean.''

''It might have, in the days of Edgar Hoover, I suppose. I don't think it would now,'' she said.

''I wouldn't put it beyond Mann.''

''No,'' she agreed. ''Neither would I. Brennan would have to be the submitting officer. He's nominally in charge, after all.''

''You'd tell me if it happened, wouldn't you?'' he said. ''I'd want to know if the bastards tried anything.''

She smiled gently at his concern. ''I don't know whether I'd tell you or not,'' she said. ''Whether I'd consider it sufficiently important. And I don't think they've done anything to deserve being called bastards. Just been a bit stuffy, that's all. And that's because they're frightened it might affect what we're doing.''

It was Brennan who brought the affair out into the open.

At Brennan's suggestion, the investment broker had driven with him along Seven Mile Beach to the Holiday Inn where a room was permanently reserved for video lectures on how to minimize tax liability—"just in case we can see anything interesting."

Farr thought the trip a waste of time but went anyway. Brennan seemed to agree, so they walked to the thatched beach bar, fashioned like the prow of a boat. Brennan insisted upon getting the drinks, and left Farr thinking how out of place he would have appeared here such a short time ago in his stiff and formal business suit. It was instinctive now to dress casually, and he enjoyed it.

"Maybe today's the beginning," said Farr, seeking conversation.

"Small-time, like I said," reminded Brennan. "That's not what we're after."

"At least it's a start," said Farr.

"I don't like what's happened between you and Harriet," announced the FBI man abruptly.

Farr had been gazing out over the beach. He turned back, concentrating his attention on the other man, aware now that the hotel visit wasn't as aimless as he had suspected. "I don't see that it's got anything to do with you."

"Of course it has!" said Brennan. "We're all here for a specific reason. So it's a complication we don't need."

"It's nothing of the sort. Hasn't had—nor will it have—the slightest effect upon what we're trying to set up."

"It's unsettling people."

"It's doing nothing of the sort," said Farr. "It's upsetting *one* person and that's because Harvey Mann had decided he was going to have a relationship with Harriet. If Mann is unsettled, then send him back to the mainland and bring a replacement; someone else can do the bookkeeping just as easily."

"If I thought I could, I would," admitted Brennan. "It would mean too many explanations to Washington. And leave Mann back there, to spread the poison."

"So your problem isn't anything to do with Harriet and me," pressed Farr. "It's office politics."

"*Caused* by Harriet and you."

"It's happened. And it's going to stay happened," said Farr, annoyed at the revolving conversation. "Bring Mann out here and lecture him."

"She had a bad experience," said Brennan.

"She told me."

"Be unfortunate if there was a repeat," said the supervisor.

Farr's anger at the man leaked away at the sign of sympathetic concern. He supposed that Brennan's role was to maintain a balance and the affair between himself and Harriet *would* have caused a tilt. He said, "This time the circumstances are different. We're neither of us married. There's no reason why it should turn out bad. And don't forget I've got another personal interest which guarantees it's not going to affect our plans."

Brennan looked steadily at him for several moments. Then he said, "Let's hope you're right. For all our sakes."

The interception of a second Gomez shipment, of one hundred and thirty kilos, was a stupid mistake on the part of the smuggler, a young man called Alvarrez who had never panicked before. But he did panic that night, en route in a speedboat from a mother vessel to one of the hidden creeks leading into Florida's Everglades, just beyond Cape Sable. The searchlight was not even from a customs launch but from a punt carrying licensed alligator hunters, who found a drifting, abandoned boat stripped down to carry the maximum amount of marijuana and cocaine in a lightweight hull and with an engine sufficiently powerful to outrun practically any U.S. navy or customs patrol boat.

Gomez's initial reaction to the seizure was to have Alvarrez killed, but on reflection he decided that such an action would convey the wrong warning to those who might follow. Racing bicycles is a popular sport in Colombia, on a par with bullfighting and cockfighting—and Alvarrez was a promising rider who was being tipped for

some sort of national recognition. Gomez ordered that both
the boy's knees be smashed, and that he then be held
captive for a long enough period for them to set naturally.
After they had been rebroken and set again, he would have
limited mobility, to spread the word, but his career as a
bicyclist would be at an end.

Within two days Gomez replaced the shipment to Scarletti,
managing an uninterrupted run through one of the smaller
tributaries off Morehead City in North Carolina. But Gomez thought of himself as a perfectionist and felt the
Alvarrez mistake important enough to explain it personally
to the Philadelphia Mafia leader.

Scarletti regarded the visit for what it was. An example
of complete professionalism. He assured the Colombian
that he viewed seizures as nothing more than an unfortunate but acceptable disadvantage of their business—a business which was proving itself to be one of the most
successful in which his family had ever been involved.
Already almost ten tons of cocaine had successfully entered the United States and a further eight tons had been
channeled to Palermo in Sicily for onward distribution
throughout Europe.

"I welcome your confidence," said Gomez. He appreciated the assurance because the Alvarrez loss had worried
him, coming so quickly after the discovery of Rivera's
treachery, which he had naturally kept from Scarletti.

"We've got something good going," insisted Scarletti
with genuine enthusiasm. "I don't see the problems as any
more than teething difficulties—small teething difficulties,
at that."

Gomez reflected that, as replacement was guaranteed,
this was an easy remark for the American to make. The
insurance had been offered as an inducement—but he hadn't
expected to lose practically one hundred and sixty kilos of
high-quality, uncut cocaine in such a short period. The
disadvantage of what he'd established was that *he* had no
insurance. He said, "I'm glad you feel that way."

"Gather you've seen Lang, in New York?" said Scarletti,

who wanted the other man to be impressed at how well informed he was.

Gomez was glad rather than offended at the American's knowledge of his meeting with the lawyer: he considered he had kept every part of their bargain and that Scarletti had advised him badly. He was anxious for the other man to know how he felt, but he did not want to anger Scarletti and affect their trading relationship. Gomez said, "I must confess, friend to friend, that I am extremely disappointed. I understood from you that he was a good man, a reliable man. So far he has done nothing for me, apart from getting me to agree to his having power of attorney over affairs I entrust to him."

Scarletti's face clouded. Gomez had impressed him and failed to be impressed in return: which wasn't the way it should be, ever.

"Will you see him again, during this trip?" asked the American.

"Of course."

"Give it two days."

When Gomez entered the Manhattan office, after the requested period had elapsed, the lawyer was noticeably subdued.

"I think I've found something," said Lang at once. "It's taken so long because I wanted to be sure it was absolutely safe. I've checked it out, even though I already knew it to be a respectable firm. It's safe. So safe, in fact, that I'm thinking of recommending it to Mr. Scarletti."

17

When it came, that moment of approach for which everything had been created and planned, it was not recognized as soon as it should have been. There were some excuses for the failure but there had also been mistakes. One of the excuses—which would never have satisfied Washington if they had inquired—was that the Cayman people were investigating two illegal money laundering schemes, one of which involved two million dollars from a group in Chicago; too late it was discovered that the money came not from drugs but from a clever computer theft at the First National Bank.

Another excuse was circumstance—although that wouldn't have impressed Washington either. When Norman Lang made contact, he did so, naturally, through Farr's Manhattan office. Farr was there at the time—gathering original documentation as part of the Chicago investigation—rather than in the Caymans, where he could have discussed it more completely with Brennan. Farr knew of the impeccable respectability of Lang's firm and of Lang himself, and made the mistake of not thinking anything illegal might be involved. So he mentioned it only in passing on the telephone to Brennan. This created the only produceable piece of evidence from the monitored telephone, but it was hardly worth producing because it came right at the end of a long conversation about Chicago: Farr simply said that

there had been an approach from one of New York's
leading legal firms—without mentioning the name—which
he thought he would check out while he was in the city,
and Brennan said why didn't he do that.

Lang requested that they meet at Pearl Street, and they
did so the day after Farr's dismissive conversation with
Brennan. Farr was impressed by the discreetly opulent
surroundings and by the cherubic, soft-handed lawyer.
Lang said that he understood from what he had read and
heard that Farr had established himself offshore; Farr went
through well-rehearsed responses and a general discussion
about the difficulty of taxation ensued. When they progressed beyond generalities, Farr became aware from several of Lang's remarks that the lawyer knew a great deal
about his firm, and had also a better-than-average knowledge of the various tax-haven countries, even for a lawyer.

"I have clients," said the lawyer. "Men who have a
substantial amount—a very substantial amount—of money
to invest. There is, however, a very essential requirement:
everything must be done with absolute and utter discretion.
I hope you understand."

The surroundings—like the lawyer's reputation earlier—
had deceived Farr. The meeting had progressed like a
hundred others he'd had in a hundred different offices.
Now, suddenly, he realized it was developing into something else. He said, "I think I understand. This would be
cash?"

Lang smiled, pleased. "All cash."

"What sort of sum are we talking about?"

"Millions," said the lawyer. "And it is not *a* sum: it
would be a continuing investment. The initial investment
would be, I would think, in the region of fifty to a hundred
million dollars."

Farr hoped he remained impassive, but he wasn't sure.
Maybe it was too soon to react, but there was only one
source from which fifty to a hundred million could be
untraceably amassed for untraceable investment. He said,
"That's a very great deal of money."

"Which is why I've asked for this meeting," said Lang. He smiled again, an attempt at modesty. "My clients seek the best legal advice, which is why they come to me. And the best investment advice, which is why I have come to you. You must understand that before today I've made a very thorough examination of the investment and brokerage firms in this city."

"That's very flattering," said Farr. Talk on, for Christ's sake, he thought.

"I've recommended you to my clients and they've asked me to see if you would be prepared to act for them."

"There are a number of legal requirements concerning currency transactions of which I'm sure you're well aware," said Farr.

"That is why the sort of discretion I mentioned earlier is necessary," said Lang smoothly. "For such discretion, my clients understand, it may be necessary to pay a slightly higher than normal commission."

"Did you suggest any commission figure?" said Farr.

"I thought fifteen would probably be a fitting percentage," replied Lang.

Farr wondered from the ease with which the bribe was offered how many times Lang had made such an approach in the past. With one conjecture came another. If he were not involved as he was, what would his reaction have been to a fifteen-million commission, no questions asked? His mind still on the figure, the broker said, "That would be very generous."

"And I repeat that this will be a continuing situation," said Lang, increasing the pressure. "The fifteen percent would be payable on every sum invested."

It was time to appear tempted, decided Farr. He said, "The percentage payments would also be in cash, naturally?"

"Naturally."

"I think it's something that I would certainly like to consider," said Farr.

The lawyer's easy smile switched on again. "I was

hoping for something a little more definite than consideration," he said.

"Then I think it is necessary for us to be more specific," said Farr, knowing it was the sort of response he had to make because to acquiesce too quickly might arouse the other man's suspicion. "The money is undeclared and must never come to the notice of the authorities?"

"That is so."

"So it's from some sort of criminal enterprise?"

Momentarily the lawyer's face clouded. He said, "I'm a professional man, Mr. Farr. Like yourself. I have clients who ask my advice. I provide that advice and for it I charge a fee. I restrict myself to the advice for which I'm asked and to receiving the required payment."

Farr wondered how many other lawyers and accountants and brokers satisfied their consciences with such a simplistic, ostrichlike attitude. A cautious man seeking protection, Farr said, "With whom would I be dealing when receiving these investments. Your clients? Or you?"

The smile returned. The lawyer believed that Farr was trying to distance himself. "There would need to be some meetings with my clients," he said. "With such large sums of money they not unnaturally want to satisfy themselves of the integrity of the person in whom they are entrusting it. But in terms of actual operations, I would expect it to come from me."

Farr, who was caught by the use of the word integrity, supposed that, if this were the sort of conversation that Lang believed it to be, then that assurance would have provided some safeguard for him. Deciding that he had shown sufficient caution, and wanting to learn more, Farr said, "You'd like a commitment today? Now?"

"Yes," said Lang. "I think we've discussed enough for you to indicate how you feel."

Just the two of them, so it would always be deniable, thought Farr. He said, "I would like to know more—need to know more—but in principle I think I shall be pleased to act for your clients . . ." He paused, deciding to maintain the caution. "Predominantly through you," he added.

Lang patted his pink hands together in satisfaction. "I'm delighted, absolutely delighted. And I know my clients will be, as well. Delighted, too, that I haven't had them waste their time today."

Farr frowned at the remark. "I'm not sure I understand."

"I told you that I carried out an extensive investigation of investment and brokerage firms in the city," Lang reminded him. "It was necessarily time-consuming. My clients, one particularly, are busy men. They are anxious to get the matter settled and, as both happen to be in New York, I suggested that, if our encounter were satisfactorily concluded, we should meet."

"Today?" demanded Farr, surprised.

Lang looked briefly at a slim gold watch. "They are arriving in about five minutes—surely you'll be able to stay?"

"Of course," said Farr, with no alternative. Things were going too fast. He'd never imagined becoming as involved as this. He'd seen his function as creating the machinery—which he'd done—but then overseeing everything from a distance. He felt hollow-stomached and wondered if this was the fear that he'd been so proud of avoiding in Boston.

As if on cue, an intercom sounded. Lang nodded into the hand-held receiver, so Farr could not hear what was announced from outside, and said, "Thank you. Please show them in."

The lawyer rose and instinctively Farr did the same, turning to greet the new arrivals, intent on the detail he guessed Brennan would demand later. Both comparatively small men, both neat and unobtrusive, both unsmiling. One darker skinned than the other. Latin, probably.

"Gentlemen, I'd like you to meet Walter Farr, the investment broker about whom I told you. I'm glad to say that he's agreed to act for us, if we decide to continue," said Lang.

The darker of the two extended his hand. Farr shook it, then that of the second man, waiting for the introductions to be completed, so he could learn the names. They weren't.

"We've only discussed things in the most general terms,"
continued the lawyer. "I thought you'd best describe the
facilities you want."

"It's very simple," said Scarletti. "The best return. No
gambling. No declaration. And everything untraceable.
You understand that?"

The accent was American, Farr noticed; the voice that
of a man accustomed to giving orders and being obeyed.

"Completely," he said.

"You've been told the sort of figures?" asked Gomez.

Definitely Latin, decided Farr; maybe Spanish or South
American. Good English but with a blurred accent. He
said, "I was told between fifty and one hundred million."

"So set it out for us," instructed Gomez. "Tell us how
you'd best invest a hundred million."

Farr shrugged, holding out his hands. "There are a
number of ways," he said. "It's very difficult for me,
without any warning whatsoever, to come up with anything definite."

"Just sketch a scenario," insisted Scarletti.

Farr realized it was a test. Lang had carried out the
vetting but now these two needed to be convinced that he
could provide what they wanted. It would have to be good
if he was to influence not just these two commanding,
unknown men but Lang as well: Farr had already determined from their initial conversation that Lang knew a lot
about currency manipulation. Farr coughed, preparing himself, and then said, "The object of the exercise is to
translate large sums of money which can't be officially
recognized into assets which can be . . ." To gain time,
he turned to Lang and said, "You're aware, of course,
what a fiduciary account is, with a bank . . . ?"

Lang responded as the broker had hoped, embarking on
a simple explanation. "It's the same as a trust," said the
man, talking to Scarletti and Gomez. "It's organized by
some banks in tax-haven countries and the beauty of it is
that the bank virtually acts as the trustee, so all the deal-
ings are done in the bank's name . . ."

". . . It separates the name of the holder from the account itself," completed Farr. "The Cayman Islands, where I am now established, operates such systems. We could establish a company in which you had whatever shareholding division you wanted and in the name of that company open a further, separate fiduciary account. We are now trading upon the established reputation of the bank. Literally. The company instructs the bank to buy shares. This can be here in America or anywhere else. I understand the difficulties of so much liquid money and, as you are operating through Caymans, I would recommend that any purchases are made here in America. It's simpler, but not absolutely essential. The order is placed in the bank's name, no one else's. All you need to do is ensure that, on the necessary completion date, the money is available to the bank to make the purchase. You do this through a New York brokerage house. The money is hand-delivered by a courier. The brokerage house wires that the deposit has been made and the money is debited from the account of the brokerage house to the foreign bank. The brokerage house merely pays the money into its account, to balance the books. Your money hasn't even left America but now you own however many million dollars worth of shares you've decided to buy. If you buy into gilt-edged in any major country in the world, your investment is just that. The main thing is that it's no longer a hoard of unusable money, but negotiable. Your gilt-edged stocks will gain you, untaxed, a normal rate of interest—say ten, maybe fourteen percent on long-term. It's not a lot—I could recommend something as safe but with a higher yield—but . . ." Farr paused, looked to Scarletti. "No gambling, you said. If you invest a hundred million and leave it at its most basic, long-term fourteen percent, you're seeing an obvious return of fourteen million dollars on your original investment, with no danger to that investment."

Farr stopped, needing to rest.

Gomez said, "That seems remarkably simple."

"It is," assured Farr. "There are, of course, more complicated arrangements. You could, for instance, not move directly through your Caymans-established fiduciary account. You could move sideways once, or twice, more. The Swiss—although their banking system isn't as secure from investigation as many people believe it to be—operate another system, known as an omnibus account. It works virtually in the same way as a fiduciary but goes one stage further, creating an additional buffer. Your Cayman company sets up the fiduciary account at one international bank—which loses your identity once—and then that bank opens up with a lawyer in Switzerland an omnibus account in the name of a second company, of which you're directors. Now you're twice removed from any association with the source of the money. I made the point of the Swiss banking system not being as secure as many people believe it to be . . ." Farr avoided directly mentioning drugs. Instead he said, "There are legal provisions between the United States and Switzerland for bank accounts to be made publicly available if the proceeds can be proved in court to have been obtainèd criminally. And seized, by the Swiss . . ."

Farr paused again, conscious of the looks that passed between the two unidentified men and also of the lawyer's approval, apparent from the way he was nodding, of the exposition. He began again. "Having distanced you twice, therefore, it would make practical sense to remain safe and insert another buffer. We do this by instructing your Swiss lawyer not to incorporate in Switzerland but in Liechtenstein. There are three sorts of company we would establish there—if you want me to itemize them individually, I will, but for your needs I would recommend the *anstalt*. Effectively, it is a corporation without any issued, and therefore traceable, shares. It is controlled by a founders' certificate, which is a bearer instrument, like a bearer check. The company does not, according to Liechtenstein law, have to be profit-making. Nor even to operate as a business. It becomes a holding or investment company. It is not subject to any sort of internal inquiry—and certainly not external investigation—and can have financial interest in foreign firms or even exercise control of them." Farr tried to gauge the men's reactions. "You asked for a scenario and I've sketched one out for you. Let's say we've gone through all the processes and you now have a hundred million in your Liechtenstein-based company. You can now, through Liechtenstein, purchase one hundred million worth of property here, a constantly appreciating and realizable asset, gain tax relief as a foreign corporation investing in America and further receive an income from the simple rental or leasing of that property. Not only have you distanced yourself three times but you've created three separate ways of increasing the value of your money and they are all yielding at the same time."

For several moments there was complete silence in the room. Scarletti broke it, the tone of his voice indicating his admiration at what had been outlined. "You could set it all up, just as you've explained?"

"Everything," Farr assured him.

"No tax at all?" queried Gomez.

"Minimal, if we were finally incorporated in Liechtenstein. The security is worth it. Liechtenstein law does not require that the names of the real owners of the company even be registered: only the name of the company and the lawyer who manages it."

"How can we retain—prove—ownership, then?" demanded the alert Scarletti.

"By a trust agreement, which you hold in a simple safe deposit box."

"U.S. tax relief, on our own invested money?" sniggered Scarletti.

"Very generous tax relief," said Farr.

"I like it," said Scarletti. "I like it very much indeed. I don't think I want to hear about any more schemes. I like the one you've just told us about."

"Me, too," said Gomez. He had a warm, grownup feeling, the sort of comfort he'd experienced on his initial visit to the mahogany room of polish smells and expensive cigar odor.

To the lawyer, Scarletti said politely, "Thank you for taking so much trouble and being so successful . . .'' Addressing Farr, the man continued, "I think we're going to have a very long and mutually beneficial relationship."

"Very beneficial," echoed Gomez, in complete agreement.

"Shit!" exploded Brennan, when Farr called him two hours later. "Holy shit!"

Brennan said shit again, when Farr returned that same night to the Caymans and went through the encounter in as much detail as he could recall in the lounge of the bungalow he shared with Harriet. They were all there, unspeaking as he talked. After expressing his anger, Brennan said, "It's *got* to be right. And we haven't got a thing. Not a damned thing! Why the hell didn't you tell me!"

"I did," protested Farr, angered himself at being criticized in front of Harriet.

"I listened to the tape," retorted Brennan. "You just said a leading lawyer."

"I thought he was straight," apologized Farr, wishing he didn't have to.

"No names?" queried Seymour.

Farr shook his head. "Although I'm sure one of them was Latin, like I said."

"They're being very careful," said Seymour. "Classically so. Not providing names is careful, and insisting on the meeting as soon as you'd agreed, to prevent any outside contact or second thoughts, is careful."

"I'll have to know the names eventually," said Farr.

"I wanted *everything*," said Brennan. "From the very beginning. You should have been wired."

"Wired?"

"I could have fixed you up with a personal system," offered the ever-helpful Batty. "Body mike, small recorder. Stuff like that."

"You weren't searched, were you?" asked Harriet.

"No," said Farr.

"Shit." Brennan's mind was apparently blocked by one obscenity. "It would have worked, too!"

"How was it left?" asked Seymour.

"Like I said: that I would work with them. And that Lang would contact me."

"To go ahead with the sort of scheme you outlined?" said Brennan.

"That's as I understood it," said the broker.

"Who the hell are they?" demanded the exasperated FBI supervisor.

"We've got Lang," pointed out Harriet. "We can start working backwards from him."

Brennan nodded. "Quietly," he cautioned. "Very quietly. We already know how careful he is. If he becomes even slightly suspicious, he'll close everything down and we'll lose him . . . lose everything." He stopped, head bent, and then looked up toward Farr. "You've got a lot of files to go through back in Washington," he said. "We've got a case, certainly; just like we set out to get. Now we need some luck."

The need was met, indirectly, through Lang, the minute efficiency of computers and the fact that a small-time mobster called Harry Peel stopped for a drink on his way back from hand-delivering to the New York attorney the cash payment for setting up the meeting with Walter Farr.

At the Hoover Building they made available to Farr a corner office which actually overlooked Pennsylvania Avenue, with a view of the Capitol. Only Brennan accompanied him to Washington and in the office on the first day the FBI man said there was no hurry and that Farr should take all the time he wanted; it would be a boring task but at the moment there was no other way.

Brennan brought in photographs not only from their own archives but from the other antinarcotic agencies—the Drug Enforcement Administration, the IRS, Customs, the Marshalls' Service and the Bureau of Alcohol, Tobacco and Firearms. At Brennan's hopeful suggestion, Farr concentrated initially upon people with convictions whose clearly identifiable official pictures were on record. Farr began diligently enough but the process was repetitive and increasingly he found himself staring up at the government building thinking how much he missed Harriet and wondering about Howard—about whom he telephoned Eastham that night, to be told by the director that there was still no improvement.

On the second day Farr isolated what he thought was a possibility and for a moment there was brief excitement until Brennan checked through the computer and discovered that the man—a Peruvian—had been murdered in Lima, eighteen months earlier.

That night Harry Peel stopped for his drink. And had several. Peel was a gofer, a trusted messenger and odd-job man for the Scarletti organization with a twenty-year history of petty crime. Ironically Scarletti had insisted upon the payment being made to Lang in person, and that the person should travel by road precisely to minimize the risk of any link being discovered. Peel reached Manhattan by midday, delivered his package, obtained a sealed and addressed receipt, and was heading south again by early afternoon, having stopped in New York to eat. His car number had already been recorded by the FBI surveillance team monitoring Lang's Pearl Street office. It was still early when he stopped at the roadhouse in Trenton, intending to have just a couple—but became engrossed in the ballgame on television and the barmaid's nice ass. She was willing to put it out, too, but it meant his having to stay until she got off duty at midnight, by which time he was quite drunk. She didn't live far away but he almost missed the slip off the turnpike, and by suddenly swerving hit a truck in front of a police car. The breathalyzer was positive and Peel spent the night in a cell instead of in the cocktail waitress's bed. Strictly in accordance with the regulations, all his possessions were listed.

Brennan's computer checks on all vehicles recorded at Lang's Pearl Street office threw up Peel's name from registers by midafternoon the following day. The FBI man was excited to find that Peel had a record and disappointed when Farr at once dismissed the file picture. It was routine to check through Philadelphia for Peel's most recent activities, which produced the previous night's arrest. Brennan was later to admit he didn't know what prompted him to telephone Trenton: it was pure luck that the arresting officer had been in the building and that the man had idly mentioned that in Peel's possession had been a sealed letter addressed to Antonio Scarletti. No, apologized the man in response to Brennan's gabbled inquiry, he didn't know what was in the envelope: Peel had been bailed and everything returned to him.

Five minutes after replacing the telephone, Brennan was in the corner office with its view of the Capitol.

"What about him?" he asked, putting a photograph of Scarletti in front of the tired-eyed investment broker.

"Definitely," said Farr at once.

That same afternoon Harriet made contact with New York. A message from Lang had been relayed through Farr's Manhattan office: the lawyer confirmed that they wanted to proceed and asked for a further meeting.

"This time we'll be ready," said Brennan exuberantly. "We've caught up and we're going to get the bastards by the balls."

"We still don't know who the other one is," Farr reminded him.

"It'll come," said Brennan. "It'll come."

18

Brennan supervised the preparations for the meeting with
the lawyer with the care he'd counseled at the Washington
identification meeting. He irritated Batty and Jones by
insisting that they check every piece of monitoring equipment in the Cayman office and then stood by while the two
technical experts rehearsed Walter Farr in the use of the
personalized recording device that the supervisor had determined was necessary. Harriet watched, too, and Farr
stood self-consciously in front of her, embarrassed at the
theatricality of it all. There was a physical discomfort, too;
although the pack was comparatively small and specifically tailored for its purpose, the investment broker was
acutely aware of it. It was essential, of course, to prevent
the system being accidentally revealed, which was difficult
with the sort of relaxed clothing to which Farr had now
become accustomed and which Brennan agreed Lang would
expect him to wear. Again under Brennan's guidance, they
selected a lightweight summer suit, to provide a concealing jacket, but discarded a shoulder holster for the recorder
because, when Brennan and Seymour had Farr reluctantly
go through a series of movements—walking and sitting
and behaving as he might in normal circumstances—they
decided that the risk of the lawyer noticing it was too
great. They substituted a pack that clipped onto his trouser
waistband, in the center of his back, which enabled the

wires to be trailed up his back and down his left arm to the
minute microphone mounted in a wristlet band, which
appeared to be a sort of metal strip people sometimes wear
to protect against rheumatism. Brennan insisted that Farr
model the pack by walking and sitting as before. Farr
protested that it was difficult to sit properly with the device
in the small of his back, but Brennan said the concealment
was so good that he would have to accept the inconve-
nience. Farr felt the wires up his back and down his
sleeve, satisfying himself they didn't cause bulges in the
thin cloth; he looked at the wrist microphone and said he
felt like Dick Tracy: Brennan said that was OK because Dick
Tracy always got the bad guys. Throughout the day—and
the night—before Lang arrived from New York, Brennan
had Farr wear the machine to become accustomed to it.
Batty had carefully explained the simple operation required
to activate it.

"I feel bloody stupid," Farr said that night to Harriet
when they were alone in bed.

"You're doing fine," she said. "It always feels strange—
is strange—the first time. Nervous?"

Farr considered the question. "I had a strange sensation
when I met them in New York, but I think that was
excitement rather than fear. I'm not apprehensive about
tomorrow: that'll just be business, after all."

Harriet came closer to him, so that she could actually
put her head on his shoulder. "I'm very proud of you."

Farr smiled in the darkness, pleased at the praise. "How
long could it take? Arrest and a trial, I mean?"

She shrugged against him. "There's no specified period. Why?"

"Don't we have something to decide, when it's all
over?"

Momentarily, he was conscious of her stiffening beside
him. "There'll be plenty of time to talk about things like
that," she said, with her customary reluctance to make
commitments.

"We *will* talk about it," he said.

"Later," she said. "Not now."

Batty went first to Owen Roberts airport, wanting to secure a discreet position for the car from which he would photograph the lawyer's arrival. Farr drove out early, too—sitting forward in his driver's seat because of the intrusive backpack—and gave no sign of recognition when he saw the FBI technician sitting easily in the car, apparently engrossed in that day's edition of the *Miami Herald*. Farr wondered where the camera was hidden. Having got there early, he had nothing to do. He went into the tiny bar, for its air conditioning more than for a drink, and contented himself with Seven-Up. The incoming flight from Miami was on time and Lang was one of the first to disembark, carrying hand baggage and with no need to wait for luggage clearance. The man was dressed predictably in his lawyer's black and the heat seemed to affect him, so that he appeared more pink-faced than he had in New York. The greeting was restrained and businesslike. Directly beyond the arrival section Farr feigned a moment of forgetfulness about the position of his car, to enable Batty to get his pictures.

"Thank God for air conditioning," said the lawyer, as they set off on the short journey to Georgetown, confirming Farr's impression of the man's discomfort.

"I'm told it gets even hotter in August," said Farr, using the movement of securing his seatbelt to activate the tape. "Think you'll have time for any sunbathing?"

Lang shook his head. "This is strictly business: I'm confirmed for the evening flight tonight."

"I'd rather thought you might stay longer?" encouraged Farr.

There was another headshake. "I think we can settle everything in a day."

How long would it be, wondered Farr, before the other man said something that could be incriminating? He said, "I was glad of the decision to go ahead."

"I think I've already made clear that my clients thought it was an impressive exposition."

"Today I'll get formal instructions? Sufficient details to go ahead with the incorporation . . . set everything up?"

"I hope so," said the lawyer guardedly.

Farr parked intentionally some way from the office, in the parking lot on Edward Street. It meant they had to walk practically the length of the road, past the courts office and the Comart store and the post office, all the while approaching the office where Jones was concealed with another camera. Lang was extremely flushed by the time they reached the sanctuary of the air conditioning.

"Why not take your jacket off?" suggested Farr, nervously aware as he spoke that it was something he couldn't do himself.

"I'm fine, thank you," said the lawyer.

Harriet and Harvey Mann were seated in the large, open-plan front office, appearing to work. Farr made introductions, to which Lang responded perfunctorily, uninterested in hirelings. They went almost immediately into Farr's personal office, where the visitor's chair was positioned perfectly for the movie camera installed in the supposed burglar alarm, in the corner of the room beyond Farr's desk.

"Right," said Farr. "Why don't you tell me *exactly* what it is you require. I'll need to know the names of people for whom I'm operating and precisely what sort of arrangement they require." He leaned forward over his desk to avoid the discomfort of sitting back against his own recorder and to place his wrist nearer to the lawyer; Farr presumed his speaking had caused the office-installed microphones to operate.

"I want a company incorporated here, to operate a fiduciary account. My clients feel, having discussed things with you in New York, that they want the company here to move sideways, through an establishment in Europe. I would expect you to arrange that, but I shall carry out the actual negotiations, once I've satisfied myself the arrangements are satisfactory . . ."

"In New York we talked of three separations," reminded Farr. "Would you want a Swiss lawyer to create an *anstalt* in Liechtenstein?"

"Yes," said Lang at once.

"From the figures we discussed in New York, we are going to have a series of interlinked companies with a very great deal of liquidity," said Farr.

"Again, my clients accept your advice about investment in America . . ." Lang permitted himself a brief smile. "I think they will feel more comfortable having their investments close at hand."

Not when the trap is sprung, thought Farr: if the money were channeled back into America, it would become liable to seizure when the case was proven, even if it had been translated into property development. Brennan—and everyone else—should be extremely pleased at the way everything was working out: *exactly* as they had hoped, in fact. Deciding it was time for the question to be asked, Farr said, "If I'm going satisfactorily to act for your clients, I'll need their names. We were never properly introduced in New York, remember?"

"Like I said in New York," came back Lang, "my clients are cautious men who enjoy discretion and seek anonymity . . ." The man hesitated. "I think our discussions—and my inquiries—have progressed sufficiently for me to be able to tell you at this stage. The incorporation of the company here will be in the names of Jorge Herrera Gomez and Antonio Scarletti. For each I have power of attorney: signatory authority."

They had it! thought Farr, feeling the excitement churn through him. They had the second name and confirmation of the first. And they knew that Scarletti headed the Bruno Family in Philadelphia—which was further confirmation that the money was illegal and that they weren't wasting their time, as they had with the Chicago business. He said, "I'll need formal proof of that. It's a requirement, you understand."

Lang unclipped a snakeskin briefcase and offered the broker a series of prepared papers. "There's a notarized proof of power of attorney . . ." the man said. "There is further a contractual letter between yourself and myself instructing you to proceed on the lines we have discussed. I would expect to receive from you, today, a contractual agreement. You'll see that my documentation requires a very detailed accounting to be maintained, certainly from this point of the operation: it is, after all, the base from which everything will emanate . . . I will accept your signature on the copy of my contract as being your formal agreement . . ." Lang waited, and Farr realized the lawyer expected him to sign immediately.

Farr studied the letter. It was a fairly standard document, setting out terms between himself and Lang: Farr would have been happier if the names of Scarletti and Gomez were included, but the power of attorney obviated the need for that, and the broker decided it would have been tactically wrong to try to get them written in. He had enough—more than enough—from today's meeting and to try to obtain more would be to risk everything. He said, "It all seems straightforward and satisfactory."

"I can assure you it is," said the lawyer with one of his faint smiles. "It's entirely legal and binding but it guarantees that all-important requirement of discretion."

"It would need to be witnessed, of course," said Farr. "Would you accept the signature of one of my staff?"

"I think so," said Lang.

Farr buzzed for Harriet. When she entered he addressed her by name, for the benefit of the tape recordings, and set out with as much verbal detail as he felt he dared what he wanted her to do. Harriet played her part perfectly, holding back from any special interest in the paper, as if she were frequently called upon to perform such a function.

"How long do you imagine it will take to establish everything?" asked Lang, as the woman left the room.

"Maybe a month," said Farr, remembering the quickness of his own incorporation. "And it's time we can usefully occupy. The essentials of the European part of the operation can be arranged while the formalities are being dealt with here. So that, as soon as we are formed here, we can trigger the formation in Switzerland and Liechtenstein.''

"Good," said the lawyer. "Very good. Everything seems to have been resolved even faster than I thought it would."

The conclusion of a deal traditionally demanded a celebration, Farr realized—certainly a deal that would apparently give him such a strong personal return. He sat back slightly, so that he could feel the pressure of the recorder against his back. Lang would expect the offer at least. He said, "Your plane isn't due out for some hours yet. Why don't we eat and maybe I can show you something of the island, now that we've concluded the business necessities?"

"That would be nice. And kind of you."

Farr had Harriet make the luncheon reservation for them, to ensure that they would know where he was going and follow if they felt like it. Although the Grand Old House was not a personal favorite, he guessed Lang might know of its reputation and want to be taken there. Because of the restaurant's closeness to the office, Farr drove first out along Seven Mile Beach, pointing out the development and saying, quite sincerely, that he believed the main island and certainly the two smaller ones were ideal property investments. Carefully playing his role, Farr said he was considering investing some of his own profits from their arrangement in the islands. Lang did not respond to the invitation but repeated the guaranteed commission of fifteen percent. They went as far as the Turtle Farm and then retraced their route, to arrive at the restaurant.

Lang was fastidious about eating as he was about everything else, ignoring anything adventurous and settling upon a steak, which he hardly touched. He refused wine, limiting himself to mineral water. Farr was careful to judge his timing, saying in the middle of the meal that he was looking forward to their partnership and wondering about the number of times it would be necessary for him to meet Scarletti and Gomez.

Lang stopped eating altogether, frowning at the broker.

"I thought you understood that I had complete power of attorney?"

Shit! thought Farr. He said, "Of course I understood. I'm just a little surprised that, with so much money involved, they wouldn't expect closer contact."

"I told you in New York that they are busy men. Señor Gomez doesn't actually live in the United States. They will decide the degree and extent of contact they require."

Farr tried to think of an acceptable way to ask the question. Finally he said, "I don't suppose any legislation or laws in Señor Gomez's country preclude the sort of arrangement we've discussed?"

"I thought the sort of arrangement to which we've agreed precluded the difficulty of internal regulations," said Lang.

He'd tried and failed to discover where Gomez lived. It would be wrong to pressure, Farr decided. "Of course. It was a thoughtless question."

"My clients have come to you because they believed you were someone who would not allow thoughtlessness," said Lang.

The investment broker was silenced by the rebuke, awkwardly aware that he had gone almost too far. Trying to recover, he said, "I think we should define thoughtlessness. I was instinctively trying to anticipate any problems, before they arose. That is why I asked the question."

Lang remained staring at him for several moments, knife and fork suspended over the plate. Finally he said, "Of course."

Farr did not think he had succeeded particularly well and was angry with himself at the original mistake and his failure to rectify it. Insistently he said, "I'm very determined that nothing will go wrong."

"Mr. Farr," said the lawyer. "If I feared anything might go wrong, I wouldn't have linked with you and your company in the first place."

Farr felt a further anger, not just at the patronizing tone

but at the belated realization that it was all on tape and
Harriet would be able to hear his mistake and his stumbling efforts to cover it. Still foundering, he said, "I
would hope that this might be the first of a series of
productive relationships between us."

"I think it might be a good idea for us to see how this
one goes first, don't you?" asked Lang, obviously domi-
nating the exchange.

"I know exactly how this is going to go," said Farr,
allowing himself the satisfaction. "It's going to be an
overwhelming success: we will achieve everything we want.
And more."

"I'm looking forward to that," said the lawyer. "Very
much."

They took their coffee in the grounds, sitting beneath
the encompassing trees and staring out over the eye-hurting
brightness of the Caribbean. Farr wondered if any of the
others had followed to take more photographs. Farr remembered Harriet's bedroom remark about being proud of
him and hoped he hadn't failed her, on the transcript. He'd
know soon enough: Brennan was attaching a great deal of
importance to the meeting.

Although there was nothing more for them to discuss,
Farr expected Lang to return with him to the office but
when he suggested it the lawyer said that they had discussed all that was necessary and that he would prefer to
return to the airport to catch a flight to Miami which would
connect with a plane arriving in Manhattan earlier than
planned.

Under the pretext of ensuring accuracy, Farr leaned
forward, for the benefit of the mike, and again went
through everything they had discussed. He undertook to
contact the lawyer as soon as he thought it reasonable to
extend into Europe. The earlier mistakes—no, he corrected
himself, not mistakes; misjudgments, at the most—unsettled
Farr and he decided against calling the office to tell them
what he was doing.

Instead, he drove directly to Owen Roberts. There were

seats available on the flight two hours earlier than that on which Lang was booked, so the lawyer transferred.

"I'm sure everything is going to work out just fine," said Lang while he waited for the flight to be called.

"I intend to make it so," said Farr.

"You won't forget my wish to conduct all the negotiations personally in Europe—call me the moment you begin to make the moves?"

"Of course not."

"We're going to become rich men." For the first time Lang allowed his feelings to intrude beyond the stiffly formal. "Very rich men indeed."

"That's what we both want," said Farr.

He drove slowly toward the island's tiny capital. He'd stumbled at lunch, certainly; but Lang appeared to have accepted the explanation. Against his blunder, there was a lot of success. He had the names, confirmation enough that they were on the right track, and written instructions to go ahead.

He thrust hopefully into the office, smiling broadly to Harriet, who looked fixedly back at him.

"You alone? Has he gone?" she asked.

"What's wrong?"

"You alone?" she insisted.

"Yes."

"Christ!" she said despairingly, as Mann emerged from the second office, followed by the cautiously waiting Brennan and Seymour. Behind them, finally, came Batty and Jones.

"What is it!" demanded Farr.

"Let me have your cassette," demanded Batty in return. "I want to check it."

Farr turned, self-conscious again, while the technician extracted the cassette, pushing it immediately into a playback machine and pressing the start button. The result was a screeching whine—an unintelligible, electronically created sound.

Farr stood gazing down at the pointlessly revolving tape, bewildered.

Batty turned it off impatiently and said, "Shit! I knew it was going to be like that but somehow I hoped. Shit!"

"What the hell *happened*?"

"We knew he was careful," said Brennan, dulled by disappointment. "But not this careful. He carried a baffler: an electronic device that defeats any effort at tape recording."

"It's not particularly complicated," took up Batty. "Works on a system of magnets and electronic impulses."

"You mean he guessed what we were trying to set up!" said Farr, his eyes moving from one to the other in the room. "That they *know*!"

"Not necessarily," said Brennan. "If he'd known, he wouldn't have come in the first place. Just careful, like I said. We were set up for everything and now we haven't got a thing. Son of a bitch!" he finished viciously.

"Oh yes we have," argued Farr. "He confirmed Scarletti to me. And gave the other name as José Herrera Gomez. He entered into a contract with me, a contract of which we've got a copy and which shows he's got power of attorney for both of them."

"It's an in-house notarization," said Seymour patiently, blinking sadly behind his thick spectacles. "We'd have a hell of a difficulty proving it in court, if Lang denied it."

"What about the films? And the photographs?" persisted Farr desperately. "Surely he couldn't have interfered with those!"

"The films are OK," agreed Brennan. "But what do they prove? He's a bona fide lawyer and you're a bona fide investment broker. He's got every right—every legal right—to come here to talk to you, if he wants to."

"Where's a bona fide lawyer going to get hold of one hundred million dollars he daren't risk declaring to the IRS?" said Farr, refusing to share their dejection. "When we get the money and place it for them, we'll be embarking on a criminal enterprise. He won't be able to deny that."

"We don't want Lang," pointed out the FBI supervisor. "We want Gomez and Scarletti and whoever else in the drugs world he's working for."

"You confirm that Gomez is a dealer?" asked Farr.

"We checked it out through Washington, although we didn't really have to because we came across the name recently . . ." Brennan hesitated, stopping short of disclosing the circumstances. "José Herrera Gomez is a large-scale trafficker who works out of Medellin in Colombia."

"It all fits," said Farr. "The man I met in Lang's office was Latino, remember?"

"Not enough fits: not enough for a court," bemoaned Seymour.

The elements continued to refuse to mesh as smoothly as they'd hoped. On the last flight that night—the aircraft which the New York lawyer was originally scheduled to catch—Washington hurriedly flew in their file pictures of José Herrera Gomez. They were only three. The first was a blurred, distorted shot, seemingly taken through the window of a moving car. The second was a photographic reproduction of an already poor newspaper picture. The third was not a grown man at all, but an already fading photograph of a youth, hardly little older than eighteen.

"Well!" exclaimed Brennan.

Farr took his time, knowing the importance of the question and refusing to be affected by the supervisor's urgent tone. "Are you asking me if I could swear to this in court?"

"Of course," said the FBI man.

"I don't know," confessed the broker. "I know how important it is. I want it to be the man and it's logically *got* to be him. But if I were on oath in a court of law—without seeing anything more, I couldn't in all honesty testify that this was the man whom I met in Lang's office."

"Damn!" said Seymour, driving one fist into the palm of the other. "Damn!"

"I need more!" pleaded Farr.

"I'll get it for you," promised Brennan. "Whatever it takes, I'm going to make this case."

Gomez was pleased. Primarily because Ramos had brought

the information to him, which meant that the man on whom he relied so heavily remained loyal. Also because he now knew who it was within his organization who'd taken the bribe and gone over to Julio Navarra.

"No doubts?" he pressed.

"None," said Ramos. "I became suspicious when Rodriquez was anxious to make more than his usual share of collection flights to Bolivia. So I put in as a copilot someone I knew I could trust. He said that as soon as Rodriquez landed in Beni, he'd always find a reason for going into town—without company. Yesterday we followed him, to Magdalena, actually saw him meet Navarra there."

Gomez thought, in passing, that he would be sorry to lose Miguel Rodriquez: the man was one of his most experienced pilots, someone who'd never lost a shipment either from the point of collection or the point of delivery.

"Want me to have him killed, as an example like the others?" asked Ramos.

"Of course not," said Gomez irritably. "While we know who it is, there's no danger. We don't have anyone in Navarra's organization, so we can't move against him. Let's wait until there's an advantage in it for ourselves."

"It would make me nervous having to wait too long," said Ramos, hand to the knife-scar.

"Maybe we won't have to."

Even the Colombian couldn't have anticipated just how quickly the opportunity would arise: that night, the instruction was routed from the Cayman Islands, via Washington, for a photographic surveillance on José Herrera Gomez. Harry Green got the assignment, of course.

19

Gomez did not evolve the plan at once. His initial reaction at discovering Rivera's treachery had been one of apprehension. It was automatic caution to have a watch maintained on the American FBI agent and his movements from the Bogotá embassy after the episode with the Colombian lawyer. When Green caught the internal flight to Medellin, Gomez's watchers telephoned from the capital, and there was independent warning from one of the immigration officials on Gomez's payroll attached to the airport. Although it was only a short flight, little more than an hour, it gave Gomez sufficient time to have his people in place when the FBI man arrived. Green was followed to the Intercontinental hotel, where he booked in. Then into the center of the town—to Calle 52, where the Drug Enforcement Administration had their offices—and back again, escorted this time by a known Enforcement agent named Kip Colby, toward the Intercontinental and the *finca* beyond which Gomez regarded as his primary home and where, ironically, José Rivera had been killed.

Gomez wasn't there, of course. He had already flown north out of Medellin before the American's arrival, taking one of his three helicopters away from the central mountains, up to the coast near Riohacha. He had an expansive villa there, set into the hillside with an uninterrupted view of the Caribbean, from the veranda of which, on more

relaxed occasions, he would enjoy watching the distant
scurrying ships and overflying aircraft and fantasizing how
many of them were carrying his product even further
northward, to America.

Now was not the time for fantasy. Now was the time
fully to recognize that Green and Rivera had talked about
him, and that the Americans were continuing the investigation despite Rivera's death. The situation was worrying but
there was no need for panic. The FBI could have learned
nothing about his current involvement with Scarletti because he'd never discussed it with the lawyer. What was
the danger then? Realistically Gomez had long accepted
that the authorities might know of him by name. What he
was sure they didn't have was a face to go with that name.
That confidence was confirmed three days after his arrival
in Riohacha, when he heard from Medellin that Green was
occupying his time around the *finca* with an elaborate camera. The information—further assurance that he was handling things properly—pleased Gomez.

It was then that Gomez started to think of Miguel Rodriquez and his betrayal to the Bolivian. Gomez knew he had
sufficient people in authority—passports, immigration,
police—to make it possible. The preparation might be
more difficult, but Gomez determined that at the speed he
intended to work it didn't matter if Rodriquez became
suspicious. He summoned Ramos at once to Riohacha,
setting out his proposal in detail and demanding that the
other man be as critical as he could, to expose the flaws.

"Rodriquez will be suspicious," said Ramos, at once.

"I've anticipated that," reminded the trafficker. "What
can he do, if he is? He won't be able to run, because we'll
be watching him too closely. He won't be able to go to the
authorities. Only to Navarra. Which is where I want him
to go anyway."

"Certainly passports are easy enough to replace," agreed
Ramos, exploring the proposal further. "We'll never know,
of course, whether they already have photographs of you."

"If they did, then why would they have a man here
trying to get more?"

"Better ones, perhaps?"

"If they need better ones, than Rodriquez's won't conflict."

"It's an uncertainty," persisted Ramos.

"One I'm prepared to risk."

"How long do you think it'll take you to spread the story?"

"Little more than days. We can guarantee the word getting back through the officials we control. We can fix people whom the Americans will believe are informers— and independent corroboration, too."

"When do you want Rodriquez brought here?"

"At once," ordered Gomez. "He's got to accept—as much as we can make him accept—the sudden deference."

The defecting pilot arrived early the following morning. Gomez greeted him effusively. They took coffee and drinks—and at Gomez's urging shared some good, uncut cocaine, because Gomez wanted it and he knew that Rodriquez would see it as a failing he could communicate to Navarra. On the veranda overlooking the Caribbean, Gomez said he was considering some changes in his operations, which the pilot must know by now from the increased frequency of the flights. Ramos was not being replaced, the man was to understand, but merely complemented by the appointment of an equal number two in the organization. Rodriquez would be that appointee. Gomez saw the greed in Rodriquez's eyes and wondered if the man was registering how simple his liaison with the Bolivian would become. One reflection led to another. Gomez convinced himself there were even physical similarities between him and the other man—height and general coloring, for instance. Certainly not enough for any direct comparison, but then it would not be done that way.

"I'm very grateful," said Rodriquez. "And I'm aware of the trust. I won't fail you."

"I know you won't," said Gomez, enjoying his own private joke.

"There won't be resentment from Ramos—any thought from him that he is being usurped?"

"I've told him already," said Gomez. "And I've told him I don't want any friction. I think it's important, though, that you get to know each other better. I want people working *with*, not against, each other. If I find that it's not working, there'll have to be changes."

"You won't have any problems from me," assured Rodriquez ingratiatingly.

"Ramos is at the main *finca*, in Medellin. I want you to go there for a few days. Get to know the proper layout of the place. How everything operates."

"Of course."

"Then I think you'd better make a visit to Navarra. I'll call him, naturally. But I think you should personally explain what you're going to be doing in the future—you won't, for instance, be making so many collections. That can be left to others now."

"Whenever you say."

The rumors started—just as Gomez intended them to—before Rodriquez's return flight reached Medellin. The carefully instructed and corrupt police and narcotic officers on Gomez's payroll filed official reports that Jorge Herrera Gomez, according to their informants, was expanding his cocaine operation and considering a big shipment. And the carefully fed informants supplied their own, matching reports independently, direct to the Drug Enforcement Offices in Medellin. Because Green was in the city and investigating Gomez himself, Colby naturally shared the information with him, which together they passed on to Washington, through their respective Bogotá offices. Green already had his instructions but from Washington came orders that Colby had to liaise with him completely and also concentrate upon Gomez.

There is a magnificent restaurant in the foothills of Medellin, built by drug money and owned, for its money-washing facilities, by a drug runner. It was to this restaurant, according to the information from all the planted sources to which Green and Colby eagerly listened, that Jorge Gomez would come to finalize arrangements for the shipments with members of the Bolivian organization run by Julio Navarra. The deception worked. The real Jorge Herrera Gomez made contact with Julio Navarra and asked for a meeting of emissaries, for a necessary discussion. Independently, Miguel Rodriquez sent a message to Navarra saying that something extremely important had happened.

By the time of the meeting at the restaurant, Green had managed to photograph Miguel Rodriquez extensively, believing the man to be the trafficking owner of the *finca* behind the Intercontinental. Ramos ensured, too, that other people in obvious evidence accorded Rodriquez the deference which indicated that he was someone of importance, such as always allocating him the largest limousine and standing back politely until he entered. When Rodriquez and Ramos kept the meeting at the restaurant, Rodriquez appeared to the watching Americans clearly the dominant participant.

Gomez guaranteed, through the already believed channels, that the identity and progress of Navarra's emissaries were recorded as they passed through Bogotá and onwards to Medellin. They were, in fact, Louis Milona and Enriques Valdeblanques, and it was an advantage Gomez had not anticipated that both men were already established as members of Navarra's organization on the records of both the FBI and the Drug Enforcement Administration.

Gomez called Rodriquez back to Riohacha just before the meeting, telling the pilot that he had approached Navarra and suggesting that Rodriquez use the opportunity to explain personally his promotion to Navarra by flying the Bolivians back across the border. This was the most dangerous moment—when Rodriquez was likely to question his abrupt elevation—but again fortunately, just as the Bolivians being Louis Milona and Enriques Valdeblanques was fortunate, the renegade pilot was conceited enough to believe the promotion justified.

Gomez later regretted having to rely upon Ramos's

account of the luncheon at the restaurant. Detailed as it
was, he himself wanted to have been there, to see everything unfold exactly as he had planned. Rodriquez had
already indicated his superiority over Ramos, and was
encouraged by Ramos's seeming acceptance of the relegation. Everyone got drunk—although ultimately Rodriquez
was to pilot a plane—and they were later than intended
descending the foothills road to regain the bottom of the
valley and the airport.

Harry Green and Kip Colby lunched that day at the
same place. They'd photographed the departure of Rodriquez and Ramos earlier, and had been aware of the deference shown by the two Bolivians in the restaurant where,
with concealing napkins, Green succeeded in taking two
pictures with a miniature camera.

Gomez's plane was in the private section of the airfield,
so there were none of the irritating formalities of an ordinary boarding—which would have been minimal anyway,
because Gomez had made sure that, on this day, every
customs and immigration officer on his payroll was on
duty. Ramos accentuated the effusive farewells for the
benefit of the watchers, and then stood back while the
executive aircraft taxied out, was almost immediately cleared
and then took off over the frowning brows of the surround-
ing foothills. To have remained might have betrayed his
prior knowledge of what was to happen. So he returned to
his car and drove slowly back to the *finca*.

Though waiting for it, Ramos never actually heard the
explosion—which he always regretted. He was never to
know that Rodriquez, drunk, flew the plane dangerously
lower than he should have done, only clearing by feet the
wraparound mountains and not gaining the required height
to detonate the pressure-controlled explosive for a mile
beyond the planned crash spot. So the disaster occurred
much further away from Medellin than it might have, deep
in the river-stitched, cauliflower-topped jungle. There was
no access possible by road and none easy by helicopter
either, because the close-packed jungle wouldn't allow any

landing for four miles from the scene. When the hopeful rescuers reached it by jungle trek, they found everybody dead and mutilated beyond recognition. This was intentional in the case of Rodriquez, which was why the bomb had been placed by Ramos directly in front of the pilot's seat. Some things were found, of course. The passports of Milona and Valdeblanques were recovered from the burned and split-apart bodies. So, too, was the passport of Jorge Herrera Gomez—which was less surprising because Ramos had placed it as far back into the tail of the aircraft as he could, wanting it to survive. Sixty thousand dollars was found—which was forty thousand less than Ramos had placed aboard. The rescuers stole the rest. The flight plan to Bogotá, for onward passage to Bolivia, had been filed and signed in the name of Jorge Herrera Gomez, the signature verifiable because he'd had a control-tower employee personally bring it to him in Riohacha for the purpose, and there were three more loyal airport employees who swore in later depositions that they had personally seen Señor Gomez board the aircraft, a perjury for which they each received ten thousand dollars. *El Colombiano* and other newspapers duly reported the death in an aircrash of Jorge Herrera Gomez, a death officially listed as an accident because of the bribe-induced reluctance—as well as the logistical difficulties involved—to put forensic experts into the area.

Ramos waited until the following day, establishing that he was unobserved, before flying up to Riohacha. He sat on the veranda, enjoying the view with Gomez, and said, "I think we did it. I think we killed you."

"You did well. Very well indeed . . ." He handed the man an envelope which contained fifty thousand dollars.

"Thank you. What's it feel like, to be dead?" said Ramos.

"Safe," said Gomez, after some thought. "Pleasantly safe."

The Cayman formation of the shell company went as

smoothly as that of Farr's corporation itself. He completed
the island formalities, made the approaches to Europe and
confirmed the arrangements with Lang, in New York,
urged on by Brennan who was anxious to get something
recorded at last on their extensive monitoring equipment.
He then insisted upon visiting Eastham and Howard's
school principal before accompanying the lawyer on the
completion stage of the operation. Green's completed file—a
bulky dossier of reports, obituary clippings and extensive
snatched photographs of Miguel Rodriquez—arrived on
the night Farr was due to leave the island.

Expectantly Brennan produced the sought-after pictures,
offering them to Farr for identification.

A lot were far clearer than the ones the investment
broker had been shown before. Farr studied them carefully, as he had before, and then said, "No. I'm sorry,
because I know how important it is. But this isn't the man
I met in Lang's office. This isn't the man I know to be
Jorge Gomez."

"Fuck it!" said the FBI supervisor. "It's the wrong
one."

The change in Howard was dramatic—astonishingly dramatic. It was a different ward—not solitary but with three
other beds—with no bars at the open windows and flowers
adding a smell of freshness to the room. The boy was neat
and pressed and freshly washed, his face glowing with
health. Farr's surprise was obvious and for several moments he found any reaction difficult. The boy laughed,
not contemptuously this time, and said, "Shocked you
again, Dad?"

"Yes," admitted Farr honestly.

"Shocked myself," said Howard. "About what I'd done.
What I was prepared to become. I'm glad you've come. I
want to say that I'm sorry. Sincerely sorry. For an awful
lot of things."

"It's all right," said Farr. Stuck with cliché, he said,
"Everything will be all right."

"I'd like to think so," said the boy. "There's still the court. And the school."

"I'm seeing Jennings later today," disclosed Farr. "I've written a couple of times but I thought he'd appreciate a personal visit."

"Which leaves the court," said the boy. "I really can't see much point in stringing Jennings along, can you?"

"We'll see," said Farr. "Leave it to me. It's great to see you like your old self."

And Howard *was* like his old self, decided Farr. Bright, eager and vibrant, as he had been in the last few months before Ann died and maybe in the immediate years afterwards, before they had drifted apart.

"It's good to *be* like my old self," said Howard. "Although I don't think Dr. Halpern is completely satisfied, not yet."

"I'm not," admitted the clinic director, when Farr met him an hour later, after promises to Howard to come again as soon as he could, and assurances from both of them about new starts.

"Why not?" said Farr, unwilling to have his happiness punctured. "He tells me he's completely detoxified. Taking part in all the activities. He's clearly sufficiently trusted to be out of security. And he tells me he's not interested in drugs anymore. So what's wrong?"

"I'm not sure that anything *is* wrong," conceded Halpern. "Howard has performed a complete turnaround. Textbook reaction."

"So where's the problem?"

"I want more time to be satisfied," said Halpern. "I accept textbooks in theory but rarely in practice."

"More than the agreed six months?"

"Yes," said Halpern.

"Howard didn't say anything about this," said Farr.

"I haven't spoken to Howard about it."

"What do you think his reaction will be?"

"It will be interesting to find out."

Farr became irritated at the psychiatrist's perpetual bland-

ness, his refusal to be shocked or upset or outraged. "I
think Howard is better," he said. "I *know* he is."

"You asked me for a professional opinion," said Halpern,
refusing to argue. "I'm giving it to you."

"How much longer?"

"Maybe three months. To be sure."

"You positive it's essential?"

"Absolutely," said Halpern. "Don't forget we can't
afford one mistake."

It seemed to be a recurring admonishment in everything
he was doing these days, thought Farr. When he telephoned Brennan at the Cayman Islands, asking the FBI
supervisor's help in persuading the district attorney, Brennan said confidently, "No problem. I can convince him on
what we've got already. Schuster will do whatever we
want when he sees the way things are going."

Farr had to drive back into Boston and then cross the
river for his meeting with the Harvard Dean.

"It's not going well then?" said Jennings.

"The doctors want more time."

"Is he studying at all?"

Farr shook his head. "He's not able, not yet. Soon
though."

"There's nothing more I can do," said Jennings.

"I thought you should know," said the broker.

"I'm grateful," said Jennings. He sighed. "Why do
they do it, these little fools!"

"I wish to God I knew," said Farr, sincerely.

"Try to convince him he has to work."

"I'm not sure I know how," confessed Farr.

20

Farr flew to Switzerland with Norman Lang beset by
conflicting thoughts. The most positive—because it was
the most important—was his increasing awareness of how
much everything was his responsibility, with little partici-
pation from the professional FBI agents. He accepted,
because he had talked it through with Brennan, that at this
stage it was unavoidable, but it was still something he
hadn't anticipated—and which he suspected Brennan hadn't
either—and he was anxious to retreat from such promi-
nence. Having constantly to operate alone—and now more
alone than ever—Farr was frightened of making a mistake
and ruining everything. Farr wished that he had some way
of knowing who his FBI watchers and protectors were
during the trip. He had been convinced by Brennan's
argument during their Caymans planning that he stood less
chance of hinting recognition and alarming someone whom
they knew to be hypernervous if he did not know the
identity of the FBI task force who would be monitoring
them throughout. But now that he was actually engaged on
the journey, Farr wished he did know. It would have given
him at least a small feeling of security.

Also, he disliked the lawyer. Lang was a humorless
automaton of a man, concerned only with the purpose of
the journey, unwilling for small talk or any social relax-
ation, despite their being forced to be constantly in each

other's presence. Farr supposed that the man's reservation could be a further indication of his caution about disclosing anything other than absolute essentials. Still Farr tried to talk as much as he could about himself—unsuccessfully inviting the reciprocal information from Lang—and did his best to be convivial when they ate or drank, but again the lawyer failed to respond, remaining as he had been during that first lunch, a nondrinker and an uninterested eater.

Farr was also preoccupied by his uncertainties about Howard. He recognized that Halpern was the expert, the man who should know, but Farr believed that the boy he'd seen at Eastham had recovered: things sometimes happened according to textbook formula, despite the doubt of experts. The complication did not stop at whether Halpern was right or wrong. Though Farr accepted there was nothing he could do until his return he still found it difficult to put his worries about it completely aside in an already overcrowded mind.

A great deal of that crowding concerned Harriet. In the thoroughly unnatural circumstances, their relationship had settled into some sort of naturalness. And had been accepted by the others with the exception of Harvey Mann, to whose animosity Farr was wearily resigned. Brennan did not seem any longer to oppose it, after the original objection; Jones and Seymour were not interested and Batty was determinedly friendly. Farr wished Harriet would not consistently refuse to discuss what would happen to them when this business was finished. He had openly told her he loved her and she said she loved him. So why did she find it so difficult to make plans? Farr decided she was behaving stupidly, for a reason he could not understand, and that when he returned from Europe he would insist they discuss marriage. Farr was sure everything would become good again—sensible and normal and good. Despite his present, understandable uncertainty, he would do what the FBI wanted and get their conviction for them. Howard would get better: *was* already better. And he and Harriet would marry. Farr smiled at the recollection of the remark that the Texan, Harry Becage, had made in the Union Club on the day this all began: he would become the complete and satisfied man again. It couldn't happen fast enough.

Norman Lang embarked upon the European trip with his characteristic attention to detail. Farr had provided him with a choice of financial lawyers in both Zurich and Geneva, because Lang had insisted the selection should be his, and only announced his decision when they were airborne after the Kennedy departure. The man chose Geneva. He had made reservations at the Beau Rivage, suites overlooking the lake, but didn't until the day of the appointment disclose which of the Geneva attorneys he had preferred. The man's name was Anton Fabre, senior partner of the most prestigious firm, which had discreet but extensive offices a short walk away on the rue de Monthoux. After they were ushered into the man's room, Farr decided that there were similarities between the Swiss and American lawyers. Fabre was quiet-talking, about sixty—someone who, after a lifetime in one of the world's leading financial capitals, had obviously known every sort of approach and suggestion concerning money and whom, now, it would have been impossible to surprise.

Not until they were in the Swiss lawyer's presence did Lang defer to Farr, and then only slightly. Farr explained the forthcoming Cayman incorporation of the company—which had been named, with intentional blandness, Sealand Investments—but added that its operations were naturally intended outside the island, through an anonymous fiduciary account to be established at the Bank of Tokyo Trust. Fabre interjected, asking about the intended liquidity of the company and its account. Farr said initially one hundred million dollars, but with constant infusions. Fabre's face remained unmoving and unimpressed. Farr continued that they wanted the Swiss lawyer to act on behalf of the company and, through the fiduciary account, create a second company in Geneva through an omnibus holding at Credit Suisse.

"With myself as the named director?" anticipated Fabre.

"Yes," confirmed Lang, entering the discussion.

"We would further like a third company, an *anstalt,* created in Vaduz, once more with a lawyer nominee."

"Quite easily achieved," said Fabre. Because it was legally required, the lawyer set out the tax requirements demanded by the Swiss government, details of which Farr had already provided before they left New York.

Fabre then asked if they wanted to specify their own Liechtenstein attorney or leave the choice to him. As with Switzerland, Lang had insisted upon a selection of names before leaving New York and said at once, "I understand that Monsieur Perlion is an experienced man in such matters."

"We're most of us experienced men in these matters," said Fabre, allowing himself the gentle rebuke. "But I will certainly move through Monsieur Perlion if that's your wish."

He had it! thought Farr, triumphantly. Not the names of the Swiss and the Liechtenstein companies, but now he knew of Fabre and of Perlion. And certainly Fabre, under Swiss law concerning the financial proceeds of criminal activities, would be required to disclose the company names.

"There will, of course, be need for legal proof of original ownership," prompted Farr, wondering if he would get more.

"A simple trust agreement, between myself and the undisclosed directors," said Fabre.

"I have signatory power of attorney," said Lang.

"How many true directors are there?"

"Two," said Lang.

So who was the Jorge Herrera Gomez? wondered Farr, inwardly churning with excitement at what he was discovering. Following the wrong identification after the Colombian plane crash, Brennan had carried out an urgent computer check and failed to locate another known or suspected trafficker of that name.

"Signatory powers for both?" persisted Fabre.

"Yes."

"Then it should be possible to complete all the necessary requirements while you're here in Geneva."

"That's what I hoped," said Lang.

The preparation and signing of the documentation was spread over days, which gave them a lot of spare time together. Farr tried, and failed, to spot anyone appearing specifically to be interested in them, who might have been one of the FBI surveillance force. Which, he supposed, indicated their expertise as trained observers, for which he should have been grateful, but which he regretted because he would have still liked the assurance of their presence. For the benefit of the Cayman recording apparatus, he telephoned to inquire how the business was going in his absence; he was able to give the name of their hotel and introduce Lang's name on the record under the pretext of listing the number of their hotel rooms if they needed to be contacted. It was one of the subterfuges agreed upon before his departure. Brennan called later and appeared to ask for the wrong number, allowing a brief conversation with the New York lawyer to be recorded—thus establishing for later court production the definite presence of Lang in Geneva. Farr found the Cayman contact frustrating because it involved his talking to Harriet in a necessarily stilted, businesslike fashion and he wanted to tell her he loved her.

Farr worked hard at including himself in every session between Lang and Fabre, never querying whether he should accompany the American—which could have invited refusal or rejection—but attaching himself automatically to the other man. It worked well until just before the end of the visit, when, as he went expectantly toward the hotel exit with Lang, the man stopped him and said that today it was necessary for him to be alone. Farr protested carefully, saying that some financial factor might come up for which the lawyer might need his advice, but Lang said that today's business was a simple matter of completing and concluding the trust agreement.

Farr remained miserably in the hotel, irritated at having

failed. He tried to convince himself that it was a minimal failure when set against everything else that he had achieved, but it was because he had managed to get so much that he felt the anger: he wanted to get it all. Now he wouldn't know the bank in whose safe deposit section Lang would deposit the document indisputably implicating Antonio Scarletti and Jorge Herrera Gomez. It would have been the last link in the chain. He wondered, hopefully, if a watching FBI man would follow the lawyer from Fabre's office to one of the banks in the city.

Two days later, Lang decreed that they leave.

"I'm glad everything has gone so well," said Farr.

"That was how it was intended to be," said Lang smugly, predictably shaking his head to the stewardess's offer of in-flight drinks.

Farr realized that, in subsequent encounters with the known Scarletti and the mysterious Gomez, his own part would be minimized and that of Lang promoted beyond its importance. At the thought of those subsequent encounters, he said, "Everything will be operational within a very short time now. There'll be the need for us to maintain close contact."

"Contact," qualified the lawyer at once. "Despite its apparent complexity, the system is comparatively simple. You said as much when we first met. Obviously the need for meetings will arise from time to time, but I would have thought everything could continue quite adequately if I simply notify you of the infusions and whatever purchases need to be initiated, with advice when the cash will be presented to your Manhattan offices."

Farr realized that Lang considered he'd served his essential purpose and could now be relegated to his rightful, inferior position. With the flush of annoyance came the recollection that this was exactly what he had been wishing for himself on the outward journey. Wanting to deflate the other man's pomposity, Farr said, "You approached me in the first place because of my investment expertise. Does that mean, now that things have been established, you won't need that investment advice anymore? I would have thought it rather essential: what other broker could be aware of your needs or your surprisingly high liquidity?''

Lang flushed, more pink than usual, at being easily caught out. "Of course," he capitulated. "We'll be relying upon you for investment suggestions and possibilities."

"So there'll need to be close contact," persisted Farr.

"Close contact," conceded Lang.

Farr had made another recordable telephone call to the Caymans office, advising his return flight, so he presumed their New York arrival was fully monitored. He considered going north to Boston to try to settle the uncertainty with Howard, but rejected the idea because what happened to Howard depended so much upon what he had just done and he wanted that settled more quickly. The time difference between Europe and America was to his advantage, so he was able to make a Miami and then a Caymans connection, completing the trip, exhausted, in one day. From Harriet's unembarrassed, uninhibited greeting Farr knew she had missed him as much as he'd missed her; she was hand-holding and proprietorially close to him while he verbally sketched out to the entire group the result of his journey.

"Marvelous," said Brennan with his quicksilver enthusiasm. "Absolutely bloody marvelous."

Enjoying the praise in front of Harriet and wanting more, Farr said, "There were some things I couldn't get, though."

"Nothing that we can't pick up from: you've made it very easy for us."

"Did your people follow Lang on that last-but-one day? The day he signed the trust agreement which will name Scarletti and Gomez?"

Brennan nodded. "He went from the hotel to the rue de Monthoux and from the rue de Monthoux directly back to the hotel, without any deviation."

"So the document isn't in a Swiss bank," reflected Farr. "I thought it might be where he'd put it."

"Looks like somewhere more conveniently close. An American bank would be just as good, for that purpose at least . . ." The supervisor paused, producing a folder of photographs with the satisfaction of a conjuror managing to extract a rabbit from the hat at his first-ever attempt. "We've got enough pictures to cover walls and make home movies for years," said the man.

Farr took some time studying the photographs that had been snatched of him and Lang in Geneva, impressed at how they'd been taken to leave no doubt about Lang's presence at all times; there were two of Lang entering the Swiss lawyer's premises which showed the nameplate on the door. Looking up to Brennan, he said, "I tried, all the time. Never managed to isolate one of your people."

"Which means Lang couldn't have done so either," came in Seymour confidently. "As was intended."

"Do you think he was still carrying a mike baffler?" said the eager Batty, locked into his unusual expertise.

When the trip had been planned, Farr and Brennan had agreed he should not be equipped with personal apparatus—more because of the dangers of its being exposed by electronic airport security checks than by accidental discovery. There had been some general talk about Farr's trying openly to use the sort of dictation machine frequently employed by businessmen, and he actually took one in his briefcase but didn't use it, determining that Lang would have identified it as something unusual. Farr said, "I don't know. I didn't consider putting it to the test. It wouldn't have worked."

"You were quite right," said Brennan, still effusive in his praise. "There was no point in risking what you'd already got."

"What now?" asked Farr.

"We channel their money and appear to do what we're supposed to do. That's Harvey's job. From now on, we take over more of the general operation."

Not before time, thought Farr, relieved. He said, "Thanks."

"Thank you," said Brennan. "You've done a terrific job. I've talked to Schuster, incidentally, in Boston. Told him just that. He's happy to extend."

Farr was too exhausted to properly make love that night to Harriet, though he was anxious to do so, physically to prove to her how much he'd missed her. The following day Farr called Halpern to say he felt Howard should leave Eastham at the end of six months.

"It could be taking a chance," warned the director.

"His schooling is at risk," said Farr.

"So is his future," said Halpern, heavily.

"He set his mind to six months," said Farr. "Having his entry postponed, after trying so hard, is just the sort of thing to put him back where he started."

"It's your decision," said the psychiatrist.

Later, at lunch in the Lobster Pot with Harriet, Farr said, "Have I done the right thing?"

"I hope so, my darling," said Harriet. "I hope so."

Gomez's temperament—his machismo—meant that he should demonstrate to the Bolivian that he had lost. He enjoyed parading himself in front of Navarra, willingly going to the Beni province instead of trying to persuade Navarra to come to him. Ostensibly the purpose of the visit was to discuss the progress of their operation, but Gomez indulged himself by openly complaining to the gold-chained, jewel-bedecked trafficker of the man's failure to maintain sufficient shipments to provide not only Scarletti direct but the European markets which had been opened, as the result of Scarletti's influence, in Palermo. Tight-faced and narrow-lipped, Navarra endured the humiliation and the rebuke. Gomez extended the insult by asking if Navarra thought it necessary for Gomez to send in some of his own people better to ensure that the consignments were maintained. Navarra said, tight-voiced as well, that it wouldn't be necessary; Gomez accepted the assurance, but his tone of voice indicated that his agreement was on a "this time but no more" basis and that he could always go elsewhere.

Gomez chose to travel directly from Bolivia to America, as always by a circuitous route—this time from La Paz south to Rio de Janeiro and then overflying the United States completely, to Toronto, then south again—and on an easily obtained but quite genuine passport with another identity. Self-indulgent again, he used the name Rodriquez.

His demeanor for his meeting with the American Mafia chieftain was quite different: not subservient or even respectful; rather, he approached him as an equal.

"It was worrying that the FBI were on to you," said Scarletti.

"They're not, not any longer," insisted the Colombian. "According to the investigation agencies, Jorge Herrera Gomez is dead."

"You quite sure about that?" demanded Scarletti, with equal insistence.

Gomez wasn't, but he chose to exaggerate. "What I did was possible only because of the number of officials I have in Colombia entirely dependent upon me," he boasted. "Some are in the narcotics division. I've had them check it out. Officially the file on me is closed."

The American smiled admiringly. "That was a pretty smart trick," he said. Almost immediately he became serious again. "Why the fuck did Navarra try to put an informant in?"

"Because he's greedy and he's stupid," dismissed Gomez. "Don't worry about Navarra. I can handle him."

"I worry about anything that can possibly upset an arrangement as sweet as we've got going," said Scarletti.

"That's foolproof," said Gomez. "We both know that. Everything is ready: which is why I wanted this meeting. I think it's time to start. I've waited too long already."

Scarletti hesitated, but only briefly. "You're right," he said. "Let's make the money grow."

21

Farr was still necessary—essential for the liaison with Lang in New York—but the day-to-day running became the responsibility of the others, mainly that of Harvey Mann, heavily assisted by Harriet. After the complete incorporation of the Cayman company and the creation of the linkup subsidiary enterprises in Switzerland and Liechtenstein, Farr made frequent trips to Manhattan, suggesting the investment possibilities to the lawyer and making sure he was on hand when the first money transfer was affected: a movement into the Caymans, and then beyond, of 75,000,000 dollars. The purchase orders had to return through the Caymans bank, which meant Farr's brokerage firm got notification of the expenditure—because the accounts had to balance—but not of the object of that expenditure. To find how that money was spent, Farr was forceful in his suggestions to Lang. They were all for property and complete details of each were made available to two separate FBI task forces specifically established to monitor any changes in the property ownership. Two task forces were hardly necessary because it was a simple matter of checking land registers and ownership records, a boring but productive job. Lang deferred to Farr's suggestion on two occasions, committing fifty million dollars of the initial installment into deals the investment broker proposed. Lang continued to trust Farr; a total of one hundred and twenty million dollars from two subsequent installments moved out through Farr's Manhattan office in courier-delivered cash deposits, which subsequently became land investments located by the FBI teams.

The concentration was on the Scarletti-Gomez operation but the advantage to the FBI of the Caymans' setup extended beyond that. The Bureau decided to go ahead and make a case against the Chicago computer embezzlers, and Harvey Mann became suspicious of three other sets of financial movements; when checked, they were found to be criminal as well, two actually involving drug money. Brennan was appointed overall supervisor, which involved his being away from the Caymans for comparatively long periods.

"He's done it," said Harriet.

"Who's done what?" queried Farr.

"Peter Brennan," said the woman. "Set out to make his name with this. Looks like he's done it. Riding on your back."

Farr frowned. They were in the bungalow, alone. Harriet had cooked dinner and they were still finishing the wine in the bottle, he in the easy chair with its view of the ocean, Harriet at his feet. "What's that all about?"

"I know how these things go," she said. "He'll get all the credit; you'll be relegated to the rank of mechanic."

"I didn't set it up for any credit," said Farr. He felt down, turning her face so that she had to look up to him. "And I benefited far more than I thought I was going to anyway."

"Me, too."

"So maybe it's time to talk about it," he said.

"Why?"

"Why not?"

She shrugged against his knee. "I don't know; I still can't believe things have worked out like this."

"Do you love me?"

She looked fully up to him. "You know damned well I do."

"And I love you. So why don't we forget all about the circumstances, which aren't important anyway, and you agree to marry me?"

"*Marry* you!" Harriet swiveled, kneeling in front of him. "You're asking me to marry you!"

Farr laughed at her. "I should be the one kneeling and you should be the one sitting down."

She didn't laugh with him. "Marry you?" she repeated doubtfully.

"Of course," he said. "What else do you think we should do?"

"I hadn't thought about it."

"I don't believe you."

"I hadn't wanted to think about it," she conceded.

"Think about it now," he insisted. "This whole thing's coming to an end, right?"

"Right," she agreed.

"So what do you want to happen when it's all over? For me to go back to Manhattan and you to go back to some West Coast FBI office, and that to be the end of it?"

"No," she said immediately. "No, I don't want that."

"So let's get married," he said. "Is there any reason why we shouldn't?"

Harriet raised and dropped her arm against his knee, the gesture of someone unable to find the right words. "I suppose not," she said. She giggled girlishly, extending it into a laugh. "No!" she said. "There's no reason at all!" She rose further and he pulled her toward him and kissed her.

He said, "That's not much of an agreement."

Harriet sat back, mock-serious, on her heels. "I am honored to accept your proposal of marriage," she said. The seriousness became real. "It'll mean leaving the Bureau?"

"Of course," said Farr. "Does that matter to you?"

"I suppose not," she said. Excitement rising again, she said, "Can I tell the others?"

"Why not?"

"Will we live in New York?"

"That's where I work. We can live outside, if you want. Certainly have a weekend place."

"I don't know what I want," she said. She tightened and then relaxed her shoulders. "I'm so happy," she said.

"So am I."

Later, in bed, after love, she said quietly, "I hoped, you know. I always hoped. But then I thought it might have just been the sort of affair where you say you love each other but don't really."

Brennan returned the following day, more hurried than usual. He called the office from the airport to ensure they were all together there, and as soon as he entered the building he smiled and announced, "We're ready to go."

"When?" demanded Seymour.

"Washington says right away. The appointment has been made with the district attorney . . ." He looked directly toward Farr. "The Bureau lawyers think it would be a good idea if you attended with me. Because everything emanates from Manhattan, it looks like a New York prosecution . . ." He included the others again. "In Washington everyone is delighted. Confident, too."

Farr experienced an odd sensation, a feeling of reluctance that everything was coming to an end. Despite the strains—and now that Howard appeared satisfactorily to have recovered—there had been an exhilaration about what he had been called upon to do. But the reluctance passed. It would be good to get back to New York, to a regulated environment which he knew and understood. With Harriet. He said, "How soon do we go back?"

"Tomorrow," said Brennan.

"As we're all together it seems like a good moment to make another announcement," said Harriet. "Walter and I are getting married."

For a moment there was complete silence in the room. Then Seymour said, "Looks like everything has worked out well for everyone."

"Guess what!" said Batty. "That'll be on tape and video. Two different systems, too."

Illogically—an illogicality he at once, irritably, conceded to himself—Farr expected the district attorney to be Alvin Schuster, whom he already knew. The New York attorney was an altogether different man—thin, constantly moving his hands and worrying his spectacles, with an unthought-out, stop-start style of talking. His name was William Harrop and Farr wondered at once what sort of impression the man conveyed in a courtroom. An FBI lawyer, Jack Webster, accompanied them from Washington for the meeting and they assembled in a rear office of the justice building, with a smoke-grimed view of back alleys. Farr thought it depressing compared with the surroundings in which he'd worked over the previous few months.

"I've read the file," declared Harrop at once, after the introductions. "Now I've got to decide if there's a case. Which is what I want you to help me with. So thank you for coming; thank you very much indeed."

"*Decide* if there's a case," said Webster, allowing the surprise. "It's a hell of a case."

"What about entrapment?" demanded the state lawyer.

"No!" refused Webster. "We were very careful about that, obviously. That's the reason for Mr. Farr's involvement. For the defense to succeed with an argument of entrapment, they have to show that we inveigled the accused into doing something—committing a crime—which they would not otherwise have considered."

"I'm aware of the definition," said Harrop.

"Then surely you can see that it isn't a defense," said Webster. "Farr created a perfectly legitimate offshore branch of his business. Through it he moved a great deal of legitimate business. The approach on behalf of Scarletti and Gomez came *from* Lang. Nothing—absolutely nothing— began from us. I'm sure they'll try entrapment. It's the obvious defense. I'm convinced a judge will find in our favor."

"You've no doubt, either, that the criminal liaison agreements between the United States and Switzerland and the Caymans will operate effectively?" persisted the nervous lawyer.

"Once we can prove, as I'm sure that we can prove, that the money channeled through both countries was the result of criminal narcotics enterprise, then no, I haven't any doubt whatsoever."

Harrop nodded, head bent over a yellow legal pad at what appeared from where Farr was sitting to be a list of reminders to himself. The district attorney looked up and said, "OK, I asked those questions because I wanted your views upon them. I'm inclined to agree with you. There's an aspect of the evidence I'm not entirely sure of, however."

"What?" came in Brennan.

"Gomez," said Harrop, shortly. "Scarletti, too, but Gomez most of all. At least with Scarletti you've backup documentation: Bureau files. The only Gomez on any enforcement files died in a plane crash . . ." Harrop nodded toward the investment broker. "And, according to Mr. Farr, the pictures of that man are not those of the person whom he met in Lang's office."

"So it's a different Gomez," said Brennan.

"Where is he?" asked Harrop, not responding to the FBI supervisor's impatience. He nodded again toward Farr. "We have evidence of a meeting in a lawyer's office, but the corroboration is only possible from Lang's staff, who might choose to deny it. There are photographs and film, certainly, of a New York lawyer named Norman Lang visiting the Caymans; and, later, documentary proof of the apparent reason for that meeting, with the names of Gomez and Scarletti on incorporation documents. All the tape recordings are scrambled but I'd never succeed in a million years getting past any defense lawyer the suggestion that it was because Lang was wired to defeat them. At the moment I think I've got a very good case for a conspiracy between a lawyer and an investment broker. The only positive link to Scarletti and Gomez is their apparent signatures upon a document giving Lang power of attorney. And our version is a copy that Lang gave to Farr, not the original . . ."

"But Farr saw them!" interrupted Brennan, his exasperation growing. "That day in Lang's office."

"I'm sure he did," said Harrop. "Just as you're sure he did. I'm considering what we're going to manage to get through in court to convince a jury—which is all that matters." The district attorney turned to Webster. "I know your commitment; your belief that you had a good case," he said. "Try to look at it from my point of view— independently. I'm concerned not with beliefs and commitments but what I can produce in court and legally be expected to succeed with . . ." He hesitated, enumerating the points. "The meeting with two men called Scarletti and Gomez is, as I've said, deniable. The photocopy of power of attorney with signatory authority is doubtful because it's not an original. I've got Lang linked with Farr in a series of tax-avoiding maneuvers but Lang is a subsidiary target. Right?"

Before the FBI attorney could respond, Brennan said, "OK! To date we've traced close to two hundred and thirty million dollars from that one source. Where does Lang get two hundred and thirty million dollars? Tell me that!"

"I wish I could. And I'd like to hope that we could persuade Lang to tell us, when he's arrested. But I can't be sure of doing so. We've got to look for evidence beyond that."

"I can't get you any more evidence," protested Brennan.

"What's the point of my seeking an indictment against a man called Jorge Herrera Gomez when we don't know *who* the hell he is or *where* the hell he is!"

Farr was bewildered by the exchange. He'd arrived expecting nothing more than a formal discussion and found— not for the first time—that Brennan's confidence was misplaced and that everything was a long way from the conclusion he'd imagined. It couldn't affect Howard, he

decided—not now. Schuster had agreed to a postponement
of any court case, before the decision to let Howard leave
Eastham and try for Harvard. So Howard—for a while at
least—was OK. What about him and Harriet? The delay, if
there was to be a delay, couldn't affect him and Harriet.
Not having entered the conversation before, Farr said to
the district attorney, "What, exactly, is it that you want?"

"Ideally, an arrest," said Harrop simply. "A seizure in
a situation of provable malfeasance—"

"Come on!" interrupted Webster, as exasperated now
as the other FBI man. "You've heard how careful these
bastards are . . ." He indicated the dossier before the
district attorney. "It's all written down there, for God's
sake!"

"I was asked, exactly, what I wanted," reminded Harrop,
stiffly. "I'm well aware I was asking practically the impossible. Short of that, I want to know who and where
Gomez is—as I've already explained—and something more
substantial linking both him and Scarletti with Lang."

"You're not prepared to go ahead on what we've got!"
demanded Brennan.

From the man's side Farr could see that Brennan was
white with anger, hands gripped with matching whiteness
against his legs.

"Your linkage is too weak at the moment," insisted
Harrop. "On what I have here"—he patted the folder in
front of him—"I'd say we could proceed against Lang but
that there was a chance of Scarletti getting himself removed from the indictment. I don't think I'd consider
moving against Jorge Gomez, whoever he is—which would
be a telling point in Scarletti's *favor*."

Farr's Manhattan office was the most convenient place
for them to go after the meeting with the district attorney
and Brennan succeeded, just, in restraining himself until
they got into the broker's rooms.

"Son of a bitch!" he exploded. "More evidence! What
the fuck more does he expect—a written confession before
we charge the bastards!"

"His objections were good ones," said Webster, more
controlled. "He's young and he's nervous and this would
be his first major national case. So we're unlucky in
drawing him: there's no way we could have foreseen that.
But his points were valid. I think we let ourselves get a
little off balance, by the success of some parts of the
operation, without properly considering the weakness of
others. I think there's enough on Scarletti. But not on
Gomez. And he's right about what he says. We can't seek
indictments against one without the other."

"None of this is my fault," said Farr, determined their
internal foul-ups wouldn't affect himself or Howard. "I
did everything and more than I was asked."

"No one's blaming you," said Brennan irritably.

"In fact," said Farr, "you misled me. I thought we
were coming here to get everything signed, sealed and
delivered."

Brennan didn't speak, looking instead at Webster. "That's
my fault," admitted the lawyer. "It was my decision to go
ahead."

"So where are we now?" asked Farr. "I don't know if
you've realized it yet, but at the moment what we've done
is create the perfect launder for millions of dollars of drug
money and just been told by a district attorney to do
nothing about it!"

"I'm going to do something about it," said Brennan, so
quiet he was almost speaking to himself. "If that frightened bastard wants Scarletti and Gomez, then I'll give
them to him."

Brennan wanted him to go to Washington but Farr refused,
further angering the already angry FBI man, arguing that
Brennan had already agreed to his going instead to Boston
for Howard's release, and that anything decided upon at
the FBI headquarters could be discussed between them
later. They parted, hostile and unspeaking, at La Guardia,
Farr turning right for the Boston shuttle, Brennan and
Webster left for Washington. Farr strapped himself into

the belt for takeoff, feeling an anger of his own. He fully believed now that Howard had been trafficking on the scale they'd first claimed, but they *had* entrapped him into setting up the financial outlet. And then, over the months, taken him for granted, treating him as if he were some contracted employee. So it was right that he should have made a stand. Farr thought—hoped—that he'd rebuilt some sort of relationship between himself and the boy, but he accepted that it was fragile and he didn't intend it to be endangered by his leaping to Brennans' finger-snap. Gathering evidence was FBI work, for FBI operatives; he'd done—and done bloody well—all he'd been asked to do.

Farr saw Halpern first, in the director's office. Halpern agreed that nothing had happened since their last conversation to make him think that Howard's recovery wasn't successful—conceding, rather, that it was everything they could have hoped for—but repeating that he would still have liked to have had more time, to be sure. Farr said again why more time wasn't available and thanked the director. Halpern said he'd be available any time, if something arose that Farr was worried about.

Howard was waiting, his few belongings already packed. He was polite and grateful to Halpern and the rest of the staff and there were jokes about neither of them wanting to see the other again.

"Looking forward to getting back?" asked Farr.

"Sure," said Howard. "How come I'm not appearing in court?"

"I got the district attorney to agree to a postponement of the hearing, for reports on the degree of your rehabilitation," said Farr, scarcely lying, hoping his story was better prepared this time.

"So I'm still due in court?" demanded the boy.

"Not necessarily," said Farr, seeing a danger of Howard trying to run if he feared fresh incarceration. "If Halpern's reports are satisfactory—and I understand that they are—and if your progress back at school is satisfactory, the possibility is of a suspended sentence, which is like probation. There's a record of conviction but you don't go to jail. In your case, you could continue on at school.''

"For what *I* was caught for!" asked the boy disbelievingly.

Farr was conscious of Howard looking at him across the vehicle. ''It hasn't been easy getting them to agree,'' he said.

Howard did not speak for several moments. Then he said, still doubtful, ''It can't have been.''

Gratefully Farr saw the signposts to Boston. He said, ''There's something I want to tell you. Talk to you about.''

"What?"

''I'm getting married again.'' Farr blurted the news out, feeling oddly embarrassed.

''You're doing what!'' The tone of Howard's voice suggested surprise, nothing more, Farr decided.

He repeated, ''Getting married. Her name's Harriet Becker . . .'' Quickly, to preempt the question, Farr added, ''Met her through work.'' When Howard didn't respond at once, he went on, still quickly, ''I want you to meet her. Get to know her. You're not offended?''

''Offended!'' said the boy. ''Why should I be offended?''

''Happens sometimes,'' said Farr. ''Kids think their parents are being untrue or unfaithful to a mother or father who died. That isn't so, in this case. It couldn't be . . .'' He stole a glance across the car. ''You know that, don't you? Getting married has got nothing to do with your mother—doesn't mean I've stopped feeling for her the way I always will.''

''For Christ's sake, Dad!'' said the boy. ''Stop apologizing to me! I think it's terrific.''

22

To have met in the Cayman suite of offices would have meant an automatic recording of their conversation, because the system could not be overridden, so the day Farr returned from America they gathered instead at the bungalow, where the devices could be turned off. Brennan's anger was still visible and it affected the others in different ways. Seymour became angry, too, but Batty and Jones showed uncertainty, believing they had wasted their time. That seemed to be Mann's attitude, as well. Only in Harriet's case did Farr, who did not have to concentrate on the New York account and had time to study them all, have difficulty in gauging a feeling.

"Madness!" erupted Seymour, when his partner finished. "Absolute bloody madness."

"Of course it's madness," said Brennan. "I tried every way by which to get the case switched to a different district attorney . . ." The man hesitated at the moment of admission. "And failed," he said. "Harrop's got the case, which means we've got a weak prosecutor who won't go forward on what we've got."

"So it's all been for nothing?" said Batty, expressing the fears of himself and the other technician. "All of this."

"No!" said Brennan. "I'm . . ." Hurriedly he corrected himself. ". . . Washington, isn't going to let this go."

"But it's a Catch-22," said Harriet. "We've given the district attorney all we've got, he won't proceed on it, we can't get any more. So where do we go from there?"

"We get more," said Brennan simply.

"That wasn't what Harrop wanted," pointed out Farr, glad he'd been at the New York meeting. "Harrop wanted Gomez—whom we know from what Lang told me doesn't live in the United States—and he wanted more, if possible, on Scarletti. Seizures, he said. How does the FBI intend to get that?"

"They intend to get it through us," said Brennan, looking directly at the broker. "Through you."

"Me!" said Farr. He raised his hands, a warding-off motion. "Now wait a minute. I did everything you asked for, maybe more. There's nothing else I can do. It's detective work now."

Brennan glanced around and said, "I wanted this meeting where it couldn't be recorded because I think we're coming close to what we've always tried to avoid. Entrapment." He said to Farr, "What do we know about Lang and Scarletti and Gomez? The motivating factor?"

Farr thought for a moment. "Money?"

"Money," nodded Brennan. "And greed. We want you to set up something that'll trigger that greed. It's got to be so big and so enticing that it'll lure them—Gomez—out from wherever they are and into a situation where we can jump them."

"Entrapment, like you said," rejected Seymour.

Brennan shook his head. "I told you we looked at this every way but which in Washington. This got as high as the deputy director. Webster's boss, too. Of course they'll plead it; they'd have pleaded it if that bastard Harrop had let us proceed on what we've got. Webster's view—the view of the entire legal department—is that we can win an argument against entrapment."

"It was Webster's view—and presumably that of the

entire legal department—that we had enough to proceed
with as it is," reminded Farr. "And Harrop threw it out."

"This has been thought through very clearly," urged
Brennan. "Believe me."

He had, earlier, thought Farr. "You told Harrop that
we'd moved something close to two hundred and thirty
million dollars for Gomez and Scarletti. You underesti-
mated. The actual figure is two hundred and eighty million
dollars; I've got forty-two million dollars commission in
an escrow account for when this is all over that's going to
make the operation self-financing! If you've thought everything through very clearly, then tell me what sort of
scheme will be big enough bait."

"You're the financial expert," said Brennan, too glib.
"We're just the investigators."

"Who don't seem to be having a great deal of success
with their investigations," said Farr.

Brennan's face tightened, but only briefly. "OK, I deserved that," he said. "I didn't expect it to shake out this
way either. I'm *asking* you to think of something, so that
we can get this thing back on course."

"This wasn't part of the original deal," insisted Farr.

"Yes," said Brennan.

"No," said Farr, as quickly. "I'll create something but
I want all charges quashed against Howard. Schuster can
have a medical report from the clinic saying that he's
rehabilitated. So I want the charges dropped. That's the
deal."

"Give me a scheme first," demanded Brennan.

"No. Give me Schuster's written agreement. And
the agreement of the court and the judge . . ." He
paused momentarily, unable to recall the woman's name.
". . .Telford," he remembered. "The agreement of Judge
Telford. That's what I want."

"You're not in a position to make demands," said
Seymour, trying to come to his friend's aid.

"Yes, I am," said Farr, as the awareness came to him.
"In fact, you're not in a position to refuse them. If you, or

Schuster, bring Howard to court, then the name becomes
public. Just how long do you think Lang would remain
dealing through my firm, on behalf of Gomez and Scarletti,
if it all came out? What would you say, Brennan, when the
defense counsel I employed asked why the case had been
in suspension for so many months?''

Brennan went white, as white as he had been in the
district attorney's office. ''You wouldn't!'' he said, his
voice very quiet.

''Put Howard through a court and see,'' said Farr. He
was exultant at the thought of protecting Howard completely; protecting his schooling completely, too.

''I'll not deal,'' argued Brennan. ''Not as simply as
that. I'll get the written orders. From Schuster and from
the court. And then I'll want to hear what your scheme is.
If it won't work—if I think it won't work or Washington
thinks it won't work—then the papers get torn up.''

He couldn't expect any more, Farr decided; without his
threat of exposure, the broker didn't think they'd risk
someone named Farr getting into the newspapers while
everything was unresolved anyway. ''I agree to that,'' he
said.

Brennan appeared suddenly to realize that the confrontation had occurred in front of everyone else. He said, ''So
it had better be good!''

''It will be.''

Later, when he felt out familiarly for her, Harriet shrugged
him away, an unaccustomed refusal. ''What's the matter?''

''I don't like it,'' she said.

''That I faced him down? The bastard deserved it: he's
been taking me for granted for weeks,'' said Farr, remembering the reflection on the Boston shuttle and glad the
opportunity had arisen so quickly.

''Of course not that,'' she said impatiently. ''I've been
waiting for something like that to happen for a long time.
What I don't like is your further involvement. You were
right. You've done what you were asked. Why the hell
can't the damned Bureau get its act together!''

He felt out again and she let him this time. Her shoulder was tensed under his hand. "Don't worry," he said. "It'll all work out OK."

"How can you say that!" she demanded beside him in the darkness. "According to Brennan, things have been going to work out OK for weeks. Months even. Only they haven't. There's always a fuck-up or something somebody hasn't thought of. I've seen it happen time and time again. People outside—ordinary people—imagine the FBI and CIA and their police forces as always efficient, super-running organizations where everyone knows what they're doing and there are never any mistakes. You know what the truth is! There are a damned sight more mistakes and foul-ups than there are successes. Believe me, I know. Because I've been involved in a lot of them."

"I think you're overreacting."

"I wish I were," said Harriet. "Just like I wish you hadn't had to go up to Boston to get Howard from the clinic and had been able to get to Washington with Brennan to see what really happened."

"I don't understand."

"I told you before that Brennan intends making his reputation on this," reminded the woman. "However and whatever. He's in too deep to let it go and he'll twist and turn anything that Washington says to keep it alive, and go for his glory."

"You really don't like him, do you?" said Farr, lightly mocking, trying to lift her feeling.

"It's not a question of liking," said Harriet, refusing to react. "I just don't trust the bastard."

"You won't have to bother, not much longer. Soon you'll be out of the Bureau and out of headquarter politics and out of everything. You'll be Mrs. Walter Farr. I told Howard about us getting married, incidentally. He thought it was terrific."

She came to him at last, turning her face into his shoulder. "I'm not going to have any secrets from you," she said. "Not ever. So I won't keep one now. I'm frightened, darling. I lost, once before. I'm terrified of losing again . . ." She began to cry, shuddering against him. "I couldn't bear to lose you, my darling. I love you so much."

It was a week before Brennan returned to the Caymans. They assembled at the bungalow again, to avoid the automatically triggered listening devices. Brennan gestured with the papers quashing Howard's convictions, but before Farr would outline the idea that he'd discussed and perfected with the increasingly frightened and distracted Harriet, Farr insisted upon reading them, to ensure they guaranteed what he asked.

"Fine," he said.

Brennan held out his hand, overly dramatic, for their return and said, "Well?"

Farr told them. It didn't take long because it was very simple, but before he finished Brennan was smiling, to Seymour and to the other FBI personnel. When Farr stopped talking, Brennan said, "It could work! By Christ, it could work! OK, we all know the entrapment argument. But accepting the risk of entrapment it could achieve everything that son of a bitch Harrop wants!"

"I think we should go for it!" said Seymour.

"We're going to," decided Brennan at once. "We're definitely going to."

Farr adopted the role of host and indulged himself, settling upon the Union Club. He arrived first to ensure that the table was sufficiently isolated and discreet, by one of the corner windows overlooking Fifth Avenue. Lang was prompt, surveying the table with the same care as Farr had earlier, and predictably declining an aperitif.

"Our relationship is working out remarkably satisfactorily," opened Farr, after they'd ordered.

"I think so, too," agreed the lawyer. "Remarkably satisfactorily."

"What about your . . ." Farr hesitated, appearing to

change his mind over the actual naming. "Clients?" he finished.

"I know them to be very pleased," said Lang. "There'll be a further one hundred million dollars soon now—under a month, I would say."

"Since my establishment in the Caymans, I've developed a number of other clients," said Farr. With other people, he would have delayed reaching the point of the meeting but with this lackluster, business-only man there seemed no purpose in procrastination.

Lang looked up expectantly, not speaking.

"There are three, particularly," continued the broker. "Seeking similar investment outlets as your two clients. With matching discretion . . ." Farr allowed the pause. "People whom I believe to be following a similar course of business . . ."

As Farr expected, Lang glanced quickly around the paneled room and then said, "I'm not sure about the propriety of this conversation. I certainly hope you haven't involved the names of myself or my clients in any discussions with these people!"

Farr shook his head, smiling reassuringly. "I've had no discussion with them whatsoever involving you and your clients. What I have had is an approach from them for investment possibilities. Just like yours was initially. They have similar sums to ascribe. In fact, that is not strictly accurate. Their commitment is considerably greater. By about one hundred and fifty million dollars."

The lawyer was still frowning. "I'm not sure why you are telling me this."

"They are seeking a consortium, to expand even further than they have at the moment . . ." Farr hesitated, deciding it was going well. "At the moment, their portfolios amount to something like seven hundred and fifty million dollars. Their approach to me has been to see if I can interest business partners in such a consortium. The necessity would have to be, you understand, for the partners to be in a particular line of business."

Lang went back picking at his food, calmer now. "I appreciate that at this stage there is a limit to the amount of information you'll be able to impart, but I wonder from exactly where in the world these clients of yours operate?"

Farr made as if to consider the question. Then he said, "They have considerable interests in the confluence of three Southeast Asian countries, Thailand, Burma and Laos. Also interests and outlets in Southwest Asia, mainly in Pakistan at its border with Afghanistan."

"I see," said Lang.

"I understand there might be interest in going beyond an investment consortium purely from the aspect of finance."

"Trading terms, you mean?"

"Yes," said Farr. "Mutual trading."

"These clients, are they Asian?"

"One," said Farr. "Two are European."

"What do you propose?"

"Nothing." Farr was purposely awkward. He'd conducted enough business negotiations to know when to stop trying to make a deal attractive and let the other side come to him. "The whole basis of our relationship is that of suggesting investment possibilities—which is what I've just done. I now look to you for a response: making the point, of course, that the potential return could far exceed anything we've so far considered."

"I don't think that's a point worth making," rebuked the lawyer. "I think I understand perfectly."

"You'll put it forward to your clients?"

"That's what they retain me for," said Lang blandly. "What they retain both of us for."

From the moment of his first identification, Scarletti was put under the maximum surveillance considered safe, and Farr's approach to the lawyer was recognized as something that might lead the FBI to the unknown Jorge Herrera Gomez, whom they were seeking. So that observation was tightened to an almost dangerous degree. It appeared to prove worthwhile.

Scarletti, like most Mafiosi, was a person of regular custom, a habitué of known and recognized establishments, usually bars and restaurants. The habit had its advantages and disadvantages. It meant that Scarletti was confident always of his surroundings; it also meant federal and local authorities knew always where to look for him. Which was another advantage for Scarletti because he *knew* they knew—which gave him the head start in the game of cat and mouse.

One of Scarletti's favorites was an Italian restaurant on 39th Street and it was from here that he left on the day he was to meet Jorge Gomez, following Lang's contact from New York. He traveled in an easily identifiable, dark-windowed limousine, which kept strictly to the speed limits and regulations, posing no difficulty for any of the tailing cars. The destination was soon obvious, so the surveillance teams radioed ahead their guess of the city airport. By the time the limousine pulled into the departure section, FBI men were already in place, with confirmation of the flight in Scarletti's personal aircraft and its previously filed flight plan, to Toronto. There wasn't time for any effective liaison with the Royal Canadian Mounted Police and so the decision from Washington—from where the pursuit was being coordinated—was to ignore Canadian jurisdiction and pick up the arrival at the airport without any reference or permission from the authorities. With more than an hour's advantage and district offices in New York, Buffalo and Cleveland, the FBI was able to flood Toronto with a team of twenty operatives, overcompensating with manpower in the absence of any sort of technological aids, even something as elementary as radio-controlled cars on secure frequencies.

The operation was efficiently mounted and would have been effective, had Scarletti maintained his flight plan. But, overflying Buffalo, the pilot requested landing permission, reporting an overheating oil-pressure gauge, and Scarletti was already on the ground and away before the FBI had the slightest idea what was happening: an engineer's report even confirmed, later, that there had been a malfunction in the gauge, caused by a blocked valve.

They met in Buffalo itself, at Gepetto's, because Scarletti genuinely preferred Italian food to any other. He arrived first and seated himself comfortably in a secluded booth, with his people buffering him front and back and occupying the immediately adjoining table in the alleyway. Gomez, who had flown by his customary circuitous route into Montreal and motored down, apologized for being late but blamed crossing difficulties at the border.

"Passport?" demanded the American.

"Congestion," reassured Gomez.

"You've considered what Lang said?"

"Yes," said Gomez, guardedly. He was excited at the apparent offer but wanted the reaction to come from the other man.

"What do you think?"

"I think it's interesting," said Gomez evasively, wanting the questioning to shift. "What's your reaction?"

"Good," said Scarletti at once, less reserved. "We've already got an operation making us big, if not the biggest. If I understand this approach correctly, we're being offered not simply a financial tie-up—which I'm not particularly interested in anyway—but a two-way trade: our cocaine for their heroin, from both the Golden Triangle and the Golden Crescent."

Gomez smiled at the other man's enthusiasm. "That's the way I read it, too."

"Which would be incredible!" said Scarletti, letting the emotion show. "Can you calculate the percentage if we got the complete handle on heroin, as well as cocaine! We'd put the Gambino and the Genovese and all the other New York families who imagine they control heroin importation into America out of business overnight . . . !" Scarletti stopped, his voice choked with the magnitude of what was being proposed. "We'd be so big we couldn't even count it!"

"We don't know a lot," warned Gomez.

"That's Lang's job. He's served us well, over a lot of time now. Maybe me more than you, because I knew him earlier. But he's never been wrong. I'd respect his judgment."

"Let him check it out, you mean?"

"Fully," confirmed Scarletti. "If Lang's satisfied, then I think we should take it further. See what they've got in mind, at least. It's too good to pass up, without looking at it as much as we can. You with me?"

Gomez had been anxious to pursue the idea but he was unwilling to disclose his true feelings to the American, reluctant to appear overeager. "I'm with you," he said. "Let's have Lang check it out."

On their way back north—ironically passing on Route I-190 the disgruntled and disappointed FBI officers who were returning after being hurriedly summoned from Buffalo—Gomez said to Ramos, "I think we should do more than rely solely upon Lang."

"Like what?" asked the scar-faced man.

"Why don't you run a check on Farr? I know Lang did, already. But that's all we've got: Lang's findings. Let's get everything Lang's got; we pay him well enough, for Christ's sake. Get what Lang discovered and go from there. I want the absolute guarantee from you."

23

Farr created a fiduciary account company—this time a shell—in the Caymans and then hid the directorships through Hong Kong, using the same system as he had for Scarletti and Gomez in Europe. Directors for the shell were FBI headquarters staff—senior division directors who had never worked in the field and who would therefore be unknown to Scarletti or Gomez and untraceable. From the delay in Lang's response, they guessed he had been very thorough.

When that response came, Farr took Harriet with him to New York; while the meeting with Lang was the main reason for the trip, he wanted to show her the brownstone and he was anxious, too, that she meet Howard.

They went up the night before the meeting. Farr had been meticulous in his telephoned instructions to the housekeeper from the island and there were flowers in all the downstairs rooms and the place was aired and clean. He stood apprehensively just inside the hall, letting her precede him from room to room, wondering in the larger drawing room if he should have had the photographs of Ann removed and then deciding that it was right that he hadn't. Harriet made the tour without speaking, returning with him to the big room, the one that overlooked 63rd.

"It's—it's—" groped the woman. "It's absolutely fabulous!"

"You like it?"

"Like it! I love it!"

"It's yours," said Farr. "From now on, this is your home."

Harriet clasped her arms across her chest, hugging herself. "I guessed it would be wonderful. But not like this . . ." She grinned at him. "You must be one of those rich guys I read about in the society columns."

He smiled back, enjoying her pleasure, "I get by," he said, joining in the game.

She reached down to a side table, picking up one of the portraits about which Farr had been uncertain. "This Ann?"

"About two years before she died."

"She was very beautiful."

"Yes," he said. "I wasn't sure whether it was a mistake."

"Mistake?" she said, frowning.

"Whether I should have had the housekeeper take them away."

"What on earth for!"

"I just didn't know how you'd feel. About seeing her pictures here and coming to this house. This was never Ann's house, you know. She died before I got this place."

Harriet carefully replaced the photograph and came across to him, cupping his face in her hands. "Stop it!" she said. "I'm not jealous of Ann. I know you loved her, just like I loved Jack—more than I loved Jack, probably. I'm not going to avoid talking about him sometimes. And I certainly don't expect you to start hiding her pictures, like you're ashamed of them. Her photographs should stay where they are, always. And you should love her—always . . ." She stopped, straining up to kiss him. "Just love me, too. That's all I ask."

He kissed her back and said, turning her earlier lightness back upon her, "You must be one of those special ladies I read about in books but never meet in real life."

They stood holding each other, content just to touch. She said quietly, "You know what I think?"

"What do you think?"

"I think we're going to have the most wonderful life together," she said. "And I think I'm going to enjoy like hell being Mrs. Walter Farr."

The meeting was in Lang's office on Pearl Street, among the mahogany and polish smells and sound-deadening carpets. Farr knew the lawyer wouldn't have come back to him if Scarletti and Gomez weren't interested, and he was sure of the attitude he should adopt.

"I've spoken to my clients," said the lawyer.

"I'm glad," said Farr.

"They consider it an interesting proposition."

"I was certain they would." He paused. "I'm not sure that I'm at liberty to disclose anything more, at this stage," said Farr. "We both know how important discretion is, after all."

Lang sighed, pressing his pink hands against the desk. "Mr. Farr," he said, "I wonder if we aren't both taking this discretion a little too far."

Farr took it as an admission of the lawyer's failure to find out anything about the dummy Caymans company; maybe the man hadn't even located the company itself. He said, "I've always taken my lead from you."

"I think we both know what the business is we're talking about," said Lang. "My clients think a tie-up with what comes out of Asia would make an ideal trading consortium . . ." The man smiled, a teeth-baring expression. "Certainly something from which we could both benefit, without any danger."

Farr tried to match the other man's smile, unsure if he succeeded. "That's what I think, too."

"So what's involved?"

"It may be a problem," admitted Farr. "My people are prepared for me to set up companies for them to invest in. But they won't trust me with the sort of liaison we're talking about. They're frightened of being ripped off. They want to meet."

"Meet!"

"Would your clients let you do all the fixing?"

"I don't know," admitted Lang. "Where could they meet? How?"

"I was told to explore the idea, with whomever I thought best to approach—which is why I came to you. To talk about it and then come back with a reaction. Details like an actual venue could be mutually decided. My people are flexible."

"My clients could decide?"

"They could suggest," qualified Farr. "We both know what we're talking about. My people are as careful as yours."

"Vung Thieu?" said Lang, wanting to boast about his investigation, "John Miofori and Albert Tripodi?"

"Yes," confirmed Farr.

"I haven't been able to find out a lot about them," admitted Lang. "Nothing, in fact."

"Which is exactly the way they want it. Scarletti, certainly, is a known figure in this country. They're not happy about that."

"You told me you hadn't discussed them by name!"

"Subsequent to our meeting," escaped Farr, still easily. "They asked whom I had approached. I mentioned only the names: that of Scarletti got a bad reaction."

"How bad?"

"I came here today because of our relationship in the past—courtesy, if you like. They'd prefer me to go elsewhere."

It was a fleeting expression, hardly more than a register in Lang's eyes, but Farr detected it: the fear of losing the commission that Lang had already calculated for himself from the linkup. The lawyer said, "Could you?"

"Yes," said Farr. Got you, bastard.

"I see."

"If Scarletti and Gomez don't want to proceed, fine," said Farr. "In fact, I'd rather they didn't. I'm not at all sure that my people will go on, Tripodi especially."

"I've told you they're interested," said Lang, just too quickly. "I'll need to go back."

"How soon?" demanded Farr, maintaining the pressure.

"Twenty-four hours."

Farr allowed a doubtful look. "Twenty-four hours, then," he agreed. "If you don't come back to me in the time, then I'll take it as a refusal. Which will be OK." He smiled. "Like I've said, I think it might be better, from my point of view. And it wouldn't affect anything between us in the future, of course." Farr detected the lawyer's envy at the thought that Farr would tie up and make a fortune with other people and that he wouldn't be involved.

"Don't do anything—make any other deals—until we've talked."

"Twenty-four hours," repeated Farr, happy with his control and manipulation. "That's what we've agreed. I'll do nothing for twenty-four hours." Farr wasn't sure but he thought he could see a sheen of perspiration on the lawyer's pink face.

"I'll come back to you, either way," undertook the lawyer.

Farr wondered if the man saw a role for himself, even if Scarletti and Gomez weren't involved. He stood abruptly, determined to conclude the meeting on his terms. "I'll be waiting."

Scarletti and Gomez arrived an hour later, in response to Lang's telephone call to the Plaza.

Diplomatically Lang stopped short of saying openly that Farr appeared reluctant to proceed because of Scarletti. He gave a brief summary of his talk with the broker, saying that the man had spoken of others interested in the linkup.

"Who?" demanded Gomez.

"There were no names," said Lang, impatient with the other man's arrogance.

"It could be bluff," insisted the Colombian.

"Where's the ante?" argued Scarletti. "It's a straight trading agreement, as we understand it. Our cocaine for their heroin. There's no benefit in their trying to drive up any stakes: there aren't any stakes.''

Gomez was irritated at having his point put down. To Lang, he said, "Did you believe him?''

"Like Mr. Scarletti has said," repeated the lawyer, "what's the point in lying?''

"What did he say about none of his people being known?'' asked the American.

"That that was exactly how they wanted it to be,'' said Lang. "The company disappeared in Hong Kong. I've checked the names out every way I can and there's absolutely nothing . . .'' He smiled briefly. "The effectiveness of the cover, incidentally, shows how well protected you are.''

"So they want a meeting?'' mused Scarletti.

"Farr thought you would, too.''

"I would," said Gomez. "Certainly for something as big as this.''

"He didn't offer any suggestions for where it might be?''

"To be agreed, mutually,'' said the lawyer.

"Medellin would be safe,'' insisted Gomez. "I could guarantee Medellin.''

"I think I could guarantee Philadelphia,'' said Scarletti. "But Medellin might be better.''

"You want to proceed then?'' asked Lang.

"I sure as hell don't want to lose the opportunity,'' said Scarletti. "What do you think about it?''

"I'm unhappy at how little we know,'' said Lang.

"Farr's proved himself, surely?'' Gomez pointed out.

"He seems to have," admitted the lawyer.

"I didn't just leave it to you, when we started checking Farr out," said Scarletti, "I asked around to see if there'd been any stories spread about, suggestions that Farr was a good guy. That's the way the bastards have operated before, with their phony companies. There wasn't a whisper.''

"Certainly Farr's company isn't phony,'' conceded Lang.

"If we could dictate the meeting place, I don't see the danger," said Gomez. "Medellin would be perfect."

Conscious of Farr's reluctance, Lang said, "What if we can't dictate the meeting place? If they don't agree to Medellin?"

Neither Gomez nor Scarletti spoke for several moments. Then Scarletti said, "We'll have to be extremely careful: it'll have to be somewhere I'm very sure of."

"Me, too. I wouldn't like Europe. Or Asia."

"Which is why they might not like Medellin," pointed out Lang.

"We're talking in circles," said Scarletti. "I want it. Tell Farr that . . ." He looked sideways, to Gomez. "You in any hurry to get back to Colombia?"

Gomez shook his head.

Scarletti went back to the lawyer. "Twenty-four hours?"

"That's what he said," agreed the lawyer.

"Like it was an ultimatum?"

"Yes."

"Don't go back at once; it makes us look too anxious. Let him wait awhile. I don't like being pressured. Tell Farr that we want to go ahead and let the suggestion for a meeting place come from them. And let's take it from there. We'll both stay in town; liaise from here."

Farr would reject them, Lang knew; he was sure of it, from the broker's attitude. Just as he was sure that what he'd learned so far was a fly-speck compared to what was possible if this thing went through. He said, "I'll do everything I can to make sure it works out."

It could not be an easy meeting—initially, at least—but the fact that it went as well as it did was entirely due to Harriet. They caught the early afternoon shuttle to Boston, Farr going directly from his meeting with the lawyer, and Howard ducked a class and admitted it. Farr accepted it. The broker wasn't sure where they should meet, so he left it to Howard. The boy chose a restaurant-bar on Memorial, across the river in Cambridge. After the handshakes and the immediate uncertainty, Harriet said to the boy, "You're looking OK. How is it?"

Howard's face clouded momentarily. "So he told you?"

The woman moved at once, not just to stem the obvious annoyance but to prevent a dispute arising between them. "Course he told me, yo-yo. I'm going to marry your father: you expect him to lie about you to me?"

The fixed expression remained and then broke into a reluctant smile. "Suppose not."

"You're not a kid, Howard," said Harriet. "We're all grown up. You had a problem, which I hope you've got over, but whether you have or you haven't we've got to get something straight between us, you and I. I'm an intruder into your family. I love your father like crazy, so much that it hurts. I don't know about you because I don't know you. If I could learn to love you, in time—and you to love me—then it would be terrific. I'd like that a lot. If not, it'll have to be a situation we need to sort out. Not with your father. Between you and me. I've made your father a promise and I'll extend it to you. No cheating. No lies. No fucking around. I want to be your friend."

The boy blinked at her in surprise. Finally he managed, "Christ!"

"You've got to do better than that," encouraged Harriet.

"You nag a lot?"

"Not a lot. Only when I think it's necessary."

"When it's necessary?"

"When it's necessary: don't smart-ass me, boy!"

Howard laughed in genuine amusement, and Farr sat to one side, his head moving back and forth between the two people—the only two people—whom he loved in the world, thinking how lucky he had been to meet Harriet.

Howard said, "I don't know how to handle you."

As if to compound his uncertainty, Harriet said, "You didn't answer me: how is it?"

"OK," said the boy.

"No, it isn't," she countered at once. "Despite the

detox and the therapy and all the determination, it isn't easy. So how is it!''

"Not easy," he conceded. "Shit, you are an awkward woman!''

"Why didn't you say so, in the first place?"

"Didn't want to."

"Why not?"

Howard did not reply for several moments. "Guess I wanted to impress you."

"Wanna know a secret?"

"What?"

"I want to impress you too." Harriet extended her hand toward the boy, but with her little finger crooked, so that he had to crook his as well. "Hopeful friends?" she offered.

"Hopeful friends," he agreed, shaking the offered finger.

"Slipped?" she demanded.

"No!"

"Sure?"

"Why the . . . !" he started, but she broke across him and said, "Because we're not fucking around, remember?"

The boy looked down into his lap, composing the words. When he looked up it was to both of them and he was serious. "OK," he said. "Honest-injun time. I thought I'd cracked it and that I could resist but now I'm not sure. So far, I have. But Jesus, it's been difficult! I've actually gone out, twice, to score: once I even got to the place and saw the dealing and managed to turn back . . ." He was now speaking not to Farr but to Harriet. "It frightened the shit out of me," he admitted.

"You didn't?"

"No."

"Then you won," said Harriet.

"That time," said Howard. "What about the next?"

"If you did it once, you can do it again."

"That sounds like the therapy crap."

"It wasn't crap," said Harriet. "There are only a certain number of ways you can arrange words to try to say what you mean. Often they come out the same way, so OK, it sounds trite. It doesn't affect the sincerity.''

"What do I call you?" said Howard.

"Harriet's good."

"You're wrong, Harriet, about being an intruder. I don't think you're an intruder at all. I think you're terrific.''

"So do I," said Farr. He made the remark in the cab, just as they were entering the cross street into 63rd: throughout the homeward shuttle they'd talked and talked again about the encounter with Howard, Farr intent upon analyzing every word of every sentence. Harriet led her way into the house, still unable fully to accept this was to be her home.

"Thanks," she said.

"You were," insisted Farr. "You were absolutely terrific.''

"No lies, remember?"

"I remember."

"I acted," she admitted. "Not much, but I acted." They had walked automatically into the main room and she turned to look at him. "You were frightened, when we got here first; when we came in and I saw everything?''

"You know I was," he said.

"So was I," she said. "I was frightened then and I was frightened when I met Howard. I wanted so much to make him like me. So I went over the top.''

"No, darling," he said. "No, you didn't. You surprised me and I'm sure you surprised the hell out of him, but you weren't over the top. You were marvelous.''

"Not even saying fuck?''

"Not even saying fuck.''

Outside the terraced house, Ramos ensured that the watching Colombians were properly emplaced and could observe the property throughout the night, as they had been instructed to do since Farr returned from the Caymans. The Colombian remained for a moment, beside the observation car, staring up at the house, in which only the ground-floor light was currently showing. Lang's investigation of Walter Farr had been extremely detailed and it was completely accurate—as Ramos knew because he'd done what Gomez ordered and checked every fact, and he had found not one mistake. But there appeared to be one oversight. There was no reference to the woman, whom Ramos knew to have arrived with the broker, gone to and from Boston with the man, and to have returned that night to the house. Maybe, thought Ramos, she was just some passing screw. Then maybe again, she wasn't. It was important he find out. He enjoyed Gomez's dependence on him: the place he had in the organization. So he did not want to fail in something as important as this.

24

Farr spent the day at the Manhattan office, finding it increasingly difficult to concentrate upon the things that Angela Nolan felt necessary to bring up. The time passed without any contact from Lang. He was growing positively nervous, concerned that he had overplayed his hand, when the call came: the relief moved through him but he was sure he kept any indication of it from his voice. Testing his strength, he suggested that the lawyer come to him on this occasion—rather than he go to Pearl Street—and Lang agreed after some hesitation. He was there in thirty minutes, which was fast, despite the nearness of the two offices.

"They want to meet," announced the lawyer.

"Oh." Maintaining his attitude of reluctance of the previous day, the broker sounded disappointed. He said, "You know the difficulty. I'll put it to my people. I can't guarantee they'll agree."

"We'd both benefit."

"I will anyway."

"Yes," said the lawyer tightly. "I've a suggestion, if they agree to a meeting. Gomez said he could guarantee absolute security in Medellin. Scarletti's agreed."

Farr registered the Colombian city. He smiled, shaking his head. "I know, even before consulting with them, that

Medellin would be out of the question. They'd laugh at me.''

Lang's concern was obvious. ''Have they suggested anywhere?''

''Hong Kong?'' proposed Farr. Brennan did not want it there at all, but Farr knew from his rehearsals with the FBI supervisor that Lang had to be convinced that some sort of bargaining was in progress.

''Gomez was specific about not wanting to go to Asia,'' said Lang. ''Nor Europe.''

''There doesn't seem a lot of purpose in continuing these discussions, does there?'' said Farr. ''Gomez particularly seems to imagine he can impose all the conditions.''

''They're not conditions,'' said Lang quickly. ''Suggestions, attitudes, nothing more than that.''

Time to concede, Farr decided. He said, ''We need something neutral, don't we? Neutral and safe.''

''Absolutely.''

''But what?'' asked Farr, not wanting to appear too well prepared.

''It's not easy,'' admitted Lang.

''There was one thought that crossed my mind.'' In immediate qualification, he said, ''Not perfect, of course. But it might go some way toward reaching a compromise.''

''What?'' demanded Lang.

''A boat,'' announced Farr. ''Let's be blunt. They're worried about arrest. What about a foreign-registered boat, in international waters? They'd be beyond any jurisdiction . . . beyond seizure.''

Lang gave one of his cat-with-the-milk smiles. ''I like it,'' he said, ''it's a good idea.''

''Maybe my side won't like it. Maybe Gomez and Scarletti won't like it.''

''It meets the requirements,'' said Lang. ''I'll tell them that. How soon will you know?''

Farr gave a purposely vague shrug. ''I'm returning to the island tonight. I should be able to establish contact within a day or two; I'm supposed to be arranging something, after all.''

"I'll know by tomorrow," assured Lang. Scarletti and Gomez were still in town, awaiting his report of the meeting.

"Call tomorrow. I'll try to get a reaction by then."

Harriet had remained at the house and Farr went through the entire meeting with her, while it was still fresh in his mind, so that he would forget nothing and she would be able to remind him when he told it again to Brennan, later.

"Wonderful, darling," said the woman. "Absolutely wonderful."

"They haven't agreed yet," said Farr cautiously. "And we don't know if Brennan will think it wonderful."

He did. They got back to the Caymans on the late plane, so it was almost midnight before they reached the bungalow. Farr recounted the two meetings without any need for prompting from Harriet and the FBI supervisor said, "You did well. Damned well."

"You sure Lang's hurting for it?" asked Seymour.

"Like hell," said Farr. "He's a greedy bastard."

"But it still comes down to Gomez and Scarletti," said Brennan. "Just how far can we go with them?"

"There's no way of telling."

"Definitely Medellin?" queried Seymour.

"Definitely." ·

"We'll run another check to satisfy that son of a bitch Harrop, but we came up with a blank last time."

"If we get an actual seizure, the background won't be necessary," said Harriet.

Brennan held up his hand, forefinger narrowed almost shut against his thumb. "We're that close," he said. "I can *feel* it. We're going to get them!"

"Let's hope," said Farr, suspicious by now of Brennan's enthusiasms.

"Five bucks says Lang's in touch before midday tomorrow."

It was a bet the supervisor would have won, if anyone

had taken it. The lawyer tried to be circumspect, on an
open telephone line, using words such as clients and mutual discussions, but Farr intruded the names of Gomez
and Scarletti, for the benefit of the recording system, and
managed to get a grunted confirmation from the other end.
Farr retained his feigned reluctance, saying that, while
there seemed to be tentative agreement from his end, his
people still wanted more details and further time to consider
the idea. Lang came back that his clients also wanted him
to come to the Caymans again, personally to satisfy himself
of the arrangements. Already briefed by Brennan about
how long it would take to set up the arrest procedure,
Farr proposed the end of the week and Lang at once accepted.

It meant spreading the operation beyond the immediately involved FBI personnel to include customs, coastguards and U.S. air force. Brennan flew to Washington to
act as liaison, leaving Seymour to organize a boat. Fleetingly the man considered utilizing one of the fleet of
seized drug-smuggling vessels held by the U.S. customs
and coastguard, but discarded the idea because of the
necessity for foreign registration, and mindful of Lang's
attention to detail. He inspected and rejected as too small a
yacht anchored off Georgetown. The second time he had
better luck, locating a British-registered—essential for the
plan—sixty-foot motor cruiser called the *Mary Ann*, anchored and available for charter in the protective lagoon
off Rum Point. Farr had to be the hirer, of course, to
satisfy any investigation Lang might undertake. He paid in
cash and went through the unnecessary ritual of providing
a victualing list; he said he would be assembling his own
crew, whose seamen's certificates would be produced to
satisfy the insurance requirements. The men—all coastguards—arrived the following day with the returning Brennan.

"We're all set," said the man, tense with an excitement
which caused him to keep smiling, as if at some private
joke. "Everything. An air force AWAC surveillance plane,
two coastguard cutters and a coastguard helicopter. Cus-

toms plane and helicopters as well. We could invade Europe with what we've got.''

''Let's hope it doesn't leak,'' said the more cautious Seymour.

Brennan clenched his fist. ''It's tight,'' he promised. ''Very tight.''

The FBI surveillance of the *Mary Ann* was fully mounted and absolute when Lang arrived. Batty and Jones were operating concealed still and movie cameras and Seymour, apparently working on the next but one mooring, had a directional microphone aimed at the cruiser, to pick up as much conversation as possible; they'd decided against trying to install an eavesdropping system on the vessel in advance of the lawyer's visit, in case he located it. Lang asked the coastguard crew to leave, which they did at Farr's instruction, and the lawyer went carefully through the cruiser, making the sort of checks that might have detected a wiring system. The man carefully studied the registration documents and noted their numbering for a later independent check, and after three hours said, ''It looks all right.''

They emerged onto the fantail of the ship and Lang said, ''It would have been better if there'd been no crew.''

''They're necessary because of the size,'' said Farr. ''And the size is essential because we've got to go beyond territorial waters to be safe from American arrest.''

''I accept the reasoning but it's still unfortunate,'' said the lawyer. ''What have they been told?''

''Nothing,'' said Farr. ''They think it's fishing, obviously.''

''I'm glad your people agreed.''

''They're not completely happy.''

''Scarletti and Gomez won't join here,'' announced Lang.

Farr wondered if Seymour had picked up the names with his extension mike. He said, ''How, then?''

''At sea, from their own boat. They want a wavelength, so they can talk on a radio and fix a rendezvous once both vessels are at sea.''

"They're not taking any chances, are they?"

"No," said Lang. "None. Will that be acceptable to your side?"

Farr wasn't sure but didn't think it would create any difficulty given the extent of the monitoring facilities Brennan had arranged; and any positional fix could easily be radioed to customs and coastguards, he supposed. He said, "I think they'll appreciate the security, too."

"It's all going to be worthwhile."

"When?" asked Farr.

"We're ready."

"I'll need to consult," said Farr. "There shouldn't be any delay."

"They're here?" pressed Lang.

"Available," said Farr, seeming to avoid a direct answer.

"There are some other . . ." Lang stopped short of saying conditions. Instead he finished, "Requests."

"What?"

"Only principals, apart from the crew."

"Just Scarletti and Gomez?" clarified Farr for the benefit of the microphone.

"Yes," confirmed the lawyer. "And no weapons."

"I don't imagine my people are foolish enough to carry weapons at any time," said Farr.

"Just so that everything's understood. Before they'll consider boarding they'll need to see there are only six people aboard: the three crew and the three they're coming to meet."

"I'll make it clear."

"And only one crewman, to maintain a course, while the discussions are taking place: he's to be at the helm at all times, of course. Nowhere near the saloon."

"All right."

The humorless smile set in place. "We work hard for our money, don't we?" said Lang.

"Let's hope it's worthwhile," said Farr.

"It's going to be," said the lawyer. "I know it's going to be."

The recording was intermittent, because of the gusting wind which frequently blurred the sound, but the photographs were sharp and Farr was able to fill in the gaps during the evening conference at the bungalow. Brennan smiled and said, "Didn't I tell you that we'd got them!"

"All we've got to do is decide the day," said Seymour, as excited now as his partner.

"Sunday," said Brennan. "We'll tell them Sunday."

"Know something I'm glad about," said Harriet, when she and Farr were in bed later.

"What?"

"The insistence upon only principals," said the woman. "It means you won't have to be involved."

"Stop worrying!"

"I can't," she said.

Batty installed a receiver set in the Caymans office, from which they hoped to be able to monitor the radio exchange and get some indication of how the seizure progressed. Brennan and Seymour were to go, as the two supposed Caucasians, Miofori and Tripodi. From the FBI offices in Honolulu the Bureau flew in a staff officer named Aoki Yoshisuke, who was of Japanese parentage: during the short encounter that was intended, Brennan was confident that Gomez and Scarletti wouldn't question the Asian origin. Batty and Jones acted as supposed victualers, carrying the provisions aboard the boat to deceive any watch Lang might have established, hurriedly adapting the vessel's existing cassette sound system automatically to record the discussions when the traffickers boarded. They also carried in the food sacks two handguns, short-barreled, six-shot .38 Smith & Wessons, concealing one in a prearranged space beneath the engine cowling lip and the other inside the wheelhouse paneling, within arm's reach of the helmsman who would be expected to be in position the entire time. Apparently to ensure accuracy—but in reality to establish a verifiable printed record—Farr telexed the proposed radio frequency for contact at sea, requesting for matching accuracy that Lang respond on the same system, which he did. Farr set the Sunday embarking time for 10:00 a.m. and Lang agreed to that as well.

Anticipating the possibility of a Caymans airport check, Brennan, Seymour and Yoshisuke flew in the day before on a New York filed flight-plan in a private Learjet, hired through a New Jersey company in the name of their supposed Caymans corporation. A chauffeured car was waiting for the round-the-island trip to Rum Point. For the benefit of any observation, Farr made as if to meet them in and conducted what appeared to be an intense, limited conversation: at the limousine door there were exaggerated handshakes.

Farr was already back in the office when the signal bleep came from the Rum Point lagoon on Batty's monitoring system, alerting them to the limousine's arrival.

"Wonder if they'll be as nervous as I am," said Farr.

"They'll be nervous," judged Harriet. "You always are, no matter how experienced."

At the anchorage, Brennan and Seymour approached the *Mary Ann* with the curiosity of people seeing it for the first time and went through a charade of greeting the already familiar coastguard crew similar to that at the airport earlier. They lifted anchor at once, setting out slightly before the notified time of ten o'clock. They fixed an immediate southeasterly course, to take them through the Windward Passage between Cuba and Haiti. At 10:30 a.m. precisely, Seymour, who was to run the radio, signaled the course and the setting that would take them past the Isle de la Tortue and south of the Turks and Caicos, out toward the Atlantic. There was an immediate acknowledgment from the unknown, unsighted vessel carrying Scarletti and Gomez. The outward transmission—on the known wavelength—was intercepted by the American navy base maintained, by diplomatic quirk, at Guantanamo Bay, in Cuba; by the second monitor point at the coastguard center in Miami; and by the already airborne AWAC plane, flying at forty-five thousand feet off the coast of Mexico.

Brennan, who knew the degree of surveillance, said to Seymour, "Think the acknowledgment would have been sufficient for a positional fix?"

The bespectacled FBI man shook his head. "Too brief," he said. "We'll have to wait."

"I hope it's not for too long: air cover's easy enough but boats need time to make the distance."

"Where will they be?" asked Seymour, consulting the chart which had to remain unmarked, against Gomez or Scarletti looking at it when—hopefully—they boarded.

Brennan came close to his partner's shoulder, tracing the map with his finger. "Coastguards are coming south, down the Great Bahama Bank; at ten the fastest cutter should have been somewhere off Jumento Cays. The second is holding back, ready to cut eastward through Crooked Island Passage if the need suddenly arises for any quick sideways movement. It's all regular patrol areas, so their sighting shouldn't cause any alarm. Customs are coming in *from* the Atlantic, as if they were returning from a patrol. Routing here is pretty regular, too."

Ahead to the east, Gomez and Scarletti were still ashore, in the shade of the jetty shed against which their hired boat rose and fell gently at its mooring; both men still wore lounge suits, making them appear incongruous in their surroundings. Gomez gave the response signal to the other boat's course information and Scarletti nodded back toward their craft and to the captain who was preparing it and said, "How long does he say?"

"No hurry," said Gomez. "They're coming straight for us. Difficult to tell the speed, from Lang's estimate of size, but he says at least an hour. Maybe more."

Scarletti was uncomfortable and growing more so. They'd flown the previous day to Caicos and crossed the passage to Turks Island to establish themselves on the most southerly atoll, early that morning. Scarletti was a bad sailor and glad of the landfall, but it was getting hot now and the insects were beginning to swarm and trouble him; the beer had been properly cool when he took it from the freezer pack but it was warm now, hot from his hands. "Maybe this wasn't such a good idea, after all," he said.

Gomez, who was only slightly less discomforted, said, "It achieves what we want."

Despite the tattered, flapping awning on the remote slip, Scarletti had to use his hand to shield his eyes against the glare off the water as he stared toward the open sea. "There seems to be a lot of ships around," he said.

Gomez indicated their own cruiser. "I asked about it. He says it's always like this." If it had been possible, Gomez would have taken a line or two of coke; it would have been unthinkable to risk traveling with the drug or to use it in front of Scarletti.

"Still busy," insisted the American.

"Just pleasure craft."

"An hour?" queried Scarletti.

"At least," repeated Gomez.

"Who the hell wants to hang around a dump like this for an hour!"

Gomez frowned at the other man's irritability. "I'd have preferred somewhere else, but this'll do," he said.

Scarletti threw away his half-drunk warm beer disgustedly and took a cold one from the pack. "It had just better be worth it, that's all," he said. "It had better be worth it."

Their man straightened from the boat, stepped ashore and walked back to the awning. He was a Cuban who called himself Orleppo, which no one supposed was his real name, and who had made six unimpeded runs for Gomez across the Caribbean. The Colombian had chosen the man because of his track record. He helped himself uninvited to a beer from the pack and said, "Sea's slack; they should make good time."

"Tell me again what we've got," ordered Scarletti.

"Pump-action shotgun, beneath the wheelhouse ledge," recited the Cuban patiently. "Two grenades in the binocular box; two handguns behind the cushions of the first seat on the left as you enter the cabin.''

''Think they'll be carrying?'' asked Gomez.

''Of course they will,'' said Scarletti, still irritable. ''Ridiculous for them not to.''

On the *Mary Ann* the helmsman gestured to port and said, ''Guantanamo current's with us: we're doing good.''

Seymour said, ''Shouldn't we make contact with the coastguards or someone? Let them know what's happening?''

''Nothing *is* happening, not yet,'' said the other FBI man. ''We're under AWAC surveillance all the time. We're not breaking radio silence, not even when we rendezvous. These bastards have got equipment that could reach the moon and back. And they know how to use it, to search our frequencies.''

''Anyone want anything to eat or drink?'' invited another of the coastguard men from the saloon entrance, off which was the galley area.

All three FBI men shook their heads. Yoshisuke said, ''I should have been playing golf this weekend.''

''Play two rounds next weekend,'' suggested Seymour.

''It was a tournament.''

''It's a shitty life,'' said Brennan unsympathetically.

''We're clear,'' said the helmsman. ''Which way now?''

''Straight on, I guess,'' said Brennan, looking down at the chart. ''We've got to clear international boundaries, to get beyond any jurisdiction.''

Seymour dialed the wavelength, sending out course and direction, and this time he extended the transmission, requesting confirmation that they could make a meeting and asking what vessel they should look out for.

Still from the mooring, Orleppo responded to the course and confirmed the meeting. Contact established, Seymour said they intended maintaining their setting and aimed to sea-anchor in a further hour: the timing, at their current speed, would put them five miles beyond any international limit. Orleppo said that he understood and closed down at once.

"Should have managed some sort of directional fix that time," said Brennan. "That took a little over three minutes in total."

On the empty jetty, Orleppo said, "They've dictated the bearing: that OK with you?"

Gomez, the supplier who had to know about such things and who therefore understood the question better than Scarletti, said, "No. Let them get there and give them some time."

"What's the point?" demanded Scarletti.

"Not getting trapped, that's the point," said the Colombian.

"I'm pissed off with all this waiting!" complained Scarletti. "It's been hours."

Gomez insisted upon their waiting a further two, until one hour after the next transmission from the *Mary Ann,* saying that they were in position and waiting, dead in the water. As Orleppo finally took their cruiser away from the jetty, Scarletti said, "OK, so what's that all about?"

"If this were a setup, everyone would be getting into position now," said Orleppo. "By waiting the extra hour, we'll make them overshoot themselves: get too close so that we'll be able to see them when we get near. This is a big flat sea and we've got visibility of at least five miles today. If I see a piece of driftwood that I don't like the look of, then I'm not going anywhere near a sixty-foot cruiser called the *Mary Ann.*"

Scarletti smiled, a rare expression for the day. "That's clever," he said admiringly.

That was also the judgment aboard the *Mary Ann* from the helmsman, who guessed the strategy. Brennan said, "Bastards!"

"We could break silence," suggested Seymour. "Warn them to keep off."

"No," said Brennan. "If they are trying to do what we think, then they'd be moving over the transmission wavelengths, too. Just waiting for us to give the warning."

"Everyone's listening to us—coastguards, navy, air force, right?" said Yoshisuke.

"Right," agreed Brennan.

"So transmit to Gomez and Scarletti again. Say we've waited beyond the time and we're considering withdrawing, because they haven't showed. None of our guys will be able to misunderstand that."

"Sure glad you're not playing golf," said Seymour, moving the dial. He waited until Orleppo responded and repeated the message twice.

On the approaching cruiser, Orleppo said to Gomez, "So—what now?"

The Colombian was wedged with his arms against the wheelhouse ledge for support, scanning ahead with binoculars. "Few ships," he said, glasses still to his eyes. "All look like fishermen." He handed the glasses sideways to the Cuban and said, "What do you think?"

Orleppo went back and forth across the area directly in front of them, not speaking for several moments. He said, "I think I don't like making meetings like this at sea. But that from what's out there at the moment, I can't see anything that looks wrong."

"You can see the *Mary Ann*?" demanded Scarletti from behind.

Gomez indicated a faint black blur practically on the horizon. "That would be the fixing. There's something else, just to starboard, but it's pretty small. I think that's the ship."

Orleppo took his cruiser closer, rods splayed either side of the main housing, a typical fishing boat seeking a shoal.

The helmsman aboard the *Mary Ann* sighted the approaching fishing boat and gave surreptitious warning. Brennan came further out on deck and stared hard across the water. From his own wheelhouse, Orleppo reported the direct attention.

"Let's get alongside," said Gomez.

Orleppo swung the wheel, bringing his ship about so that he approached from the stern. He hove to, with about ten yards separating them. Seymour and Yoshisuke joined Brennan on the *Mary Ann*, and Gomez and Scarletti emerged from the cabin and confronted the strangers across the intervening water.

"We've waited too long," shouted Brennan. "What the hell!"

Gomez gestured to Orleppo to take the boat closer, his hand against the binocular box containing the grenades. Aboard the *Mary Ann*, the helmsman kept the boat steady and the two other crewmen went fore and aft, dropping fenders for the linkup. Orleppo brought his boat expertly alongside, taking back his engine so that the last moment the swell completed the maneuver.

"Like I said, we've been waiting," repeated Brennan.

"We wanted to be sure," said Scarletti.

"So?" said Brennan.

"OK," said Gomez.

"Why don't we stop wasting time?" said Seymour.

Gomez crossed first in a fluid, agile movement. Scarletti followed, more awkwardly. The aft area was briefly crowded and Gomez said, "There was an agreement."

"I know," said Brennan, nodding to the two crewmen fore and aft. Both stepped easily into the smaller vessel, head-jerking to Orleppo. The Cuban made a gesture in response, his hand close to the shelf edge beneath which the shotgun was clipped out of sight.

On the *Mary Ann*, Brennan led the way to the cabin. There was the briefest hesitation and Gomez and Scarletti followed, then Seymour and Yoshisuke.

"Tripodi," said Brennan, in self-introduction. He nodded toward his partner and the Japanese. "Miofori and Thieu."

"Scarletti," offered the American.

"Gomez," said the Colombian.

"Let's talk," said Brennan.

"It's your deal," said Scarletti.

"You got coke?" said Seymour.

Gomez nodded.

"How much?"

"Much as you want," said Gomez. "You got heroin?"

"As much as you want," offered Brennan.

"Distribution?" said Scarletti.

"No problem," said Brennan. "Let's talk specifics. How much coke could you supply?"

"It's a question of how much you want," said Scarletti. "Ton? Two tons. Just place the order."

"Could you move a similar amount of heroin?" said Brennan.

"Like that," said Scarletti, snapping his finger. "I've got tie-ups throughout America. Countrywide." He looked at Yoshisuke. "Shipping from the Golden Triangle?"

Yoshisuke nodded. "Bringing it out through Thailand," he said. "Got good chemists. Purity's high."

"How high?" asked Gomez.

"Ninety, nearly all the time," said Yoshisuke. "How's that sound?"

"Good," said Scarletti.

"Tell us about the coke?" said Seymour.

The question was never answered. Seymour's radio message threatening to withdraw had warned the other boats, but the coastguards had still been extremely close. They diverted, running a parallel course until the AWAC reconaissance plane reported the contact and then they resumed too soon the heading. Orleppo saw the approaching cutter, not even needing glasses to identify it. He recognized it at the same moment as one of the coastguard crewmen from the *Mary Ann*. Orleppo hesitated, moving first toward the binocular container for the grenades, then changing his mind and going for the shotgun. He managed to get it clear of its securing clips before the coastguard man got to him without time to grasp it properly, holding it in only one hand pointing toward the deck. Orleppo tried to lift up, but the coastguard seized the barrel and the Cuban fired. The blast jerked the gun out of his insecure grasp and threw the coastguard off balance. The shot spread through the fantail, shattering part of the rail. The main force hit the second coastguard, who was trying to move into the fight, fracturing his left thigh.

From the *Mary Ann* the sound of the explosion and the injured man's scream appeared almost simultaneous.

"What the . . . ?" said Scarletti, thrusting for the cabin door. Yoshisuke, moving sideways, tried to intercept the man, but the American clubbed out backhandedly and caught the FBI agent awkwardly, so that he collided with Seymour. Gomez was only slightly slower. He kicked out, catching Seymour in the groin, and was at the door before Brennan jumped at him awkwardly, only managing to get an arm half around the Colombian's throat. It was sufficient to keep Gomez from the door, however; Brennan's weight threw him forward so that they both fell through the hatch and out onto the deck. Seymour was still writhing on the floor, retching, but Yoshisuke leaped over the two struggling men and kicked out at Scarletti, catching him in the back of the knee and bringing him down in a stumble against the coastguard helmsman, who fell away from the wheel, jarring the boat against the smaller craft. The Japanese didn't attempt to do anything more; instead, he snatched at the engine cowling, hauling it up and seizing the hidden Smith & Wesson. He fired harmlessly out to sea, wanting only the sound of the shot: it achieved the purpose. Scarletti stopped, foolishly astride the rail, trying to get back into his own boat, where the coastguard had already knocked Orleppo unconscious with the rifle butt; and Brennan rolled away from Gomez, who pulled himself against the bulkhead and then stopped moving, staring up at the gun.

The nearing coastguard vessel, with a customs launch now visible about five hundred yards behind it, started sounding its siren; the noise screamed across the water and then the helicopters fluttered in, equipped with floats so they could land on the gently rising and falling swell.

"Hurt bad?" Brennan called across to the uninjured coastguard in the smaller cruiser.

"He took it in the leg," said the uninjured man. "Bleeding a lot. Thank Christ for the helo."

Brennan waved to the settled machine, indicating the smaller ship alongside and beckoning it closer to evacuate the injured man. From the cabin behind, Seymour emerged, still bent forward in pain.

"You OK?"

"Caught it right in the balls," said Seymour. "Hurts like a bugger."

Brennan took the second gun from the wheelhouse cowling, easing himself onto the helmsman's seat. He went from Gomez to Scarletti and then back to Gomez again. "Know something, assholes?" he said. "You just been busted."

25

Events developed so quickly after the high-seas seizure
that it was later difficult for Farr logically to separate them
into days and weeks. There was a kaleidoscope of legal
meetings and chartered air flights and arguments followed
by apologies followed by arguments. But throughout he
was with Harriet, so none of it seemed to matter.

The most frantic period was immediately after the seizure, from the moment of the flashed radio signal from
which, waiting apprehensively in the Caymans office,
they realized everything had gone well. Self-consciously,
they shook hands with each other, and Harvey Mann actually apologized for some of his earlier behavior and admitted he never thought it was going to work, and the FBI
personnel took a series of congratulatory telephone calls
from their Washington headquarters. From the calls Harriet gathered that the attorney general himself wanted to
announce the arrests but was being persuaded, with difficulty, against doing so until everyone was detained. The
operation was well coordinated and came without serious
mistake—which was surprising, considering the number of
arrests necessary. Lang was seized at his Westchester home.
The computer embezzlers were picked up in a series of
house swoops throughout Illinois, and the members of the
minor drug ring that Mann had detected were all arrested
except for one Cuban who must have seen the sudden

271

arrival of cars in Brooklyn and fled, never to be caught. The coastguards and customs men took the *Mary Ann* and the traffickers' cruiser back not to the Caymans but to Miami, which meant a late arrival and caused the attorney general to miss the prime-time television slot he wanted—and Brennan said the man could kiss his ass. In the immediately succeeding days, there were protests from the Cayman authorities at how the island had been used, but the publicity generated by the arrests minimized any effective outrage, although Washington apologized. The business closed, of course, and Farr and Harriet set up permanent house in the Manhattan brownstone. Harriet offered her resignation from the FBI but was persuaded first by Brennan and then by an interview at the Washington headquarters to delay her actual departure until the grand jury hearings and the ensuing trial, so that she could appear as a witness still employed by the Bureau.

An encounter that Farr remembered clearly, with no confusing overlay from other events, was the conference just prior to the grand jury hearings, with the nervous district attorney, William Harrop. The lawyer asked them all to attend, because it was a planning meeting for the indictments, and it was the first time for several weeks that Farr had seen the other members of the group, apart from Harriet. There were smiles and greetings but Brennan was serious-faced, giving Farr the first hint that things weren't going as well as the FBI supervisor wanted.

"Review time," announced Harrop, when they had assembled. "And as we're all together for the first time since the actual seizures, I want to congratulate you all on an absolutely first-class operation. That's not just my opinion: I was in Washington earlier this week, talking to the attorney general himself."

"Everyone's happy then?" demanded Brennan.

The district attorney concentrated upon the man. "You know from our earlier meetings the answer to that," he said.

"I'd like everyone else to hear, as well."

"Let me set it out as completely as I can," said the lawyer. "We've held Scarletti and Gomez on fifteen different charges, predominantly conspiracy to import and distribute cocaine and heroin. Under the seizure legislation agreements we've got the Cayman Islands and Switzerland to open up the records, so we can establish an effective chain. Lang is linked and charged on every count. We didn't think there was sufficient evidence to tie in the captain of their boat, Orleppo, but he's charged separately with attempted murder and assault with a deadly weapon . . ."

"Sounds pretty complete," said Seymour.

"It's complete but there could be problems," warned Harrop. "I just can't quite understand the strategy they're adopting, not now. Lawyers for Scarletti and Gomez are obviously going for entrapment: they've already tried at prehearings to get everything quashed on the grounds of high-seas seizure, beyond territorial waters, but the fact that an agreement exists between England and America permitting such boarding got that thrown out."

"So where's the problem?" asked Farr.

Harrop smiled at him. "Something that I consider is going to involve you quite a lot," he said.

"I don't understand," said the broker.

"The fact is that the coastguard and customs people arrived too soon," said Harrop. "What we've got on the tape is good—certainly for Scarletti, who appears to have done most of the talking—but I'm not happy about Gomez. Sure, we've got access to company records, attesting to a number of directorships for someone called Jorge Herrera Gomez. But you couldn't identify the photograph you were later shown; in fact, you said quite categorically that the person pictured on the records to be Gomez wasn't the man whom you met. But you *did* meet him, just that once, in Lang's office. It comes down very much to a question of positive identification in court. Whether you can say that the Gomez we seized on the ship is the Gomez you met in Lang's office."

"But the tape was good," insisted Brennan.

Harrop shook his head in immediate contradiction. Appearing to have anticipated the dispute, he handed to them all transcripts of the conversation that had occurred in the saloon of the *Mary Ann* and then said, "Go through it, while I play the tape." The man depressed the start button, sitting back to watch as they obediently followed the recording.

"Introductions were fine, establishing the names," said Harrop, itemizing the points. "Neither Scarletti nor Gomez responds to the invitation when Brennan invites them to talk. Instead it's Scarletti who invites . . ." The lawyer stopped and then replayed the tape. Into the room clearly came the voice of the Mafia chief saying, "It's your deal," then Seymour's question about coke.

"There!" said Seymour eagerly. "I asked him and he said he did."

"No, he didn't," said Harrop. "The next voice on that tape is yours again, asking how much."

"He nodded!" insisted Seymour. "We've got three witnesses, me, Brennan and Yoshisuke, who can swear to it."

"It makes entrapment an easy defense," insisted Harrop. "The only identifiable remark that can be attributed to Gomez after this is in reply again to your question. He seems to be agreeing that he can let you have as much as you want and asks about heroin. That's the strongest entrapment argument on the whole tape. It's the sort of argument that got DeLorean off. Gomez's lawyers are going to plead that he was enticed into a situation by the temptation of making a lot of money but that normally he wouldn't have considered any such enterprise."

"Bullshit!" exploded Brennan. "We all of us know that's absolute bullshit."

"I know we do," agreed Harrop. "A lot of defense arguments and pleas *are* bullshit. Too often they succeed."

"You said this was going to involve Walter a lot," the alertly apprehensive Harriet reminded him. "Do you mean that, if he can't identify the man in court, Gomez could go free?''

''I think there's a possibility of it.''

''Holy shit!'' said Brennan. ''We came to you with a good case before and you said you wanted seizures, and we get you the seizures and still you tell us it's not guaranteed.''

''Yes,'' agreed Harrop. ''That's exactly what I'm telling you. I don't want anyone to have any illusions about this. We've got a damned good case: one that everyone is extremely happy with. But it's not a fait accompli by any means.''

''Lang can't plead entrapment,'' insisted Seymour.

''I don't think he can,'' agreed Harrop. ''I suspect that his defense will be ignorance of the money source, acting as a professional man in good faith.''

''And taking his payment in cash!'' jeered Brennan. ''That isn't going to work!''

''No, I don't think it is,'' said Harrop. ''I just think that's about the best he'll be able to mount. He's got bail, incidentally. It was refused but he applied to a judge in chambers.''

''What about Scarletti and Gomez?'' asked Mann.

''No.'' Harrop shook his head. ''They're being held separately, only able to communicate through their respective lawyers.''

''When's the grand jury convene?'' asked Seymour.

''A week's time,'' said Harrop. He smiled, in contrast to his usual nervousness. ''I gave you all the bottom line,'' he said. ''I'm sure it's going to go fine, just fine.''

Gomez made contact through his lawyer, whose name was Winthrop, with Ramos in Medellin, but there was a delay in the Colombian reaching New York because of the care he had to exercise in entering. Winthrop was uncomfortable with the further demand that Ramos be allowed to accompany him during one of the final briefing meetings.

The exchange of pleadings had taken place between the

district attorney and Winthrop, so the defense lawyer had an indication of the prosecution's case. He went through it with Gomez, as Ramos listened intently, going into detail to the extent of recounting some of the tape-recorded evidence he believed the prosecution to possess.

"You think entrapment will succeed?"

"It's got a good chance," offered the lawyer.

"I want more than a good chance; I want a certainty."

"Identification is the key," said Winthrop. "Your meeting that day with Farr, in Lang's office; it establishes you as someone embarking with premeditation upon a criminal enterprise. If that hadn't taken place—if you'd managed always to deal through Lang—I think we'd be in the clear, with what they've got."

Gomez indicated Ramos and then said to the lawyer, "Give us a few moments."

Winthrop, who was only thirty and saw his role in the defense of a case that had received so much publicity as a takeoff point in his career, looked uncertainly between the two men. "*I'm* your defense attorney, right?"

"Other business," said Gomez. "Nothing to do what what we're discussing here."

Winthrop went to a far corner of the interview room and Gomez said softly but vehemently to the other Colombian, "You were supposed to check, independently of Lang! Stop me getting set up! You let it happen!"

"I did check!" insisted Ramos. "There was nothing I could have done; they spent a lot of time and money."

"The man Farr . . ." said Gomez. "He can't identify me."

Ramos nodded. "How?"

"I don't know!" said the furious Gomez. "I'm shut up here, for Christ's sake! You make it work. That's why you're here."

"You want him hit?"

"Of course not," said Gomez. "He's got to stay on, for the jury to hear. I want a proper acquittal."

"Lang's report talked of a son," reflected Ramos.

"I want it guaranteed; no more mistakes."

"I'll try," promised Ramos.

"You'll do it," insisted Gomez.

"OK. I'll do it. It'll mean bringing some people in."

"Bring as many as you need. And fast." Gomez nodded toward the hovering lawyer. "Go through everything he's got; there might be something in what the prosecution has made available."

"Soon now," said Harriet. "At last."

"I'll be glad finally when it's all over," agreed Farr. "I want to get it done with and for us to settle down. Be normal again."

"I want that, too," said Harriet.

"I thought we'd take a vacation, straight afterward," said Farr.

"Where?" asked the woman, surprised.

"Wherever you want," said Farr. He hesitated and said, "In fact, why don't we make it the honeymoon? There's no reason for us waiting before getting married, is there?"

Harriet smiled at him slowly. "None, darling," she said. "In fact, I think it would be a good idea for it to happen as soon as possible."

Farr frowned at her across the lounge. "What does that mean?"

"It means I'm pregnant," said Harriet. "I'm going to have your baby."

Less than a mile away from Farr's 63rd Street house, Orlando Ramos stretched the cramp of concentration from his shoulders, staring over the trial dossier made available to him by Winthrop. He had practically decided he would have to go for the boy alone and almost missed the extra when it came, because it was in a separate file not considered relevant to the main thrust of the evidence—which, in strict accuracy, it wasn't. Harriet Becker's announcement, picked up by the Cayman monitoring system, that she and Farr were getting married. She must be the woman he'd seen constantly with Farr at the Manhattan house, Ramos decided—so he even knew what she looked like. Ramos checked his watch for the arrival of the people he was bringing in from Colombia. Providing they got through immigration without difficulty, everything should go according to plan.

Ramos rose, sighing in sudden irritation. After all he had done for Gomez, he didn't deserve to be treated like shit. He'd sort everything out, now that he knew the way. And then Gomez would apologize: they were blood relations, after all.

Scarletti was held in Albany. The day of Gomez's meeting with Ramos, Scarletti also made his private arrangements with the intention of getting an acquittal. He had already considered it might be necessary, before the briefings with his trial lawyers. That was why he hadn't pressed as much as he could have done—and as they advised—to obtain bail. Jail was an excellent alibi. They would obviously suspect that he'd blown Norman Lang and his notarizing bank clerk away, but they'd never prove it. Everything would be difficult to prove, in fact.

26

There had obviously been meetings in the office since the disclosure of what he had done, but only with individual members of the firm—in particular, with Hector Faltham, to whom Farr felt he owed an apology. Faltham had accepted it, saying that he fully understood now, and that he would like time to consider Farr's offer of a full participating partnership. Farr decided upon a general conference in the week before the court hearings, which he guessed were going to occupy him as much as the Cayman organization, and which meant that the operation in Manhattan was going to continue to be the others' responsibility for some time yet.

Angela Nolan maintained her customary record of arriving first, and three men—Paul Brent and Richard Bell, in addition to Faltham—came together. As they grouped themselves around the large oval table—the same table, he recalled, around which they had assembled when he'd announced his decision to go into the Caymans—Farr thought he discerned a change in their attitude toward him. It was a distancing—not from annoyance at what he'd done without informing them, but from some sort of respect—maybe admiration—for the part he had played. Farr decided that, if his guess was right, then he was embarrassed by it. None of the explanations he had given them individually had been complete, so now he openly told them about Howard's arrest and what he'd been called upon to do because of it and how, until now, it had been essential to keep his activities from them. He assured them that he had done nothing to bring the firm into disrepute, and recounted the reaction that he'd entrusted Angela to obtain, since the intensive publicity, from their regular, established clients—the majority of which was congratulation and only a small minority, less than two percent, was even vaguely critical. Farr insisted that this role—but, more importantly, that of the firm—would be made abundantly clear at each and every court hearing, because that was part of the deal he'd made. The court hearings would occupy him for some time, but he hoped it would not be for too long. When it was over, he intended returning to the business as they'd known it before and trying to put as far behind him as possible the events of the last few months. As it was tell-everything time—and because he was feeling so good about it—Farr also revealed to his immediate working partners his marriage plans. Angela Nolan remained impassive.

"Quite an experience, one way and another," said Brent.

The attitude *was* admiration, Farr decided. He said, "And one, believe me, that I would have liked to avoid, apart from the opportunity of meeting Harriet."

"What about Howard?" asked Faltham.

"I've not been up as much as I would have liked, but I've kept in touch by telephone. Both with him and with the school. Despite all the foreboding, it looks as if he's managing to stay straight. There'll be the chance for more time together, when it's all over."

"You're going to become even more of a celebrity then than you are at present," said Bell.

Farr shook his head. "No. I did it because I had to, and I'm going to give evidence because I have to. But I'm not going to indulge in any of this ridiculous personality stuff . . ." He hesitated. "I know I don't have to say it, but if any of you get any approaches from the media, about me, I'd appreciate your refusing them."

There were nods from the people grouped around him
and Brent said, ''Sure. Whatever you say.''

''You talked about it taking up more time,'' said Faltham.
''What sort of time? Weeks? Or months?''

''I don't know, not yet,'' said Farr. ''Only weeks, I
hope.''

''I think what you did was very brave,'' said the woman,
expressing the feelings of the rest. ''Very brave and
courageous.''

''It wasn't, not really,'' said Farr. He looked around at
them. ''Wouldn't you have done the same, if one of your
kids got into trouble and there was a way to minimize the
damage?''

''I guess so,'' said Faltham. ''I'm just sure as hell glad
it didn't happen to me and I didn't have to make the
decision.''

''I think that goes for all of us,'' said Brent.

''Let me tell you,'' said Farr. ''I wouldn't want it to
happen to anyone. Thank Christ it's almost finished for
me.''

After the full meeting, he went through with Angela
Nolan only the things that she considered absolutely essential, deciding that until the court hearings were over it
would be pointless—and distracting—trying to involve
himself fully again.

Farr lunched early with Harriet at a bistro near Lincoln
Center and they bought tickets for a Verdi concert there
that weekend. He asked her to go up to Boston with him to
see Howard, but Harriet said the sickness had been particularly bad that morning and she still wasn't feeling completely better—and anyway Brennan had called that morning,
saying he wanted to see her. Concerned, Farr asked why
she didn't change gynecologists to someone better known,
but she laughed at him and told him not to worry, it
happened to everyone. Farr originally intended to eat with
Howard and catch the last shuttle back but said now that
he wouldn't; he didn't think he should let the boy down,
but he'd get back as soon as he could. She told him once

more to stop worrying and that she'd be waiting at the house when he got back.

Farr managed the three o'clock shuttle. Things were good, he decided. He'd gone through a period the like of which he never wanted to experience again, but it seemed to have come to a better conclusion for him than he could have hoped. He was almost stupidly happy with Harriet—indulging in love words and love gestures and meaningless gifts that would have been juvenile if they hadn't been so important to both of them—and Howard was OK. Farr paused at the thought. Maybe it was too soon to be absolutely sure of Howard—he remembered the detention doctor at the time of Howard's arrest saying that drug addiction was like alcoholism, and Halpern's depressing cure statistics—but in his present ebullience Farr thought it was going to work out as well as everything else had done.

Jennings was waiting for him at the school, as arranged, and Farr decided he had every reason for confidence about Howard. Jennings had maintained practically daily contact with St. Marks, monitoring particularly the boy's class attendance. He had not missed one lesson and his grades had actually improved.

"Looks like you—and he—are one of the lucky ones," said the man. "I'm glad we did what we did and kept the place open."

"I'd already decided how lucky I was," said Farr.

He picked up his son at the dormitory-house entrance and they went to the cafeteria at Howard's suggestion. Farr was initially surprised—expecting the boy to want to go into town—and then became aware of the attention of a lot of other students. Embarrassed for the second time that day, he realized that Howard was showing him off. When he accused his son of it, Howard said, "Why not? Aren't you somebody to be proud of?'

"It's good to hear you say it," said Farr. "I'm not much interested in the attitude of other people."

"So it was a deal, wasn't it?" said Howard.

"Yes," said Farr.

"You could have been hurt!"

"There was some talk about that in the beginning," remembered Farr. "Thank God it didn't turn out that way."

"What was it *like*?" demanded Howard. "Really like?"

Farr stared down into his coffee cup, thinking about the question. He smiled up and said, "Actually, it wasn't really anything different from what I do all the time. They were just men with an awful lot of money they wanted invested."

The boy seemed disappointed. "But they're big-time hoods: Scarletti's a Mafia don, according to what the Boston papers said."

"I was only actually with them on one occasion," said Farr. "Wish I could make it more dramatic for you."

Howard smiled around the crowded cafeteria, nodding and smiling to some people who immediately answered his look. "It's dramatic enough," he said.

"I saw Jennings," said Farr. "He told me the grades were good; improving even. Thank you."

"I guess I've got a lot more to thank you for," said the boy.

"How do you feel about a half brother or sister?" asked Farr.

The boy looked at him quizzically. "What?"

Farr told Howard about Harriet's pregnancy and of their intention to get married almost at once. Howard giggled disbelievingly, and said, "You're putting me on!"

"In seven months," insisted the broker.

"Holy shit!" said the boy.

"Why the surprise?" asked Farr, feigning offense. "I'm not that old."

"It's just . . . I don't know . . . I just never thought of that happening, even though you were getting married."

"Well it is," said Farr. "She's not having a particularly easy time, so I thought you could come down to New York more often. I'm not moving around anymore, so we'll be there pretty permanently."

"Great idea," said Howard. "Having a baby! Holy

shit!'' The boy became serious. ''Hey, how do you feel about it?''

''I couldn't be happier,'' admitted Farr. ''So much has been happening lately that it's only in the last few days that I've had time to work out precisely what it all means. It's all come out pretty well—bloody well, in fact.''

Howard reached impulsively across the table for his father's hand, the crowded surroundings forgotten. ''I know I've said it before, one way and another. But I want to say it again. Just once. Thanks, for what you did—for all of what you did. I won't forget it. And I'll try like hell never to let you down again.''

''It's going to be a difficult standard, never to make some sort of mistake,'' said Farr. ''I just don't want it to be one particular sort.''

''It won't be,'' promised the boy. ''Wanna know something?''

''What?''

''I don't even think about it anymore. I used to, a lot, when I first got out. Difficult, like I told you it was. But not now. There's a lot about, from other guys, I mean. Be the easiest thing in the world, to start again. But I haven't. And I won't.''

''Like I said,'' repeated the broker. ''It's all come out bloody well.''

Howard said he understood about dinner and Farr managed the six o'clock flight back to La Guardia, jammed into the home-going commuter flight. He bought a copy of the *Globe* and a paperback but couldn't concentrate on either. He'd make Harriet go to another gynecologist; ask around among people in the city and insist that she put herself in the best care possible. He smiled at his own reflection in the night-darkened window; he was going to spoil her more than she knew it was possible to be spoiled.

Farr was practically at the exit from the arrival corridor, where it widens out to the baggage reclaim and car-rental desks, when he became conscious of the P.A. system blaring his name. He stopped, searching curiously for the

information desk, wondering what it was. Harriet had
mentioned a meeting with Brennan so maybe they wanted
to involve him as well. The girl smiled when he identified
himself and said there had been a telephone call, from
someone who hadn't left his name. Before getting trans-
portation into the city, he was to pick up a message from
the message board. Farr felt the first flicker of unease as
he approached the wired, pin-stuck message pedestal, seeking an envelope under his surname initial. It was a long
business envelope and his name was neatly typed, even
with a first initial. Urgently now, Farr ripped at it and then
stood staring down at the words which had been created by
letters cut out from newspapers and magazines—an ap-
proximate type-size maintained—to make two words: FOR-
GET GOMEZ.

Farr's hand shook, not from immediate fear but from
lack of understanding. He could comprehend the approach—
there'd been enough discussion and conferences about it—
but not why it should happen here, at the airport. He stared
hurriedly around, deciding he was under observation, and
then back at the paper. He didn't know what to do, what it
meant. Maybe Harriet would. Certainly Brennan. That's
what he had to do: reach Brennan and tell him. Maybe the
district attorney, too. Farr looked at the telephone bank,
but at once dismissed the idea of standing in a public
place, pumping dimes and quarters into a slot and chasing
Brennan around God knows where.

The broker hurried from the terminal, ignoring the shared
taxi rank for a cab of his own, anxious now to get home.
The bulk of the expressway traffic was home-going, in the
opposite direction, but there still seemed to be a lot ahead,
slowing them. Farr sat with his hands tight against his
knees, in irritated impatience, several times taking the
paper from inside his jacket and staring down at it in the
intermittent light of the highway illumination, as if he
expected to learn more from repeated reading.

Farr became aware of the cars—police vehicles with
their lights flashing and unmarked limousines, around the

block—long before he reached his house, and actually had
the door open before the cab stopped moving at the ob-
struction, unable to get any nearer. He ran froward, uncaring at the shout of the unpaid driver, and as he got close
two men in civilian clothes moved to intercept him. Then
their faces opened in recognition and they made some sort
of gesture to another vehicle and Brennan and Seymour
emerged, running as Farr was.

"What's happened?"

"Where the hell have you been!" said Brennan, instead
of answering.

"Boston," said the broker. "Harriet knew."

Farr was conscious of the looks that went between the
two men and shouted, "Harriet! Where's Harriet?"

"Let's go inside the house," said Brennan.

"Where's Harriet!"

"Inside."

Farr slipped and fumbled the key in his anxiety, hurrying into the main room and turning immediately to confront them. "What happened!"

"A lot. Too much," said Brennan awkwardly. "Lang was
shot down, about three hours ago. Leaving his office in Pearl
Street. Shotguns. Died instantly . . . The notary too . . ."

"I don't care about Lang," cut off the broker. "Where's
Harriet?"

"We don't know," admitted Seymour. "We had a
meeting but she didn't keep it. We came here but couldn't
find her. We've got an all-points alert for her and it hasn't
turned up anything . . ."

"We think she's been snatched," completed Brennan,
abruptly.

For several moments Farr said nothing. Then he managed, "Oh God. Oh, my God."

"We weren't so sure, until about an hour ago," said
Brennan.

Farr blinked at the man, trying to concentrate. "What
happened an hour ago?"

"We thought they might go for you: it's obvious, after

all. Hit every sort of panic button and thought of Boston. Alerted our office there. Howard would have been their contact . . .''

". . . *Would* have been!'' interrupted Farr once more, aware of the qualification.

"They can't find him,'' said Seymour. "Not at school, dormitory, anywhere where he normally hangs out . . .''

". . . It's too soon to be sure,'' came in Brennan, in attempted assurance. "He could be a hundred places. It just doesn't look good.''

Farr felt emptied, devoid of any reaction or response; he was unable to grasp the enormity of what they were telling him. "What . . . I . . . there must be . . .''

"You're safe,'' said Brennan, misunderstanding the need for reassurance. "You're going to have someone with you even when you go to the john. We've already got a wire on the telephone here. Mail intercept, too . . .''

". . . But why . . . ?''

"Remember, we don't know yet; we're not sure. But, if they've got Harriet and Howard, then the purpose is to pressure you. When it comes, we want to get it. Immediately. And when it does, we'll get them back. Remember that: we'll get them back. Safe . . .''

Farr remembered several things, in fact. The first was the envelope and the paper with its cut-out message. Then he remembered all the guarantees and promises that Brennan had made since the beginning, guarantees and promises that had failed or had to be revised. He tightened his arm against his body, so that he could feel the outline of the envelope. And decided to say nothing about it.

It was training not to resist when resistance was futile, so Harriet didn't at the sudden moment when she was bundled into the car, too quickly even to scream an alarm at any passerby. She tried to control the fear, to be the professional she was, and one of the initial realizations was that they were professionals, too, not holding the gun against her body, where to fire it would have killed her—

because what good is an immediately dead hostage?—but instead against the very side of her knee, which was far more frightening because they could have fired then, shattering her kneecap and crippling her for life but not wounding sufficiently to kill her. The professionalism decreed that she note and remember everything, so she tried to memorize what the four men looked like for a later description, and she noted the bridge they crossed and recognized Queens and the waterfront roads, on the little-used section of the wharves, where the redevelopment was taking place and where there were no ships and therefore no activity. The one to the left, who wasn't holding the gun to her knee, had his hand across his body anyway, against her breast, feeling her up, but she didn't pull away because another part of the training was to avoid their anger and keep everything as calm as possible.

Ramos, who was the one holding the gun, gestured her out of the car when it stopped and into a warehouse alongside one of the empty, decaying wharves. It was a vast, echoing place but just inside the part against the water's edge there were what had obviously once been some sort of administrative offices. Most of the windows were broken and there was the drip of water from some leaking pipes and a smell of dampness and rot. As soon as Harriet entered, she saw that two of the divided rooms had what seemed to be comparatively new mattresses on the floor and a supermarket sack of groceries. Alongside the grocery bag was a six pack of beer and a bottle of wine.

Discerning, from the respect that the others showed to him, that Ramos was the leader, Harriet turned to him, attempting to prevent any nervousness showing and said, "So, OK. What do you want?"

"Cooperation," said Ramos simply. "If there's cooperation, then everything is going to be all right." He indicated the furthest office, where there were no side windows through which she might have attempted an escape, the only exit being through the outer rooms they were to occupy. "You're there," he said. "Get in."

The Colombian who had sat on the other side watched her enter the secure room and said, "I want her. I know she wants it, too. Liked it, in the car."

"Not yet," said Ramos. "Later."

Howard's prison was near the water, too, but much smaller than Harriet's, a hurriedly discovered and entered disused boathouse on the Charles River, close to the Longfellow Bridge. There was no division of rooms and the only bedding was some wet, rotting canvas of long-ago sails and some survival jackets from which the padding had leaked.

They thrust him with intentional roughness ahead of them into the place, knowing how insecure it was and wanting to frighten him into immediate acceptance of his captivity.

"It's my father, isn't it?" said the boy defiantly.

"Motherfucker," said one of the Colombians.

"A brave guy who fucked you!" said Howard, stupidly forcing the defiance.

The Colombian who'd spoken hit out suddenly, pistol-whipping the boy across the face, splintering his nose and sending him screaming back onto the canvas. The concern of the men was at the noise rather than the injury, and a second man said, "You shouldn't have done that."

The spokesman said dismissively, "He had to be frightened. So now he's frightened . . ." He stared around the stinking hut. "Hope we don't have to stay around here too long."

27

The gangland slaying of Norman Lang made feverish the already intensive publicity on the eve of the court hearing, so that it dominated every newspaper and occupied every television newscast. By the second day the Bureau acknowledged the kidnap, but managed to suppress publicity. With Harriet—one of their own officers—it was easy. In Boston it was explained that Howard had made an abrupt disappearance before, when he went into the Eastham clinic—although Farr insisted that the FBI tell the truth to Jennings, up in Boston. Farr's house became a fortress, a crowded place of openly armed men shielding him completely, taking every telephone call and opening every piece of mail, angrily impatient for the kidnap demand that only Farr knew would never come. It had been more impulsive than instinctive to withhold it from Brennan, but having done so Farr realized that he couldn't produce it now because his earlier failure proved his willingness to cooperate. And it was right that he should cooperate. Too many of Brennan's assurances *hadn't* been fulfilled and with two people—the only people—in the world whom he loved, Farr decided that he could not take the slightest risk.

The day before Farr was scheduled to testify to the preliminary hearing, he was smuggled in under armed escort for the last conference with the district attorney,

Brennan and Seymour. They met, as before, in the Justice building and as soon as Farr sat down Harrop said, "I know how it is for you; how it goes beyond Howard. I'm very sorry."

"Thank you," said Farr.

"The lack of contact doesn't make sense," protested Seymour. "There should have been something."

"They obviously feel it isn't necessary," said Harrop. "That the killing of Lang was the message."

"How does it leave us?" demanded the determined Brennan.

"Weak," said Harrop, at once. "We had the best case of all against Lang, and I'd already been getting signs from his counsel that he was prepared to plea bargain and turn states' evidence—which would have guaranteed everything . . ." The lawyer hesitated, looking sympathetically at Farr again. "And, although Miss Becker's evidence wasn't vital, it was corroborative of some of the transactions between the Caymans and New York, and now I don't think we're going to have that . . ." The man made another pause, still looking at Farr. "So," he said, "everything devolves now almost entirely upon you. Certainly—I would say—in the case of Gomez."

"Scarletti?" queried Brennan anxiously.

"Mr. Farr's already positively identified Scarletti in a deposition," the district attorney reminded him. "With Scarletti we're in better shape; I'd have liked it to be stronger, but I think there's enough. Just."

"We should have been more careful," said Brennan in bitter recrimination. "We knew what sort of bastards we were dealing with. We should have anticipated it and mounted some sort of protection."

"There was nothing we could have done about Lang," pointed out the other FBI man. "He hadn't actually turned states' evidence. He was still a charged defendant; his counsel wouldn't have let us within a million miles of him."

"What about Harriet?" demanded Farr, with a bitterness different from Brennan's.

"We've had witnesses interfered with before," said Seymour. "Members of the public. Never one of our own people. No one's ever risked moving against a member of the Bureau like this. And I can't understand why they've moved against your son, instead of you. So much of this doesn't make sense."

Could they have done something if he'd given them the letter: traced somebody through fingerprints that might have been on it, for instance? A possibility, Farr supposed. But only a possibility. Still, it was something he couldn't have risked putting to the test. He said, "How long will I be on the stand?"

"All day," said Harrop. "Not longer, I wouldn't have thought. They're taking a chance, making a grand jury appearance; normally their attorneys advise against it, until the full hearing. Indicates they're going for a nonreturn of an indictment."

What would happen if a formal charge were returned against Gomez anyway? wondered Farr, in a sudden surge of despair. He said, "They've been kidnapped, right? I know you've said you'll get them back but what are the odds? No bullshit."

The other three men looked awkwardly from one to the other, each unwilling to be the person to reply. It was Brennan who finally responded. He said, "There's no average, no way of knowing, in a case like this. If we get a break, establish contact, we've got a chance. Hint a deal, talk about the penalties—which can frighten the shit out of them, despite their probably being professional criminals."

"That's pretty fair summation," endorsed Harrop. "We'll keep a public lid on the kidnapping—say nothing at the trial—until there's contact."

Farr was glad he had repeated the question. It was the sort of reply that Brennan had given before, the night of the Boston return, but now he had the district attorney's confirmation: officially there wasn't a chance in hell of getting them back. It was confirmation, too, that what he'd done—and intended to do—was right.

Seymour said, "Forgive me if, by being frank, I'll be brutal?"

Farr swallowed, looking at the second FBI man. "Yes," he said.

"Like Peter said earlier, no one's ever risked moving against the Bureau like this because they know damned well that it becomes a personal thing, for every one of us," said Seymour. "They know we'll go on, for as long as it takes, to get whoever it is back. And they know best of all that, if they cause that person any harm, we'll tear the bricks out of the houses to get at them."

"What are you saying?"

"That we've got to accept that Scarletti's or Gomez's people—or both—have got Harriet. And Howard. To pressure you. OK, so they'll risk the pressure but there's no way they'll risk causing them any permanent harm."

"You sure of that?"

"We're sure of that," supported Brennan.

He wasn't, thought Farr; he wasn't sure of anything anymore. He said, "I hope you're right. Dear God, I hope you're right."

"Don't . . . ." began Harrop carelessly, but managed to stop before he said "worry." Awkwardly—the nervousness at once surfacing—he said instead, "I'm sure everything is going to work out all right."

Now it was Farr's turn to look at each of them in turn. He said, "I wish I were."

So efficient had been the sealing off of 63rd Street in general, and Farr in particular, that the broker's arrival for the grand jury's hearings was the first opportunity for the media to get within photographic or shouting distance. He entered completely enclosed in a kraal of protective agents, blinded by the camera flashes and television lights, unable to decipher the babble of screamed and shouted questions. It was, anyway, a passing, unimportant impression: Farr's mind was concentrated upon the examination room, and who he would see in it.

After the flustered entry there was an abrupt, surprising calm. Still phalanxed by his FBI protectors, he was hurried through footstep-echoing corridors to a witnesses' anteroom where, almost absurdly after the previous days' unremitting close attendance, he was left momentarily quite alone. Then Harrop entered, through a door different from that which led out onto the corridor.

"OK?" asked the district attorney.

"Of course I'm not OK," said Farr, the strain breaking through.

"Sorry. Thoughtless. There's nothing, incidentally. No news."

"I know."

The lawyer shifted uncomfortably just inside the entrance to the room. He jerked his head in the direction of what Farr presumed to be the hearing chamber. "Going well in there," he said.

"I'm glad for you," said Farr.

Harrop retreated, backing through the door. "You'll be called immediately," he said. "A few minutes."

Farr turned away as the door closed behind the man, irritated by Harrop's blatantly forced behavior. Farr did not believe in God, so there was no normal difficulty if he had to lie under oath. It came down to practicalities, and the only practicality was keeping Harriet and Howard alive. If that meant a drug trafficker escaping justice, then, Farr decided, he couldn't give a fuck. He had already decided, weeks and months ago, that he had done all and more than had been demanded of him. Only Harriet—saving Harriet—mattered. Farr became at once hot with embarrassment at the way his mind automatically organized priorities: Harriet *and* Howard, he corrected himself.

Farr was frightened when the summons came from the court usher. Frightened because it was the moment when he would see for the first time—because Harrop had insisted that no official record photographs be shown, to prevent a

challenge of collusion when it came to identification—if
the man seized aboard the *Mary Ann* was the man he
knew from the encounter in Lang's office as Jorge Herrera
Gomez.

It was. Farr made the identification as he entered. Farr
had steeled himself for the recognition, tensed against
there being any reaction. The turmoil in his mind made it
momentarily difficult to control his thoughts. The predom-
inant one was that he had made the right decision in not
disclosing the demand note. The FBI method would have
been complicated and possibly confused in the way he was
already familiar with—half starts and changes of direction—
and all the time Gomez's men would be aware of the hunt
and doing something stupid. This course was simple: he
understood, and Gomez knew he understood, and everything would be OK.

He took the stand, swore unhesitatingly to tell the truth
and sat where he was told. Harrop was directly in front of
him, with Scarletti and Gomez to the right, flanked by
their counsel. Also to the right was the stenographer. The
grand jury—the group who had to decide whether there
was sufficient evidence to form an indictment and bring
the two men formally to trial—was assembled to his left in
two tiers.

For the benefit of the official record, Harrop unnecessarily
explained the procedure and then embarked upon the evidence, beginning not with Howard's arrest and the FBI
pressure but by suggesting that the FBI approach had been
without motive: a law-enforcement body had merely asked
a public-spirited citizen for assistance. It would make his
intended perjury easier, decided Farr, if he agreed that it
was as the district attorney suggested it had been. Increasingly Farr took over the narrative, not needing Harrop's
prompting, recounting without difficulty from his precise
financier's memory the details of Lang's approach, his
meetings with two men named Julio Scarletti and Jorge
Gomez and the European tour to establish their companies.
He confirmed the names and the holdings of those compa-

nies and the money transacted through them, and was grateful that the attentive district attorney insisted that everything Farr had done had been in the furtherance of the FBI investigation and never for personal gain, and produced the details of the escrow holding into which Farr had deposited his cash commissions. Several times during the difficult explanation of money transfers and sideways movements of currency, Harrop took him back, to repeat and clarify, determined for his case that there should be no misunderstanding.

Farr was conscious of walking a tightrope; he knew it would be wrong for him to give the protracted evidence without looking in the direction of Scarletti and Gomez. So he did so deliberately, and then frequently, as he got more fully into his account and felt more relaxed with his surroundings. It was statue looking at statues: Farr tried to remain impassive—difficult because of the hard churning hatred he felt for Gomez—and the two men sat in apparent calm, regarding him with matching blankness. Farr's difficulty went beyond his detestation for the Colombian: he was numbed by his inability to make some sign to the man that he was going to comply and to receive an indication that Gomez understood as well, and that Harriet and Howard would be freed as soon as he met the ransom demand.

Harrop led Farr through the documents, making the photostats available to the jury, and the broker verified them, only half concentrating, knowing that the moment could not be long coming.

"Mr. Farr," said the district attorney. "There was an occasion, very early on, when you had a meeting in the office of Norman Lang with two men?"

"Yes," said the broker.

"Two men introduced to you as Julio Scarletti and Jorge Herrera Gomez?"

"Yes."

"And for those two men, with the knowledge of the authorities, you created a situation whereby they could export large sums of money from the United States of America?''

"That is so.''

"Money you came to understand to be the proceeds on narcotic trafficking and dealing?''

"I did believe that,'' said Farr.

"Will you look around this room, Mr. Farr, and tell the jury if you recognize Julio Scarletti and Jorge Herrera Gomez?''

It was not the way Farr had expected the question to be put and he hesitated, looking back to the two men, flanked by their counsel. He said, "I recognize Scarletti.''

Harrop was watching the jurry expectantly. He turned his head sharply, and said, "Scarletti!''

"Sitting there,'' said Farr, indicating.

Now it was the district attorney's turn to hesitate. Slowly he said, "What about Gomez?''

Farr stared directly at the Colombian for several moments. Then he said in a strong voice, "No. This is not the man whom I met in the office of Norman Lang.''

There were several reactions. Harrop twisted, frowning at Brennan and Seymour, and there was a head-jerk, too, by Scarletti, who looked first to Gomez, then up at Farr, then back to Gomez. Farr was conscious, as well, of an exchange of looks between the jury.

"Mr. Farr,'' said Harrop hurriedly. "I want you to be quite sure about this. You are positive that the man whom you met in the lawyer's office is not the man here today, brought before the jury in the name of Jorge Herrera Gomez?''

"Quite sure.'' He'd done it, thought Farr. It had been remarkably easy and he felt no guilt whatsoever.

Ramos was the first to have Harriet and then the others followed, and because they were drunk three of them took her at the same time. She was only half conscious when Ramos returned from making the telephone call, to learn what happened at the hearing.

"Everything went as planned?" said the man who had groped Harriet in the car on the day of the kidnap.

"Perfectly," said Ramos.

The man gestured toward the back room, to the curled-up figure of the woman. "What about her now?"

"We'll make an example," said Ramos. "Show everyone we're untouchable." He wasn't just doing it to show the Americans, thought Ramos; he was doing it to prove to Gomez he hadn't failed after all.

It took a long time for Harriet to die, because they all abused her again before the attack. Not as long, however, as it did Howard, because when the boy realized they intended to kill him anyway, he tried a frenzied escape and badly hurt one of his captors, partially blinding the man with a kick, so they determined he should suffer. Which he did, terribly.

28

The grand jury returned indictments on all counts against
Julio Scarletti but failed to agree on Gomez, who was
immediately freed. Farr saw it all on television in his
blockaded house, overcome with relief at the sight of the
slim, saturnine Colombian being hurried away from the
court, face shielded and a ring of men keeping photogra-
phers and reporters from him. The broker kept switching
newscasts, to remain constantly up to date, and on ABC he
saw the departure of Gomez on a Bogotá-bound flight,
within hours of his release. How long before he heard?
wondered Farr. There would be a confrontation with Brennan and the district attorney, he supposed: Harriet and
Howard would obviously know the connection between
their captors and Gomez and from that Brennan would
know he'd perjured himself. It was conceivable that they
might consider some sort of action against him for perjury,
although Farr doubted it because it would deflect from the
ongoing prosecution against Scarletti. Farr did not give a
damn, not about any confrontation or legal action. He had
done the only sensible thing.

He moved impatiently around the house, alert for the
sound of the monitored telephone that never rang, unable
to settle anywhere for long. He poured a drink he didn't
want and finally forced himself to remain in the main
lounge, where the larger television was, so that he could

watch the later broadcasts. They contained nothing beyond what he heard earlier but it was at least a way to occupy himself. He went finally to bed, because there was nothing else to do, but not to sleep. He took off his shoes and lay dressed on top of the covers, not wanting there to be the delay of even minutes when the news came. He tried to read but couldn't concentrate, so he stopped bothering, lapsing into a half-doze from which he kept blinking awake at the smallest house-sound or noise from outside, in the guarded street or beyond. He got up early, when it was only half-light, and showered and changed—doing both quickly, in case the call came—and made coffee and went back to the television, for the early newscasts. Because it remained the major story, the indictment against Scarletti and the freeing of Gomez was repeated but there was no further development overnight.

He would give it until ten and then call Brennan, Farr decided. He guessed that the FBI supervisor would contact him the moment he heard anything, but at least he would be doing something; it was the inactivity as well as the uncertainty that was irritating the broker. No later than ten, definitely.

Brennan would create hell when Harriet and the boy were freed and the man discovered what he'd done. Farr expected it and decided he could not give a fuck; only one priority, he thought again, in familiar litany. He knew Brennan did not fully believe him—Seymour and Harrop maybe, but not Brennan. That had been obvious from the meeting afterward, in the district attorney's chambers. Farr had rigidly maintained his insistence that Gomez was not the man he'd met in Lang's office, knowing they couldn't prove otherwise. But Brennan's attitude was suspicious and accusatory; he subjected Farr to a virtual interroga-tion, until Harrop pulled the man back from some of the cross-questioning, and even then it hadn't stopped. I hope to hell you haven't done anything stupid, Brennan had said, in parting. Despite the apprehension, Farr smiled, sure that he hadn't. Farr was not worried about Brennan.

He could withstand any anger and attack from the FBI man—even official accusation, if they felt strongly enough to make any sort of case out of it. Anything, just as long as Harriet and the boy were OK.

Today, thought Farr; please make it today.

The arrangement was that he would not answer his own telephone; that one of the FBI men would respond, pretending to be staff, for the proper monitoring facilities to be triggered and the source traced during the apparent delay in connection. Farr had become accustomed to it—although he continued to start instinctively toward the instrument at the first sound, then held back. Because the routine was familiar by now, he was surprised at the quickness with which a bulging-stomached man named Edmington, who was that week's FBI supervisor, came into the room after taking the call. The quickness was not the only unusual thing; Edmington was usually polite—almost excessively so. In the past he had always knocked; this morning he did not.

He seemed flustered upon entry, as if he had forgotten his usual manner. "Oh, you're here. It's Brennan: he's coming. Soon."

Farr smiled in anticipation. "They're OK?"

"Brennan's coming."

"I didn't ask that," said Farr. "I asked if they're OK."

"He won't be long."

"Isn't it about Harriet? Howard?"

"I don't know," said the other man. "He just called and said he'd be here soon. That he wanted to talk to you."

Farr looked uncertainly at the FBI official. The attitude was understandable if Harriet had explained what had happened and Brennan—and the Bureau—knew how he'd lied, on oath. He said, "Do you know if they're OK?"

"No," said Edmington. Hurriedly, he said, "I mean, we didn't talk about it. He's coming."

Brennan arrived soon afterward. The FBI supervisor entered abruptly, with Seymour behind him, but, once

inside the house, the man seemed unaware of their surroundings, stopping immediately as if unsure of their way
and staring around the lobby. Farr was expectantly at the
drawing-room door, gesturing them forward urgently, looking beyond them for Harriet—this was her home, after all.

Neither Brennan nor Seymour responded at once to the
encouragement. Both remained where they were.

Farr looked between the two men and said, "They're
OK? You've found Harriet? And Howard?"

Still there was no response. At last, they moved. There
was further awkwardness, neither seeming sure if they
should sit or stand. Brennan said to Farr, "You got a
doctor?"

"Of course I've got a doctor," said Farr, confused.

"Maybe we should get him," said Brennan.

"Get him? Why . . . ?" Farr stopped, conscious of his
own stupidity. ". . . They hurt . . . ?"

"We weren't thinking of them. Not of Harriet or Howard," said Seymour quietly.

"I don't . . ." started Farr.

"I'm sorry," said Brennan. "I'm really sorry. I didn't
think—hoped—that it would be like this."

"Like what?" After the emotions of the preceding weeks
and months, Farr expected to have some reaction. Incredi-
bly, he didn't. It was as if he were suspended above it all,
an uninvolved observer of the conversation and interaction
of himself and Brennan and Seymour. Not waiting for
Brennan to reply to one question, Farr posed more. "You've
found them, haven't you?" he said. "They're all right?"

"They're dead," said Brennan.

There was a long silence, which was finally punctured
by Farr with a wail of echoing, plaintive despair. "No! Oh
dear God, no!"

"Sorry," said Brennan. "All I can say is, I'm sorry.
How we're both sorry."

"That wasn't . . ." started Farr. "You said you could
find them," he completed. "Get them back."

"We did everything we could," said Brennan. "There was so little."

"Fucking liar!" erupted Farr. "You did fuck all! Nothing! Let them die."

"It won't mean much, not now," said Seymour. "But it was true what I said during the meeting with the district attorney. Harriet was one of us and so it was an attack upon one of us. We *did* take the bricks out of the houses. We had every informant and streetman and contact on the entire eastern seaboard turned over and shaken, for just a clue. There was nothing: believe me, there was nothing."

Farr began to cry unashamedly; his nose ran, too, and he sobbed and he didn't care. "They shouldn't have died!"

"They have," insisted Brennan. "Don't run from it, not from the truth. They're dead. I always feared they would be but I tried to convince you—convince myself— that they'd be all right. That it wouldn't happen."

"You didn't say," said Farr emptily.

"Of course I didn't say."

"Conviction was too important?"

"Would it have helped?"

"Would anything have helped?"

"That was the problem," admitted Seymour. "Nothing would have helped. Certainly not telling you what it was going to be like."

Farr shut his eyes, against the men in the room and against what they were telling him and against the possible mistake he'd made—although he still wasn't sure it was a mistake—and against what it meant.

"We want you to agree to something," said Seymour, seemingly from a distance.

Reluctantly Farr opened his eyes, knowing they were still there and that what they were telling him still existed: that Harriet was dead and that Howard was dead. "What?" he asked dully.

"Harriet's got a relation. An uncle. Lives in San Diego. What about Howard?"

Farr tried to concentrate. "I don't know what you mean."

"Is there any other relation, apart from yourself?" said Brennan.

Farr frowned, still not understanding. "No," he said, slowly. "Ann's dead. So are her parents—my parents, too, before he was even born."

There was an exchange of looks between the two FBI men. Brennan said, "We've been in touch with Jennings at the school. Halpern, too. If you're willing—in the circumstances, we could get the coroner to agree to their providing the identification."

"What?" demanded Farr, his voice hollow.

Brennan said, "We think it would be better for Jennings or Halpern to do it."

"How bad?" said Farr, increasingly feeling the witness to someone else's conversation.

"Bad," said Brennan. "I'm sorry. Very bad."

"For Christ's sake stop telling me that you're sorry!" erupted Farr. "You couldn't give a fuck!"

The other men refused to argue with him; react in any way. Seymour said, "Is it OK with you if we have Jennings or Halpern carry out the identification?"

"No!"

"Walter," said Brennan. "I'm not going to try to pretend there's been anything like friendship between us. Try to defend or explain anything, even. Let's just say we got thrown together. There've been some foul-ups, but I always tried to keep it straight—as straight as I reasonably felt I could. Now I'm being completely straight. Let's do it our way: we're trying to help."

"What did they do to them?"

"You don't want to know."

"Don't be so fucking stupid!"

"Don't you be so fucking stupid," came back Brennan. "Don't do this to yourself."

"I won't agree to either Jennings or Halpern identifying

Howard,'' said Farr. ''I want to do it. I want to identify
Harriet—to see Harriet—as well.''

Brennan made as if to argue further but stopped at a
headshake from Seymour. The bespectacled FBI man said,
''Please. Don't do it.''

''Yes!'' insisted Farr.

They went to Boston in an FBI plane, a small executive
machine with only six seats but surprisingly luxurious,
leather-seated, and with what appeared to be a cocktail
cabinet at the rear. It was the sort of detail that registerd
with Farr in his suspended state, rather than where he was
going or what for. He was almost oblivious of the landing
and the journey into Boston, but the moment he entered
the building to which they took him he realized that it was
the one he'd gone to the night of Howard's arrest, when
the boy had hunched in the detention cell and asked him to
get drugs and made Farr wonder if they'd be able to
establish any sort of relationship ever again.

The mortuary was brightly white and smelled of formal-
dehyde and antiseptic. An attendant led them to the wall of
tiered racks, like giant filing cabinets. When they got to it,
Seymour said, ''Let's not do this. It isn't necessary. There's
no point.''

''I want to be the one.''

There'd been warning enough and despite the unreality
of his feelings, Farr had tried to be prepared—but he
wasn't, not at all, for what he saw. The anguished despair
moaned from him, in a desperate, wailing sound, at the
sight of his son. Because of the beating, everything was
obscenely bloated, not just Howard's face but his body as
well. There was no nose or ears and there were brutalized
stitch marks where his mouth had been secured, to en-
close something. Against the grotesque distortion, the bullet wound in the temple appeared surprisingly neat—con-
siderately, the attendant maintained the covering sheet over
the hugely swollen body.

''You've got to say yes,'' insisted Brennan.

''Yes,'' said Farr and then he vomited, hardly able to

turn away from the tray upon which his son's body was laid. He used the edge for support, retching and vomiting further, crying as well. The three men—Brennan, Seymour and the attendant—stood back, not so much to distance themselves but to give him room for his grief. Seymour even offered the broker a handkerchief, for his face and eyes, and after he'd used it Farr looked unsure what to do with it. Aware of the mess he'd created, he said to the attendant, "I'm sorry." The man shrugged and said, "It happens. Forget it," and Farr wondered—seizing details again—whether it often did.

Farr was unaware of their leaving the building or of entering the bar or of ordering the whisky he found cupped between his hands. "I should have listened to what you said."

Brennan and Seymour did not speak.

Farr said, "Harriet? Is Harriet like that?"

"Yes," said Brennan. "Don't do it. Don't try to see her."

Farr had to grip the glass tightly and needed to keep his head bent over the table for some moments, to stop the urge to cry again. Then he said, "No. No, I won't."

"I guess it's not much satisfaction—will never be—but at least we got the indictment against Scarletti," said Brennan. "He has to be the one responsible."

Except that it wasn't Scarletti, Farr knew.

The Colombians went home from America by a variety of different routes. Gomez flew first and direct. Ramos was pleased with the way it had gone and decided he deserved a reward, so he stayed three days in Haiti, because there was a brothel in Port au Prince specializing in very young girls, and Ramos's preference was for very young girls. It meant that he was the last to arrive in Medellin, which was the way he wanted it; everyone assembled to see him get the proper recognition for freeing Gomez. He telephoned from Bogotá and when he got to the *finca* in the Andean foothills he saw that they were assembled like some recep-

tion committee in the courtyard with its green, floral centerpiece. Ramos descended smiling from the car. The men
he'd summoned to America—both groups—were gathered
in a half-arc, and all the guards whom Ramos controlled
were waiting. As he approached, Gomez emerged from the
house, as if he'd been waiting as well. Ramos stayed
smiling in anticipation of the greeting.

"Motherfucker!" screamed the trafficker. "You were
supposed to see it didn't happen! You let me get arrested
and go through a fucking hearing! Do you know what
they've seized; that I can't get seven hundred and fifty
million dollars!"

Then he hit Ramos, a clubbing punch that so took
Ramos by surprise that the man stumbled backward and
then fell in front of everyone. As Ramos lay in the dirt
Gomez kicked him low in the stomach, so that all the
breath was driven from him and he writhed in pain. Through
misted eyes Ramos saw Gomez turn away from him and
stride back toward the main house.

29

Farr's grief was absolute. He retreated within himself, reacting automatically to outside events but practically unaware of them or of the people concerned. Angela Nolan and Faltham organized Howard's funeral and escorted Farr to it—with the now customary FBI protection. Brennan and Faltham explained the circumstances to the San Diego uncle, who was not close to Harriet and who therefore agreed to her being buried on the East Coast as well. Howard was buried in the same plot as Ann, and Farr arranged the purchase of an adjoining space for Harriet. Her funeral took place after that of his son.

Farr made no effort to leave 63rd Street for almost a month—no effort to do anything, in fact, not bothering to shave or to bathe or to change his clothes. He wouldn't have troubled to eat if the housekeeper whom the FBI finally allowed back into the house hadn't prepared things for him; even so he scarcely touched the food, oblivious to what it was. He drank too much in the first week, mostly Scotch, wanting to numb himself—it worked, to a degree, but it began to make him sick, and the hangovers worsened, so he reduced the intake, physically hurting instead of physically numb, which wasn't the way it was supposed to be.

Faltham maintained daily contact by telephone and came to the house at least three times a week. He made no comment on Farr's personal neglect. He concentrated entirely upon the business, insisting that Farr discuss things with him and forcing the broker to respond with an opinion, making Farr accept work as the support and turn away from the internally eroding self-pity. Farr rejected his friend's efforts initially, wanting to turn everything over to Faltham and get out. He told Faltham to draw up the transference documents, which Faltham refused to do—just as Angela Nolan refused when Farr gave her the same instructions. Between them, the woman and Faltham worked hard at diverting Farr from his determination to quit to achieve instead what they wanted: his return to the business. Individually they hinted and argued that there could not be the sort of change that the broker wanted until there had been what, in a limited or public company, would have been an annual general meeting, where they could examine the profit or loss of the business. It worked. Farr began to take an interest in the work that Faltham brought to 63rd Street, and Faltham began to complain at the difficulty of transporting files and dossiers between the two places and of the disadvantage they suffered at the house by not having computers available.

Faltham received the warning of Farr's return from the FBI, because the broker told them what he intended to do, and the Bureau insisted upon checking out the security of the floor with its view of Battery Park and the trade center. It enabled Faltham fully to prepare the entire staff—the clerks and the secretaries, not just the senior investment personnel—so that when Farr emerged from the elevator there was no surprised reaction whatsoever to his reappearance. From the first day of Farr's return, they burdened him with activity and decisions, but cleverly, so that it was impossible for him to suspect that he was being patronized or spoon-fed: the portfolios and investments needed examination and choices genuinely needed to be made. Angela Nolan, who had maintained his personal section of the business during the man's absence, was the most closely involved, but Faltham was constantly present as well, and when the pressure began to slacken upon Farr, after he'd reviewed everything the woman had done, it was Faltham who devised the way to sustain it. Appearing to follow Farr's wishes about the transference, he had the senior and junior brokers in the firm submit their activities for review, for an overall assessment to be made of success and viability. It meant concentration from early morning to late night for Farr, and Faltham and the woman watched with increasing satisfaction Farr's further emergence from the cocoon in which he attempted to wrap himself.

At a meeting with Faltham the day before the review with the senior managers, Farr said, "Seems we've got a pretty sound operation running here."

"Always knew we had," said Faltham. "Thought what you're going to do, when you leave?"

Farr gave an uncertain movement of his shoulders. "Maybe go back to England."

"You haven't been back to England for twenty years," said the other broker. "It would be like a foreign country to you; *is* a foreign country to you, in fact."

"Maybe stay here then."

"To do what?" persisted Faltham.

"Don't know. Haven't thought about it."

Faltham hesitated, wondering if he could go as far as he wanted. Chancing it, he said, "I think Harriet and Howard would have expected your grief. But they wouldn't have wanted you to become a recluse because of it."

Farr winced, as if the sound of their names caused him physical pain. "There's a lot you don't know," he said.

"I think I know enough to say that," insisted Faltham.

"Thank you," said Farr. "For all you've done."

"Like you said," reminded Faltham, "it's a pretty sound operation. Pity to jeopardize it."

"That wasn't what I meant," said Farr. "You've been a good friend. I recognize it—and I'm grateful."

"I don't want to take over," said Faltham. "I want things to stay as they are. Your getting out would be like running away. I don't think it's necessary; in fact, I think

it's stupid. Drama for the sake of drama; there's already
been too much of that.''

"You're being very honest," said Farr, in mild rebuke.

"Why don't you be?" invited Faltham.

"How?"

"Still want to quit?"

Farr smiled, near embarrassment. "No," he admitted.

"Good," said Faltham briskly. "Let's have the meeting, because we've prepared for it after all and it'll be a
worthwhile review and afterward go on . . ." The man
hesitated at the last moment but then finished. ". . . like
we were before.''

Which is what they did. Scarletti's trial was the only
interruption but when it came Farr was glad. He had
recovered sufficiently from the deaths of Harriet and Howard and had become irritated at the FBI protection and
wanted it over. There was the blaze of pretrial publicity,
and this time it continued through the trial because the
grand jury had been a closed hearing but the trial was
public. He saw Brennan and Seymour and Harrop again
for the pretrial preparation, and the district attorney kept
to his word and publicly exonerated Farr's firm of any
criminal activity. The murders had emerged by now, of
course: no mention was made of Farr's involvement with
Harriet, but Farr became a focal point of the trial because
of what had happened to the boy. After the trial there were
television and newspaper requests for personal interviews,
and two different legal firms made contact on behalf of
publishers who wanted him to write—or have ghostwrit-
ten, if he preferred—a book on what had happened. Farr
rejected them all. At the trial itself Farr spent almost a
week on the witness stand, cross-examined again and again
by Scarletti's lawyer, whose name was Manson. The man
concentrated, predictably, upon Farr's identification of
Scarletti—about which the broker remained adamant—and
during the questioning it emerged that Manson had attempted to subpoena Jorge Gomez but failed because the

American court writ had no validity in Colombia and the man had refused to attend voluntarily.

Farr was surprised—and pleased—at how successfully he endured the pressure. Only on the first day—responding to Harrop's lead about the creation of the company, when he remembered his and Harriet's arrival on the island—and then at the beginning of Manson's cross-examination—again distressed by memories of the beach-side bungalow—did Farr come near to any sort of breakdown, but he managed to prevent it both times. Because he was a primary witness, the judge ordered him to remain in court in the event of any reexamination arising from a later point, and so Farr was there when the jury, after a comparatively short retirement of only three hours, returned the guilty verdict and the judge imposed a sentence upon Scarletti that totaled eighteen years. He also imposed seizure orders on the property and investments made in the name of the company Farr had established for the man, further ordering that the other named director, Jorge Herrera Gomez, should forfeit his investments unless that named director appeared before an American court successfully to argue that the money had been obtained from a source other than criminal activity. There were further comments about the smashing of a major Cosa Nostra family and the promise that such activities—particularly drug trafficking—would continue to be vigorously pursued by the country's enforcement agencies. Farr sat listening, anxious for it finally to end—glad, at last, that it had.

Something lifted from his shoulders when he rose, with dutiful respect, for the judge to leave the chamber, and he watched Scarletti being led away and the court break up. For no more than seconds—he was once more able to control and disguise it—the grief was worse than at any other time during the trial, at the awareness that this would have been the moment when he and Harriet would have finally been able set about a new, untouched, unendangered, unimpeachable life. He became aware of Brennan beside him, urging him into the side conference room. Obediently Farr followed. Seymour was there, with the other three FBI technicians who formed the Caymans operation, and Harrop as well. The district attorney had arranged drinks, Californian champagne as well as hard booze, and busied himself about the room filling glasses. When he turned from the prepared table, his own drink in his hand, he looked at the broker and said seriously, "This wasn't how it was meant to be—not as any of us would have wanted it. Walter Farr did something no one else could have done and all of us here in this room know the personal cost. So this isn't a celebration; it couldn't be. It comes down to thanking Walter. He has already had our sympathy. Now he has our thanks . . ." The lawyer raised his glass and everyone responded. Farr wished they hadn't, because he felt self-conscious and irritated.

The broker smiled distantly and muttered, "Thank you." He wanted desperately to leave this room and these people whom he never again wanted to see. Brennan came up, extending his hand, and, self-conscious still, Farr responded.

"Like I said before," reminded the FBI supervisor. "It's not much of a satisfaction. But now we've done it. At least you know that the person responsible for killing Harriet is going to serve a minimum of eighteen years."

"Yes," remembered Farr. "You said it before."

Jorge Gomez acknowledged the mistake but at first only privately, to himself. Ramos deserved the humiliation: he *had* been told to double-check Lang's findings and he *had* failed, costing Gomez the arrest and the indictment hearing but worst of all seven hundred and fifty million dollars because the fucking judge knew full well that to attempt to reclaim the money would provide the proof they'd been too stupid to get from elsewhere. But Gomez acknowledged, too, that he'd acted upon impulse, in the frustrated heat of an angry moment, before he'd properly had time to consider and assess the full implications. He had escaped— escaped the sort of incarceration that Scarletti faced and which had always been his secret, wake-up-in-the-middle-of-the-night terror. But only just, by the imperceptible width of an empty shadow. He would never be so lucky again—which meant that with whatever passport or whatever identity he chose to travel he could never again maintain the frequency of the previous visits to America. They had taken photographs and fingerprints and, although his counsel had demanded their return for destruction after the grand jury clearance, Gomez knew damned well that the bastards would have taken duplicates and that his profile was recorded on every monitoring facility the immigration and customs authorities possessed. He needed an emissary, someone whom he could trust absolutely and who was accustomed, and free, to move about to reestablish the vital contacts. An emissary like Ramos, who was family—a blood tie. Ramos had his limitations, certainly; he was not able to operate as brilliantly or as effectively as Gomez knew he could on his own, but he was still capable.

Gomez was reluctant to make the apology, however, and so he tried initially to find someone else. He deputed a total of three, all of whom failed to make any sort of proper contact with American outlets, and because of the near embarrassment—the relegation of his name and reputation among the American families who mattered and the openly laughing traffickers in Colombia—Gomez stopped trying. It had to be Ramos, as he'd known it had to be Ramos for a long time but had refused to accept it.

Ramos responded to the summons like the loyal and well-paid employee he was supposed to be, halting deferentially as he entered the main room of the *finca*. Gomez urged the man further in and personally poured the drinks. Anxious to get it over, he said, "I was hasty, after returning from America."

Ramos used his drink to cover his reaction, guessing what the meeting meant but wanting everything to come from the other man. Bastard, he thought.

Reluctantly Gomez said, "I shouldn't have done what I did that day; I was upset after everything that happened. It was a mistake."

"Yes," said Ramos, sure of his advantage now.

Gomez's discomfort worsened at his awareness that Ramos knew. Bastard, he thought, in turn. He said, "I want to apologize. Restore things as they were between us."

"Yes," said Ramos again, determined to make as much as possible of the moment.

Gomez had to turn away on the pretense of going again to the drinks, to control his anger at the other man's awkwardness. "So how is it?" he said, with his back to the other man. "Can it be like it was before?"

Ramos's face was prepared by the time Gomez turned back, feigning relief that the temporary misunderstanding had been resolved. "Of course," he said. "I've been waiting for this moment."

Gomez came across the room and enveloped the man in an embrace, which Ramos reciprocated, each perfectly concealing the distastefulness they felt at the physical contact with the other.

"Forgive me," said Gomez.

"Of course," echoed Ramos. Bastard, he thought again. The attack—the shaming—had been in front of everyone and the apology in private, known only to the two of them. And too late—far too late. Ramos had already made contact with Julio Cesar Navarra and there had been two meetings between them, at La Paz and at Santa Cruz. And another one was planned, in two days' time.

Ramos suffered from the altitude of La Paz. He felt perpetual near-nausea and a lightheadedness after just one drink. Still he held back from the recognized remedy, the tea mixed with the official coca from which the unofficial cocaine was refined, nervous of feeling out toward the fire. Navarra had decreed the Sucre Palace for their meeting place and Ramos found a suite waiting when he arrived. He was expectant now, as he stood gazing over the bustling Avenue 16 de Julio, impatient for the Bolivian. Ramos was determined to repay Gomez for what the man had publicly done to him; and to make him suffer far greater humiliation.

The Bolivian trafficker arrived boisterously, heavy with gold and protectors. He insisted that the bodyguards come into the suite with him, but the two conspirators withdrew to the window area to discuss the reason for Ramos's visit.

Navarra heard Ramos out and said, "I don't understand how this is going to make it easy."

"He's dependent upon me," insisted Ramos.

"He can't be *absolutely* dependent."

"He hasn't got any choice. He's marked now and he knows it."

"How are you going to do it?"

Ramos smiled at the other man, savoring the thought. "My way," he said enigmatically.

"Kill him?"

"Something better than that," said Ramos.

A week later Ramos successfully entered America through the circuitous route via Canada. The Canadian crossing was chosen because Ramos's destination was Chicago and the Accadio family. But the Colombian did not stop at Chicago. He went instead directly to New York and spent a lot of time on 63rd Street ensuring that the FBI surveillance and the protection had been removed. He also established the regular movements of Walter Farr.

Ramos made the approach on the third night, fifteen minutes after seeing Farr enter and watching the lights prick on throughout the house. Farr personally answered the chain-secured door, frowning through the restricted gap.

"I know who killed the woman," announced Ramos. "The boy, as well."

30

Farr had considered vengeance, of course. It had been his all-consuming, never-discarded desire in those unwashed, uncaring weeks, immediately after the deaths, when he retreated inside himself. He had fantasized about going to Colombia on some sort of suicide mission, seeking Gomez out and killing the man, careless of his own fate. Even after everything Faltham and the others had done, the idea still recurred, a daydream he was rational enough to accept could never come true because he would never succeed on his own.

Now Farr gazed fixedly across the room at the strangely still, hard-bodied man whom he'd admitted to the house fifteen minutes earlier, trying to keep other thoughts out of his mind, recognizing the chance he had never dared hope for and determined not to lose it. The approach, and the man, had to be genuine because there was nothing whatsoever for him to gain. A falling-out of thieves? That was the obvious conjecture. Just as it was obvious that, if the man knew as much as he boasted, then he had to have been very much, perhaps personally, involved in the slaughter and mutilation of Harriet and Howard. Farr swallowed against the bile that came into his throat. The only thing that mattered was getting Gomez. Anything else was a distraction. For the moment at least.

"You want Gomez arrested?" queried Farr. "Jailed?"

Ramos smiled at the prospect. "It would be the ultimate humiliation for him."

"You could provide sufficient evidence of trafficking?"

"As much as you—or the FBI—want."

"Where is he living?"

"Medellin. He has houses there. I could tell you where," offered Ramos eagerly.

"Why not go to the Colombian authorities?"

Ramos laughed openly at the naiveté, stretching out his hand to form a cup. "He's got everyone like that in Colombia," he said. Ramos waved his hand. "That's his favorite expression, his boast. If I went to the authorities, it would be me who was arrested. Killed probably."

"Why have you come to me?" demanded Farr abruptly.

"I told you."

"Tell me again."

"OK," said Ramos, moving into his carefully rehearsed lie. "I'll admit it, I've worked for him. Still do, for the moment. I didn't realize, for a long time, what sort of man he was. How evil. The killings—of the woman and the boy—finally convinced me."

Farr gripped one hand over the other to control the shaking. The desire that was surging through him was to leap across the few feet separating them and pummel and beat and smash and kill the lying bastard. Had he actually touched Harriet? Howard? Tight-lipped, he said, "Tell me about that?"

Ramos looked curiously back at the broker. Then he said, "There was never any intention to let them go. They were as good as dead the moment his people got them. He said he wanted an example made."

"Said to you?"

Ramos shook his head quickly. "I wasn't involved. You must believe me. He has trained men—killers—to do that sort of thing. He laughed about it when he got back to Medellin. That's how I know."

"He trusts you?"

"Absolutely."

Farr shook his head. "I can't believe, having been arrested once, that he would take another risk."

Ramos smiled conspiratorially. "Money's the key," he said. "Money and his vanity. He tried to be number one and he failed. The other traffickers in Colombia are laughing at him. That's why he's sent me here, to try to set something up with the Chicago family. That's important for his pride. And it's important, too, to recover his money. You washed it; you know how much he lost. He'll be careful—far more careful than he was before—but if the lure is big enough, he'll finally go for it."

"And when he does, you want me to set him up for the FBI?"

Ramos nodded. "You did it once. You've got a personal reason for doing it again."

"Yes," agreed Farr reflectively. "I've got a reason for doing it again." The broker was quite in control now and confident that he could remain so. He said, "I'd need a lot from you."

"Anything you ask."

"How often could you get here—not necessarily New York, anywhere in the United States? I could always meet you."

Ramos gave an expression of uncertainty. "It depends how things go in Chicago. Probably once a month. How long would it take to set things up?"

"I don't know," said Farr, purposely vague. "I don't know yet exactly *what* I could set up." As the thoughts came to him, Farr hurried on, "He'll look for reassurance. If he thought other people—people he respected or knew at least—were channeling their money the same way, he'd probably be more inclined to go along."

"I suppose you're right," said Ramos doubtfully. "What are you asking?"

"Do you know such people; other traffickers?"

Could he achieve everything—get rid of Navarra and Gomez and take over the whole empire—in the same move? For a fleeting moment, Ramos experienced a sensation of faintness at the overwhelming prospect. He said, "It is possible."

"Think about it," urged Farr.

"You could fix it with the FBI?"

"Of course. There hasn't been any contact since the trial but it's only a matter of a telephone call." He stopped, frightened that the control of which he was so sure might be slipping. He forced himself on, "Don't forget that Harriet Becker was an FBI agent. The Bureau wants whoever did it."

"I must be kept out of it absolutely," insisted the Colombian. "I'll provide everything they want . . . do anything . . . but I mustn't be involved."

Farr saw the opportunity. "Why don't I be the liaison? If I'm the link beween you and the Bureau—if there's no actual contact—you should remain quite safe."

"That's good," agreed Ramos anxiously. "That's very good."

"There'll need to be a method of contact."

"No." Ramos wanted as much protection as possible and remembered what had happened to Gomez and Scarletti when they'd permitted a connection as tenuous as Norman Lang. "Nothing must ever come from you. Always from me. I've said every month; every month I'll make contact."

"Things will come up in between," protested Farr, who didn't like the uncertainty.

"They'll have to wait."

Don't lose the chance, thought Farr. Refusing obviously to concede, he said, "We'll see how it goes; something might be necessary, later."

"We'll see," agreed Ramos, who had no intention of changing his mind. Remembering the computer printout duplicates and telex monitoring, the man added, "And here. I'll always make it here."

"All right."

Ramos suddenly started forward on his feet, the menace almost physically visible. "Don't try to trap me. Ever," he said. "I'll never come unprepared. I'll watch. For a long time. I'll know, if there's any sort of monitor or surveillance.''

"What purpose would there be for me in trapping you?'' asked Farr, scoring. "It's Gomez I want.''

"Just so that you understand.''

"I do,'' said the broker.

"About a month, then?'' said Ramos, rising. "I can't be specific, but that's what I'll try: maybe three weeks, maybe five or six. Think about something meanwhile.''

Arrogant bastard, thought Farr. He said, "Sure, I'll think of something.'' He already had. It needed further, proper consideration. And detailed, extremely detailed, planning. But it could work.

"You'll call the FBI?'' said Ramos.

"At once,'' said Farr, who was not going to involve the Bureau until it suited him. He remembered how Howard looked in the mortuary. And always would.

The Chicago meetings went better than Ramos thought they would. The Accadio people were interested but cautious, aware of what had happened to Antonio Scarletti and wondering openly whether it was because of his association with Gomez. Ramos came prepared. He negotiated with Tony Accadio and pointed out that the lawyer who made all the arrangements and all the mistakes was Norman Lang—Scarletti's lawyer—and not anyone connected with Gomez. It was a convincing point, reinforced by the further argument that, having made the mistake of becoming entrapped by Scarletti's ineptitude, Gomez was the person who extricated himself and was now fully back in business, while Scarletti—whose appeal had been dismissed—was just beginning an eighteen-year jail sentence.

"You make a lot of sense,'' agreed Accadio, a heavy, fleshy man whose perpetual cigars were always destroyed by his nervous chewing at one end rather than by the glowing heat at the other.

"We made a mistake,'' said Ramos, in apparent confession. "We teamed up with the wrong people and we almost suffered because of it. Which is why we're making the offer to you. You want it? OK, we're in business. You don't, no hard feelings.''

It approached overconfidence but the Chicago don was impressed. He said, ''I think we want it. You'll be responsible for delivery into America. And Europe, if necessary?''

''That's the offer.''

''It's good.''

''Do we deal?''

''We deal.''

Conscious of the stakes, Ramos planned his return to Colombia with the care he was giving everything else. He took the train from Chicago across to the West Coast—playing the tourist in the observation car as they crossed never-ending Kansas—and from San Francisco booked the first stage of a Caribbean cruise, which enabled him to disembark in Panama City, beyond the interest or jurisdiction of U.S. customs, and fly from there to Bogotá. It was ironical that Panama was the country in which Farr had decided to establish himself, for what he intended to do. He was actually staying in the Intercontinental, with a view of the canal, when Ramos's ship disembarked by tender. Ramos, in a hurry, went straight to the airport.

31

Farr was sure he had thought everything out by the time he got to Panama. He could remember as if hearing a recording everything that Ramos said during the surprise Manhattan encounter, but remained particularly aware of the warning of Gomez's nervousness, because of what happened before. Panama, calculated Farr, was the best choice to allay that nervousness. It was, after all, immediately adjacent to Colombia—which, he hoped, would give Gomez the impression of being close to the control of his money. And it was an established and recognized tax haven he was confident he could manipulate. He hoped that, when everything was established, it would be as convincing for Ramos.

Farr was working backward along the essential chain. He chose first a lawyer named Francisco Zarak, who had an office on the vía España. Farr was reminded, as they talked, of the meeting he had attended with Lang, months before, when he had established the initial company for the Colombian through the Swiss outlets; he decided that what he was doing would not have been possible if Lang were still alive. Farr explained that he wanted a company established for which Zarak would be the named holder, acting on behalf of Colombians. Such an arrangement was perfectly legal under Panamanian tax law, and Zarak, a neat, summer-suited, unresponsive man, dutifully copied down

the details. Farr provided Medellin as the city of domicile
and explained that, in the early operating stages, he expected the company to be a holding institution, receiving
large sums of money for the creation of liquidity to make a
major purchase. Farr produced a bank draft—purchased in
cash and made out to bearer and therefore untraceable—in
the sum of 250,000 dollars for the opening funding and
establishment costs. It was his own money and he didn't
expect to get it back—knew he couldn't get it back—but
regarded it as a justifiable expense. It took only a week to
prepare the formalities—the most important of which was
a verifiable date for the forming of the company—and in the
times between the meetings with Zarak, Farr sought out
another lawyer, for the formation of the other necessary
company.

The second lawyer's name was Roberto Meiss, and he
had an office on the Plaza Cinco de Mayo, where Farr's
hotel was located. Farr's approach to the second Panamanian was quite different from that to Zarak. Farr announced that he was on an investigatory visit, acting for
clients who were considering setting themselves up in the
country but wanted to be sure of its advantages before
making any commitment. Meiss was an urgent, plump man
who smiled a lot, bulging his cheeks, an immediate contrast to Zarak. The man went carefully through the schemes
available and Farr politely listened, as if he were unaware
of them, and at the end of the explanation he thanked the
man and said that it certainly seemed as if the benefits
were better here than in any of the Caribbean islands so far
considered; he would have to report back, of course, but he
felt that Meiss could expect another visit very shortly.

Farr initiated other inquiries before flying south, and by
the time he returned to New York, the necessary information was waiting. He had chosen Hawaii with the same care
as Panama, considering that it fitted what Ramos would
expect—and that it would also interest Gomez and whoever else was involved. There were several development
schemes on the main island, two of which he marked as

possibilities, but he was far more attracted to an elaborate prospectus for the adjoining island of Maui. Farr isolated that as the best choice—because the money-washing opportunities were greatest there.

Farr was ready three weeks after Ramos's visit. He was on the lookout for flaws and decided it was feasible—not perfect, but feasible. Now all he could do was wait. He was impatient as he had been before, finding the normal operations of the office irksome. It gave him time, at least, to consider the office. He decided he would not behave as he had before—certainly not toward Faltham, who had shown him such friendship during the past few months. Farr supposed that there could be some personal danger. So Faltham and Angela Nolan and all the others who had been so loyal should be protected. He'd go through with the ownership transference after all, so that if anything did happen to him, the firm—and the people—wouldn't be endangered. Farr realized that he would have to tell Faltham what he was doing.

Ramos called on the Wednesday of the fourth week from an untraceable pay phone. Farr said he wanted the meeting and the cautious Colombian told the broker not to leave the house for the next few evenings. Farr said he wouldn't. Ramos came unannounced on Friday.

They went as before into the main room and the Colombian demanded at once, "You've worked something out?"

"I think so," said Farr.

"What?"

"Panama," said Farr. "It's close to Colombia, which I thought important. It's a bank secrecy country. There's no tax on foreign-sourced income of either companies or individuals. It permits shareholders' or directors' meetings in any location, so Gomez wouldn't have to leave Colombia. And it allows companies to be established in lawyers' names. I've been down, checked it all out. There's a lawyer named Roberto Meiss, with an office on the Plaza Cinco de Mayo. He'll act, if we want him to."

"Gomez has got to *come* out, if the FBI are going to be able to make an arrest," protested Ramos.

"What about someone else being involved in the company?" said Farr. This was vital to his plan.

"I've got an idea," said Ramos. "A Bolivian. I was waiting until today, before taking it further."

Farr offered the other man the development details he'd obtained for Hawaii. Ramos looked down and then frowned up, for an explanation. Farr said, "That's how we get Gomez out, into FBI jurisdiction. Because Hawaii is America. You said the lure had to be big enough and I think this is. There are several choices, but I think Maui is best. It's a leisure complex, between Hana and Keanae. They're inviting staged investments, but if we could propose enough money I think we should go for the whole thing. It's got every advantageous argument, as far as Gomez is concerned. He'd be buying from a foreign company into American real estate, so he'd get tax concessions. And, like I said, Panama doesn't tax foreign-sourced income, so the profits wouldn't be touched. He'd be making money both ways. Being a leisure complex, hotels and amusements and bars, there would be dozens, maybe hundreds, of tills. He could wash any money he liked, as if he were in a laundromat."

Ramos smiled in admiration at the presentation. "All to set Gomez up," he said, regretfully. "Seems too good to throw away."

There was always the greed, thought Farr. He said. "There are a lot of other things just as good. Maybe even better."

Ramos made as if to speak, to make the approach for which the broker was hoping, but then he changed his mind. Farr said, "Well, what do you think?"

"The bait's good, like I said," congratulated the Colombian. "What about the FBI?"

"I told you what their reaction would be," reminded Farr, seeing another opportunity. "But there are problems."

"Like what?" demanded Ramos, instantly concerned.

"If we can get him out to Maui, then fine, we've got an arrest. But on what charges? Sure I can assemble the details of the currency transactions, like the first time. But then we had Scarletti: evidence of criminal activities within the United States. Gomez would be committing no crime, trying to buy into a real estate development in Hawaii through a foreign company. There has to be the way of showing that the funds of that foreign company were generated from here . . .'' He paused and then reminded the other man, ''Last time here you said you could provide evidence . . . Everything they wanted, you said . . .''

Ramos stared across at the broker, considering his response. He remembered giving the undertaking but it had been automatic, without real consideration of what he was saying. He supposed that, to make it work, he had to provide details of the Accadio connection but he had hoped to continue with that after he replaced Gomez and Navarra. He said, ''It wouldn't work without that?''

''You don't have to ask the question,'' pressed Farr. ''Look at it logically. Where's the criminality?''

Again there was no immediate reply. Then Ramos conceded, ''I suppose you're right.''

''They need evidence,'' reiterated Farr.

The demand off-balanced Ramos, who found it difficult at once to see the advantages over the disadvantages. It would be the second organized-crime group in America to be brought down, and this time it would create a tidal wave rather than the ripple that had spread through the families the first time. But tidal wave against whom? Ramos thought, pleased as the answer immediately came to him. Gomez had been involved with Scarletti and, publicly at least, it would be Gomez involved with Accadio—doubling, or maybe tripling, the humiliation, among the Cosa Nostra in the country where Gomez wanted to appear the big man. With no danger to Ramos himself. No danger whatsoever. He would have to be cautious directly afterwards: not emerging too soon, obviously to fill the gaps and pick up the pieces. And he wouldn't have to emerge too soon. If he deposed Gomez and Navarra at the same time, then the combined operation would be his—the cocaine monopoly would be his—and he would be able to afford to sit back and just wait for the American outlets to come to pay court to him. He looked up toward the broker, his considerations complete. He said, "No problem with evidence. No problem at all."

"Who is it this time?" prompted Farr gently.

There was the briefest hesitation, at the moment of commitment, and then Ramos said, "Accadio. They operate out of Chicago. A known family."

"How's it work?"

Ramos swallowed, reluctant at the increasing knowledge the other man was obtaining—he supposed there was no alternative, but it made him nervous. "Simple. The stuff is couriered in through all sorts of routes. They distribute."

"And you collect the money?" said the broker. Farr thought he knew enough to make the guess but that's what it was still, a guess that could have been wrong, and he was apprehensive of the reply.

The now perpetually hesitating Ramos looked silently at the broker for several moments and then said, "Yes. I collect the money."

Farr was ready. There was no indication of the inner satisfaction, the fitting of another link into the chain that had begun in Panama. Instead, hurrying the man beyond the admission, he said, "Excellent. Absolutely excellent."

"Why?" asked Ramos suspiciously.

Farr accentuated the frown. "Don't you think another bagman might have wanted details? This way it stays exactly as it should: strictly between us."

Ramos's face relaxed. "You're right." Everything was unfolding far more clearly than he had hoped it would; Farr was a clever, devious bastard.

Farr hadn't expected it to be quite so easy. He said, "Everything depends upon you now. You've got to persuade Gomez and whoever your Bolivian is to go ahead with the formation of a company. And pass on to the FBI, through me, the connection with Chicago."

"You'll get it," promised Ramos.

So, thought Farr, will you.

"No!" erupted Faltham.

"That's the way I'm going to do it," insisted Farr.

"You're mad," said the other broker. "I really mean that. Mad. You know what happened last time, for Christ's sake. And the FBI—the professionals—were involved then. Harriet and Howard still got slaughtered."

"I never got the impression that the FBI were very professional," said Farr.

"That's crap and you know it," rejected the other man. "I won't let it happen."

"But I'm going to bring the FBI into it," said Farr. "I've explained that."

"Bring them in now!"

"I want to get the man who killed Harriet and Howard," reminded Farr. "The only contact I've got is someone who takes two days to check out this house before he'll make an approach. It's got to be my way for it to have any chance of success."

"They'll kill you," said Faltham, with forced calmness. "You know that, don't you? They'll kill you like they killed Harriet and Howard."

"No, they won't," said Farr. "It's a one hundred to one possibility. But because it's even a possibility, I want the transference to go through. So that the firm and everyone in it will be protected."

Faltham sighed at the other man's obduracy. "When in the name of God is this all going to end?" he said. "And how?"

"This time," promised Farr. "It's going to end this time. And with the proper sort of punishment."

32

Anxious though he was to replace not just Gomez but Navarra as well, Ramos proceeded with the necessary caution, fully aware that just one miscalculation would ruin everything—which meant that the idea must come from Gomez, rather than be suggested to him. Ramos guessed it wouldn't take long and it didn't; it happened within days of the first successful shipment to Chicago and the resulting payment, of thirty million dollars.

"It's got to be invested," insisted Gomez. They were in the coastal villa at Riohacha, with four girls they had flown in from Medellin. Gomez insisted that Ramos share the villa and the women, to show the man just how much their old relationship had been reestablished.

"After last time!" said Ramos, the reaction already prepared.

"So things went wrong—it happens," said Gomez. "This time we'll be more careful. Not take recommendations from the Accadio people, for instance."

"You want me to do it?" anticipated Ramos.

The trafficker nodded. "But I'll want to check every step of the way—no mistake like last time."

"Sure," said Ramos.

"You did well, making the Chicago contact."

"Thank you," said Ramos. "Looks like it might work good."

"I'm glad everything's OK between us now," said Gomez. "I need someone like you, whom I can trust."

"Everything's going to be fine," said Ramos, for his own satisfaction. "Just fine."

It was a week before Ramos felt he could justifiably go to Bolivia and he let the initial meetings with Navarra proceed as the Bolivian grower expected, restricted to talk about availability and profits and the new tie-up with the Chicago family. It was only on the last day that he brought up the subject of Gomez's investment and he did so as if the company formation had actually been initiated and Gomez knew about the Hawaiian leisure complex.

"How much profit?" demanded Navarra.

"Double, from the prospectus I've seen," said Ramos. He allowed just the right hesitation and added, "Interested?"

"Would it mean getting into some sort of partnership with Gomez?"

"Initially," smiled Ramos. "But Gomez isn't going to be around for long, is he?"

Navarra answered the smile, seeing the point. "Which means things could revert to single ownership."

"Exactly," said Ramos. "Why not have your lawyers check Hawaii out?"

"You could guide me through, to get alongside Gomez?"

"He's asked me to coordinate the whole thing," said Ramos. "So it's no problem. Still like you to get an independent assessment of the investment, though. Satisfy yourself it's OK."

"We'll talk further."

Ramos flew from La Paz to Venezuela, so he could make the American entry from a country that did not attract as much customs interest as the source countries of Colombia, Bolivia, and Peru. He collected another payment—thirty-three million dollars this time—from Chicago and carefully watched Farr's house for almost two days before making the approach. The Colombian disclosed Navarra's identity for the first time, and Farr agreed it had been a good idea to allay any suspicion by suggesting that Navarra

should have the leisure complex checked out independently. The broker lied easily, saying the FBI were already
creating an operation on the island, and at Farr's urging
Ramos outlined the details of the Accadio connection.

"How soon can we establish in Panama?" demanded
Ramos.

"As soon as you like," said Farr. "Could you go down
this trip?"

Ramos hesitated. "I guess so."

Farr was alert to the other man's doubt and hurried on,
wanting to get advantage from it. "I'll come down as well,
of course," he said, as if it had been agreed that he
should. "Introduce you to Meiss and make sure nothing
goes wrong."

"Yes," agreed Ramos, and Farr hid his relief at the
ease with which he'd crossed the one uncertain hurdle:
it was essential that the Panamanian lawyer accept him
as someone with authority to act for Gomez and Ramos.

They flew down the following day, on separate planes at
Ramos's insistence, which Farr was glad about because he
did not want to spend any more time in the man's presence
than was necessary. Meiss repeated the earlier lecture for
Ramos's benefit, and this time Farr paid more attention
than on the first occasion, intent upon Ramos. The Colombian gave a reasonable impression of understanding, but
the broker didn't think he did, not completely, and was
encouraged by it. Ramos's open confusion came when
Meiss asked how funds were to be transferred from the
United States into the company—which was how Farr had
planned it would be and the reason why he hadn't spoken
about it to the man. Farr allowed sufficient time for Ramos's
uncertainty to become obvious and then said it would
either be by direct money transfers, through his investment
company, or by bearer checks negotiated through money
exchanges—and Ramos hurriedly agreed. Farr came in
again when Meiss. asked about signatures on necessary
formation documents, explaining that they would be

couriered in and out of Colombia for separate lawyer
examination and notarized signatures—and once more
Ramos agreed. Meiss took the instruction and undertook to
establish the company and the following day Farr flew
northward to New York, confident things were going just
as he wanted them to, and Ramos flew south to Colombia
under the same impression.

Gomez was still on the coast, so Ramos flew directly to
Riohacha from Bogotá. Gomez had brought in different
women, two of them black, which was becoming his
increasing preference, and when Ramos arrived he heard a
lot of laughter and shouting. He entered the room with its
panoramic view of the Caribbean and saw the little hill of
cocaine at once and then the smaller lots, set out on their
individual onyx blocks, already chopped and segregated
into sniffing lines.

"We're partying," said Gomez, unnecessarily.

Ramos went further into the room, recognizing the additional advantage, striving to keep the surprise from showing. He'd overlooked Gomez's preference for what they
produced: once, he remembered, it would have been unthinkable to imagine Gomez doing coke. The man had
positively despised the traffickers who became users themselves, sneering at their weakness and stupidity. Ramos
wondered how affected the man was. This was good stuff—
maybe ninety percent—not cut by glucose or quinine or
other shit. Ramos was sure it was going to make easier
what he intended. He refused the offer to do a line, taking
whisky instead and heavily watering it down. Gomez took
both the black girls to bed in the afternoon and so it wasn't
until early evening that there was any conversation between them about the American trip. Gomez was tired
after the lovemaking and suffering the immediate post-
snorting depression after a cocaine high, so that absolute
concentration was difficult. Ramos explained completely
the details of the Panamanian company—stressing that
Gomez was going to have the chance to decide for himself
because all the papers were being ferried into and out of

the country—and produced all the information about the Maui investment as if that had arisen through his discussions with Meiss. Tired and as distracted as he was, Gomez still identified the problem, pointing out that the money they had so far earned and could put into Panama for reinvestment fell far short of what was necessary to take over the leisure complex. Ramos saw as his biggest problem getting Gomez to accept the suggestion of Navarra being involved and had tried—and failed—to evolve an argument different from the one that lured the Bolivian.

"You need a partner," he said simply.

Gomez frowned, trying for the point. "Accadio?" he said.

Ramos shook his head. "Not after what happened with Scarletti. Surely we want to stay out of any American linkup."

"We do," agreed Gomez.

"What about Navarra?"

Gomez laughed disbelievingly. "Get involved with that bastard!"

There was no other argument, Ramos decided. He said, "You'd have the company and the Maui investment and his money if anything happened to him."

Gomez laughed again, but differently this time, approvingly. "That's got a good sound," he said. "I like that."

Ramos thought it would be wrong to press any further. He said, "Why not think about it, when you've had chance to read more fully what the prospect is? And had time to consider the company details. You might decide against any of it."

Gomez blinked owlishly, in dissipated exhaustion. "I don't think I do," he said, "I don't think I do at all."

After the near disaster with José Rivera, Gomez limited his involvement with Colombian lawyers to a wary minimum, briefing them to consider the advantages of a Panamanian corporation—with a possible additional partner—and examined completely the potential of the Hawaiian investment. It took three weeks. Both reactions were favorable.

Gomez made his approval into another party—this time at the main Medellin *finca*—with another carousel of women but, more importantly for Ramos, with miniature pyramids of cocaine in all the main rooms. The sexual, alcoholic and narcotic hangover was such that it was two days later before Ramos was properly able to take their conversation beyond Gomez's simple agreement. He flew the same day to Bolivia, with instructions to inveigle Navarra, if possible. It was easy because, by the time of Ramos's visit, the Bolivian supplier had already received an independent report from his own lawyers about the attractions of the Pacific investment. At Navarra's urging, Ramos—sufficiently aware of the details by now—actually met the lawyers and took them through the construction plans of the proposed Panamanian company. Then he remained unoccupied in La Paz for a further day while Navarra engaged in his separate, private consultations, finally to emerge saying that he wanted to proceed but that he needed his lawyers to visit Panama City, meet the attorney there and fully satisfy himself. With no alternative, Ramos agreed, promising to make the arrangements and summon the men. So good was the encounter that Ramos risked asking Navarra if he would consider visiting Maui if everything went through, personally to examine his purchase. Navarra said that of course he would—that he'd actually insist upon it—and Ramos knew that warm-milk-in-the-veins feeling that comes in anticipation of a complete triumph. It was difficult not to overreact but he managed to resist it by not going up to the United States until his necessary money-collecting visit, but once there he made immediate contact with Walter Farr, needing to boast to someone how successful the planning had been.

Farr, who in the interim had made three visits to Panama, one essential, the other two simply to get Meiss accustomed to his presence and to accept completely that he was working and acting on behalf of the Colombians, was ready for the approach. It was a simple, mechanical operation although Farr absented himself when the men actually flew in from La Paz, letting Ramos be the intermediary for the introductions.

"It's all worked!" exulted Ramos, on the night the lawyers left: he and Farr remained, as had become the custom, to examine the events of the visit, eating in the rooftop restaurant of the International, the lights of the city spread out below them.

"Not yet," said the more guarded broker. He was excited as the Colombian but controlling the euphoria better.

"What's wrong?" demanded Ramos.

"Overconfidence, at this stage."

"What about the FBI?"

"They're ready," assured Farr. "I still need all the details of every trip. Amounts, couriers, methods of distribution. And, of course, the money; it's the money details I need, to establish the commission of crime within the United States . . ." Farr made the pause, as if the awareness suddenly came to him, in an afterthought. "And the authority," he said.

"What authority?"

The broker looked up at the other man, appearing surprised at Ramos's lack of understanding. "When we met Meiss, the first time, we arranged that the funding of the company would be through me. Either through my own organization or through bearer checks or money exchanges."

"Yes," remembered Ramos, doubtfully.

Farr produced the Panamanian authorization, to obtain which had been the reason for his last, essential trip to Panama, sliding it across the table toward Ramos. "If I'm going to act, then I need this signed," he insisted. "It's my power to act in your name. Without it, Meiss won't be able to accept from me . . ." He paused. "And you can see it *is* in your name. I'm not trying to cheat you."

"We didn't discuss this," protested Ramos.

"It's a detail," said Farr dismissively. "Read it. It's a transference document, nothing more . . ." He waited until Ramos became frowningly engrossed in the paper and added, "If you don't want me to act, don't sign. I thought that was the arrangement. Without it we've wasted our time."

"Of course it's the arrangement," said Ramos, irritably. "I just thought we'd covered everything."

"Everything that's important, we have," said Farr. "This is just necessary officialdom: lawyers protecting themselves."

Ramos hesitated a moment longer and then scribbled his signature and Farr knew the last hurdle was cleared and he was running now for the tape.

Ramos said, "Is that it? We're all ready now?"

"Oh no!" said Farr, abruptly. "I'll deposit for Gomez but there'll need to be matching infusions of capital from Navarra. We need to build up a liquidity around five hundred million dollars to enable the approach to be made for the complex. I'll need to be kept in the closest touch possible about how the lawyers are progressing: I've got to let the Bureau know blow for blow, don't forget. And I've got to know the moment either of them decide to make a visit in advance of the one we've got to set up for them. I've got to know your visits to America and I've got to receive the money and I've got to go on being kept informed about all that happens with Accadio."

Ramos nibbled his bottom lip, worried by the demands. "I'll do my best," he said.

"If you don't do more than your best, none of this is going to work," warned Farr.

They shared a car the following day to the airport and Farr watched the Colombian catch the scheduled flight to Bogotá, which left two hours before the New York connection. The broker waited until he was sure Ramos had departed and then emerged from the airport without attempting to check in, hurrying back into the city for a meeting with Francisco Zarak at the vía España office.

"You know how I feel about this!" protested Faltham.

"There's nothing to worry about."

"There's everything to worry about," insisted Faltham. "It's madness. Stark, raving madness."

"You've already said that," reminded Farr. He offered the signed and legally valid certificate of ownership to the other man and said, "Congratulations. You've just become the holder of a pretty impressive brokerage company."

Faltham made no effort to pick up the document. "And you know how I feel about that," he said.

"I want you to have the insurance," said Farr. "All of you."

"When?" demanded Faltham.

"Not yet," said Farr. "There's got to be the buildup of liquidity. And everything has got to happen in the right sequence, of course."

"And if it doesn't—if one thing goes off at half-cock— then it collapses like the pack of cards it is and they'll come for you," warned Faltham.

"I know," said Farr, quietly. "That's why it's important that I get everything right, isn't it?"

33

Farr utilized two ways to move from America into the Panama company the huge sums of money that Ramos provided, on his cash collection runs. Primarily—because the amounts were so large—he employed the loophole in America's Currency and Foreign Transactions Reporting Act, which does not require any notification to the authorities of money moved abroad if it is a wired transfer. But he also purchased anonymous bearer checks from banks through the major East Coast cities and made frequent and regular visits to Panama. Increasingly, Meiss extended the visits to a social level, initially lunches and then a weekend visit to the lawyer's estate at Chitre. It was on the next deposit visit after the Chitre weekend that Farr produced also the power of transfer document that Ramos had provided. On that visit, too, he had a longer than usual meeting with Francisco Zarak.

As the time passed, Ramos became less nervous, although rigidly maintaining his one way method of contact, during the American visits. Throughout the transactions, Farr kept a meticulous record of the infusions into Panama, knowing from what Ramos told him that Navarra was matching Gomez's payments and wanting to be able to act when the sum reached what was necessary for the Maui purchase.

A Ramos collection of twenty million dollars established sufficient liquidity.

"Sure?" demanded Ramos.

"Of course I'm sure," said Farr. He produced his figures, offering them to the Colombian for confirmation. "I'll move this over the next few days. Providing Navarra matches, then there's enough. There's no reason why the lawyers can't go ahead."

"What shall I do?" asked Ramos.

"Give me a week," said Farr. "Then tell Gomez and Navarra there's no reason why they shouldn't complete. All the lawyers need do is confirm the Panama balance."

"They've got to go there!" insisted Ramos.

"That's got to come from you," said Farr, with equal insistence. "The moment you contact me, telling me the visit is on, I'll alert the Bureau."

"I hope no one fouls up," said Ramos, frightened at the approach of the actual commitment.

"They won't, providing your information is accurate," said Farr.

"They both trust me, Gomez and Navarra."

"So it shouldn't be difficult?"

"No," agreed Ramos, the doubt still obvious. "It shouldn't be."

Farr transferred the bulk of the last payment by wire, as usual, but personally took down one hundred thousand dollars in bearer checks. But this time, as well as making the deposit, he invoked the document that Ramos had signed, explaining to the now friendly lawyer that the instructions were from Colombia, actually from Señor Gomez himself. Farr remained overnight for the meeting with Zarak, but was able to catch an early enough plane back to America still to be able to call the FBI in Washington, seeking Brennan. The FBI supervisor responded the following day. The man was in Washington and because it was so close he was able to get to New York in the afternoon, after Farr told him the information that was available.

It was late evening before Brennan finished reading everything Farr provided on the Accadio family in Chicago. The

balding, neat man stretched back in his chair and nodded
agreement to Farr's offer to freshen his drink and said,
"OK. So you want to tell me what this is all about?"

The broker indicated the disarranged dossier lying at
Brennan's feet. "Evidence of a major drug importation
operation," he said.

"So how'd you come by it?"

Farr shook his head. "I went public last time. Look
what it cost me. That's all there is. It's enough to start an
investigation, isn't it?"

Brennan looked down at the folders. "We could subpoena you."

"Which would make me a hostile witness, so I'd need a
lawyer of my own. He'd have to ask me about how the
original thing was set up, in the Caymans, which didn't
happen the way it was explained in court. It might give
Scarletti grounds to appeal to the Supreme Court," said Farr.

Brennan looked at the broker across the rim of the glass.
"You've really thought this out, haven't you?"

"Like I said, that's all there is. You won't have a
money trail, like last time. But you should be able to get
enough evidence."

"On the phone, to Washington, you said you wanted to
trade," reminded Brennan. "What is it you want in return?"

Farr told him, aware as he talked of Brennan's change
of attitude, a stiffening in the chair in which he sat.

"In court you testified that it wasn't the Gomez you
saw in Lang's office."

"I know what I testified in court," said the broker.

"So why this!"

"I just want to know, that's all."

"No," refused Brennan. "That's not all."

"Again, that's all there is," said Farr, in a refusal of his
own. "You've got some sort of monitor, haven't you? If
not your own people, then someone at the embassy? Drug
Enforcement people, perhaps?"

Brennan sat for a long time without replying. Then he
said, "So that's how it was!"

Farr stared back at the man, saying nothing.

Brennan said, "You going to tell me what you've done?"

"No," said Farr.

"I'll need a reason to initiate protection again," said Brennan.

"I didn't ask for protection; don't want it," said the broker. "All I want is what I've asked for."

"Stupid son of a bitch!" said Brennan.

"Fuck you!" said Farr.

Ramos let the suggestion emanate from Gomez and was himself the recognized and trusted liaison between the Colombian and Navarra, who agreed to proceed. Both sets of lawyers flew to the islands, basing themselves in Honolulu and commuting when it was necessary to Maui. Ramos decided he'd been extremely clever, choosing the way to get Gomez and Navarra into American jurisdiction and subsequent arrest, planting the idea of a necessary visit—for a purchase of such magnitude—in the minds of the lawyers for them to do the persuading, instead of himself. Because even after they were arrested and jailed, no suspicion had to be attached to him: he had to be clean, to continue. A week before the intended visit, the separate teams of lawyers returned respectively to La Paz and Medellin, for the necessary authority to initiate the deposit payment from the Panamanian company established by Roberto Meiss, against the full settlement figure. The Maui developers required twenty percent, which was fifty million dollars against the agreed and negotiated completion sum of two hundred and fifty million dollars.

When the lawyers called by appointment at Meiss's office on the Plaza Cinco de Mayo, the Panamanian looked at them in obvious bewilderment.

"What are you talking about!" demanded Meiss. And produced the accounts which showed the company to be just under twenty thousand dollars in credit.

Epilogue

Farr stared down at the photographs, wanting to feel something but feeling nothing at all, neither satisfaction nor revulsion nor disgust. Would it have been better if he could have identified either man from the bloodied mess? He didn't think so. It was easier to remember Howard's mutilated body. And imagine Harriet's.

"Ever seen anything like that?" asked Brennan.

"No," said Farr.

"Both in Medellin," said the FBI supervisor. "They're used to violence in Colombia but our man there, a guy called Green, says not even the authorities know anything like this. Autopsy reports say there wasn't a torture they hadn't been subject to before they were killed. They actually—"

"I can see." Farr did not need an explanation.

"Jorge Herrera Gomez and a guy called Orlando Ramos," continued Brennan. "There was some dental information—just—and some sort of fingerprints. We had Ramos on photo record, too—from the time when we first tried to identify Gomez's man."

"They must have suffered," said Farr, handing the pictures back to the other man.

"Difficult to imagine just how much," said Brennan. He waited in vain for the broker to speak and then went on, "Authorities think it was some sort of gang war, between rival factions . . ." The American stopped again. Still Farr did not attempt to speak. "They've no idea what it could have been about. The war, I mean . . ."

"Probably never will have," said Farr. "These things don't seem to become public, do they?"

"You have any idea why it could have happened?"

"None at all," said Farr. It would have taken only days, he thought; maybe it was the *same* day that Navarra's lawyers learned there was no money left. Farr intentionally made it as easy as possible for Navarra's attorney to trace from the transference document in Ramos's name the second company created by the lawyer Francisco Zarak: the company registered in the name of Jorge Herrera Gomez and Orlando Ramos weeks in advance of the other by Farr's two hundred and fifty thousand dollars, with the sole object of cheating Julio Navarra of a hundred million dollars. The Bolivian might have exacted his own revenge for what the man imagined to have happened but he was never going to be able to recover his money. Farr wasn't surprised at the extent of the torture.

"You wanna know something?" asked the FBI man.

"What?"

"I don't believe you. I just wish to hell I knew how you made it happen."

Farr refused to be drawn into any boast.

Brennan sighed, resigned. Abandoning the attempts, he said, "Looks like we're going to be able to bring something against the Accadio family. It'll take some time, but I think we can do it."

"I'm glad," said Farr.

"You want to keep these photographs?" asked Brennan. "No."

The FBI man stood, replacing them into his briefcase. He looked down at the broker and said, "I wish—after what you did—that you could bring them back, Harriet and Howard. But you can't, can you?"

"No," Farr finally conceded. "I can't bring them back."

Postscript

Malcolm: Let's make us medicine of our great revenge.

Macduff: He has no children. All my pretty ones?
Did you say all? O hell-kite! All?
What? All my pretty chickens and their dam,
At one fell swoop?

SHAKESPEARE, Macbeth